FIVE FARTHINGS

Also by Susan Sallis

Rising Sequence:
A SCATTERING OF DAISIES
THE DAFFODILS OF NEWENT
BLUEBELL WINDOWS
ROSEMARY FOR REMEMBRANCE

SUMMER VISITORS
BY SUN AND CANDLELIGHT
AN ORDINARY WOMAN
DAUGHTERS OF THE MOON
SWEETER THAN WINE
WATER UNDER THE BRIDGE
TOUCHED BY ANGELS
CHOICES
COME RAIN OR SHINE
THE KEYS TO THE GARDEN
THE APPLE BARREL
SEA OF DREAMS
TIME OF ARRIVAL

FIVE FARTHINGS

Susan Sallis

This edition published 2003
by BCA
by arrangement with TRANSWORLD PUBLISHERS
a division of The Random House Group Ltd

CN 115047

First reprint 2003

Copyright © Susan Sallis 2003

Typeset in New Baskerville by
Kestrel Data, Exeter, Devon.

Printed and bound Germany by
GGP Media, Pössneck

For my family

Prologue

I'm supposed to be writing this as a therapy but, to be honest, I don't need that sort of thing any more. My mother once called it psycho-nonsense; now she says it would be better if I got everything straight and the best way of doing that is to write it down. She even wants me to do it like a diary, day by day, but I know that wouldn't work. Things don't seem to happen day by day. There's an event, then a long pause, then two or three things come together. So I'm going to write it as it happened. It's almost like a detective story except that there doesn't seem to be just one guilty party. In fact by the time I get to the end it may well be that no-one is guilty. Nevertheless, it all happened. We made it happen.

Detective stories are about people and this one is no exception. Most of these people lived in the small town in one of the Mendip valleys where I was born and brought up. There were my parents, Monica and Donald Maslin: they were wonderful, everything parents should be. Dad was head of the local primary school. Mum did everything – decorated, gardened, got up a ladder to point a chimney . . . very practical.

And there was my sister, Jennifer. Ten years younger than me. Beautiful, sophisticated, funny . . . my daughter loved her. Jennifer lived twenty-five miles away, in Bristol.

At first I thought the story began with the death of my father. He died of oesophageal cancer in November 2000. It was diagnosed the previous August and he had an operation and some treatment but there were secondaries.

I felt as if a huge axe had fallen and severed time. Everything was cut off, finished. Life had to start again. Maybe that was the beginning of it all. But nothing actually happened until the following March. So that is where I am going to start.

Anyway, back to the cast list. Mum had a friend, Alicia, who was married to Ray. They featured a lot in my early childhood.

I had a good friend too, Jean Parslow. She was married to Jock and they had four sons.

And there was me, Jessica Tavener. Aged thirty-five. Married to Matthew Tavener. Lucy Tavener was four and then five when it all happened. She is our daughter.

Matthew was always called Matt; he started selling double glazing sixteen years ago for a firm in Bristol. That was in 1985 when the double-glazing boom was at its height. Then he set up his own factory and office on the new industrial estate just outside our little town and I went to work for him. We were married in 1991 but Lucy was not born for another five years. Matt wanted to clear some of the bank loan and get a house for us. So we waited. And though we tried for a bigger family, nothing happened. We didn't mind too much; we were happy.

Matt employed a factory manager called Sam Clarkson. Sam was a craftsman, especially with stained glass. He was also steady, reliable, very predictable. Until he was pitchforked into this detective story.

Two other people were concerned in the plot. A man called Jerry Jerome who lived in a place called Marcroft in Wiltshire. And our local hairdresser, Marilyn George. They had their roles; finally they were important too.

However, the leading actors were Mum; Ray; Jean, Jock and their children; Jennifer; Sam; Matt, Lucy and me. We very nearly destroyed each other. We have the scars to prove it.

And it all started that dreary March of 2001 when I found the first clue and began to ask questions.

One

The rain was bitterly cold that day; aggressive, too, because the wind blew every which way and you couldn't hold an umbrella against it, so the raindrops shot you in the face and made you blink. It was great to open the door on Marilyn's salon, hear the bell ping a warning and have the new girl come to take your coat and ask if you wanted a cup of tea.

I'm not that keen on having my hair done, but Mum thought it would be a treat for me and she'd paid in advance and was back home looking after Lucy and probably doing the ironing, and if I did what she had suggested and called on Jean on my way home, she might even have vacuumed for me. Anyway, there are bits of the hairdressing routine I like and the shampoo is one of them. Marilyn didn't do it, of course; she was the stylist as well as the owner. I had the new girl, who told me her name was Amanda and thought she had been in the same class as my sister, Jennifer, and did I want conditioner. I said yes to make it all last longer. Amanda definitely had the touch; I could have been shampooed all afternoon.

'I remember when Jennifer was your bridesmaid,' she said, combing the conditioner into my wet hair. 'I thought you were marvellous letting her wear trousers.'

'They were pure silk,' I murmured. 'And really they were sort of culottes.'

'She'd never wear a skirt,' Amanda reminisced. 'She was always in trouble about that. Miss Gormley was the clever one. She told her she could wear trousers as long as her grades were above average.'

'And they always were.' I smiled at the ceiling. Jennifer was stubborn but fair.

'Well, I should think so. What with you behind her. And your father being a teacher and everything.'

I didn't say anything to this. I couldn't have helped Jennifer if I'd tried. And Dad, well, dear Dad, he'd probably had enough with trying to coach me, let alone his awkward baby. God, how we all missed Dad.

Amanda rinsed and massaged some more as a treat, or probably because Marilyn wasn't quite ready with the scissors. Then she swathed me in towels, asked me again about a cup of tea and led me through the archway and into another chair. I sat down and smiled into the mirror at Marilyn. This was the bit I didn't like. The mirror was omnipresent and depressing.

Marilyn smiled back. She wore black – they all did – which set off her natural blond curls. She was ever so slightly overweight but it didn't matter; she had a terrific presence. When Jennifer was sixteen she went through a terrible period of seeing other people in terms of defects. The woman with the spots. The dog with one eye. Worst of all, the man with stained trousers. We were all out together and saw Marilyn on the other side of the road. 'She looks like a ship under full sail,' commented Jennifer. And Dad smiled and said, 'Yes. Isn't she beautiful?' It was the end of Jennifer's critical period; she looked again and said, surprised, 'Yes, she is, isn't she?'

Marilyn said now, 'How would you like your hair, Mrs Tavener?'

I grinned. 'Like yours, please.'

I'm dark with very straight hair, so this was meant as a jokey compliment. We came to some arrangement and it seemed I wanted to look like a singer I hadn't heard of. Marilyn cupped her hands around my head and used words like bell-shaped. She then clipped back various wet lumps of hair and set to work with comb and scissors. I looked down at my lap.

'How's that dear little baby of yours?' Marilyn asked coyly.

'She's not really a baby any more. She goes to school next September.' I knew she wasn't really interested in four-year-old Lucy but I couldn't resist talking about her. 'She's got such a good memory. She recites poetry all the time. "Hey-diddle-diddle", "Row the Boat" and "Incy Wincy Spider".'

'And what about her gorgeous daddy?'

'Oh . . . gorgeous. He can say, "Hey-diddle-diddle".'

Marilyn actually laughed. 'I bet. And he can row the boat too.'

We both laughed indulgently. Unexpectedly she said, 'Don't worry, dear. Couples have been playing that game since Adam and Eve.'

It took me a minute to realize that there might well be an adults-only version of the rhyme. I blushed.

She swept on without pause. 'I think we'll have an uneven cut here. To fall around the face, so.' She slicked a sliver of hair to my chin and looked in the mirror. 'D'you know, I could keep you looking as sexy as this if you came every four or five weeks.'

I puffed an apologetic laugh. 'I can't really afford it, Marilyn. And anyway, it wouldn't be me. Sexy, I mean.' I managed to look at my reflection. It wasn't in the least sexy.

Marilyn resumed her cutting. 'It would give you confidence. You haven't got enough confidence. Now your sister, she's got all the confidence in the world.'

I didn't comment. Jennifer is beautiful and very intelligent as well as confident. She goes to hairdressers all the time, and beauticians. Mum's best friend, Alicia, said that she was getting so sophisticated she looked older than me. There are ten years between us. Mum said easily, 'Yes . . . Jessica won't change. She's got a schoolgirl face.'

Marilyn told me about her latest holiday. A cruise to Barbados. 'I swam on New Year's Eve, can you believe,' she said. 'There was a panto on board. And carol singing . . . Oh, it was lovely.'

I'd been happy that Christmas; I'd felt guilty about it until we took Lucy round to Mum's in the afternoon and Mum said, 'Isn't it great that we can be like this? I'd feel we were letting Dad down if we were miserable.' And Matt swung Lucy around the Christmas tree and grinned. 'This is what Dad has left us – his enormous contentment.'

I smiled up into the mirror at Marilyn's reflection and tried to nod.

'Head still.' She stood behind me, took a lock in each hand and pulled it under my chin. 'I had a go at that karaoke thing. Some chap who reckoned he was a theatrical agent wanted to sign me up.' She gave her throaty laugh. 'I asked him if he had a casting couch!'

I rolled my eyes at her, not liking to ask her right out whether he did have a casting couch and whether she would have used it. She knew exactly what I couldn't say and primmed her lips. 'That would be telling. You know me. I've been around. Two or three times, actually.'

I wanted to ask her why she'd never got married. Didn't she want a family and a home of her own? But I remained silent.

She put a plug into a socket on the wall and started the business of blow-drying. It was noisy so there was no more talk but time to think. And as she reached for the hair spray she said suddenly, 'It doesn't mean a thing. None of it. I wouldn't ever get serious and hurt someone.'

And for some reason I said, 'I know. My father said that you were beautiful. And he meant more than skin deep.'

She stopped spraying and stood for a moment, poised, the can at the ready.

'Did he? Did he really say that? How lovely.'

She put the can back on the shelf and got the hand mirror for me to see the back of my head. My hair looked good. Really good. I consciously lengthened my neck and dropped my shoulders.

'Thanks a lot, Marilyn,' I said.

'You should come in regularly,' she repeated, fetching my coat and leading the way to the till. 'I could do wonders with you. You've got one of those faces . . . You could still be in your twenties.'

I laughed as I fished for my purse. She sounded like Svengali. A blond, beautiful, overweight, female Svengali. I never know how much to tip and while I was still trying to work something out she leaned across and put a hand over my purse.

'I don't want it, Mrs Tavener. You telling me what your father said . . . that's set me up, that has.'

She even came to the door and adjusted the hood of my anorak. And I went outside into that awful driving rain and felt warm.

I didn't intend to go and see Jean, simply because I didn't seem to do it any more. Besides, I wanted a proper cup of tea with Mum and Lucy in my own home. But as I drove past she was just getting out of her car with about six bursting plastic bags from Hartford's, the supermarket, and she looked so awful and I felt so good that it seemed really mean not to pull in and give her a hand. We've been best friends since primary school back in the Seventies and she was so desperate and sweet when Dad died. I remember her sobbing, 'I'm meant to be brave and buoy you up and all I do is cry!' And I wept back, 'I'm sick of people being cheerful! I'm in some kind of a pit and I can't get out and you come down there with me.'

Even so I hadn't seen her since Christmas.

She gasped when she saw me. 'You're an answer to a prayer, Jess! Can you fish my key out of that pocket . . . no, that's the car . . . yes, that one. And just take this, and maybe this . . .'

We eventually got inside the front door and dumped

13

everything and started to laugh. I told her she looked terrible and she thanked me sarcastically and suggested I might look the same if I had been slogging round the supermarket all afternoon trying to find food to suit four and a half children – the half being her husband, Jock, who was probably coming home that weekend. I told her where I'd been and while the kettle boiled she studied me as I carefully pushed back my hood.

'Not bad. Where did you go?'

'Marilyn's, of course. Where else?' Our little town wasn't exactly overflowing with hairdressers.

She looked surprised. 'Well, I just thought you might have tried that new place on the high street.'

I shrugged. 'Dad liked Marilyn.'

'Men do.'

It was such an untypical remark I stared at her. She gave an apologetic grin, said, 'Sorry,' and turned away to make the tea. I didn't think she was sorry at all but at that moment Marilyn didn't interest me that much, so I just laughed and picked up Jean's mac and a couple of the bags and began to put things away, and then we sat at the kitchen table and smiled at each other through the steam of the tea and she asked about Lucy and really listened when I told her about 'Hey-diddle-diddle' and things. I did ask about Jason and Simon and the twins but she said fine except for the asthma which got her down worse than it did the twins. They'd had asthma since they were seven and they were ten now.

'If they can handle it all right perhaps you shouldn't worry so much,' I murmured, trying to be positive.

She drained her tea and put her mug into the sink.

'Get real, Jess. It's pretty tough sitting by their beds praying for another breath for them.'

'Oh Jean, I'm so sorry, babbling on about Lucy. I don't mean to be heartless.' I reached for her hand. 'It's just that you manage so well that you fool me into thinking everything is all right!'

14

'I don't manage well at all. Jason called me a wet wally yesterday.'

I laughed. 'Well, you were pretty wet just now but you're no wally.'

Unexpectedly she put her face in her hands. 'That's exactly what I am, Jess. You don't know the half of it. I am the biggest wally south of Birmingham.'

It was a phrase coined at school and we both laughed. I hoped Jean would then be able to talk for a while, get it out of her system, but as usual at her house there was an interruption. It was the twins arriving from school. They looked all right to me, boisterous as ever, very healthy. They were both redheads like Jock, both wore braces on their teeth and it was impossible to identify which was which. Nat was good looking when he smiled and Tony was not but they made a real effort not to smile very often. Tony was the extrovert, however, and planted a kiss on my nose as soon as he had dropped school bag and anorak on the floor.

'Aunty Jess. You look nice. Really nice. Are there any more biscuits, Ma?'

'I got some this afternoon. Jess put them in the tin. How are you?'

Nat allowed himself a smile and was instantly beautiful; he nodded. Tony, scrabbling at the biscuit tin, said, 'Fine. We've been fine, haven't we, Nat?'

Nat said, 'The Ventolin works in the day, Ma. Honestly.'

They milled around getting some food together, asking about Jason and Simon who were at the comprehensive and were going to be late home. Nat sent his love to Uncle Matt and Lucy and then they were gone into the living room, from where, very shortly, the television could be heard. It was always like that. Matt said it reminded him of machine-gun fire: a sudden lethal burst, then a lull. Jean had had Jason five months after her marriage to Jock – they had both been twenty. Simon had arrived two years later, then the typical lull and three years afterwards the twins had burst on to the scene.

I said, 'I'd better go.'

Jean tried to grin. 'Can't take it, eh?'

'Mum's there on her own.'

'Yes. Of course. How is she?'

'Marvellous. It was her first Christmas without Dad and she was determined . . . you know.'

'Yes.' We went down the hall to the front door. I called out goodbyes to the twins. She said, 'Did she mind? You going to Marilyn's?'

'She popped in and made the appointment.' I grinned. 'She paid too!' I opened the door on to that relentless rain. 'Anyway, she loves babysitting. She would never mind.' I ran to the car clutching the hood of my anorak under the chin.

Jean called after me, 'Jock will be home next week!' Jock works on the oil rigs off Scotland.

I let go my hood to wave happily. It flew off and the wind whipped my hair upwards. I was still laughing as I drove into the garage.

Mum said, 'Oh, it still looks wonderful, idiot! You don't wreck a hairdo with one puff of wind. Not one of Marilyn's hairdos anyway. You remind me of someone on television. It's really special.'

Lucy said, 'Mummy's got new hair.'

'What d'you think of it, darling? Doesn't Mummy look beautiful?'

Lucy loved all the attention. She rushed around showing me what she and Gramma had done all afternoon. I told her Nat sent his love as I admired the strings of paper dolls, cut by Mum and crayoned by Lucy.

'I'm glad you popped in on Jean,' Mum said comfortably. 'I think she needs female company now and then.'

'Jock's coming home next week,' I said, holding the glue stick in Lucy's little fist as she stuck the paper dolls into her scrapbook. Mum made a face and I laughed. 'She thinks he's great and that's all that matters.'

'Will he sit up with the twins when they get an attack in the night?'

'No. But he makes her happy. He really does.'

I could tell Mum was unconvinced, but she had Jennifer going round that evening and wanted to get home to deal with some veal that was marinating. She shrugged into her coat and scrabbled around for car keys.

'Listen,' she said. 'You should start back at the office. Matt's had to manage by himself all this time and it's not fair. You know I don't mind coming along in the afternoons to look after Lucy.'

'What about your outings with Alicia?'

Alicia is to Mum what Jean is to me and she'd been wonderful since Dad died. They went to the cinema in Bath or Bristol every week, had lunches out . . . talked. It struck me as Lucy and I found her bag and gloves that this was the big snag about normal life: there was never any time to talk things through.

Mum said, 'Alicia would come here. And anyway the clocks go forward soon and the evenings will be light. We can do things then.'

'You've got an answer for everything.'

Mum was already fighting her way through the rain to her car. She knew I didn't want to go back to work so she quite deliberately wasn't going to give me time to talk about it.

Matt was early; I hadn't even peeled a potato. He danced us around the room, Lucy screaming with delight while he nuzzled both of us frantically. We half fell on to the sofa and lay there panting.

'D'you realize, four years ago we could have gone upstairs now and stayed there till the morning?' he enquired.

'You wouldn't ever – ever – have dreamed of missing out on a meal!'

Lucy crowed, 'Jelly! Jelly!' and Matt groaned, 'Not jelly again!'

We all went into the kitchen and started cooking. We did it every evening but that particular evening I filed away for future reference because it was so special to us. We had each other. I thought of Jean, anxious and on her own; Mum, coping wonderfully, but still on her own; even Jennifer, beautiful and sophisticated but probably often on her own. I told Matt how happy I was and he looked up from mashing the potatoes and said, 'Well, that's good because I was hoping you'd go down to the office later and have a look at the VAT return.' I flipped a tea towel over his head and told him he'd been talking to Mum, then got the chops out of the oven. I'd always worked for Matt; that was how I'd managed all this so-called compassionate leave. And of course I would go back to work for him – he'd already brought home stuff for me to look at – but the bottom had fallen out of the double-glazing business and there wasn't that much work to do. Anyway, I thought that as soon as Lucy was asleep we would be going to bed. I directed his attention to the rain still drumming on the kitchen roof.

He said, 'You should go. I'll put Luce to bed. Slippers by the fire. You'll feel good about it. I promise you.'

So he had been talking to Mum and he was serious. And they were both such very special people . . . I had to do it.

An hour later, very reluctantly, I left him with Lucy and the washing-up, got the car out of the garage again and drove up the side of the valley to the Goose Bump, then down to the industrial estate in the next valley. Like all these places, it was out in the wilderness right in the middle of sheep country.

The security guard came out of his office, umbrella up, and peered at me with surprise.

'Didn't expect you, Mrs T.,' he said. 'Mr T. said you might be down to have a look at the tax but with this weather and all . . .' He tried to hold his umbrella over the door as I got out but I made a run for it.

'Thanks, Bob.' I stood inside the door, taking off my

mac. 'I know he wants me back at work, but on a night like this . . . it's ridiculous.'

Bob shook his head dourly. 'Business not good, Mrs T. The VAT inspector coming to look at the books, you know.'

I didn't know. I hadn't wanted to know anything much outside our immediate family circle. Matt, Lucy, Mum, Jennifer, they were the only people I was interested in. Even Jean . . . until this afternoon I hadn't seen Jean for months.

I went into the office; it was perfectly neat, papers everywhere but in tidy piles. A bottle of spray polish stood on the filing cabinet and a duster nearby. I had always kept things clean and it touched me that Matt must have gone on dusting. Maybe he'd vacuumed too; the carpet tiles didn't look bad.

It was the first time since Dad died that I'd prepared a return. As I pulled the invoices out of the cabinet, I realized with a shock how dilatory I had been. No wonder Matt – and Mum – wanted me to get back in the saddle. After all, it was our business and, since the boom of the Eighties, it hadn't been roses all the way by any means. We'd bought our house, which was only one notch above 'modest'; we had two cars, and we'd sorted out money to cover Lucy's needs in the future. But when they built the enormous new estate on the hill, the builders decided against double glazing and though we put in a tender for single glazing it must have been too high because they went for a firm in Bristol. Matt jokingly asked Jennifer if she'd sleep with the building contractor; strangely enough, she did meet him at some party, but as Dad said, 'If it's that sort of set-up, you don't want the job anyway.' The truth was, of course, that the double-glazing boom was over. Like many firms in the late Nineties, we pared our admin staff down to two – Matt and me – so that we could keep the factory going.

In other words I knew darned well my input was overdue,

and as I switched on the computer and assembled the invoices in date order I felt a twinge of something like shame. Had I used Dad's sudden death as an excuse to cocoon myself with Lucy and 'keep an eye' on Mum? Matt was always so cheerful; he never came home and said he'd had an awful day. When he went off for a couple of days to drum up business or keep an eye on a particular job, he no longer assumed that I would take over at the office. I started to enter the outgoings and whispered, 'Sorry, Dad,' and then stopped that too in case it was me being sentimental. Jennifer had accused me, the week before, of being 'cosy'. I knew it wasn't a compliment.

I worked solidly for two hours. After the VAT form I started on some filing and the more I did the more there was; I would have to come for a couple of hours every day to get things in order again. I had worked in this office for a dozen years and I was angry with myself for letting things slip so badly. I went over to Matt's desk and started to sort that out as well. Silly things – putting the paper clips into a container, rubber bands into another, sketches into a pile. I paused at those. Matt was a good artist and there was a detail of what looked like a baronial hall somewhere with tall, arched windows. A very difficult job but interesting too. I thought I would ask him about that when I got home. I came across another, similar. Then, startlingly, a drawing of Dad. Matt rarely sketches people but when he does he enhances some special feature in the way a caricaturist does, highlighting some little quirk that immediately identifies the subject. This time it was Dad's stance – slightly bowed, enquiring, interested. Dad had a knack of really listening to what anyone said. He was a wonderful teacher; the children in his care had been so lucky.

I felt my eyes filling because Matt had seen Dad properly. I wished he had shown me this sketch but of course I knew why he hadn't. He hated to see me cry. I made up for it then, sitting in the office, looking down at it, letting the tears roll down my face, thinking that I must show it to Jennifer. And Mum.

So I found an old cardboard folder and put it carefully inside and looked at it again, smiling slightly. Dad was absolutely there for me. And what was more, he was standing in that baronial hall below the high arched windows. I smiled mistily; Matt had made sketches in a bid for a contract and then – presumably because he hadn't got the job – he had doodled Dad in the setting. I sniffed and blew my nose and dabbed at my eyes and started to shuffle the other drawings into a pile. Then I realized there were other sketches of people; other views of the hall too. A refectory table running almost the full length of the floor space; a minstrels' gallery; a rose window. A woman sat at the table. I didn't recognize her at first. But in the next drawing there was the same woman, looking up at the minstrels' gallery, head flung back, full-bosomed, wearing a straight black jacket to her knees with trousers beneath and ridiculously high-heeled shoes. Marilyn.

I put the two drawings together; both were of Marilyn. Why on earth had Matt doodled sketches of Marilyn and Dad on one of his bids for business – and both in the same setting?

I frowned and slipped the Marilyn drawings in with Dad's, then put a rubber band around the folder. I wouldn't show them to Jennifer or Mum until I'd had a serious word with Matt. And it would have to be serious; none of his joking about having married a private eye. And I would have to come back to work properly. Dashing in at the last minute to prepare the accounts was not good enough. There was a backlog of stuff to put on the computer and the files were in need of a good sort-out. I sighed. Maybe it was for the best. Mum would love to look after Lucy on a regular basis – and perhaps I needed to 'get real' as Jean had said.

I put the file on the passenger seat, switched on front and rear windscreen wipers and set off slowly through the rain. It seemed to be slapping the car quite hard and I wondered whether it was turning to snow. Surely not snow in March . . . the snowdrops were over, the crocuses still braving the March winds. We needed the spring now. Dad had been dead for four months; we all needed to look forward. Suddenly I wished I hadn't found those drawings. I had a feeling they might drag us all back. I drew up at some temporary traffic lights guarding road works. An ambulance roared past me, blue lights flashing. It was another reminder of that day last summer when Mum had telephoned, saying she couldn't have Lucy for me in the afternoon and could I cancel the office for a while, or maybe Jean would fill in? She had been almost incoherent and then after my questions she was suddenly very calm. 'Dad had a barium X-ray yesterday. He has a growth. He is going into hospital this afternoon and they will operate tomorrow.'

I bit my lip fiercely. The lights flicked to amber then green and I grated into first and moved around a fenced-off hole in the road. Traffic was being diverted through the town. The rain was softer now, the wipers collecting it more slowly. It was snow. The first of the year. Still very wet but definitely snow.

I drove through the centre of our small country town. Even here many of the shops were steel-shuttered against vandals. But tonight in the wet snow there were no signs of dawdling youths; the fish-and-chip shop across from Marilyn's was dark and the Red Fox hadn't closed yet so its customers were also out of sight. I turned into Acacia Avenue, past Jean's house where all the lights were blazing as usual, up to the war memorial and the church and the stocks and – much too close to the old part of the town – Hartford's, the hideous new supermarket. But beyond that point the fields rolled into the headlights. I knew they were full of lambs and hoped for their sakes that the snow would not settle. Then right into Dip Lane and the small group of labourers' cottages, all privately owned and extended, double-glazed, one with a swimming pool. I felt guilty that one of them was ours. But thankful too.

Lucy was in bed, my slippers by the fire, sandwiches on a tray. Matt had obviously only just sat down with the paper but he leaped to his feet and took my bag and coat and snuffled into my neck.

'Did you know it's snowing?' I asked, smiling at him, so pleased to be home and away from everything dark and fearful.

He didn't know. He was like a schoolboy, flinging open the front door and letting the big splattery flakes break on his face and outspread hands. I dragged him back in.

'Idiot. You'll get soaked.' I held him around the waist and pressed my face against his wet sweatshirt. 'Don't you dare catch cold!' I kissed him fiercely. 'Keep yourself safe! D'you hear me?'

He laughed at first and then was tender. 'Don't be frightened, darling. Everything will be all right. Just hang on. That's all you have to do. Hang on.'

He knew so much. He had this zest for life. He had made a wonderful Christmas for all of us and now . . . I could see what he was doing.

'I know what you're up to,' I whispered against his face.

'What am I up to, Sherlock?'

'You're easing me back into work again.' I bit his ear and he yelped. 'Did Mum say something to you?'

'Like what?' He was running his thumbs across my back, very firmly. He should have been a masseur.

'Like I'd had enough time back in the womb?'

'Maybe.' He kissed me; a very serious kiss. 'Shall we go to bed?'

'It's only half-past nine. And those sandwiches . . .'

'We could get up again.'

'I love you, Matt Tavener.'

So that's what we did and afterwards we sat on the floor by the dying fire and for once Matt was quiet and still. I told him that I was only halfway through the return and would go back tomorrow. 'And next week I'll come most afternoons. Mum said . . .' I murmured on, pausing now and then to listen for Lucy. Then I was quiet too and I thought of the sketches I'd brought home with me, and when we'd finished the sandwiches I went into the hall and rummaged in my bag. I took just the one from the folder and came back to the fire.

Matt said, 'I love the way you move. You're not lithe. In fact sometimes you're almost awkward . . .' I protested and he shook his head. 'No. Stop it. I want to think about it. All right, not awkward. Kind of angular. It – it's great the way you bend.'

I laughed helplessly. 'As far as compliments go you are zilch,' I told him.

But he wouldn't give up. 'You got up – and got down again – like a . . . not a giraffe. A camel. Like a camel!' He beamed at me even as I whammed him with a cushion. And then of course we were laughing as usual and I nearly didn't show him the sketch. But then I did. It was the one of Dad. For some reason I left the ones of Marilyn in the document case.

He stopped teasing me and held the sketch towards the light of the fire. For quite a while he looked at it. I knew he had loved Dad. He couldn't remember his own father and his mother had married again – twice. We didn't see much of her.

He said slowly, 'It's him, isn't it? Just how he was. Did it upset you?'

'Yes. But in a good way.'

'I know.' He sighed and put the sketch behind us on the seat of the sofa.

I waited but nothing else came. I said, 'Why did you do it?'

He was surprised. 'I've drawn Dad lots of times. You know that.'

Still I didn't mention Marilyn. 'Yes, but in that setting. It looks like an abbey or something.'

'It's Victorian, built in the style of an abbey – just a folly, really. In Wiltshire.' He stretched. 'I think we might have the job. They've asked me to go and look at it again. It's stained glass and Sam's rather keen to have a go.' Sam runs the factory for us. Matt could do stained glass but Sam is an expert.

I was completely diverted. 'Oh Matt. It sounds wonderful. So much more exciting than a big modern estate. Significant and special. You know what I mean.'

'I know exactly what you mean. But it will take a long time. Most of the spring and summer, Jess. I'd only be home weekends.'

I made a face. 'That's why you and Mum want me to get back in the saddle! Devils. Both of you.'

He kissed me again. We did a lot of kissing that night. 'Can you bear it?'

'Listen, Matthew Tavener. Why should you think I need special care and attention? Mum doesn't get it. Neither does Jennifer.'

'I think you three women care for each other.' He gave me a funny little grin. 'Sometimes you frighten me. You're so strong. The Triumvirate.'

'Idiot,' I said. And then, 'How long will you be away?'

'If I get the job . . . well, you know. How long is a piece of string? It depends on how much they want the job done properly. It can't be hurried.'

I breathed deeply. I was determined but a bit scared. I relied so much on Matt. 'All right. And home weekends, you say?'

'Every weekend.'

'All right. If you can do it, so can I.'

He wasn't overjoyed; he just said, 'I love you.'

We were quiet again, gazing into the fire, holding each other. Then we began to sit up, stand up – lots of quips about camels – and clear up.

I said, 'I can't remember you going there before . . . This place in Wiltshire. And Dad too.'

He smiled ruefully, picked up a plate with one hand and hugged me to his shoulder with the other. 'There's so much you've blocked out, Jess. Don't worry about it now. Let's go to bed.'

'Yes. All right.' It did suddenly feel too much. I would think about it all in the morning.

We crept upstairs again, looked in on Lucy, stared at each other across her bed because she was so beautiful. And then we went into our room with its fitted wardrobes and just before we switched out the light Matt said, 'The trouble with death is you lose sight of the human being. It's as if they're set in a kind of amber, with all their good points highlighted . . . I've done that with Dad. We simply see him as that thoughtful, concerned man.'

I nodded. 'And he was so much more than that.'

Matt nodded. 'And less too.'

I didn't have time to think about that because he got out of bed again and opened the curtains. 'So that we can see the snow,' he said.

We were both asleep immediately.

Two

Two weeks later Mum brought Alicia round. The clocks had gone forward by then and it was a bright windy afternoon. They planned to take Lucy for an outing with her new trike.

Alicia was quite excited. 'There's a toy shop just opened in the high street. One of these activity places with a ball pool and a wooden train layout. Lucy will just love it!'

'Not to mention Gramma and Aunty Alicia,' Mum said.

'That trike is hard work.' I demonstrated the safety restrainer. 'Whether she pulls you or pushes you back, it's never easy.'

'Stop fussing, Jess.' Alicia always talked to me as if I were still ten. 'We don't mind, do we, Monica? We've got tickets for the ice show in Exeter this evening and your uncle Ray is going to drive us there and back so we don't have to worry about a thing.'

'Isn't he going to the show?' I enquired. I knew darned well he wasn't but now and then I feel Alicia needs reminding that he's her husband rather than an unpaid companion and chauffeur.

'Darling, he just hates things like that!' Alicia laughed merrily and Mum shook her head at me.

They were going out of the door and I had kissed Lucy and told her to be a good girl when I remembered to ask Mum about the Wiltshire Project, as I now called it.

'Must have been after school broke up at the end of July.' I didn't pinpoint it more by saying that it had to be before mid-August because that was when they discovered

Dad's lump. 'It's a village near Avebury. Did Dad say anything about it? Only Matt thinks we might have the job.'

Mum paused momentarily and Lucy yelled as the restraining rod brought her to an abrupt halt. Alicia went to the rescue.

'No, darling. I don't think Dad went anywhere just then. He was having such difficulty swallowing his food he tended to stay at home.' A shadow went across her face as she remembered. Of course I wished I hadn't said a thing.

'It doesn't matter. I just thought how pleased he'd be . . . You know.'

Alicia took the restrainer and allowed Lucy to scuff her way along the footpath. Mum smiled in my direction and followed her, and I went indoors to put on my fleece and find my bag. I said aloud into the mirror, 'Why don't you keep your mouth shut sometimes?'

Matt had gone to Avebury to meet the owner of the folly. He'd wanted me to go with him but I thought it was too early in the negotiations.

'I'm not asking you as my wife but as my business partner,' Matt protested. 'You should meet this chap as soon as possible. Sam as well.'

But in the end he'd gone on his own because I still hadn't finished the VAT return and the threat of a visit from the inspector put everything else in shadow.

My entire concentration was on the computer screen when Sam came in.

'Thought I might have a word with Matt,' he said diffidently, hanging on to the door and letting a gale blow in.

'He's gone to Wiltshire. That job.' I didn't want to take my mind off the figures before me but I hadn't seen Sam for months so I risked a welcoming grin. 'Come in and shut the door, for goodness' sake.'

'March. Comes in like a lamb, goes out like a lion,' he commented, standing in front of the radiator.

'I think it's the other way round, Sam.'

'Well, perhaps. Perhaps not.' Sam fidgeted. 'Shall I put the kettle on?'

That surprised me. I looked up properly. 'Oh. Yes. All right. That would be nice.'

'OK.'

He disappeared behind the curtain that masked the usual sink and electric kettle mess. I tried to pick up the thread of those figures. He called something over the curtain and when I didn't reply he came back out.

'Have you got any tea bags?'

'No.' I had meant to bring some in every day and every day I had forgotten. 'Sorry.'

'What about milk?'

'Not that either.'

'OK.'

He was gone, shutting the door carefully. Damn. I hadn't opened my mouth enough this time apparently. Sam was a good man, an old-fashioned craftsman, the solid counterpoint to Matt's brilliance. It was fascinating to watch Matt make sketches of his ideas, and then to see Sam's hands convert the ideas into reality. I shut my eyes tightly in exasperation because now I'd offended him, and I'd completely lost the plot on the screen. Then I calmed down a bit and went back a page and started again. I was there when the door opened and Sam reappeared clutching tea bags and milk.

'Where from?' I asked, amazed because the nearest shop was Hartford's.

'Pinched it from next door. They've got masses.'

He went behind the curtain and I finished my entry, pressed 'print', and then found time to smile at the sheer unexpectedness of Sam Clarkson. He was not, after all, so predictable.

'Sorry about all that.' I got up. 'Let me.'

'It's done.' He emerged with two mugs and put them on the desk well away from all the papers. He summoned a smile. 'I'm glad to see you back.'

'I should have come back before. Things have piled up a bit.' I took my tea and smiled back at him. 'Nice to see you, Sam. How is Daisy?'

'Fine. Almost there now.'

Belatedly I remembered that Sam and Daisy were expecting a baby. I felt awful; I really had shut the world out of my life. I'd been introduced to Daisy and liked her. She had come to work on the farm behind the industrial units and Sam had met her there.

'Is she keeping well?'

'I think so. But . . .' His smile became apologetic. 'She says she's scared.'

'Of course. Everyone gets scared.'

'But Daisy? She was out helping with the lambing last month.'

'That's probably why she's scared. The real thing.'

He nodded and looked down into his tea. 'We had a row. First one. I said she shouldn't go . . . when they rang from the farm. And as soon as my back was turned, off she went. I was angry. I've heard it's dangerous . . . infections.'

'Infection from the animals, d'you mean?'

He was embarrassed and could only manage a quick nod.

'I think it's just in the early stages of pregnancy.' I tried to sound clinical. 'There's a danger of the baby aborting. But she's all right.' I hesitated. 'Did you mention your . . . fears?'

He nodded again.

I said, 'Perhaps that's why she's scared.' I didn't wait for an answer to that one. 'Shall I pop in to see her, Sam?'

He was so grateful I knew that was what he had wanted all the time. He said eagerly, 'Take your little girl with you. Cheer her up, that would.'

'Oh Sam, of course.' I forced the tea down and smiled again. 'Of course I will. Tomorrow morning?'

'That would be nice. I'll tell her.' He picked up my cup, fitted it into his and took them to the sink. I heard him rinse them out and made a mental note to clean up the so-called kitchen and thank the unit next door for the tea bags and milk. He emerged from behind the curtain and made straight for the door; a man of few words.

I said, 'Hang on, Sam. Any message for Matt?'

'No. I'll see him when he gets back. Just wanted to know what was happening about the stained glass.'

'That's what he's doing today. It's all a bit . . . uncertain.'

'Yes.' He hung on to the open door again and the wind started to lift the papers. I sat on them. He said, 'Bit too rushed for my liking.'

'Hardly rushed, Sam. Last summer when he saw the job first.'

Sam raised his brows. 'Oh? I didn't know. First I heard was just before Christmas. Ah well. We'll have to wait and see.'

He was gone and I got up and shuffled everything into place and found paperweights. Then I cleaned the kitchen, washed up the cups and took the milk and tea bags next door, where they were really nice and wanted me to keep them. I eventually got back into the office and filed the printouts, and then I sat down at the desk and pulled out the folder containing Matt's sketches and laid them carefully side by side.

Mum hadn't remembered Dad going off to Wiltshire with Matt, in fact she had simply dismissed the idea. And now Sam knew nothing of the trip either. He thought the first call had been made just before Christmas. And yes, Matt had been away for a night in December. He had been worried and insisted that Mum come and stay the night. Surely I had wanted to know where he was going? Was I so wrapped up in my personal cotton wool that I hadn't been interested enough to find out more? And why on earth had Matt sketched Dad and Marilyn in some un-identified stately home or abbey or whatever? Dad, maybe.

31

Marilyn . . . no. I was going to have to ask Matt to explain. And I didn't want to. And I didn't know why I didn't want to.

When I got home, Alicia was giving Lucy her tea and Mum was putting away toys in the living room.

'She wanted to show Alicia every blessed thing she possesses,' Mum said. 'And she's got quite a lot, hasn't she?'

'Matt keeps bringing things home. And you and Dad were pretty bad.' Mum's face stilled for a moment and I went on quickly, 'I'm glad she wanted to show everything to Alicia. When she gets a present she usually goes for the box rather than the content.'

We all had a cup of tea and then Ray arrived in the car and off they went. I took Lucy upstairs to have a bath. I told her about our visit the next day and she wanted to take a toy for the new baby; I had to explain it was still in Daisy's tummy but we could take a toy and leave it for later.

Lucy said, 'Was I in your tummy?'

'Yes.' I floated a plastic duck through the suds.

'Warm,' Lucy commented.

'And safe,' I agreed.

That night Matt told me that the Wiltshire Project was clinched.

'He signed the agreement and paid the deposit. It's a lot of money. He must be rolling in it. He's planning an enormous amount of work. I want you to see it soon before anything gets started.'

I was washing up. 'Sam should see it first. He dropped by this afternoon to ask about it. He seemed a bit wary about the whole thing.'

'Sam's always cautious, you know that. But he'll love it. When I showed him some of my first designs, I could see him sort of homing in on them. He can't wait. He worked for a whole year at Ely Cathedral, you know. Restoration, that sort of thing.'

'He said it seemed to be a rushed job.'

'Hardly. Anyway that suits us, Jess. You will have realized by now that we're pretty near the edge.'

I was a bit surprised. 'The VAT's still high.'

'VAT is retrospective. We've got nothing much on now and no future jobs. Except this one. And this is going to be a good one for us.'

'Yes.' I could see that. And prestigious too. 'I'm sorry I've taken no interest in it, Matt. I really am. I remember you going off before Christmas and Mum staying with me and I don't think I even asked you about it.'

He was up in a minute, his arms around me. 'Darling. Nothing was important to you then. Of course it wasn't. Something cataclysmic had happened and everything else was . . . meaningless.'

He was so right. I turned in his arms and kissed him and found myself crying quite helplessly. He was horrified. He carried me into the living room and put me on the sofa and dried my eyes with the tea towel and asked whatever had brought this on.

'I'd forgotten Daisy was having a baby!' I wept. 'And I haven't lifted a finger to help out at work. I didn't even know about the Wiltshire Project. And you told me you looked at it last summer and Dad came with you, and he didn't and you only saw it before Christmas!'

Somehow Matt sorted all this out. He sat back on his heels and surveyed me frowningly.

'I would have told you if Daisy hadn't been all right. And the Wiltshire Project wasn't even a project until today.'

'And Dad? You said you'd sketched him in the folly . . .'

'Darling, I don't think I did. Can you remember exactly what I said?'

'No, of course not. But I got the impression you saw this abbey place last summer—'

'Which I did. I stayed two nights. Looked at it, made some sketches and very rough estimates, went back the next day and talked to Jerome—'

'Jerome?'

'A. K. Jerome. Heard of him? He calls himself an entrepreneur. Likes to be called Jerry.'

'He sounds . . . risky.'

'Yes. I rather think he is. Sam's right to be cautious. But he wants this badly and, dammit, he has signed a contract.'

'So you saw him last summer. But Dad wasn't with you?'

'I'm sure I never said he was.'

'The sketch – the background – was of the abbey.'

'Love, I did hundreds of sketches. Literally. Used them afterwards as doodle pads.'

I felt so small and mean and ashamed. I said, 'I see. I'm sorry. I'm really sorry, Matt. I can't think why . . . what . . .'

'Listen, Jess. You're coming back to life. Picking up the reins again. It will be strange and often a bit scary. You've never been keen on certain aspects of business' – I snuffled a laugh and he kissed me – 'but you'll get used to it. Don't start beating yourself up, darling. Talk to me more.'

'It's difficult. There's not a lot of time and when there is, I don't want to be wasting it talking about the firm.'

'Is there anything else? Now? Come on. Stop acting like a camel with the hump and just tell me!'

Of course I laughed but then I blurted it out. 'There was a sketch of Marilyn. Right next to Dad's. As if they were linked in some way. And of course with the same backgrounds, I naturally thought you'd done them in the same place.'

He looked blank. 'Who the hell is Marilyn?'

'The hairdresser. She was taught by Dad. She thought the world of him.'

'Who didn't? But yes, I know who you mean. He said she was like a galleon so I sketched her that way.'

'You've captured her just as you captured Dad. And you don't even know her. You're a born artist, Matt. You should have gone down that road.'

'Maybe. And we could have starved in a garret together.'

'Anywhere with you . . .' I was nearly weeping again. It

must be hormones. 'Thank you for sorting me out, darling. I'll try not to be quite so stupid in future.'

'Don't talk like that about the woman I love,' he said sternly.

I think later we watched some television. Then, later still, Mum rang to say she was back home and had enjoyed the ice show.

The next day was a great success. Lucy took to Daisy instantly and produced the baby's present, a stuffed rabbit knitted in angora wool, and explained just why it was so extra-special. She didn't see the irony of a rabbit being used to knit a rabbit. Neither did Daisy. 'It makes it almost like a real rabbit!' she exclaimed, leaning over her bump to receive it. 'The baby will know the feel of rabbit fur almost as soon as he's born.'

'Do you know it's a boy?' I pounced.

'Oh no. I want it to be a surprise.'

'Like Christmas,' Lucy said, nodding wisely.

'Yes. Just like Christmas.' Daisy beamed at both of us. 'After we've had our drink and biscuits would you like to see the nursery? Sam's done most of it but I've lined the cradle and done some stencils and things.'

We sat round the Formica kitchen table and Daisy poured orange juice and coffee and produced Hartford's biscuits. Then we went upstairs and admired the nursery and I could practically hear Lucy's brain working out a decor for her own room.

As we left I remembered that I was supposed to be instilling confidence somewhere or other.

'Listen.' I held the door against the roaring wind. 'If there's anything you want to talk about . . . the labour or anything . . . please get in touch.'

Daisy smiled and held her hair down with one hand.

'It's just so nice to see how it will be afterwards. When the baby starts having a life of his own. At clinic and relaxation and all that mother and child stuff all we talk about is

labour. Sam can't think of anything else. I feel sort of . . .
trapped. If you know what I mean.'

'He's probably scared stiff,' I said, suddenly understanding.

I gathered Lucy up and put her in her seat in the car.
Daisy waved and closed the door and I drove off and
thought that Matt had never ever made me feel claustrophobic or trapped in any way.

Mum was busy that afternoon so Matt and I took Lucy into
the office and found her a pile of scrap paper and her
crayons. She had always loved coming into work with
Daddy and drawing like he did and she hadn't lost that
over the past four months. She sat at his desk and worked
away for nearly an hour before her concentration gave
out and she wandered off to look at the photographs in
the outer room. Sam had come back to talk to Matt and
they were at the big drawing table with paper spread
everywhere, compasses, set squares and makeshift aids like
heavy books, an ashtray, even the teacups. I put the kettle
on and gathered up Lucy's drawings.

'Is it cold out here?' I asked her as I settled on one of the
standard plastic chairs. 'I've put the kettle on and I'll make
you a hot drink when it boils.'

She wasn't cold, of course. She climbed up on the chair
next to me.

'Those are my drawers,' she said, looking at the bundle
in my hand.

'Drawings,' I corrected. 'I thought you could tell me
about them. What's this one?'

'My room. That's my new bed. That's the armchair
Gramps bought me. That's the doll's house and the little
tiny tiny tiny teacups . . .' She rambled on, explaining
everything in careful detail. 'And that's the dangly thing.
Like Daisy got for the baby.'

'A mobile? You haven't got a mobile.'

'No,' she agreed.

'And your birthday has gone.' She had had the bed for her birthday.

'Yes.' She sighed. 'Can you have two birthdays?'

'Not really. But you can have treats.'

She said no more. I knew very well that the next time Gramma told me what a good little girl she had been, she would suggest a treat. I hugged her, laughing, and then turned up the next picture. It was of two stick people side by side.

'Ah. Who are these?'

I thought it would be Mummy and Daddy; it could have been Gramma and Gramps because she remembered Gramps all the time. It was a shock when she gave me a very definite answer.

'Gramps and Marry . . . kin.'

'Do you mean Marilyn? From the hairdressing shop?'

She nodded vigorously. 'I did it the same as Daddy's picture.'

'Oh.'

'Is it good?' she asked confidently.

'I don't know.' She was crestfallen and I said quickly, 'It's a very good picture. I just hadn't thought of the two of them . . . together.'

She drew down her mouth so that she looked the image of Matt.

'Mustn't waste paper,' she reminded me.

'No. Of course not.'

'I don't want it. You can have it, Mummy. But I want the one of my room.'

'Yes. I expect you do.'

I went back to the pile of scrap paper, intending to add the stick people to the others. And there on the top, copied by Lucy, was another of Matt's doodles. Same people, same setting, but this time together. And they *were* together, whatever he said. Dad was bending towards Marilyn looking into her eyes and she was standing very upright, looking straight back at him. I knew it didn't

37

mean a thing but it gave me quite a jolt. Logic was one thing, feeling another. And Matt had got feeling into this sketch.

Jennifer came round that evening. I had made a lamb casserole and while I peeled potatoes and laid the table, she and Matt bathed Lucy. The sounds from the bathroom were riotous. I smiled. It was good that when she was with Lucy, Jennifer could drop the successful businesswoman image. Once, when she announced she was off on a business trip, I had asked her where she was going. She had replied crisply, 'To the top, Jess. To the very top.' I don't think I ever discovered where the business trip took her.

She dished up while I went upstairs to settle Lucy down. Matt was looking damp and dishevelled; needless to say Jennifer was still immaculate. She was dark like me and had kept her hair fairly long so that she could twist it into all sorts of shapes and still have that sleek look. Lots of people thought she was a ballerina when they first met her.

Lucy was already heavy-eyed; for her it had been a hectic day. She didn't go into her usual Goblessmummyanddaddy routine so I thought Matt must have already heard her prayers. He knew they got to me with their final 'please look after Gramps'.

Jennifer was satisfyingly ecstatic about the lamb.

'Darling Jess. This is marvellous. Better by miles than the ragout they serve at the hotel. You should have been a chef.'

'Hang on.' Matt was grinning, happy for me. 'If she'd been a chef she wouldn't have applied for the job of office manager at the glass works and we would never have met.'

'Office manager!' Jennifer scoffed.

'It was in the Eighties,' I reminded her, 'when everybody was replacing their windows. There were five girls besides me. And later I took on another woman to cope with Sam's work.'

'Yes.' She turned her mouth down. 'I was only twelve then, I suppose. I had forgotten that it was big business for a time.'

Matt smiled. 'Booms are always followed by slumps. The information technology scene will find a different level soon.'

'Yes.' She pushed the rest of her lamb to the side of her plate. 'That's why I'm thinking of getting out.'

I looked at the discarded lamb and wished we still had our old cat. I hate waste. Matt solved that one by reaching over for her plate.

He said, 'What are you going to do?'

She smiled at him and didn't answer for some time. Then she said, 'I'm thinking of doing what you two did when Jess was twenty-five. I'm thinking of getting married.'

That really got me and I yelped my astonishment, excitement and sheer pleasure. Dad's death must have hit Jennifer worse than it hit me simply because she had no-one to share it with.

'Who?' I stared at her with my fork in mid-air. 'Do we know him? Someone at the office? Who?'

She was mildly surprised. 'I haven't met him yet so I can't answer any of that. But I've got a blueprint. I'll know.'

'What on earth d'you mean?'

'It's obvious. I don't want handsome but I couldn't stand plain or downright ugly. Although of course there are some types of ugliness . . . The main thing is, he must be successful, powerful and rich.'

Matt was laughing through a mouthful of lamb.

I said, 'But you must know heaps of men like that. So presumably you have someone in mind?'

'There's something else I left out. I need to fall for him. All the men I know leave me rather . . . cool.'

'So what are you going to do?'

'I'm going to look for him, of course. He has to be somewhere. I've been seconded to a kind of think tank.

Starting next summer. We're going to look at the future of intercontinental communications. I shall meet a lot of contenders.'

'Contenders?'

'Possible husbands,' she said patiently. 'Suitable men.'

Matt swallowed and said, 'Good God.'

'It's so cold-blooded,' I added.

'Remember how Jane Austen's characters met suitable men? At Bath Assembly Rooms or at arranged meetings in country houses. What's so different?'

I stared at her. 'I don't know. But it was . . . I mean, this is . . . Times have changed.'

She shrugged. 'Don't worry about it. If it doesn't come off I'll probably slot into a new committee anyway. Life is full of possibilities.'

Which was quite true, of course. But as I cleared the table and carried in the apple charlotte, I knew that possibilities also meant tragedies like Dad's death. I felt insecure again; vulnerable.

Matt teased Jennifer unmercifully about what he called her forthcoming marriage. Finally, when she remained perfectly good-tempered about the whole thing, he said, 'OK, you put all the info into the computer, tap the enter key. What if Mr Right refuses to respond? Won't play your game?'

She smiled at him. 'I think you know that's pretty un-likely, Matt,' she said.

'Well, I know you've had more . . . what shall I call them, boyfriends? – than I've had hot dinners, but surely you don't want that type? Once you've got them jumping through hoops, you lose interest.'

She opened her dark eyes wide. 'Yes. You're perfectly right. So . . . there's something else for the blueprint. I don't want a yes-man.'

He shook his head and said again, 'Good God.'

We finished eating and Matt said thoughtfully, 'I think you should come with me to Avebury. Jerry might be your

40

man. And anyway, you could make sure he abided by our agreement and paid the bill on time.'

'Coffee?' I asked quickly. I didn't like the way this discussion was going.

'No, thanks.' Jennifer smiled up as if to reassure me it was all a big joke. 'That was the best meal I've had for ages, Jess. Thanks.' She got up and kissed me, which was really unusual. 'I'd better go,' she sighed. 'All good things come to an end.'

I said, 'Have you rung for a taxi?' She usually took a taxi when she came to us. She enjoyed red wine.

'No, I'm staying with Mum for the night. I thought you might drive me round there.'

'Of course.'

'Does that mean I wash up?' Matt asked.

She said, 'Of course,' then laughed as she made for the bathroom. She was more than a match for Matt and he acknowledged that when he kissed me and muttered, 'Oh Jess, I'm so glad I married you.'

'She was only fifteen then,' I said, laughing.

'You know what I mean.' He hugged me and then she came down again and we got into our coats and went outside.

The wind had actually dropped. It was good to be able to stand up straight. It took less than ten minutes to get to the Old School and of course there was never any difficulty with parking. Mum and Dad must have bought fifty large flower pots but there was plenty of room still in the playground. We went through the back door into the cloakroom and then into the hall. The lounge light was on. You could see through the original glazed door. When the tiny infants' school closed, Mum and Dad had bought it and had hardly changed it at all. Jennifer and I had grown up with plenty of space and loads of tiny corners, very low lavatory seats and a drinking fountain. It had been idyllic.

I was about to call out to Mum when Jennifer half turned and gripped my arm, whirled me round and propelled me back into the cloakroom. She was amazingly strong. And she had acted very quickly. But not quite quickly enough.

'I think Mum might be having a little weep,' she said lightly. 'You get off, Jess. You'll see her tomorrow, I expect, won't you?'

She didn't wait for an answer. I was in the playground again and the door was closed against me. Yes, against me.

I stood there in the darkness trying to get my breath. I was nearly hyperventilating and I cupped my hands to my face and did all the right things. And then I leaned against the old red sandstone wall and looked around at the shapes of the flower pots and the swings and my car. And another car. Not Mum's because she always put hers in the old bicycle shed. I walked slowly towards it. It was Ray's car. And Alicia's, of course, except that she never drove it because Ray took her everywhere. I leaned against it for a moment; I seemed incapable of standing alone and unsupported. Then I went back to the cloakroom door and tried it. It was locked. Jennifer had locked me out.

I was furious. I banged on it like a child, both hands at once, palms down. Jennifer must have been the other side of it and she opened it before I could make much of a noise. She was furious, too.

'What are you playing at?' she hissed.

'Jen, stop it! That's Uncle Ray's car out there. And it was Uncle Ray. With Mum. In the sitting room. It was Uncle Ray with Mum. Just now.'

She said, 'Of course it was! For goodness' sake, Jess, pull yourself together. And try to grow up. Ray was kissing Monica. And they'd rather be alone. So clear off!'

I stammered like a schoolgirl. 'Ray is Alicia's husband!'

'And Alicia is Mum's best friend. They share everything. All right?'

I made a moaning sound. 'They can't! What about Dad?'

Jennifer said with laboured patience, 'Dad is dead, Jess. Now go home and talk to Matt about it. He'll explain everything.' She grabbed me by the shoulders and turned

42

me again. 'It's not the end of the world, darling. You've got Matt. That's the important thing.' She gripped my shoulders. 'Drive carefully, Jess. Remember, this is no big deal.'

I stumbled to the car and collapsed into it. She was right, of course. Mum had doubtless wept and Ray had comforted her . . . No big deal.

But all the way home I kept remembering that sudden glimpse of her in someone else's arms, her small head tipped back, her hands around a man's head, holding it.

Three

I didn't tell Matt. I'm not sure why; perhaps this was what he'd meant when he'd told me to talk to him. But I couldn't tell him about Mum and Uncle Ray. Or, as Jennifer had put it, Monica and Ray. Trying to remind me that they were people before they were mum and uncle. And anyway Ray wasn't a real uncle.

And Alicia. Jennifer had almost implied that Alicia condoned whatever was going on, didn't mind sharing her husband with her best friend. It was ghastly; my thoughts were so incoherent I couldn't finish one before another crashed in. No, I couldn't have talked to Matt that night.

He was amazed I was back so quickly. He'd thought I would stay and have a coffee and what he infuriatingly called 'a girlie chat'. He waited for me to throw a cushion or something, but I hardly heard him. He was still dealing with the pile of washing-up and I muttered something about a bath and went upstairs.

He made love that night with a kind of urgency as if he knew I wasn't with him and he was trying to call me back. Afterwards I left my head on his shoulder and told him I was sorry.

'Why? Why are you sorry? What are you sorry about?' I didn't answer properly and he said, 'Is it Jennifer? Has she said something to you?'

'No.'

'It's this husband business, isn't it? I could see it was putting you right off.'

'I don't know.'

'I was joking about taking her to Marcroft. I wouldn't dream of jeopardizing the whole contract by exposing Jerome to the wiles of your sister!'

'Marcroft?'

'The name of the village. Very old.'

'Sounds pretty. Marcroft.' I savoured the name. 'They'd probably be a match for each other, wouldn't they? My sister and your Jerry Jerome. You make him sound fairly tough.' I thought we had found something we could talk about.

He said consideringly, 'I'm not so sure. He seems to have quite a few women around him.' He gave a laugh, short and critical somehow. 'A man of mystery is Jerry Jerome. That's how he likes to appear, I rather think.'

'Tell me more.'

'You're getting sleepy,' he accused.

'Maybe.' I wasn't in the least sleepy.

'All right. Tell you what, I'll draw him for you. Tomorrow.'

'Lovely.'

Dear Matt. He rolled away from me and was asleep in about three minutes. I spent the night trying not to think. It's not possible.

The next day he got up early. He was meeting Sam at the glass factory and they were going to get colour samples to take to Avebury. He brought me a cup of tea and was suddenly anxious because I didn't make any effort to get out of bed.

'Are you all right?'

He drew the curtains carefully and spoke in a whisper. Lucy's bedroom door was always open and though she slept deeply we crept around like mice in the mornings, hoping to have an extra half-hour to ourselves.

'Yes. Fine.' I made a great show of stretching and yawning. 'What's the weather like?'

'Windy.' He came to the bed and kissed my nose. 'You didn't sleep.'

'No. Obviously neither did you.'

'Like the dead.'

'How do you know that I didn't then?'

'I just know.' He grinned suddenly. 'Bags under the eyes. Pudding face.'

'Oh Matt.' I could have wept at his obvious effort to cheer me up. He was so transparent.

He drew away and his grin settled into a smile. 'You're beautiful. And I love you.' He stood up and shrugged into his jacket. 'Listen. Why don't you take Luce round to Mum's and have the afternoon off? You've been working too hard.'

'Don't be silly. I'll see you this afternoon.' I had wondered during the night whether I would cancel Mum and just stay at home myself with Lucy. Now I knew I couldn't do that. I must behave as usual, otherwise she'd know.

The house was creakingly quiet after he'd gone. When I heard the clock strike eight I got up and put on my dressing gown and looked out of the window. The crocuses were flying their tiny orange and blue flags under the silver birch and the snowdrops weren't quite over. The daffodils were late; just as well with these awful winds. Next autumn I would transfer the bulbs to the little lawn on the left where there was some protection from the herbaceous stuff. They could drift down towards the path and the washing line . . .

Before that thought was over I turned quickly and made for the bathroom. It was going to be very difficult to block out all thoughts of Mum kissing Uncle Ray when Dad had been gone only four months . . . but somehow I had to do it.

Lucy woke ten minutes later and came downstairs on her bottom, step by step, her dark hair in little overnight rats' tails down her neck. I waited in the hall with a bundle of post that had just arrived.

'It's cold,' she discovered, standing upright. 'I've got bumps on my feet.'

'Slippers,' I reminded her automatically and without hope. Lucy had at last accepted that shoes must be worn out of doors. Indoors she still preferred to go barefoot. She went ahead of me into the kitchen, walking on the sides of her feet. 'Where's Daddy?'

I told her, then fetched the cornflakes while she settled into a chair at the table. Since Christmas she had become suddenly independent; I remembered this time last year when she had lifted her arms, wanting to be picked up all the time. I felt a sudden pang: my life had centred entirely on Lucy, the house, the garden; Matt coming home each evening; Mum and Dad babysitting at weekends so that we could go out together . . . so simple, so secure.

Lucy said, 'Shall we go and see Daisy today?'

'I don't think so, darling. We went yesterday. Maybe next week?'

'That would be nice. Let's go shopping.'

'Yes. But just food. Vegetables mostly.'

'We could look at the mobies.'

'Mobies? Oh, you mean the mobiles. I should have told you. Mobiles are really just for very small babies who can't sit up and play with their toys.'

'Why can't little girls have them to make their rooms pretty?'

Lucy was at the 'why' stage. I told her there was no reason on earth why little girls shouldn't have mobiles and perhaps she should design one. She was used to that word; it gave her drawings more importance. She nodded sagely and shovelled a piece of banana and one cornflake on to her spoon.

The whole morning was a struggle. Getting us dressed and into the car and down to the town. Back again with chicken pieces and vegetables for a stew. Lucy was right, it was bitterly cold. I felt myself cringing against the wind as we unloaded the boot and hurried indoors. We'd

47

seen no-one we knew, thank goodness; but the phone was ringing when I eventually slammed the front door.

It was Matt.

'Darling. Something unexpected has cropped up. Mr Jerome is here.' He broke off and gave a laugh. 'Sorry, Jerry. Jerry is here.' So 'Jerry' was obviously in the office practically sharing the phone call. 'He wants Sam and me to pop down to Marcroft with him to discuss some of these colours.' Someone said a word in the background and Matt laughed and repeated into the phone, 'Pronto.'

I said stupidly, 'Marcroft?' I'd already forgotten what he'd said last night.

A voice boomed something and Matt said with meaning, 'Marcroft Abbey, Jess.' He said in a lower voice, 'All right, darling? He wants to take us in his limo but I'll insist on the car so that I can be back tonight. Don't worry.'

I replaced the receiver slowly. It was time for lunch.

Mum arrived early before I'd really thought through whether I would stay at home all afternoon by the fire. I saw the car arrive and felt a jab of panic: what was I going to say? She would guess I knew . . . What if Jennifer had told her anyway? She hadn't. Mum came in the back way, hanging on to her bag and clutching her scarf but full of life, sparkling. Yesterday I would have told her so, congratulated her, asked her why . . . Today I said nothing.

She said, 'This wind is . . . exhilarating! I feel like your crocuses, going with it. You know?'

'Go with the flow,' I said as brightly as I could. 'Come in by the fire. Lucy is making some designs.'

I hadn't seen her looking like this for ages. It was quite horrible. The sooner I got away to the office the better. She looked over Lucy's little arm at the spidery scrawl which was a 'mobie' and entered into one of those long conversations that Lucy loves. Then she took off her coat and sat down.

'You carry on, darling.' She glanced up, smiling. 'We won't be going to the shops today, it's too windy. We'll try and make a practical model of this design.' She turned to Lucy. 'Isn't that what Daddy does?'

They were off again. I went upstairs and got ready.

I wasted the first half-hour at the office. I looked at my figures from yesterday and they meant nothing. So I made some tea and went next door to borrow milk again, then I looked at the sketches Matt had done of Dad and Marilyn, then I took them over to the waste-paper basket and very deliberately tore them in half and dumped them.

I was standing there looking down into the basket when the door opened and Jennifer was blown in. She slammed the door shut and stood with her back to it, breathing deeply. 'Bloody weather,' she said.

'I thought you'd be at work. The think tank or whatever you said.'

'I told you. Next summer. These things take time. I'm still working on statistics for the consumer company. I've just come from work.'

She went over to my desk and pulled off a pure silk scarf and black kid gloves.

'Any tea?'

I remembered I'd made some and not drunk it. I went behind the curtain and made some more. When I came out Jennifer had retrieved the torn sketches and put them together on my desk.

'These are good. Why have you ditched them?'

I shook my head. 'They're Matt's doodles. If we kept them all we wouldn't have room for any technical drawings.'

'May I take them? I'll do a photocopy.'

'Yes, I suppose so. Yes, of course.'

'Where's Matt now?'

I told her and she grinned delightedly. 'He sounds terrific, this Jerry Jerome! Absolutely in command.'

'He's got the money,' I said sourly.

'Well, of course.' She sat down and cupped her tea in her hands. 'D'you know, I really would like to meet him. A

Victorian folly designed to look like an old abbey . . . sounds really interesting.' She looked at me consideringly. 'Listen, Sis, ask Mum to take over at home and let's go and surprise them.'

'Matt's on business, Jen.'

'He'll be over the moon to think you couldn't last a day without him. And Jerry will just love it that your sister had to meet him!'

'Stop being so brazen.' But she was making me feel better somehow. 'Matt will be home tonight anyway.' She made a face and drank some tea. I said, 'I know you're being silly just to take my mind off Mum. What did you say last night? What did she say?'

She drained her mug and put it down with a bang. 'Lovely. Thanks, Jess. Well . . . I said, "Would you like a coffee?" And she said, "I thought I heard you in the kitchen banging about." And Ray said, "Hello, Jennifer. No coffee for me, thanks, I must be getting home." And Mum said, "I'll just see you out. And yes, I'd like coffee, Jennifer. Thank you." Then when she came back in she said Alicia had a cold which she had caught at the ice show so Mum had cooked for Ray. She grilled lamb chops. She wanted to know what we'd had for supper and—'

I said loudly, 'Shut up!'

She smiled. 'Come on, Jess. I thought this was how you'd be. Mum has known Ray longer than she's known Alicia. She can't cry too often with us because it'll drag us all down. So what is more natural than to talk to Ray about Dad and then cry on his shoulder—'

'Jen, he was kissing her! She was kissing him!'

'So? It's called comforting. One human being comforting another. I think it's wonderful.'

'You bundled me out of the way quickly enough.'

'Darling, it was a private moment for Mum. And precious. If you'd gone in there with that shocked face, it would have completely spoiled it for her. Made it awkward with Ray in the future. Messed up her friendship with Alicia.'

'But you absolutely shoved me outside! And locked the door!'

'Sometimes you're a bit too much like Dad. You expect too much of people.'

'Dad was completely non-judgemental!'

'He never judged, that's true. But people who were close to him, who knew him, they also knew what he was thinking.'

'He never thought ill of anyone.'

'You mean you didn't encounter his disapproval. Of course you didn't. You were the good sister. He'd had you to himself for ten years before I came along.'

I swallowed, staring at her. 'Did you . . . encounter . . . this disapproval?'

'Of course. Surely you realized that he wanted me to go to university?'

'Well, you were the clever one. Why not? And anyway when you got your first job he accepted that. Didn't try to talk you out of it.'

'No. But he had ways of letting me know about his disappointment.'

I was silent again, biting my lip.

She said, 'It's OK, Jess. I loved him like you did. We just had a different sort of relationship. He was a very complex man.'

I'd never thought of him like that. Straightforward was the word I would have used.

She smiled and put the pieces of Matt's sketch into a folder. 'That's why I want these. I want to look at them carefully.' She glinted up at me. 'Wouldn't it be a scream if Dad had a thing about Marilyn George?'

'A scream?' I echoed faintly.

'I know it's crazy. But it would amuse me.' She smiled at no one. 'I think it might amuse Dad too.' She turned back to me. 'Now look. You're all right now about Mum and Ray, aren't you?'

'I'm not sure. I didn't sleep. It was awful.'

51

'And now it's not.'

'I suppose . . . No, it's not.' I smiled back at her. 'Thanks, little sister.'

She began to gather up her stuff. 'I must fly. If you won't come with me to Marcroft Abbey I suppose I'll have to go home and get ready for work again tomorrow.'

'Come home with me. We can all eat together. Mum as well.'

She smoothed each finger into a glove. 'Well done. But I won't. She doesn't know I'm here and she'd want to know why.'

Unexpectedly, she came over and kissed me. 'She's only human, Jess. And so was Dad. Pedestals are for saints.'

I watched from the window as she ran for her car, bent double but still graceful. Then I went back to clear up the teacups. I'd thrown away my first cup because it had gone cold and I hadn't drunk this one either. I thought: I'll go home and have one with Mum.

They were surprised to see me so early. Mum had found a couple of wire coat-hangers and she and Lucy were doing a *Blue Peter* job with cut-out fishes, butterflies and birds. I made tea and found some cake and we sat around the fire and 'took a break', as Mum put it. I could feel peace and strength flowing back into me as they described how the mobile would look. Mum stood up and held out her arm and Lucy put the hook on to her outstretched finger so that the coat-hangers displayed their trailing cut-outs satisfactorily. I blew gently and everything moved around. This was what life was all about: no wonder Dad had loved children so much. They were reality.

We were well into the evening when the telephone rang. 'That'll be Daddy,' I said as I ran for it.

It was Daisy, Sam's wife.

'Is there any news of Sam?' she asked, her voice quavery.

'No, not yet. Are you all right, Daisy?'

'I think things have started. My waters have broken. I didn't want to ring for a taxi or anything just yet. Hoped Sam would be here.'

'I'll be with you. Ten minutes. Phone the hospital.'

She sort of sobbed. 'Oh Mrs Tavener, will you? Oh . . . yes, of course. I'll phone. Contractions are about ten minutes . . . Is that normal?'

'Yes. Absolutely. And I'm Jess.'

I had no idea whether ten-minute contractions were normal or not, especially as her waters had broken. What was Matt playing at, keeping Sam away from home at such a time?

Mum said, 'I'll stay as long as you need me, love.' She turned to Lucy. 'Isn't this exciting? Daisy's baby is coming!'

So I drove over to the industrial estate again, past the glass factory and down the lane through the farm to Daisy's cottage. The wind seemed to have scoured the land up here; the sheep were huddling together for the night, and the cry of the lambs sounded like Lucy used to at bedtime – that need for the security of the womb again when darkness fell. I shivered and turned in at the gate of Two Lanes Cottage.

Daisy was sitting well forward at the kitchen table. She had made tea but not poured. Two cups waited. A case was standing just inside the door. She smiled wanly.

'I didn't want to be a nuisance but thanks ever so much. I didn't know what to do quite. It's funny, all those ante-natal classes and I don't know what to do!'

'Well, it looks as if you're all ready to go so you're doing fine.'

'I rang the hospital—' She dropped her head on to her chest and stopped speaking. I took her hands and urged her to pant. Eventually she loosened her grip and raised her head. 'Thanks. It's easier with you here. Thanks.' She made an effort to push back her chair. 'The hospital said to

53

come in as soon as you got here. So . . .' She stopped speaking again and dropped forward on to the table. Less than two minutes. I took her hands again.

She said, 'Jess, I'm not going to make it to the car. Or upstairs. I'm so sorry . . .'

I threw cushions in front of the Aga, covering them with a tablecloth. It could have been like something out of a Victorian novel except that I was no midwife and there were no boiling kettles. And there was a telephone on the wall.

The hospital said an ambulance was on the way and not to panic. I switched on the lights, fetched a table lamp and plugged that in too. Daisy was on her side, rigidly still, trying to breathe quickly. I knelt by her, forcing myself to remember four years ago and Lucy's birth.

She said suddenly on a long gasp, 'It's no good. It's coming. I have to bear down.'

She rolled on to her back. Somehow she had got out of her maternity stuff; I pulled it away and took her feet on to my shoulders and her hands in mine. I think she instigated this; I can't remember. There we were in the time-honoured position, fighting – labouring, of course – to bring another human being into the world. Daisy's face was inward-looking; she did not see me. Her concentration was almost frightening. Just over a week ago she had helped to lamb some sheep and she knew exactly what was happening in her own body. She needed my presence, my hands and shoulders; but she was the one.

I told her when the head was crowned. She appeared not to hear me; her eyes were closed and she was gathering strength for the next enormous push. I thought that when that came, so would the baby. But it was not that time and she fell back, panting and somehow less purposeful. I tightened my grip.

'Daisy, come on. Don't let go now. He's almost here . . .'

I watched the muscles in her abdomen begin to contract again. There was something terrifying about this

54

involuntary spasm, the way her body was taking over. I yelled at her, 'Use this – it's coming – use it!'

She opened her eyes and looked at me, almost startled. Then the pain was on her and she clung to my hands and pushed.

The baby slithered on to the waiting towel without any help from me. It was a boy. Daisy stared down between her legs. We both stared.

Then Daisy said quietly, 'Hello, Watt. I thought it might be you.' She smiled widely. 'It was my dad's name. Walter. I know it's not fashionable but . . .'

'Oh Daisy, it's lovely.' I wanted to cry so much.

Daisy said, 'Make sure the air can get into his nostrils, then wrap him up. We'll wait for them to come and do the rest.'

That was what we did. He was so red and so cross with us, all we did was smile and laugh down at him. When the ambulance arrived they couldn't get over us. 'Hysteria,' said the young female paramedic, getting down to business straight away. But the best bit was yet to come.

'What's his name?' she asked, cleaning him expertly.

'Watt,' said Daisy.

'What's his name?' she repeated.

Daisy looked at me and I looked at Daisy. Then we really did burst out laughing.

I watched the tail light of the ambulance bounce down the lane and disappear from view. They had said it was a textbook labour and all due to the exercises Daisy had done religiously, and the fact that she had been with animals for most of her life and knew exactly what was happening. It had certainly been quick; I could remember more about Lucy's arrival now and it had been nothing like this. I smiled up at the cold March night sky, then I went back and tidied up and put the cushions in a dustbin liner. I wrote a note for Sam and left it on the kitchen table, put all the lights out and climbed into the car. The wind had

55

dropped and the enormous night sky was full of stars. I looked at my watch; it was almost midnight. It had been eight o'clock when I arrived. I couldn't believe it. Four short hours and there was an extra person on this earth.

I drove home slowly. The lights of Bath made an orange glow in the sky. That was where Daisy and Watt were going. I turned off and drove past the factory again, and across the ridge we had always called the Goose Bump, then down towards our little market town. I didn't need to go through the town; we were just the other side of the Goose Bump, but for some reason I wanted to see the place that Watt would call home. At one time there had been stocks in the main high street; now there was a wooden seat bolted down against the vandals. Opposite the market hall was a small Woolworth's, our modern equivalent. Then came a bookshop and Marilyn's and a few charity shops. After a junction a small street ran off to the left, with tall Victorian houses and modern bungalows in the big gardens. This was Acacia Avenue, where Jean lived. Dad had called it Conglomeration Street because of the varied architecture. I hesitated momentarily, with the idea of calling on Jean to tell her what had happened. But I didn't. As I went past I saw all the lights were on again. Perhaps they never switched them off.

I went past the church and then Hartford's and suddenly I was in the country and the night took over once more.

Mum was waiting up, of course, avid for news. I drank the cocoa she had made and told her everything. We were back together again; in fact we were closer than before.

'Matt rang,' she said, still smiling after hearing the 'Watt' joke. 'You will have guessed by now – they're staying the night. This Mr Jerome is at the Armstrong Arms and he's got them all rooms there. Five star, Jess. He's some important man.'

'Yes, I gathered as much. I'm surprised Sam didn't ring during the evening.'

'I told Matt that Daisy had gone into labour so Sam has probably been ringing the hospital all evening.'

'Poor Sam. Matt should have held out about coming home. For Sam's sake.'

'We'd better ring him, hadn't we? I've got a number.'

I got through without difficulty and Matt came to the phone. He was contrite but I could tell he was also extremely annoyed.

'Darling, what's been happening? Did you actually deliver the baby? Sam was completely incoherent. Just took the car keys and left!'

'Oh good, he'll be there by now. I'm so glad.' I told him I hadn't actually delivered the baby but I'd been there. 'I was sort of the welcoming committee, I think.' The euphoria was still with me but I was dog-tired. 'I'll tell you all tomorrow, Matt.'

The annoyance surfaced. 'I haven't got a car,' he reminded me. 'Sam took the bloody car.'

'Oh darling. Shall Lucy and I come and fetch you?'

'No need. Your sister has offered to drive me home.' He waited for my exclamations and when I said nothing, he said sharply, 'Did you know she was going to join us?'

'My God, how did she find you? She wanted me to come. Then she said she'd go back to Bristol. And now . . . how did she *find* you?'

'Went to Marcroft. It was mid-afternoon. We were still there. She had some story about you being upset and wanting to see me but knowing I'd be cross so she came herself . . . I don't know. It was some cock-and-bull yarn to get herself introduced to Jerry. Of course she's got Sam's room now. Can you believe it?'

I said wearily, 'Yes. She wasn't worried about me. Not really. She latched on to the fact that Marcroft was an abbey and she was intrigued . . . oh Matt.'

'She's bitten off more than she can chew, Jess. Jerry was not a bit happy about her arrival. He wanted us here for a couple more days. He likes to think he's paying the piper and calling the tune. When Sam just took my car keys and disappeared he wasn't in the least interested in Daisy and the baby. And when Jennifer then said that she would have Sam's room and drive me back tomorrow, he said nothing at all. And Jerry Jerome's silences are very . . . significant.'

'Listen, Matt. You don't like him and you don't trust him. Don't do this job.'

'We can't afford not to do this job, love. It gets better all the time. Sam is over the moon. He's talking of renting a flat here for Daisy and the baby so that he can work all hours.'

'Oh, well then . . .' I thought about it and said almost viciously, 'Let Jennifer do her stuff. See what happens.'

'It's out of my hands, Jess.' There was a pause. Then he said, 'Darling, please don't be unhappy. If Mum is sleeping with Ray she's obviously sorted it out in her head. We've got to accept that.'

'Sleeping with—' I cut off quickly. Mum was in the kitchen doing herself a hot-water bottle. 'What on earth has Jennifer been saying to you?'

There was another pause. Then he said, 'My God, has she been spinning me a yarn?'

'I think so.'

He said, 'Listen, my love. If I promise not to take any notice of what your sister says, will you do the same?'

'Well . . . all right.'

'You won't believe a word she says?'

'Oh lord, Matt. I suppose not. Unless she can provide me with – with evidence.'

'Never mind evidence. Proof.'

'Yes. All right. All right. Darling, I must go to bed.'

'Yes. Take care of yourself, Jess. I love you.'

'Me too.' Mum was in the doorway looking at me quizzically. 'Mum sends love. G'night.'

He said something else then was gone. I replaced the receiver.

'Jennifer's down there. Sam's driven straight to Bath.

She will bring Matt home tomorrow.' Mum started making incredulous noises. I said, 'I know. I've got to go to bed, Mum. Didn't sleep last night.'

'Of course. Of course, my love. I'll see you in the morning.' She put out the light in the kitchen. 'Trust Jen!' she said.

And we went upstairs.

Four

I slept on and there was a note from Mum to say she'd taken Lucy shopping and would hang on to her for the rest of the day.

Matt and Jennifer arrived at midday; she came in for coffee and the bathroom. She was almost gleeful, not remotely apologetic.

'He's the one! And I've made an impression. He's baffled.'

I said, 'You're wearing something different. You were wearing your blue power suit yesterday.'

'Darling, I had a case in the car.'

'Why didn't you *say*? Why didn't you tell me what you were going to do?'

'Because I knew you'd be like this!' She hugged me, which was most unusual. 'Where's Lucy?'

'Mum's taken her for the day.'

'Thought there'd be a row, I suppose.' She smiled round at Matt coming in behind her looking as if he had slept in his clothes. 'Matt, cheer up! You're home at last. And if I hadn't arrived, you'd still be at the hotel dancing to Jerry's tune.'

She disappeared upstairs and I put my arms around Matt. 'I'm sorry,' I whispered into his ear. 'I really had no idea—'

He kissed me; he smelled of toothpaste.

'The awful thing is, she's probably right. He thought he'd got Sam and me for as long as he wanted us.'

I drew him down to the kitchen. I'd cut sandwiches and the coffee only needed pouring.

He said, 'I had one of those English breakfasts. Jerry said you'd never speak to him if he didn't make sure I was well fed.'

'Didn't you mention you never have more than toast for breakfast?'

'Of course.'

'What an overbearing man he sounds.'

'That's the word.' He chuckled. 'When Sam upped and left he was put out but when Jennifer turned up he began to wonder what was going to happen next.' He met my eyes and grinned and the next minute we were laughing. He held out his arms and I went into them and sat on his lap. Happiness seeped through me warmly. All the mysteries and anxieties of the past week melted away. I'd slept for ten hours, the wind had dropped and already the daffodils were upright again.

He murmured into my ear, 'I love you.' Then he asked about Daisy and I told him that Mum had phoned the hospital before I was awake and Daisy was well and Watt was well and Sam had slept in the car below her window and had breakfast with her.

'He's a good man,' Matt said contentedly. 'He won't let Jerry sit on him.'

'Neither will I,' Jennifer said, coming into the kitchen. She held up a hand as I began to stand up. 'Stay where you are, Jess. Looks cosy. I must be off. No, I won't have coffee after all.' She made for the front door and I got up anyway and followed her. 'I had yesterday off but not today. They will be wondering where I am.'

'You'll find a reason, I daresay.' I should have been seriously annoyed with my sister but that morning annoyance was not on the agenda. I even pecked her cheek before she got in her car.

'No problem.' She gave me that glint of a smile again and then said, 'Jess, he's the one. And I am so going to enjoy myself! It'll be like *The Taming of the Shrew* in reverse!'

I watched her settle herself in the driver's seat and snap on her belt. She could have given lessons in how to get into a car with a minimum of fuss. I waved her off and felt a little less cosy about everything. Her avid interest in Matt's new client might make life difficult for Matt and Sam.

But that day and the next and the following month . . . they were all so good. So very good. I stopped thinking about Dad and Marilyn and Mum and Ray. It was more fun to concentrate on Jennifer and Jerry and Daisy and Watt.

That day we had the sandwiches and Matt changed into jeans and sweatshirt then showed me his latest designs. We knelt on the floor in the lounge while he pieced them together like a jigsaw.

'We'll make a workshop in the minstrels' gallery. We need to be right out of the way of any other work going on.'

'You didn't say anything about a minstrels' gallery. Sounds more like a baronial hall.'

He grinned. 'Matter of fact, Jess, it's not that old at all and it's no more an abbey than Hartford's Superstore. It's an odd conglomeration . . .' He stopped and looked at me. 'Your dad called Jean's street Conglomeration Street – d'you remember?' I nodded and he went on, 'He'd be tickled pink at this place. Everything has been tacked on to a tall shell and Jerome is going to continue in the same vein. Bedrooms, bathrooms, a sauna, a pool, stables . . . you name it, they're all going to be added.'

'Stained glass in all of them?' I asked incredulously.

'No. Only the original "abbey".' He grinned. 'But there's still heaps of work for us, Jess. Sam is all fired up.'

'And so are you.'

'I think so. It's just . . . him. Jerome.' His grin died. 'I can't seem to stand against him, Jess. Sam is unaffected – he ignored him last night. Just asked me for the keys and left. I could have gone with him but I didn't. If Jennifer hadn't turned up I'd still be there.' He stared blindly at the drawings on the floor. 'Jess . . . I'm weak.'

I laughed. He tried to tell me how serious he was but I ignored all that.

'Who do you think has kept us going these past few months? Made us enjoy Christmas. Kept the firm afloat . . . just.' I kissed him. 'Landed this contract and put up with this ghastly man. Would you call that being weak?'

'You don't know. I'm putty in his hands.'

'No. You're putty in *my* hands.' I started kissing him in earnest and he relaxed against me and closed his eyes.

'Call me Putty,' he murmured when I let him speak.

'Dear Putty. You're tired out. Let's go to bed.'

'Oh Jess. If only. I've got to get these drawings down to the office. Photocopy them.'

So we went together and spent the rest of the afternoon working. There was no word from Sam but Mum rang to say she'd take Lucy home and put her to bed if it would help. When we got back it was really late and Mum was looking exhausted so she stayed the night again in the spare room.

The next two or three weeks were so busy, so . . . intense, somehow. Sam and Daisy brought Watt home and we went to see them and they came to see us; I got all the paperwork up together at the office and the VAT man duly arrived and looked through everything and was perfectly nice; Mum and Lucy bought a splendid mobile for Lucy's room and Lucy gave the coat-hanger arrangement to Matt for the office – just ordinary everyday things but happening in a kind of Technicolor. I mentioned this to Mum and she suggested that we were coming out of that awful shut-in stage of grief and seeing things properly again.

She said, 'I remember when your grandma had the cataracts removed from her eyes – she couldn't believe how full of colour everything was! Even the double yellow lines in town made her gasp with surprise.'

'Oh Mum.' We had lost dear Gran so soon after that operation. That too had been a sad time. But we had recovered . . . or maybe we had adapted.

Mum said, 'I know. Don't think about it, just enjoy it.'

So I did. And when Matt came home from one of his mad dashes to Wiltshire it was like another honeymoon. We would chase each other around the house and Lucy would yell encouragement and we would gather her up between us and dance madly. When she'd gone to bed Matt would tell me how things were going at Marcroft. Towards the end of April, Sam and Daisy moved to a flat just outside Devizes and Daisy's mother went with them. Matt said it was temporary; company for Daisy.

'Once you're up there – in the minstrels' gallery – you're in a world of your own. Jerry's always interrupting, of course, but he's given up on Sam. Sam doesn't even hear him, he's completely absorbed in the work.'

I chuckled. I hadn't even met the ubiquitous Jerry but I didn't like him, and Sam's cavalier attitude was heartening to say the least.

'Any sign of Jennifer?'

'No. But Jerry goes to Bristol at weekends. He's got property there. And I think he's involved in some new development. So he could be seeing Jennifer.'

'Well, Mum hasn't seen her and neither have I. She must be . . . busy. I just hope she knows what she's doing.'

'She knows exactly what she's doing,' Matt said.

I nodded, reassured.

So April came to a close. It was a Monday. The weather was brilliant. Lucy played outside; Mum and I had tea under the silver birch. Matt had finished up at the office and left for Marcroft. A car drew up outside and Alicia came round the side of the house and crossed the lawn to join us. She was wearing very high heels and I told myself it didn't matter because they would aerate the lawn. She had a lime-green linen suit on. She looked wonderful.

I patted the garden bench. 'Come and sit down. I'll fetch more tea.'

She shook her head. 'I mustn't stop. Monica, you can guess what's happened.'

I glanced at Mum; it was obvious she had guessed.

Alicia went on, 'I had to come and say goodbye. When you weren't at the Schoolhouse I knew you'd be here.' She turned to me. 'Darling, I hope you don't think badly of me. Your mother disapproves, of course, but you're young and more open-minded.' She paused and then said, 'You don't know, do you? I thought Monica would have said something. Over the years.' She gave a helpless little shrug. 'I've been in love with someone else for a long time, Jessica. He's in the theatre and it wasn't practical . . . Anyway, I'm joining him at last. He's got a part in a television soap. In the States. We shall live over there. I think your uncle Ray understands.'

I was stunned. The glimpse I'd had of Ray and Mum – Ray and Monica – through the lounge window at the Schoolhouse had long been explained away by the theory that Mum needed comforting. It seemed, quite suddenly, that it was the other way round.

Mum said levelly, 'In other words, Marcus can now afford to keep you.'

Alicia turned pink but she said determinedly, 'Don't let's fall out, Mon. We've been friends for so long. And you always knew about Marcus.'

Mum sighed. 'Sorry.' She stood up and gave her friend a wry smile. 'Oh dear. I shall miss you. Thank you for what you've done these past months.'

They hugged. Alicia said, 'Will you be all right?'

'Should be me asking you that question.' Mum managed a little laugh, then drew away and looked into the carefully made-up eyes. 'Yes. Yes, I shall be all right, I promise. What about you?'

'Well, you know I'll be all right whatever happens.' Alicia turned to me again. 'You look absolutely flabbergasted, Jess. Did you have no idea? Ray and I have been so – so separate. I thought you would have guessed.'

I managed to speak normally. 'No. I had no idea.'

'Will you wish me well?'

'I – I – of course. Always.'

'Oh Jess.' She hugged me then. 'I shall miss you all. Your lovely beautiful Matt and your gorgeous little girl. It's been such fun.'

It occurred to me that Alicia had always been fun. Unexpected presents and exciting outings. I hugged her back.

'We shall see you again, surely?'

'Of course. Oh, of course. One of the best things about life is that you never know what is around the corner!' She picked up Lucy and smothered her in kisses. 'I'll send you things. Another mobile for Lucy. And candy. See – I'm already speaking American! Candy – candy kisses!' She buried her face in Lucy's dark hair and I knew she was near tears.

Somehow we got to the gate and put her into her car. It was piled high to the roof with luggage. As we waved her goodbye I said to Mum, 'I'm amazed she didn't get Ray to drive her to the airport.'

'He would have done too.' Mum turned away sadly. 'Another chapter closed.'

'Let's go back and have more tea,' I suggested. I looked at Lucy. 'You can pour if you're very, very careful.'

Lucy smiled. 'Put some in my teapot for me,' she said. 'Then you won't worry.'

I marvelled at such reasoning but of course I know all mothers think their children are unusual.

Mum said, 'Just half a cup then. I must get home in case Uncle Ray calls.'

I said, 'Oh. Yes. Of course.'

Mum must have thought I was empathizing because she touched my arm gratefully. 'Thank you, darling,' she said.

I rang Matt at the Armstrong Arms that night. Sam and Daisy had wanted him to stay with them but Jerry had insisted on the hotel and I think they were probably relieved. Watt was doing splendidly but they didn't get much sleep.

I told Matt about Alicia and he laughed – he actually laughed.

'Trust her! I've often wondered, haven't you? She practically ignores Ray when they're together.'

'Well, that's Alicia. I didn't think it meant that their marriage was on the rocks.' I was annoyed with Matt for taking it so light-heartedly. 'And what about poor Ray?'

'Poor Ray, my foot. He'll find someone else, mark my words.'

I thought with panic that probably he had already found someone else.

He said, 'Jennifer turned up today. Jerry brought her into the nave – that's what he's calling it now, by the way – to tell her what he planned to do. He knew we were in the gallery. He was showing her off. I stood up, about to call down to her, and he was kissing her. Possessively. She pulled away and walloped him!' He chuckled. 'I did a Sam. Sat back down and got on with my work. Now she's gone and he's in a foul mood.'

'Oh Matt. How awkward for you. D'you want me to phone her?'

'Of course not, darling. She's playing games with him. And he knows it. We can't interfere with their sexual shenanigans!'

I didn't know what to make of it. Alicia and Jennifer. I tried to echo his chuckle. 'So long as you can cope with the moods . . .'

'I can cope. I've only just got back from Sam's. The baby's gorgeous. Daisy's not well though.'

I was delighted to talk about Daisy, and then Watt and Daisy's mum and Sam. Compared with Alicia and Jennifer, they were so blessedly normal.

The next Monday was the May Day bank holiday. Matt hadn't come home that weekend and was planning instead to work through till the following Friday when he would take a long weekend. We hoped to drive down to Lyme Regis or Beer and all get into the sea. The weather was wonderful.

Mum phoned early.

'Darling, I know I was going to come round but Uncle Ray has suggested taking me into Bath for lunch. D'you mind? He's so lonely.'

I did mind. But on the other hand, if I hadn't seen them that awful windy night in March, I wouldn't have minded at all.

'Of course not. It will be lovely there today, down by the river.'

'It will, won't it? I'm looking forward to it.'

It had been Alicia who had given Mum her small outings; now it was Ray.

Mum said, 'Darling, why don't you pack a picnic and drive over to Marcroft? Take the country roads. Shouldn't be much traffic.'

It simply had not occurred to me; Matt had never suggested it and it was not a familiar route.

'Matt's working. I don't know whether he'd want Lucy and me around.'

'You need not interrupt him. It would be a chance to see the abbey and call on Daisy and the baby.' She paused. 'Just a thought.'

'Well, yes – I suppose I could go and see Daisy. Matt does the trip in under two hours.'

So that's what I did. Full of trepidation, I rang Matt and couldn't get him and time was going on, so I put it to Lucy and she was all for it. I hadn't done a long drive for years; I had to find a map and plot some kind of course and make a lunch . . . plenty of drinks . . . It was exciting. And the alternative was . . . well, not exciting. There were two or three other houses in our fold of the hills but on a bank holiday everyone else would be out and about. It was such an ordinary thing to do but I hadn't driven off like this by myself for years. This was definitely an adventure. Lucy loved it. And, suddenly, so did I.

The countryside was beautiful; some of the lanes were so narrow that the hedges brushed the car either side. I avoided the A roads and did not touch Frome but went across country through villages with double-barrelled names like Vencey Deverell and Sutton Moorside, and then on a hill overlooking the Plain we stopped and had our picnic. I spread out the map and showed Lucy where we'd come. She had brought her wax crayons and she marked the lanes with a red one.

'Where does the line go next, Mummy?' she asked.

'Well, there's Marcroft . . .' Matt had highlighted it long ago. 'And if we keep to the edge of the Plain for a while, we'll get to this place. It's called Overton Edge. Then we can cut through Marlborough Downs and it should bring us out just . . . there!'

We packed up and I strapped Lucy into her seat again and off we went.

There was plenty of traffic around Avebury. I was glad to leave it behind and cross the busy Marlborough road and head into the wide Wiltshire countryside around Wansdyke. We came upon Marcroft suddenly: two or three houses, a garage, a church and the imposing Armstrong Arms. I stopped for petrol at the garage and enquired about the abbey; it was still a mile away down a rutted lane that was going to be murder in the winter. I thought Jerry should be spending some of his money on having his road surfaced properly. But as the abbey hove into view I could see why he wasn't bothering. Three four-wheel drives were parked outside an arched porch, huge vehicles that could obviously cope with eighteen inches of mud; there were no signs of Sam's old car or Matt's Cavalier.

'Is this the place, Mummy?' Lucy enquired. She was getting tired and so was I. I pulled up behind the other cars and switched off. The silence was wonderful; Lucy could appreciate it too. We sat there with the windows right down, breathing in the stillness. We were used to the more bracing air of the Mendips. This was subtly different, laden with the scent of flowers, almost tangible.

'It smells of coconut,' Lucy said. She had recently won a coconut at a church fête and had not liked it.

'It's gorse, I think.'

'Is Daddy here? Can we see him?'

'Of course. I think he must be around here somewhere. Shall we go and find out?'

'It's a venture, Mummy,' she remarked as I unlocked her straps.

'Yes. A proper adventure,' I agreed. I knew we were both a little nervous.

Inside the porch it was blessedly cool. The inner door was wedged open but there was no sound coming out and our arrival had not been noticed. We walked into the abbey itself and stood still, looking around us in the gloom.

I could see immediately why Jerry called this the nave. It was like the body of a church, a long, fairly narrow space overlooked by a clear circular window at the end, facing east. The light from this round window laid a solid bar of sunlight like an aisle the length of the nave. More white light from the side windows made a grid across the flagged floor. I could understand why Jerome wanted some colour in this stark interior. Stained glass would make such a difference; I had never seen a building that called out for it more than this one.

Staircases rose from left and right of the nave to serve the gallery. The intricate stonework was amazing and even after our eyes grew accustomed to the sudden shadow we continued to stand and look.

Lucy whispered, 'It's like a magic castle, Mummy.'

It certainly was like an illustration in one of her books and perhaps that was where the builder had got his inspiration. Beneath the window, where an altar might have been in a real abbey, there was a large slab of stone and it was possible to imagine the Sleeping Beauty stretched out upon it. Perhaps it was the long and unaccustomed drive through the sun-drenched countryside, but this sudden transition into what seemed like a film set felt surreal.

I said aloud, 'I need a drink.'

My voice echoed around the cavernous interior and, as if it had set in motion some ancient mechanism, two heads popped up from the edge of the gallery. The first belonged to my sister and the second, I assumed, was that of A. K. Jerome . . . Jerry Jerome in fact. It was a well-shaped head.

Jennifer squeaked – very untypically because she always pitched her voice low, 'Jess! For God's sake!' She turned and spoke in a quieter tone. 'It's my sister. Jessica Tavener. Matt's wife.'

The other head said, 'I gathered most of that.'

They both stood up, so that I could see their upper bodies. They must have been lying down. On the floor. My sister was . . . tousled. Jennifer is never tousled and I hated it. And what it suggested. On the other hand, Jerome was almost immaculate. He wore a short-sleeved shirt tucked into jeans – yes, I noticed that. And his darkness. He was very dark and he had a long, narrow, clever face. I did not like him.

He said, 'I'm pleased to meet you, Jessica. And the young lady must be Lucy.'

His polite words made me unreasonably angry. 'Where's Matt?' I asked without acknowledging his welcome.

Jennifer said, 'Well, he's – he's somewhere. He'll be delighted. So pleased. But why have you come, darling? Is everything all right?'

'Perfectly.' I was tight with anger and my voice showed it. Jerome gave a little laugh.

Jennifer tried again to get control of whatever was happening. 'Thank goodness.' She smiled sideways. 'This is Jerry. Jerry Jerome. He owns the abbey.' She was already relaxing. 'Shall we go down, Jerry? Introductions at this height are a little difficult.'

His smile was broad and amused; he looked her up and down – below the level of the gallery wall.

'You wait here, darling. I'll go and escort the ladies up to our level.'

His implication was so obvious it was . . . horrible. Either Jennifer had shed her skirt or she was so rumpled that I would know immediately what they had been up to. I hated the whole thing. He was deliberately cheapening my sister.

I said swiftly, 'Please don't bother, Mr Jerome. We've come to see Matt. We'll go and look for him.' I took Lucy's hand in mine. 'Come along, love. Let's go and find Daddy.'

We were out of there so quickly Lucy didn't have time to utter a word. I knew she would want to go up those stairs to Jennifer – she loved her aunt – and the stairs and gallery were so inviting. I didn't give her a chance to protest. As we went back into the porch, we both heard Jerome laughing aloud. We almost ran to the side of the building and along the edge of a wonderful sweep of grass towards the back.

Lucy panted, 'Mummy, you're going too fast.'

I said, 'I know. Sorry, darling.' I slowed and stopped. It was terrifically hot and the tall abbey building was casting its shadow on the other side. We sheltered in the shadow of a mock buttress and looked around us. No sign of Jennifer following, no sign of life at all except for two or three sheep munching the grass.

Lucy said, 'Mummy, let's go and see Aunty Jenny. Then we can look for Daddy.'

I took a deep breath. I'd put myself in rather a silly position. After all, whatever Jennifer got up to on a bank holiday was nothing to do with me. I wanted to get back to the car, where there was a cool drink in the thermos. And then we could drive on to wherever Matt and Sam were.

I said, 'I think Aunty Jenny would prefer to be left alone for a while, Lucy. But we'll go back and fetch the car. It's too hot to walk.'

'It's big, isn't it?' Lucy peered down the green slope to

where the Victorian structure gave way to lower, more modern buildings. She led the way back past the sheep and a little stand of trees I hadn't noticed before. 'It's all by itself too.' She stood by the car door and waited for me to help her in and strap her up. Thank goodness no-one appeared. It was quiet and thickly still again. She looked at me with her dark eyes. 'I don't like it here, do you?'

I tried to smile reassuringly and got into the driving seat as quickly as I could without seeming panicky. The engine started and I thrust the gear stick into first and trundled into the deep shade of the abbey.

Lucy said, 'Poor Daddy.'

We found him quite quickly, before the whole thing assumed nightmare proportions. The abbey was joined to the modern buildings at a right angle and on the other side of them were woods. We recognized the Cavalier immediately. Lucy shouted, 'Daddy! Where are you?' And Matt emerged from the trees, looking incredulous. And wonderfully familiar.

I ran to him and clung on to his T-shirt as if I were drowning.

'Oh Matt . . .' I pushed my face into his shoulder. 'Matt, I just thought it would be nice to have a picnic.'

'Darling, what's happened? What's wrong?'

'Nothing. Oh Matt, I'm so pleased to see you!'

'Why didn't you phone? It's been too much for you.' He held me hard. 'I'm pleased to see you too. So pleased.'

Behind us, Lucy protested at her safety harness and we pulled apart and went to rescue her. We were laughing but I could have wept too. And then, from the trees, Sam appeared.

'My God, it's Mrs Tavener! I was asleep . . . sorry.'

It was suddenly all right again. Lucy launched immediately into an account of our 'venture', Sam smiled, Matt laughed out loud and I started to unload the remains of the picnic. The strange, Gothic scene enacted by Jerome and Jennifer from above, for Lucy and me down below, faded into proper perspective. We moved into the shade of the trees where Matt and Sam were cooling some bottles in a wonderful clear stream; I handed round the rest of our sandwiches while Lucy took off her sandals to paddle. At some point during that halcyon afternoon I tried to tell Matt about the humiliation in the abbey.

He nodded. 'I know. He gets up to all sorts of tricks like that. Yet he can be a wonderful chap.' He sighed deeply. 'Perhaps you'll pick up some of his other qualities during dinner.'

'What do you mean, darling? I can't stay very late. This really is an adventure for me!'

He picked up my hand and put it to his lips.

'I know. You must come and stay at the Armstrong. You can't go back tonight. Give Jerry a chance to redeem himself too. And there's Jen. You should have a word with her, darling.' He gave me a wry smile. 'I can't handle your sister.'

'She won't listen to me.' I looked at his bent head. Behind him Lucy sat waist deep in water while Sam found flat smooth pebbles for making a dam. I didn't want to leave, that was certain. But I didn't want to be in Jerry Jerome's company ever again.

Sam provided a solution.

'Come and have dinner with us,' he said in his flat voice. 'We can get fish and chips or something. Daisy would love that.'

So that was what we did. We drove in convoy to Devizes and then I followed Sam to one of the flats that had been the married quarters for army families during the war, while Matt peeled off to buy our supper. We sat around the kitchen table and talked about everything under the sun. It was a wonderful evening, shared with people who were ordinary in the best sense of the word. All the small and disturbing things that had happened during the last few weeks were completely sidelined. Daisy and Sam, Matt and

74

Lucy, Daisy's mum cooing over baby Watt: they were the sort of people I knew and liked and respected. This was my world.

Matt found us bed and breakfast at a pub not far away and we spent a wonderful night together. It was like another honeymoon; days compressed into those eight hours. When I drove back towards Midsomer Norton the next morning, I was deeply and consciously whole. A whole person, made so by another whole person. I thought of Alicia and her unknown Marcus; I thought of Ray and even Mum finding comfort where she could. I thought of Jennifer playing with fire, already singed if not burned. Even Jean, alone most of the time and so terribly anxious about the twins' asthma. None of them had the kind of certainty that I knew then. They would have called me smug. Even pious. Perhaps I was. I wondered, as we sped homewards that Tuesday, whether I might be pregnant again. That would be wonderful.

All that week I looked forward to Friday when Matt would be home and we would pack ready for our trip to Beer. We'd finally decided on Beer during the early hours of Tuesday morning. The shingle beach shelved quickly into a crystal sea and we could use our dinghy to paddle between the rocks and look down at the shoals of tiny fish and the bigger ones of mackerel. Lucy would love it; we'd been there before her birth and found a farmhouse where the food was excellent.

Friday came. The weather held. Mum rang to say she and Ray were going to London to see a show. I was all right about it, I think. I can't remember. I have to be quick and write this down but it is hard.

Matt rang and said he was bringing Daisy and her mother home for the weekend. Sam would be staying on. I was to expect them about teatime.

At six o'clock the policeman, the one with the broken nose, knocked on the door. For a second I didn't know why. And then I knew. Since then, that policeman has been round lots of times. His name is George something. I can't remember that either.

I do remember him standing there in the porch. Behind him was Lucy's tent, which I'd put up an hour before. He held his cap under one arm. The sun glinted off some silver on his shoulder. There was a woman police officer with him.

She said, 'Mrs Tavener? Mrs Jessica Tavener?'

I said, 'Yes.'

She said, 'May we come in?'

That was when I knew.

Five

Marilyn said, 'If you'd come more regularly we could have kept you looking absolutely super. As it is, your hair is out of condition.' She pursed her lips at me in the mirror. 'Listen, as it's so hot, would you like it really short? You could take it all right.'

I nearly told her I didn't care what my hair looked like, but of course I didn't.

'Yes, OK.'

She nodded. 'It will help. Strengthen it.' She began to cut and I looked down at my lap. Beneath the nylon gown my fingers deliberately unlaced themselves and laid themselves flat on my knees. Now was going to be the tricky part. Amanda, who had given me a wonderful shampoo and massage, hadn't spoken a word. That's how it took most people; it was as if they were terrified of me. As if I brought bad luck with me. So many deaths in such a short time: my father, my husband, my friend and her mother . . . It was terrible, tragic, incredible.

And now I was caring for my friend's baby. Was I fit to look after him? I often asked myself that question. But Sam never had. He'd always said, 'Thank God . . . oh, I mean it – thank God you're here for poor old Watt.' He hadn't even asked the first question, which should have been, 'Will you look after Watt while I get things together?' Jean had commented once, disapprovingly, 'Sam Clarkson is on another planet.' I knew she was right but I understood; it was how I coped too. Wrap yourself up . . . make a cocoon.

The police had brought Watt that terrible day, 12 May
. . . the Saturday after the bank holiday . . . and he'd been
with me ever since. More than three months. I'd been in a
cocoon for three months. A tight cocoon. Claustrophobic.
Perhaps, eventually, suffocating. Oh yes, I understood Sam
very well indeed. I'd watched him all through the funeral;
he'd stood like a ramrod, his gaze fixed on some point in
mid-air, and when the dreadful familiarity of some of the
phrases had got through, he had blinked and then refixed
that sightless gaze. And I had done the same. 'I am the
resurrection and the life . . .' Blink hard, refocus. '. . . and
is cut down like a flower . . .' Clench fingers into palms
then blink and refocus.

But then, after the joint funerals, Sam had gone to work
and continued in a way to keep his gaze fixed on the
middle distance. And I had had Watt. Watt was a link with
my other life. I had been there when he was born and
he had been with Matt when Matt had died, and Daisy,
and Daisy's lovely mum . . . A transporter lorry carrying
eight spanking-new Ford Fiestas had lost its way and was
using the narrow lanes that had been created for horses
and carts. I could imagine it so well, though I rarely did
– I did not dare to in case the cocoon was damaged
irreparably: the tall flower-choked hedges masking the
lorry's height as it took up all the road around the bend.
Perhaps Watt had been crying; perhaps for one terrible
instant Matt had been smiling sideways at Daisy's mum.
We would never know. Lucy had said it didn't matter how
it happened. She had wept distractedly and until Watt
arrived she had been like me without my cocoon, shocked
and disbelieving one minute, overwhelmed with grief the
next. And then Watt had come. Helpless, bereft just as she
was, he had taken her finger and held on to it tightly as
babies do. And she had looked up from his face and said
quite clearly, 'It doesn't matter how it happened, Mummy.
Jesus was there.'

From that moment we coped in our own ways. Mine was

the cocoon. Maybe hers was too. But it was from that simple discovery she had made for herself that she picked up her life again. And I had no choice but to do the same. One thing we had in common: she knew, quite matter-of-factly, that Matt was still around. And I must have known, because I often spoke to him. I didn't speak to Dad or Daisy or Daisy's mum. Just Matt.

No wonder people were terrified to speak to me, unable to find a word or a gesture.

But now . . . Marilyn strode in where angels might fear to peer from beneath their halos. Marilyn was not terrified.

There was a respite while she used the electric clippers. I glanced up quickly and then down again. I looked like a Mohican.

She put the clippers down and went for the scissors.

'So. How's the baby?'

'Fine. He can sit up on his own now.'

'Who's got him this afternoon? Your mother?'

'No. My friend.'

'Oh yes. Jean Parslow. I know.'

She used exactly the same tone of voice as Jean had used about her last winter. She was staring at my hair, frowning.

I said jocularly, 'Is it that bad?' I might not care what I looked like at the moment but I certainly didn't want to be bald.

She cleared her throat. 'Well, you tell me. I think it's just terrible if you want to know. It's too much for you. You've got your little girl not even at school yet, and now someone else's baby.'

I realized the misunderstanding at the same time as I realized she was on the verge of tears.

I said, 'Oh Marilyn, don't worry. It's like my mother says. Doesn't give me time to think. And that's good.'

Marilyn recovered and started on my hair again in earnest. 'I'm not so sure about that,' she said. 'Time . . . all right, I can see that you don't need too much of it. But you haven't had enough. Not enough time to grieve. Not properly.'

I glanced up again. It was amazing to discover that she really cared. She really did care.

'Grief . . . you don't need *time* for it.' She deserved a proper answer. 'It's a way of life. This is how it will be now.'

'No.' She sounded very definite. 'No. You think that now. But you won't always. It's just that . . . things will be different.'

'Yes.'

I didn't believe her, of course, but there was no point in trying to describe the kind of void in which I moved these days; cooked, shopped, fed Watt, helped Lucy with her 'designs'. I was so cheerful it hurt.

She asked me to lift my head and I did and saw that she was indeed crying. She realized I had seen her tears and said briskly, 'You have lost a lot of hair, Mrs Tavener. Are you eating properly?'

Her kindness was almost too much but I managed to say brightly, 'Of course. I have what the children have and that is very healthy. Watt has already begun to take some solids. They start early these days.'

'You must watch yourself. That's what I meant about having time. You're giving all yours to the children.'

Mum should have been saying things like this. She hadn't. Probably Mum knew that I didn't want time for myself; I didn't care about myself. It had been Mum who rang and said starkly, 'I've made an appointment at Marilyn's. Your hair is a mess.'

'Mum, don't be silly. I don't care about my hair. And Ray isn't keen on you having the children.'

Mum didn't deny this. She said, 'I ran into Jean and she says she'll have the children.'

'For goodness' sake, Mum—'

'Do Lucy good to mix with her boys.'

That shut me up. Lucy was marvellous with Watt and loved him unequivocally. So much so that she had declined a place at nursery school and it was going to be tricky to get her to go to the village primary school in ten days' time. Watt was filling the gap her father had left; she was filling the gap that his mother had left for him. Maybe a session with Nat and Tony Parslow would be a good thing.

Mum said quietly, 'You needn't worry about Marilyn putting her foot in it, Jess. She is . . . she is full of grief herself. She would love to see you.'

'Why? What's happened to Marilyn?'

'Nothing recently. But she knows what it's like to lose someone you love.'

That made me think. It was so obvious; practically everyone I knew had lost someone. And one thing I had that perhaps others didn't . . . I knew that Matt still loved me. I still felt that. Loved.

So I'd dropped Lucy and Watt off at Jean's in Conglomeration Street and come into the salon, dreading this conversation. Now, suddenly, I didn't. There was something about Marilyn. Straightforward, almost simple. I wished that I was the sort of person who needed time to grieve.

I said quietly, 'I just go from day to day, Marilyn. That's all I can do.'

She stopped snipping and held my head so that our eyes met for a long moment in the mirror. Hers were brimful of tears. Mine were so dry they were scratchy.

She said, 'I promise you it will get better.'

Her words were so convincing that I wanted to give her something in return. 'My father always said you were a good person, Marilyn,' I said.

She half smiled. 'I don't believe you.'

'He said you were beautiful. I told you before . . . He meant inside as well as outside.'

She blinked. Then she swallowed. She said, 'I didn't realize . . . Didn't you mind? When he said that?'

I was genuinely surprised. 'Why should I mind?'

'Well, you know – Marilyn George. Not got a good reputation, has she?'

'Reputation? I've heard she's a wonderful hairdresser and she's got a heart of gold.'

'Oh yes. The tart with the heart. I've heard that too.'

I was shocked out of my lethargy. 'Marilyn, nobody talks about you, if that's what you mean. You are . . . you. Special. My father saw it. Everyone sees it.'

I held her gaze; her eyes were intensely blue. It struck me that she was probably a natural blonde.

She tightened her mouth against the tears and then practically simpered.

'You're like your dad, you are. Gift of the gab.'

I forced a laugh; she laughed back. The next minute, for some absolutely unknown reason, we were both laughing our heads off. It was hysteria but it was unexpectedly good. To laugh with someone, share something, even if neither of us knew what we were sharing. We pulled ourselves together quite quickly, of course, and Marilyn turned again to my hair with determination.

'If I do a really short cut the thin bits won't notice. And it might encourage some new growth. You've got the sort of face that can take a crew cut.'

'Crew cut?'

All right, so I didn't care what I looked like, but a crew cut?

When it was done I had to look at it. It was a shock. It was so severe and unapologetic; a bit aggressive; lots of grey showing. I widened my eyes.

'It'll take some getting used to. But it's good. Really good. It's a new start. This is the new Jessica Tavener. OK? Tough and independent and able to cope.'

I said without thinking, 'Matt won't like it.'

She put her hands on my shoulders and her chin practically on top of my head. She said with complete certainty, 'Your husband would love it. It's making a statement – that's what they say, isn't it?'

'Yes. But what kind of a statement?'

'That's up to you in the long run. But first of all, it's saying that you've given some time to yourself. This afternoon has belonged to you.'

We got to the desk and the till and the next appointment.

'Yes, I will make one,' I decided suddenly. 'I'll need to keep it well trimmed, won't I? Six weeks?'

'Five. And you might like to consider a colour.'

But I shook my head definitely. 'That's part of the statement. I'm going grey.'

Marilyn grinned. 'Good for you,' she said.

I drove round to Jean's and found her sitting in the kitchen jogging Watt on her knee. He was not happy. I swung him on to my shoulder and nuzzled into the side of his tummy. Jean was transfixed.

'My God. What has she done to you? All that lovely hair . . .'

'Not much any more, Jean. This might encourage more growth.' I held Watt aloft and he looked down at me and gurgled a laugh. 'This is the new me!' I told him and he screamed with delight.

Jean put the kettle on and fetched mugs. 'She's done you good, I'll give her that.' She didn't sound a bit pleased. 'But it doesn't suit you, Jess. You're the feminine kind. Perennial schoolgirl, Jock always says. That's gone with the wind – or with the scissors, I should say.'

'Where's Lucy? And how has Watt been?'

'She's gone up to play with the electric train. Watt wasn't keen on her leaving him but I insisted.' She grinned. 'He's no good at logical argument, is he? All he can muster is a disagreeable snuffle.'

'He's had a rough time of it. All he knows now is that he's all right when his two women are around.' I sat him on my knee and took his hands and he pulled himself upright and screamed with joy. 'Look at this! Who cares about logical argument when they've got muscles of steel!'

Jean poured tea and watched us. She said, 'He's a lucky little devil. It could have been very different.'

'You call him lucky?' I glanced at her soberly. 'Let's hope the sort of luck he's had will last him a lifetime.'

'You know very well what I mean. He's lucky and Sam's lucky. How is Sam by the way?'

I told her; it didn't take long. Sam was desperately unhappy and working his socks off to go on with the Marcroft project.

'You're reacting very similarly,' she said sadly as she put my tea within my reach and outside Watt's. 'I sometimes think I'm going mad.'

I widened my eyes at her and she shrugged. 'Do you think I don't miss Donald and Matthew? Your dad was like an uncle to me. And your Matt . . . well, he was a ray of sunshine and I'm very much in need of sunshine. As you know.'

It was the first time she had admitted that her life was not perfect. The first time she had called my father by name. It was certainly the first time she had ever spoken of Matt as being a ray of sunshine.

I sighed. 'Grief makes you so selfish. Somehow you can't share it. I can't share a thing with Mum, for instance.'

'That's because of Ray,' Jean said matter-of-factly. 'He's coming between you, I expect. It's bound to happen at first. But he's a perfectly nice chap and you'll get to like him eventually.'

I really was shocked this time. I'd been surprised several times that day but this was more than surprise. Jean spoke of Ray as a fixture; not as needing or giving comfort, but as a permanent fixture.

I said quickly, 'Never mind all that. What about you? The boys? Jock?'

'Jason and Simon . . . I suppose they're all right. They come in and eat and go out again. The twins still have asthma.'

'They cope with it. We walked over to the field the other

afternoon and they were tearing around like lunatics.'

'Oh yes. They cope with it. Apparently I don't.'

'Who says?'

'Jock, of course. Comes swanning in every two months. Lots of sex, a few almighty rows and off he goes again.'

'And you want someone super-sensitive, gentle, erring on the feminine side—'

'Don't laugh about it, Jess. You had your father and you had Matt. You simply don't understand.'

I almost goggled at her. Nobody had spoken to me so critically since 11 May. It was as if she'd slapped my face. I frowned and left what she'd just said hanging in the air.

'Why do you row?' I asked instead.

She wasn't going to have second thoughts and apologize. She said, 'He didn't like me having an abortion.' There was this awful pause. She shrugged. 'That's what I mean, Jess. Every two months, lots of sex. And I am not having any more children.'

There was nothing to be said. I thought of how difficult it had been to conceive Lucy and how nothing had happened afterwards. I had hoped, that wonderful night of 7 May in that B and B near Devizes . . . but then again, how on earth would I have felt about it, really?

'I've shocked you. I'm not surprised.' Jean gathered up the mugs and went to the sink and said very deliberately, 'Donald was not shocked.'

I held the edge of the kitchen table. 'You told Dad?'

'Yes.' She looked round with a wry smile. 'See what I mean about missing him?'

I was angry, I don't know why. I said tightly, 'You could miss him as an uncle, of course. As well as a confidant.'

'I do.' Her voice was terribly sad. 'Actually, I miss him most as a friend.'

'Fair enough.' I heard my own voice, one I used regularly, hard as nails. I hadn't thought of my father as a friend; he had been so much more than that. Well, of course he had; he was my father. And if he had friends, and he did, then I hadn't included *my* friend in the list. Surely my mother had been his best friend?

I said, 'Tell me something. As his friend. Was Ray . . . seeing Mum . . . then?'

'When? Certainly not when he was ill. But yes, before then. I think so.'

'Oh God. What about Alicia?'

'She was carrying a torch for Marcus Adams. The actor, you know.'

'But . . . she went everywhere with Mum. Did everything with her.'

Jean shrugged again. 'If Jock came on to you and you fancied him, would our friendship stop you? It's something quite separate, Jess. It doesn't make Ray or Monica into some kind of Judas figure.'

I said stupidly, 'Jock? You mean, your Jock?'

Jean said wearily, 'Let's drop it. Bring Watt upstairs and let him see the train set.'

So we went. It was all highly unsatisfactory. I needed to ask about a dozen more questions. I was angry and upset and – yes – betrayed. Whatever Jean said, I felt betrayed by my mother. And my father. I caught sight of myself in a mirror on the half-landing. I had that silly bewildered look that made me into the perennial schoolgirl. I tightened the muscles in my face and set my mouth. Damn it, I would be aggressive: I would look aggressive and I would be aggressive.

Grief is strange. It's not just one thing, one emotion. Sadness and loneliness and terror are its chief constituents. Sadness and loneliness go together, and loneliness and terror go together. Sadness and terror don't mix too well. Sometimes loneliness is a completely separate issue. Sometimes not. Terror can be born of the loneliness, and sadness can lead into loneliness. Was that why Mum and Ray . . . ?

I woke up in the early hours of the next morning, streaming with sweat, my heart thumping madly, my hands shaking, tears streaming down my face. I was out of bed before I had taken another breath; I assumed Watt had woken me and I made for the cot over by the window. He lay like an angel, upflung arms, violet eyelids and lashes sweeping his cheeks. He didn't know. Didn't understand.

I put my forehead on the top of the cot and wept. 'Daisy . . .' I clapped a hand across my mouth but still in my head I was saying, 'Daisy . . . oh Daisy . . .' I looked at him again. 'He's five months. He's got two wonderful bottom teeth and he's lovely. Daisy, he's just lovely. Oh my God . . .' How was it I could weep like this for Daisy and Watt and not shed a tear for Matt?

The thought of him reared up. I longed for him so much that I sank to my knees still holding the bars of the cot. I wished I could die, then and there. But of course I couldn't because of Lucy and because of Watt. Because of them there was no way out at all. Perhaps there wouldn't have been anyway. I would never know.

I did what I had done before so often during the past few months: I visualized the grief inside my head; I allowed it to flood my chest again so that more tears pressed hotly against my eyes; then I forced it down, through my abdomen and my legs and into my feet, and I earthed it. I took a deep breath and lifted my head and knew an exquisite moment of complete peace.

And then gravel rattled on the window and I knew what had woken me.

It was Sam. I let him in and took him into the kitchen while the kettle boiled. It was the end of August and it had been a lovely day but at 2 a.m. it was chilly, and I held my hands over the kettle while I looked at the top of Sam's head drooping over the kitchen table. He looked like one of those ancient whipped horses; it wasn't just his head that hung, every muscle in his body seemed to be exhausted, done for.

'I'm sorry, Jess,' he said for the third time. 'I'm really

sorry. I couldn't take it any more. It all seemed so . . .
pointless.'

'You did the right thing.'

They were the kind of words Matt would have used. The
deed was done; Sam had taken to the road after midnight
and come to see his baby. So it must be the right thing to
do.

'Him and his precious abbey. Stained-glass windows
in a building that's just over a hundred years old . . .
pretentious, pseudo. What does any of it matter anyway?'

'It doesn't,' I agreed.

He knuckled his eyes. 'It's like bloody fiddling while
bloody Rome burns!'

I made tea and poured and passed him a cup.

'I wish I was a farmer. Like Daisy. I could go into the
fields and do some work that meant something.'

I said quietly, 'D'you remember when she helped with
the lambing last winter? You were afraid for her. But that's
why she did it. Because it was so – so significant. For her, it
was the beginning of birthing Watt.'

'I was such a damned fool.'

'No, you weren't. She understood.'

'God. I'm so thankful you got to know her, Jess.' He
lifted his head and picked up the cup of tea. 'None of this
would be possible if you and Lucy hadn't gone in that
day. Made friends.' He closed his eyes and breathed in
the steam. I did the same. The warmth ran through all the
canals behind my face. He said, 'Thank you, Jess. Do I say
that often enough? I am deeply thankful. All the time.'

'Yes. You do say it enough. Too often. I know how you
feel.'

We sipped companionably for a while and I warmed up.
I drew out a chair and sat opposite him. He was studying
the ridged grain of our old kitchen table, his thoughts
miles away. He wasn't easy with me, conversation never
flowed, but we could sit silently now without embarrassment. I looked at him carefully; he was thinner than when

I'd seen him two weeks ago, and then he'd been thinner than the time before. He probably wasn't eating. His straw-coloured hair needed the sort of cut I'd just had. I wasn't the only one in need of a new beginning.

I said, 'What's happening, Sam? Have you got time off?'

'No. I should be working in' – he glanced at the clock – 'five hours' time. Jerome will be coming in at midday to see how it's all going.' He sighed. 'I'm sleeping in the abbey now. Except that I don't sleep. I couldn't take it any more. Had to reconnect in some way. See Watt.'

'Good idea. Before you go upstairs . . . d'you want a sandwich?'

'No, thanks. D'you mind if I stay the rest of the night?'

'It didn't occur to me that you would do anything else.' I finished my tea. 'Listen, Sam. Why don't you sleep in my bed? I'll go in with Lucy and try to keep her quiet in the morning. Sleep as long as you can. And then take Watt over to the cottage and be by yourselves for a couple of days. Have some time off. Reconnect. Like you said. Reconnect.'

He stared up at me for some time. Then he nodded.

'I'll do that.' He stood up. Suddenly there was an air of purpose about him. 'Yes . . . that would be a good thing to do, wouldn't it? Thank you.'

He left the kitchen and I heard him take off his shoes in the hall and start up the stairs. He'd managed half a cup of tea.

Lucy was surprised to find me on the top bunk the next morning. I hadn't slept so I was able to stop her from galloping into my room and waking Watt and – maybe – Sam. We went downstairs and she changed the calendar date and found the card which said 'sunny and warm' and slotted it into place. She hadn't even looked through the window; we'd had a run of golden days.

'Mummy, I don't think I'll start school next week. I should stay at home with you and look after Watt.'

I had anticipated this and had wondered how to deal with it. Now I was able to say honestly, 'Well, Luce, I think your uncle Sam is going to take Watt back home for a bit. So you needn't worry about that.'

She said apprehensively, 'For ever?'

'I don't know. We must wait and see.'

She ate her cornflakes and drank some milk. Then she said, 'You'll be lonely, Mummy.' That was true; it occurred to me that that was very true. 'I'd better stay home and keep you company.'

'Well . . .' It was amazing how quickly answers sprang to my lips. As if I'd always known them. 'I rather think I should get back to work, honeybun. There will be a lot of stuff piling up at the factory.'

She said soberly, 'Daddy wouldn't like that, would he?'

It was so great the way she could talk about him. I wished I could. As it was, I just shook my head. I could so easily have told her that Daddy would want her to go to school and learn things; she would have agreed instantly. But that kind of pressure was out. So I just waited.

She heaved a sigh all the way up from her small bare feet and accepted unalterable facts.

'All right. I'll go to school. Nat will still be there and he says he'll keep an eye on me.'

'Nat? But what about Tony?'

'No. He's going to the big school. He says it's their way of splitting them up. Because when they're together they get up to things.'

'Oh dear.' I could imagine it. Their interchangeability must be a teacher's nightmare. But how had they decided which twin should go ahead while the other stayed behind? I was surprised Jean had said nothing about it yesterday. But then Jean had been so odd.

'Ackcherly . . .' Lucy looked up at me, her dark eyes alight yet slightly veiled at the same time. 'I think it's a secret but it's so funny.' She started to giggle helplessly. I joined her. I had thought I would never giggle again after the police called in May, but dear Lucy had me giggling within a fortnight.

'What?' I spluttered. 'What have they been up to now?'

'Promise you won't tell?'

'Promise.'

'Well . . .' She controlled herself somehow and gave me a garbled tale involving a kind of Shakespearean identity swop on a daily basis. One day Tony would go to Cherry-trees and Nat would go to the junior school; the next day vice versa. 'They'll have to have meetings every night so Tony knows Nat's lessons and Nat knows Tony's lessons.' She gave up trying to explain and keeled over again. I joined her.

All right, if I'd been sensible I would have had a 'chat' with the boys about their plans for anarchy. But I'd always had a soft spot for them. They coped so well with their asthma, their older brothers, their absentee father and their over-anxious mother. Why shouldn't they have a bit of fun at the expense of authority? It wouldn't last long.

Sam came down eventually with Watt bathed and dressed. Lucy was outside playing on the swing and he took his toast and went out to talk to her. He was good like that. I watched them through the window while Watt mumbled on a rusk in the high chair that so recently had belonged to Lucy. I could feel despair coming on again and concentrated fiercely on the two outside. Lucy was giggling and I knew that was good for Sam. I wondered whether she was telling him the secret. And whether he would find it unutterably trivial, like his work.

He came back in after a while and cleaned up Watt and collected some stuff for him.

'Thank you for this, Jess.' He stood holding the baby carrier in one hand, sundry bags in the other. I don't think I've ever seen anything so poignant. He said, 'I know I'm leaning heavily on you and Lucy. Can you bear it?'

I nodded once. He opened the front door and went

down the path to his car. I followed him with a couple more plastic bags.

'There's food in here,' I said. 'Frozen chops. Things like that. Sort it out when you get home. Please eat.'

'Of course. This is real. This is what I need. This is what I really need.'

'I know.'

We looked at each other, admitting our shared agony. He strapped Watt's carrier into the front seat. Watt gurgled happily; he loved going out in the car. Sam straightened and turned to peck me on the cheek. I turned my face so that our mouths met. There was a startled moment. Then I pressed against him, longing for him to hold me. He didn't.

I stood back. 'Sorry. Please take care. Ring me if you need shopping.'

He got in the car and drove off without another word. I stood there. I didn't know how I felt. Rather brazen. I told myself with determined flippancy that it was the new haircut. Then I went into the back garden to ask Lucy if she wanted lemonade or milk.

Six

The playground was almost empty. We'd come this way often in the past few weeks so that I could refer to it as 'your playground' and 'your school', but now that it really was Lucy's playground it looked completely different. Very empty indeed. The new children arrived in staggered groups and at staggered times; it was ten o'clock on a Thursday morning and she was only here until three, but five hours was an enormous span of time in a completely different environment. I could feel my heart pumping uncomfortably. It had done that off and on ever since Sam had left; I should be used to it by now.

Lucy said, 'Where's Nat, Mummy? He said he'd be here.'

'He's in the middle of lessons right now, darling. It will be playtime soon and then he'll come into the playground.'

She seemed to accept that all right and she didn't drag back as we crossed the big asphalt space and went in through the cloakroom. The smell was so nostalgic I could have stood in the middle of the coats and shoe bags and howled. Every peg was identified with a picture; when we had come for Open Day last term Lucy had chosen a wheelbarrow, and there it was surmounting an empty peg and an empty gridded space beneath.

Lucy greeted it with positive pleasure. 'That's mine!' She reached up to hang her bag on the hook. 'I'll keep my blazer on for now.' She pursed her lips judiciously. 'It might be pinched.' I widened my eyes at her and she nodded. 'Nat warned me.'

The irony of it almost overwhelmed me: Lucy's bag

containing her trainers, hanging there proclaiming ownership of a peg and embroidered vividly with her name, 'Lucy Tavener'; and the first lesson learned – don't leave anything precious around because it might be stolen. Modern lessons.

The secretary appeared and surged forward to greet us. She was new since Dad died, and so was the head. That was good, no trailing baggage.

'It's Lucy, isn't it?' She looked at the shoe bag. 'Well done, you remembered your own picture. And do you remember me from the Open Day, Lucy? I'm the school secretary and my name is Mrs Rose. That's easy, isn't it?'

Lucy nodded but did not smile. Apprehension was rising again.

Mrs Rose said, 'Would you like to show Mummy your classroom? And she can meet your teacher and see where you're going to sit. Come on, follow me.'

We trailed after her. It was not a new school; it had been the senior school when the village was a village. Then they'd built the big comprehensive on the outskirts, closed the infants' school and sold it to my parents, and used this one for the juniors. The corridor running from side to side seemed endless and the classrooms led off from it. The girls' cloakroom was one end, the boys' the other. At the far end of the corridor we could see some of the older children filing outside for netball. They were only ten-year-olds but they looked enormous.

The first door was propped open and just inside it a small boy was loudly announcing his intention of going home immediately. Mrs Rose fielded him as he emerged.

'Not just yet surely, Andrew?' She smiled at him. 'I particularly hoped you'd be around to show Lucy Tavener where you sit and where the books are kept and where you go at playtime.' She crouched to his level. 'This is Lucy. She lives right up on the Goose Bump so she doesn't know many people in town.'

Lucy and I were blocking the door so he couldn't scoot

past us. He looked up at me and then at Lucy and heaved a huge sigh. I felt for him. We were all trapped by some kind of institution and we just had to resign ourselves to it.

He said ungraciously, 'All right. Come on.' He held out his hand and, amazingly, Lucy released mine and took it. Behind him Mrs Sparrow, who had been at the school a long time and knew better than to interfere, smiled at me dismissively.

'Welcome to you, Lucy. We left the door open for the ten o'clock people. Just two more to come and then we can get on. Perhaps you'd close it now, Mrs Rose?'

Mrs Rose closed it and we went back to her office. Mrs Ingram, the head teacher, was dealing with the other two children in the cloakroom; she waved as we went past. It was all in a day's work to them. To me it was one chapter ending and another beginning; it was enormous, awful.

Mrs Rose offered me coffee, which I declined; she 'filled me in' and I didn't hear a word she said, and then quite suddenly I was outside again and going through the gate just as the bell went for playtime. What would Lucy do now? Would the boy – Andrew – escape and take her with him? I decided to linger.

A voice said, 'I've been here at least ten minutes. Come on, don't hang around. We'll have coffee and maybe lunch.' It was Jean. I was so pleased to see her I really did weep.

'I knew you'd be like this.' She passed me a tissue. 'It's really awful, isn't it? I can tell you she'll be fine – they'll all tell you that – but you won't really believe it.'

I sniffed and blew. 'I will if Lucy tells me.'

Jean took my arm as we crossed the road. 'She might not at first. After all, she's leaving you and Watt to have fun by yourselves. Jason hated the thought of me and Simon being on our own at home. He used to tell me that the other boys kicked him and that no-one told him when it was time to go home. I found out later he was having a whale of a time.'

We went past Hartford's and crossed the road again to go down Acacia Avenue.

I said, 'Watt isn't there any more. Sam has taken him home.'

She looked at me sharply but made no other comment until she had unlocked her door and stood aside for me to go down the hall. Then she said, 'So you really are on your own. Oh Jess.'

'Marilyn said I needed time to grieve. I've got it.' I spoke lightly but my words seemed to echo along Jean's hall and into the kitchen. It occurred to me that when I got home today I would not have to keep up any kind of front at all. I could run through the house wailing . . . I could fling myself on the bed in a paroxysm of grief.

I sat down at the kitchen table and looked up at Jean. She put a hand on my shoulder and gripped hard. 'Listen. You can go up to the factory. Pick up the reins again. That's something worth doing. For Matt.' She stood there holding my shoulder and eventually I nodded. Then she moved to the kettle and began the time-honoured ritual. There was nothing else to say, so we were silent; that was unusual too. At home I was cocooned in sound: from Lucy, from Watt, from myself. Now, this silence had a soothing quality. Jean's presence was enough.

We were halfway through our coffee before she spoke. Then she said, 'How was Sam?'

'Devastated. He couldn't stick it any more. He walked out.'

'For good?'

I shrugged. 'Who knows? He certainly doesn't.'

She sighed. 'Poor man. Still, I'm glad he didn't stay on with you and expect you to look after him as well as his son.'

Jean could say things that sounded unbearably hard. I began to tell her how important Watt was to Lucy as well as me.

'I know, I know. But he's important to Sam as well. I wouldn't want anyone to forget that.'

She looked at me meaningfully and I nodded. 'Of course, Watt is his child.'

'Anyway' – she put our mugs in the sink – 'he can't give up the job in Wiltshire. It's the only way you can survive.'

I took a breath. 'Yes, I suppose so. But I'm not sure. I mean, I'm not sure whether he can go back . . . whether he's able to go back.'

She sat down again. 'A breakdown, d'you mean?'

'I don't think so. But there's Watt.'

She frowned. 'Are you saying you can't cope with Watt any longer?'

'No. What I'm saying is that he might not want me to look after his baby . . .'

She was incredulous. 'Don't be daft, Jess. You're the ideal person. I don't really approve of the whole arrangement but from his point of view . . . What has he said? Has something happened?'

I nearly told her that I'd made a complete fool of myself, then couldn't find the words. Anyway, since Jean had told me about the abortion she wasn't quite the same friend I'd known at school.

I said, 'He's not interested in the job any longer. He's interested in living at Two Lanes Cottage and bringing up his child. That's all. As if it isn't enough.'

'Yes. All right.' She stood up again. 'Now, d'you want to go and have some lunch at the pub?'

'No. Thanks, Jean, but I must go home for a couple of hours. I didn't clear the breakfast things and I need to get something going for our meal tonight.' I too stood up. 'I've left the car outside the school. Better make tracks.'

'I'll walk back with you. I need to go to Hartford's anyway.' She took my arm and walked me out of the house as if I were an invalid. 'And listen. Take no notice of Marilyn. You mustn't give yourself time to grieve. You must get back in harness. A proper timetable. Mornings at the factory . . .' She proceeded to fill up my day for me. I was glad to get in the car and head back to the hills and home, although the prospect of the messy kitchen and the emptiness was not appealing. I had time to think about myself and I didn't feel well. Slightly sick, a bit of a headache. Nothing awful but not right.

I left the village and started the long twisting climb up to the Goose Bump. That was when it happened. Suddenly, out of the blue, my head began to vibrate. Then, without warning, it started to rattle. I told myself it was a jumble of all the advice I was getting: Marilyn thought I should have time, Jean thought I should go back to work, Mum wanted me to have my hair done. Sam probably thought I was wanton. But it was more than that and I was frightened. I tried to laugh it off by imagining the top of my head being lifted by my crew cut and someone stirring the contents with a wooden spoon. By the time I turned into the drive my whole body was thumping and there was a car parked in the lane and I didn't want to see anyone at all . . . I switched off and peace descended. My head belonged to me again. I opened the car door.

'My God, you sounded like a tank coming down the road! Did you know your exhaust has dropped off?'

I looked up. It was Jerry Jerome. The very last person I wanted to see.

I said stupidly, 'I thought it was my head. I thought I was having a stroke.'

'No. You're all right.' He took my arm; I wanted to shake him off but actually I found myself leaning on him quite heavily. 'Come on, let's get you indoors. I'll see to the car later. Where's your little girl?'

'It's her first day at school.' I mustn't cry. Not in front of this awful man. 'I haven't even washed up the breakfast dishes. You can't come in.'

He laughed at that, took my key and opened the door. I was childish enough to try to close it in his face but of course that didn't work. I led the way into the living room;

at least that was fairly tidy. The sun shone through the windows at the back and highlighted the dust motes but I was shivering with cold.

He said, 'You need a hot drink. Where's the kitchen?'

I sat down heavily. I was thankful about my head but I knew something was wrong with me. My legs weren't working properly.

'I've just had coffee. I don't want another drink.' I couldn't bear him to see the chaos of the kitchen, Lucy's crusts and Watt's high chair pushed into the corner. 'Did you want something? I haven't seen Jennifer for three weeks.'

'I haven't seen her since your husband's funeral. My visit has nothing to do with Jennifer.'

I looked up at him and the room moved around in an anti-clockwise direction. Luckily he stayed still. 'Have you and Jennifer . . . finished?'

He shrugged. 'Who knows? She blames me for your husband's death.'

I was astounded. Jennifer and I had never talked about the accident. 'But . . . why?'

He shrugged again. 'If he hadn't been working for me he wouldn't have been on that road when the transporter was . . . also on that road.' His voice sounded tight and hard. I'd heard my voice sounding like that. I knew then that he also blamed himself.

'That's absurd,' I said. 'He might well have been on that road. He went all over the place to get work.'

He sat down and as I lowered my gaze the room slowed to a halt.

'That's . . . generous of you, Jessica. May I call you Jessica?'

'I suppose so. What is it you want? I have to be back at the school at three and there's such a lot to do.'

'I want to know where Sam is. And when he's coming back to work.'

I didn't want to think about Sam.

99

'He's in his own home. I don't know when he's coming back to work.'

He moved impatiently. 'I understood you were looking after his baby. So there must have been some arrangements made?'

'No. None.'

He shifted again then spoke slowly and carefully. 'Listen, Jessica. Life has to go on. You understand that because of your little girl. It's very hard but that's the way it is. Sam cannot run away.'

'I think he already has.'

'You cannot allow that.'

'Sam's actions are nothing to do with me.'

He sat up straight. 'Then they should be. Good God, woman, he is threatening your livelihood! You depend on the glass company and this is the biggest contract you've had for the last three years. If it goes well it'll open up a new market for you.'

I said, 'Can't you see? Can't you understand? I'm not interested in this big and wonderful contract! I wasn't very keen from the outset. But now . . . it means nothing. Absolutely nothing. And Sam has obviously reached that point too. He had to get away. Re-establish his life – his real life.'

He was silent. I could hear him breathing. I shifted my gaze and caught sight of Lucy's swing on the lawn. I concentrated my whole mind on Lucy. What was she doing now at this minute? It was one o'clock. They would have finished school dinners and she would be in the playground. Please God let her be all right.

Jerome began to speak, still slowly but not as if I were an imbecile.

'Jess, I do understand. I was tactless. Of course the work routine seems worthless at this time. Of course. But we're talking about the future, my dear. Your little girl's future.'

'Her name is Lucy.' Matt must have spoken of her often but Jerome had forgotten Lucy's name.

'That's right. Lucy. Matt adored her.'

I didn't want him to speak of Matt. I went on staring at Lucy's swing.

'I can see that if I mention money you will despise me. But we all have to have it, Jess. And she will have to have it too.'

I didn't say anything. I had more or less agreed with Jean an hour ago that I would go back to work. But if I had to work for Jerry Jerome, I couldn't bear it. I wondered whether I could bear it anyway. Like Sam, I wanted nothing else to do with it. But . . . was Jerome right? We had some money behind us, I knew. The solicitor had explained it to me but I hadn't listened.

He went on in that gently persuasive voice. 'But it's not just the money, is it? Matt built up the business from nothing. And he was terribly interested in stained glass too. Sam had the better techniques but Matt loved the historical aspect.'

Matt had been interested in everything; that had been his great quality. But no way was Jerome going to make me cry and admit he was right.

'Matt – surely Matt wouldn't want you to let everything go? What are you going to do, sell it off?'

'Of course not!' I replied instantly.

'Well then, what?'

'I need time. I haven't worked anything out yet. There was Watt. And now school.'

'All right. And if Sam comes back I assume there will be Watt again. So you need to start addressing these problems. A childminder or nursery while you're doing the office stuff.' He paused and added, 'Matt said you were a whizz in the office.'

I almost shouted, 'Stop talking about Matt! He's nothing to do with you any more!'

'All right,' he said hastily. 'Let's stick to now. First things first. Will you go and see Sam and find out when he's coming back?'

'No!'

'Will you go into the office and sort out the paperwork?'

I took a deep breath and let it go. Then I stood up and went to the window. I could sell the house. But . . . I needed the house. Lucy needed her own swing and her own stairs to bump down every morning. Anyway, hadn't I already decided that I would go back to work? I gripped the window ledge; everything in the garden had started to move. Anti-clockwise again.

I said desperately, 'Yes. All right. It's too late today. I'll go tomorrow.'

'Good girl.'

I swung round. 'It's nothing to do with you. I had already decided to go back.'

He too stood up. 'Sorry. I don't mean to interfere.'

'Then please don't. You've made your point and I've made mine. You can leave now.'

He held the edge of the mantelpiece. He seemed strangely hesitant, which I knew was unusual.

He said, 'You said you hadn't blamed me for your husband's death. Yet you obviously hate me. Why?'

I stared at him until everything was still again. I was used to being polite and tactful. Dad had always called me his little diplomat. Yet I had spoken frankly to this man and it had been good to do so. I took a breath.

'You're a control freak,' I said. 'You wanted me to see that the first day . . . the day I came down to the abbey. Matt didn't like it and neither do I. Obviously Sam has had enough too.'

He looked genuinely surprised. 'I never thought . . . I wanted us to be one solid group. I thought Matt was . . . pretty marvellous. Sam too. I thought we would be . . . a family.'

I hardly heard him. I hadn't ever been this brutally honest before.

'You've come down here today to take me over, haven't you? I was supposed to cry on your shoulder and you would

102

comfort me and tell me what to do. And I would do it. Exactly as you said. Well, I haven't cried and I'm certainly not going to intrude on Sam's privacy. And if I go to the factory it will be because I was going anyway.' I paused for breath. He was looking fairly stunned. 'You don't know anything about normal life, do you, Mr Jerome? You tell other people what to do because you can't cope with it yourself. Thank God Jennifer saw that in time!' Suddenly I was tired out. 'Look, you'd better go. I have to phone the garage about my car. I'm sorry to be rude but there is a lot to do.'

He pushed himself away from the mantelpiece and stood uncertainly for a moment.

'I was going to ask you to send Jennifer my best wishes.'

'Yes. I'll do that.'

He smiled wryly. 'Thank you. I'm sorry if I . . . but you do see what I mean? It's – it's Lucy's birthright. Yes, that's it.' He was pleased with the phrase. 'It's Lucy's birthright.'

I almost laughed because it was so pathetic. I said, 'And it's your precious abbey. Your status symbol.' I opened the door. He went outside, looking very flushed.

'That's what I meant . . . We're linked.' He paused. 'Are you going to be all right? The car and everything?'

'Yes.' I watched him get into his car. It was one of the four-wheel drives I'd seen last May Day. I thought – I actually thought, at that moment – that I was going to be all right.

Then he leaned out of the window and said, almost diffidently, 'I liked him. I liked him very much, Jess. And I liked your father too. It must be a terrible time for you. I do understand that.'

It didn't kick in at first. His words wandered around my mind as I went back in and made tea and cleared up the kitchen, and then when I phoned the garage and met the mechanic in the road and asked about a courtesy car . . . All the time I was thinking that there must be some explanation. I was looking for that explanation until the time came to take the new car down to meet Lucy. Then of course I had to push it to the back of my mind and give her every bit of attention I had. The only good thing to come out of the meeting with Jerry Jerome was that I stopped worrying about the way inanimate objects moved around me anti-clockwise.

Lucy emerged from the cloakroom blinking as if she had not seen light all day. Then she spotted me and bounded across the playground to the gate.

'Can I go to tea at Andrew's house, Mummy?'

I hugged her and took a plastic folder from her.

'Darling, you haven't had an invitation. We don't even know Andrew's parents.'

Andrew was sheepishly greeting a girl in a long flowered skirt and halter top. Surely an older sister. But she approached me and introduced herself.

'I'm Stella Bearwood. Andrew would like Lucy to come to tea, but actually we're going to his grandmother's today. Can we make it next week? I haven't got a thing in the house until we've been to Hartford's.'

She was Andrew's mother.

I said, 'Oh please . . . they've obviously got on well. That's great.'

'Andrew started last week. He hasn't really settled down yet. But he seems perfectly happy today.'

Lucy said earnestly, 'Mrs Sparrow says I'm a good fluence on him.'

She sounded unbearably priggish. I laughed. So did Andrew's mother, Stella Bearwood.

We drove home contentedly. Lucy was thrilled with the 'new car' but didn't want to keep it, thank goodness. She told me about the letters in the plastic folder, four of them in one bag and seven in the other. 'They spell my name, Mummy. I can play with them tonight and tomorrow night I can start to trace them.'

'But you can write your name already,' I reminded her.

'Yes. But you have to do it properly, Mummy.'

I was glad when she giggled as she said this.

She told me that Nat had approached her during dinners and asked out of the side of his mouth if she was all right. She'd told him yes, and after that he had avoided her like the plague.

'Sounds normal,' I said.

She looked at me. 'Does it mean I can only be friends with him when I'm in his house?'

'I suppose so.'

'Oh. Well, that's all right. Because then I can play with his train set.'

It looked as if Jean was quite right and Lucy was going to enjoy school, discover its multilayered rules and accept them without question. That was a big plus.

Even so, when she went to bed she murmured, 'It's so nice to be back home, Mummy. Only tomorrow at school then it's the weekend and we can do what we like.'

'Would you like to have Andrew here to tea?'

She looked shocked. 'Oh no. I didn't really want to go to tea with him. I wanted to have my tea with you.' She smiled sleepily. 'Besides, we ought to go and see Uncle Sam and Watt.'

I had to nip that in the bud immediately. 'I think Uncle Sam would like to be left alone for a few more days,' I whispered.

She said nothing to this. Maybe she was asleep. But she had a way of using silence as an argument.

I went downstairs and immediately outside to tackle the weeding. I didn't dare be still. I toyed with the idea of phoning Mum and asking her again whether Dad had gone to Wiltshire a year ago just before he became ill. But she had been so definite before. And Sam hadn't known. I remembered his surprise when I had said something about

Matt's first meeting with Jerome. And Sam was incapable of lying.

I pushed the tip of the trowel far into the earth in search of a dandelion root and frowned at myself. Was I implying that Mum could lie to me? She had certainly kept her friendship with Ray a secret. But if there was something Mum wouldn't tell me and Sam couldn't tell me, who else was there? There was Marilyn, of course.

I found the end of the dandelion root and removed it whole. Yes, there was Marilyn. I couldn't ever ask her such a question but there was Marilyn. And if she'd been at Marcroft with Dad last summer, then it meant Matt had been . . . I don't know. Colluding? Was that why he didn't want to tell me? Oh God . . . I stood up suddenly and spilled the trug, scattering weeds everywhere. I looked across the boundary hedge at the high undulations of the Mendip hills. Somewhere in the next fold our neighbours were having a party. They had installed a swimming pool soon after we moved in and only used it once or twice a year. They had asked me to their 'pool party' but I had cried off because of Lucy and school. Now I wished I had kept her up and we had gone.

I gathered up the weeds and took them down to the compost bin, then put the trowel and trug in the shed. It was getting dark. I toyed with the idea of ringing Sam and telling him I would go to the office tomorrow as soon as I had taken Lucy to school. But I couldn't face his embarrassment. I could phone Jean and thank her for this morning. Or Mum, just to see how she was.

It was a relief when the phone rang just as I was washing my hands at the kitchen sink.

It was Jennifer. I was so pleased to hear her I was effusive.

'Hey,' she protested, laughing. 'It's me. Prodigal sister. No need to go over the top.'

I said feebly, 'You know how it is. Getting dark. Nothing on telly.'

She stopped laughing. 'Oh Jess, I'm sorry. I ought to be back working in Bristol, keeping in touch. I don't seem to be able to do anything right, do I?'

'Shut up. I like you the way you are.'

'Do you? Do you really? I thought . . . you know. Black sheep.'

'*Black sheep?* I've never thought of you like that! You are the adventurous one – enterprising – and so beautiful.'

'You're going over the top again.' She laughed briefly. 'You know what I mean. That business with Jerry. I've never apologized for that. It made you sick, didn't it?'

I sighed. 'Oh Jen. I'm sorry. Was it that obvious? You do mean at the abbey, don't you? I've hardly thought about it since—'

'Well, not surprising in view of what happened straight after.'

I remembered what had happened straight after. That wonderful night in the bed and breakfast in Devizes when I had hoped so much I might have conceived another baby. She didn't mean that, of course.

'Yes . . .' I cleared my throat. 'Well. It was him. I hated the way he was so obviously laying claim to you. You've always been so much your own person. And with him you weren't.'

'No. True. It was just sex. And afterwards . . . I haven't seen him to speak to since the funeral. I think I hate him.'

'He was here today.' I waited for her staccato queries to die. 'Yes. In person. In his enormous car. He was waiting when I got back from school. I'd blown the exhaust on the car so you can imagine . . . I thought it was my head dropping off!'

I laughed and after a bit she joined in.

'What did he *want*, for goodness' sake?'

'Sam back at work. Me back in the office.'

'Sam?'

'He's left Marcroft. Couldn't bear it. He's taken Watt and gone home. I don't know for how long.'

There was a pause while she assimilated this.

'So you haven't got Watt. And Lucy has started school. Oh Jess.'

'Lucy is fine. She likes school.'

'I didn't doubt she would. Somehow you have provided all the security she needs. I don't know how you do it, Jess. But you do.'

I was amazed. But I couldn't dwell on that now. I said, 'He was all right, actually. I was a bit rude but he took it in his stride – put it down to grief, I expect. I didn't realize I could get away with so much by pleading grief.' I tried to laugh but it didn't come out right.

'Jess, I could take a day off next week. Spend it with you. Would that be any good?'

'I'd love to see you, of course. Let me know when. I want to start at the office tomorrow.'

She said slowly, 'So you're doing exactly what Jerry wants? Have you asked Sam to go back too?'

'I intended to go back anyway. I have to do something. And the Marcroft job won't last for ever. We can go back to double glazing.'

'Don't you see – he won't let you. He'll find other work to do with staining. You'll always be beholden to him.'

I said, 'You really have turned against him, Jen.'

She was silent again for a while then said, 'I don't know. I'm sort of scared. And I've never been scared before. By a man.' She drew a breath. 'Listen. I'll ring you again when I know I can come down. It will be lovely to see you. And to be home for a few hours. London is no fun in this nice weather.'

I said, 'It's grand here in the hills.' Then I blurted, 'Jen, did Matt take Dad to see Marcroft Abbey last summer? Before he was ill?'

Again that silence. Then, 'Did bloody Jerry tell you that?'

'Not exactly.'

'Don't believe a word he says, Jess!'

'Did he?'

'Did he what?'

'Did Matt take Dad over to show him the abbey?'

'I don't know, Jess. I hadn't met Jerry then – I didn't know a thing about Marcroft.' She paused. 'Does it matter? What did Jerry say?'

'No, it doesn't matter,' I said tiredly. 'Whatever he said, it doesn't matter.'

'All right. I'll see you next week. Don't worry about Jerry. Don't worry about anything.'

'Good night, Jen.'

'Good night, big sis.'

I had started to replace the receiver but I think she said, 'I love you.'

Seven

Lucy had been at school for three days when the terrorist attack happened in New York. I drove her down that Tuesday, watched her make her way into the cloakroom – she didn't need, or want, my company any more – and managed two hours in the office before going home to tidy up and think about something for supper. I didn't switch on either radio or television; I had to concentrate on what I was doing, even if it did seem fairly mindless. So it was not until I reached the school gates at 3 p.m. that I heard the terrible news. It was difficult to take in. The other mothers were grief-stricken, horrified, and something else as well: frightened. There was a feeling of being beleaguered. We stood close together by the school gates; they told me about it and I asked incredulous questions and they told me again. Stella Bearwood said, 'You know what it's like in a way, don't you? Half your family wiped out in a single blow.'

I said slowly, 'I'm not sure. Fate can be aggressive, of course, but this? Other human beings plotting and carrying something through . . .'

That evening I watched the detailed coverage. I couldn't leave it alone. Strangely, I did feel a kind of kinship; some of the physical weight I carried around with me was being shared by thousands of other people. And my loss was no longer a stigma; people spoke to me in Hartford's and at the school gates. We could share grief in a positive way. It really was very strange. Lucy knew about it, of course; there was no way any of us could keep it from the children. It was obvious that Andrew Bearwood was completely fascinated by the scenes of the collapsing towers. Lucy said, 'We can think about other people now, can't we, Mummy?'

And perhaps that was what it was. The spotlight of grief shifted; we were able to externalize our own tragedy. When we had to set aside the awfulness of the New York disaster and get on with our daily lives, we could set aside our own disaster as well. Life would never be the same again and we accepted that.

Lucy went to tea with Andrew Bearwood and came home caked in mud from the stream which ran through their garden. They had built a dam, had a fight with the boy who lived next door, eaten fish fingers for tea, drunk cocoa and watched an Australian soap on television. It had been wonderful. I knew that I would have to ask Andrew to tea with us and wondered what excitements we could offer him. Lucy said she would show him how to make a mobile with two coat-hangers and some baking foil. I got some sausages from Hartford's and made sure there were baked beans in the cupboard. Stella Bearwood said to me that it was the war spirit. 'You've got to carry on, haven't you? It's the only way we can fight back.'

It even helped with what I called my 'Sam mortification'. After all, what did it matter whether I'd made a fool of myself or not? The only problem was that over the past four months I had grown to love Watt. And so had Lucy. I was afraid Sam might not want to let me look after him again.

On the Thursday, Jennifer's car drew up outside the house at eight o'clock in the morning.

'I had to come early to see my favourite niece!' She scooped Lucy up on to her shoulder and for once didn't mind when her hair fell out of its chignon. 'Oh, it's good to see you, Lucy Locket. How are you? How's school? How's Mummy?'

'Fine. Fine. Fine.' Lucy snuffled into the long neck. 'Oh, you smell nice. It reminds me of the old days.'

Jennifer's dark eyes met mine. We didn't smile.

We had breakfast and Jennifer made us laugh, talking about her new job at the 'stink tank'. We didn't mention New York. It occurred to me that Jennifer might well have known some of the office workers there. But she was her usual self.

'We're at the stage where everyone is trying to prove how clever they are,' she explained. 'A bit like school probably.'

Lucy shook her head. 'It's not cool to be clever at school,' she informed her aunt. 'And you mustn't cry. And you mustn't talk to the big children. And you mustn't leave your blazer on your peg in case it's pinched.'

'Oh dear. What a lot of things to remember.' Jennifer took Lucy's hand. 'D'you know, it hasn't changed much since I was at school. Except for the blazer. We had our names sewn inside the collar so no-one would take the wrong blazer.'

'Oh, that doesn't make any difference. We have our names in everything, but nothing is safe.' Lucy sighed deeply. 'It's the modern world.'

Jennifer and I burst out laughing and Lucy laughed too and then tried it again. 'It's the modern world – the modern world—'

'Calm down,' I said. 'Shall we take Aunt Jennifer to school with us so that she can meet Andrew?'

Lucy nodded and then told Jennifer about Andrew's stream and the dam and the fight and the fish fingers. We drove down to the village and after Lucy had disappeared into the cloakroom Jennifer said, 'You're so lucky to have her, Jess. She's . . . wonderful.'

'I know. Actually I would have gone mad without her. Seriously.'

'I don't think you would. But I can see she makes things possible.' She took my arm as we walked back to the car. 'You know, Jess, I used to think your life was incredibly boring. But I see now that the small things are the big things.' She laughed and waved her hands helplessly. 'I mean the small things, like having Andrew wotsit to tea and weeding the garden, they're the important things. You've got it right.'

We got in the car and started back home.

'Jen, I'm flattered by your approval.' I grinned sideways at her. 'The thing is, dear sis, there's nothing else to be done except what is right under my nose. So I'm doing it.'

She laughed. 'I know. It's just that when that idiot Jerry comes and tries to sort you out with a few digs, I could spit. Don't let him upset you, Jess. He's good at that. You're doing the right thing.'

'I take it you had a row.'

'Yes. I've finished with him. I was a fool. I thought he was special.'

'Is there anyone else?'

'There might be, but I rather think he's unattainable. In any case, I couldn't settle for one person.'

We drove on over the Goose Bump and started to talk about 11 September. I was right, Jennifer had known two men who worked for an insurance company in the World Trade Center. There was no news of them.

She said, 'Don't let's talk about it, darling. It must make it worse for you.'

I tried to explain but then agreed it was better to speak of something else.

The weather was not quite as beautiful; there might even have been a ground frost in the night. I told her about my plans for replanting, then I thought of the winter and shivered. I must order logs and coal and get the garage door fixed . . .

When we sat down together to drink coffee, I told Jennifer about Sam.

'It's so damned awkward.' I tried to laugh. 'All I wanted was a cuddle. And he obviously thought . . . well, he couldn't get Watt and himself into the car quickly enough.'

Jennifer was silent for some time and then she said, 'You don't feel anything for him, do you, Jess?'

'Sam? Of course not. He – he's just Sam. Anyway, he was so close to Daisy . . .'

'That need not stop you.'

I said patiently, 'Jen, I have no special feeling for Sam.'

'It's just that . . . Well, it would be so suitable, wouldn't it? But if you don't have any attraction at all . . . that's it, I suppose.'

It was a question. I frowned at her in exaggerated exasperation and she said, 'All right, all right. Subject closed.' She sighed. 'As for this small . . . incident . . . he'll know how you felt. Credit him with a little imagination. He'll turn up here or ring you and you'll be back to how you were before.' Jennifer smiled ruefully. 'I'm not at all sure that's a good thing, mind you, but if it's what you want . . .'

'Lucy adores Watt. And as there's no chance of brothers or sisters of her own, he's a gift.'

'Come on, Jess. Lucy's got a boyfriend! She's getting a life already.'

It was my turn to smile. 'The thing is, Jerome was right – we need this job. And when it comes to it, Jen, I can't let Matt's firm go down the pan, can I? So Sam and I have to work together.'

'That's fine. Sam will come round, you'll see. And I think you'll work well together. If Hateful Jerry does get you other contracts, you'll be the ideal person to go out there and "seal the deal"! Seriously, Jess, you've got Matt's way with you, open and frank. But you've got something else now that Matt didn't have. These last terrible months have given you a kind of independence.'

I asked sadly, 'Am I toughening up, Jen? Is that what you're saying?'

'Maybe I am. But not in the way you mean. You've got a special sort of strength. A solid core. Any future client would find that reassuring.'

'Really? Well, I suppose time will tell.'

I asked her about her new job but she was strangely

uninterested. She used to make Matt and me laugh with impersonations of her colleagues. Now she said, 'They're academics really.' She looked at me consideringly. 'I don't quite know what to do with my life, Jess. Do you think I'm too old to go to university?'

I stared at her and could feel a smile dawning. 'Oh Jen, Dad would be so pleased.'

'Yes. That's one of the things that holds me back.'

'Jen!'

'Sorry, darling. I know you still think of him as the best father in the world.'

I was silent. There were too many questions in my mind these days for me to be sure of anything or anyone.

She said, 'What I meant was, I would do it for me. Not for Dad. Not for anyone else. Just me.'

'All right. That is absolutely good enough. And my answer is – I think it's the best idea you've had for ages. Go for it, Jen. What sort of course did you have in mind?'

'History.'

'*History?*'

'English history – some European, of course, because it all dovetails. But mostly medieval.'

'I had no idea you were interested in history. But you were so damn good at every subject—'

'I got interested in it when I was at Marcroft.'

She was staring into the fire. It was cold enough for me to light it. I kept quiet.

'Matt and Sam. They used to talk about some of the stained glass. They had books on medieval art. Matt could make anything interesting.'

I nodded dumbly.

She gave a little laugh. 'Actually, Jess, I wondered . . . Later, maybe, I could put some money into the firm and kind of research stuff?'

I couldn't believe it. It opened up new possibilities. I could feel a tiny germ of excitement deep below my diaphragm.

I breathed, 'Jen. It would be the best thing I could ever imagine. I'm only a glorified office worker, and though Sam has the techniques I don't feel – especially at the moment – that he has much interest in the firm. With you at the helm—'

She said quickly, 'I don't want that. No more helms. I want to do something practical. Maybe produce drawings—'

'Like Matt did,' I whispered. 'Yes. You were wonderful at art too, weren't you?'

'No. Stop it, Jess. You're taking it too fast and too far. The history course at Bristol is a three-year one . . .'

'I know. I know. But I can't help it. To be able to envisage some kind of future . . . it's wonderful, Jen. If it comes to nothing – if you change your mind – we're no worse off. But for now, this moment, it's so exciting.'

So she let me talk hypothetically until it was time for lunch and then we met Lucy from school and on the spur of the moment brought Andrew back with us. The people with the pool were going to drain it for the winter and suggested the children use it for a last swim. Andrew had to wear his underpants so Lucy wore her knickers and they splashed in the shallow end for twenty minutes and then came in, shivering, to dry by the fire with Jennifer while I cooked the sausages and beans.

We took Andrew home and Jennifer met Stella, then we called on Mum – blessedly alone – and Lucy went to bed very late.

She said wonderingly as I tucked her in, 'We're happy, aren't we, Mummy?'

I put my mouth against her forehead and closed my eyes. 'Yes, darling.'

The next day Jennifer had to leave really early to beat the traffic, Lucy overslept and I had a headache. How quickly things change.

*　　*　　*

I went to the factory straight after dropping Lucy at school. I wanted to go through Matt's sketches; I needed to understand what Sam had been doing down at Marcroft. I wanted us to complete the job there. I was full of urgency. If Stella was right this was the only way I could 'hit back'. I took another aspirin as soon as I reached the factory, and by the time I had lifted all Matt's sketches from the drawer the headache had gone.

There was nothing very helpful in any of the sketches. The windows were there, diamond-paned and empty. No colouring, nothing. But Matt must have produced a portfolio; Jerome would have insisted on that. And Sam needed something to work from . . . Sam.

I dug my arms into my jacket again – the weather was definitely colder – and went out into the complex and down the road that led past the bathroom wholesalers and the paint shop to the factory. Sam's foreman was a tiny whippet of a man who had actually worked at glass-blowing years before. His name was Billy.

'Mrs Tavener!' He beamed at me. 'I was beginning to think you'd all deserted the ship!' He didn't call it a sinking ship but that was what he meant. 'No sign of Sam for nearly a fortnight. Tried ringing him at Marcroft and got choked off. Tried the cottage and nothing. What's happening?'

We walked down the narrow passageway between carefully stacked rows of glass panels.

'Sam's having a much-needed break.' We stopped by what looked like a billiard table. On top of the green baize lay a pattern of glass pieces. On the other side of the aisle was an alchemist's workshop: a Bunsen burner and a crucible. Some ingots of lead were stacked alongside. There was a similar contraption down at Marcroft; reproducing medieval windows required medieval methods.

I looked around. 'Obviously the work is all going ahead.'

'Well, until ten days ago,' Billy said. He was disgruntled, understandably so.

'I'm sorry, Billy. I could easily have popped down and kept you informed.'

'It's up to Sam to do that,' he said stubbornly. 'He's the one who pays my wages.'

'But you realize what a rotten time he's having.'

'No worse than you, if I might say so.'

'Much worse than me, Billy. I've got my daughter and up until last week I had his son too.' I looked at him. 'And I expect you've heard that Mr Jerome is not the easiest of men to work for.'

'Well, yes. I had heard . . .' He was somewhat mollified, I could tell.

'The thing is, I haven't been taking any interest at all in the work – the actual work down at the abbey. Sam must feel completely isolated down there. I thought if I could get my hands on my husband's portfolio, I might begin to understand some of it and be of help to Sam.'

'Sounds good.'

'I take it Sam has the portfolio? I mean, it wouldn't be here, would it?'

'No. Sam has brought in individual sketches and I've made 'em up under his supervision. 'Tisn't my line of country, really.'

'Oh come on, Billy. You're not a double-glazing fitter or just a cutter. I've seen some of your work, remember.'

'Thanks, Mrs Tavener. But as far as the lead work goes . . . I'm learning as I go along.'

'You're a craftsman. You'll do it.' I sounded more confident than I felt. The crucible and the lead and the Bunsen burner were not reassuring.

'Well . . .' Billy breathed in and drew himself up to his full wiry height. 'Well, I must say I feel better for seeing you. I'm getting on with one or two domestics' – he meant replacement windows in people's homes – 'but after that, nothing's come in as far as I know.'

'There are some enquiries in the post. I wondered if Sam would go and have a look at them.'

Unexpectedly, he said, 'Why don't you go, Mrs T.? Sam hasn't got the gift of the gab. Not that I'm saying you have, but you're the boss now. And women in the workplace . . . well, it's all the thing, isn't it?'

I remembered what Jennifer had said; I was surprised and very pleased.

'I'll do that, Billy. Thank you.' I grinned. 'I look on that as a vote of confidence.'

'So you should. You lived with the boss after all. Some of his talents must have rubbed off!'

Matt's talents had been his very character: his warmth and understanding. People had gone for that. I didn't have it.

I said, 'I'll go on down to Two Lanes now and see about that portfolio. Then I'll come back and sort out the enquiries. I'll be in touch, Billy.'

I went back for the car and drove out on to the high tops of the hills, remembering how Daisy had gone out last winter to help with the lambing. I had met her only half a dozen times but I had been there when Watt was born and I had been pretty certain she would be glad to know he was with me. And now he wasn't – and just because I'd been weak enough to turn into Sam's arms, he might not be again.

I pulled up behind Sam's old car. The bonnet was still warm as I passed it so I guessed he had not long been home. Why hadn't he called in at the factory to see Billy?

He opened the door before I reached it. He was still in a leather jacket, and behind him I could hear Watt crying.

'Jess . . .' He had called me a formal Mrs Tavener until that time I had turned up at the abbey. 'We've just been down to Hartford's to get some milk and stuff. Watt is hungry.'

'May I feed him while we talk?' He hung on to the door and I said, 'We've got to talk, Sam.'

'Yes. Of course.' He stepped back and I went through.

The kitchen was as I remembered it, neat in a used sort of way, smelling of bleach. Watt's car seat was on the table and he stopped crying as I went up to it. I was absurdly pleased to see him and went right over the top.

'Darling Watt, Aunt Jess has missed you so much . . . so much, little man. Are you pleased to see me?'

Behind me Sam said repressively, 'He stops crying when something new happens. They brought a clutch of chicks in from the farm and he was delighted.'

I suppose I could have been cut to the quick but it struck me as amusing and I chuckled as I picked up the dear familiar bundle and put him over my shoulder where he could smell my neck and recognize me.

'D'you hear that, Watt? You don't know the difference between chickens and your aunt Jess! What have you got to say to that?'

He chuckled too and went on chuckling as I sat down and took off his nappy.

Sam said, 'He's not smelly.' His voice was tight with resentment. 'I thought you were going to give him the bottle.'

He had got it ready; it was wrapped in a towel on the table.

'Yes, I am, of course. But I usually take off his nappy when I feed him so that his legs are free to kick.' I picked up the bottle and he clamped on to it. 'I'm sorry, Sam. I did it that way with Lucy. I thought maybe she would associate being free of all that bundle with the sheer pleasure of feeding.' I made a wry face. 'She's never picked at her food so I assume it worked!'

He sat down suddenly and put his elbows on the table and his head in his hands. 'Sorry. I'm really sorry. He's been such hard work. I know he's missing you and Lucy and it seemed terribly wrong . . . I was determined to keep him here until he got used to me. It sounds so childish—'

'Of course it doesn't!' I was so emphatic that Watt stopped his sucking, lost the teat and searched for it frantically. 'Sorry, sorry, Watt.' I smiled at Sam and said in a much lower voice, 'It doesn't sound childish at all. It hurts you to let me look after Watt because I'm not Daisy. I understand that perfectly.'

'Do you?'

'Of course. But, Sam, I never ever – for one moment – forget that Watt belongs to you and Daisy. I promise you that. It makes him, if anything, even more precious.'

He lifted his head and looked at me. He reminded me of someone who was drowning and resigned to it.

'He cries such a lot. We don't sleep at nights. Sometimes during the day we both have a few hours.' He looked around. 'D'you think he knows this is home and that his mother isn't in it?'

'No. I don't think that, Sam.' I removed the bottle and let the air run back into it. 'I think he's hungry.'

'But I keep offering him a bottle and he turns his head away.'

'I'm sorry, Sam. I should have told you. He's on solids now. I get those little jars. Or I whizz up fresh vegetables in the food processor.'

'But he's only five months!'

'Nearly six. And he's a big baby.'

The contents of the bottle had gone and I righted him and rubbed his back. He grizzled but for the moment he was full enough.

Sam said, 'Tell me what to get.'

'I'll get you in some jars. I have to go back to the office to collect some enquiries, and maybe make some calls if there's time. But after I've met Lucy I'll pop into Hartford's and come straight back here. What else do you need – for yourself?'

'I'm all right, thanks. I picked up some tins of soup earlier.'

'Is that all you're eating?'

'It's all I want.'

I hung Watt over my shoulder where he burped milk on

to my jacket. I gathered a basin and cotton wool and baby cream and sat down again to put another nappy on him.

'You can't go on like this, Sam. Daisy would be so annoyed with you.'

He was shocked into silence. I said quickly, 'It'll be better when Watt is satisfied. Once you have a quiet night you'll have the strength to cook a meal, go for a walk, enjoy each other.'

I waited but still he said nothing. I took a deep breath. 'Sam, there's no easy way to say this. Have you left Marcroft for good?'

He was shocked again. 'I don't know. I hadn't thought.'

'Jerome came to see me and asked me about you.'

Sam's face darkened. 'How could he? Only four months . . . How could he?'

'It's his pet project . . . his Gothic abbey with its stained-glass windows. But, as he pointed out, it is also our livelihood.'

'We can do without him and his bloody abbey!'

I smiled. 'It's good to hear you getting angry, Sam. And yes, we can do without him, but he could open doors for us. Get the firm on its feet again and going in a new direction.'

He looked at me while I burped Watt again and then put him in his bouncy chair. Then he said slowly, 'You sound different. Are you getting over it?'

'You know better than that, Sam.'

'But you are different. You're not afraid to look into the future.'

'Perhaps it was when I got angry with Jerome.' I smiled. 'And Jennifer, my kid sister, came yesterday. Left this morning. She . . . invigorated me!'

He raised his brows. I remembered that he knew Jennifer from her relationship with Jerome. I grinned. 'And, of course, Lucy has started school and made a new friend.'

He managed a glimmer of a smile at that.

'We've got to look into the future, I suppose. Because of

them.' He looked down at Watt, who seemed to be on the verge of sleep. He said, 'Yes. I'll go back. Give me another few days, Jess. Then I'll go back.'

'Fine.' I stood up briskly. 'Get some sleep while Watt does. And Sam . . . do you know where Matt's portfolio might be? I really need to get an idea of what's going on down at Marcroft.'

'It's in the car. But I can tell you. When you and Lucy come back, I'll put you in the picture.'

He too stood up and came with me to the door. I felt again that terrible need to put my head on his shoulder and feel his arms holding me. It would mean nothing but it would mean everything too. He held the door wide.

He said flatly, 'Jess, do you want us to get married eventually?'

I was so surprised – shocked – horrified – I hardly knew what to say. I stammered dissent but even to my ears it sounded false.

He said, 'It's just that it would be such a sensible thing to do. Comfort. Pooling our resources. Sharing our pasts. Completely. But it could never be anything else. I couldn't put anyone in Daisy's place. Not ever. But if that is good enough . . .'

I kept my body absolutely straight. Outside the midday sun was low already and very orange.

'Don't you think it's the same for me?' I said in a low voice.

'I'm not sure. Matt was . . . all things to all men. I'm so inward-looking. Narrow-minded, I suppose.'

'Yes. Yes, perhaps you are.'

'Jess, I didn't mean to hurt you. It's just that I thought you might have thought . . .' He stumbled to a halt.

'Matt was certainly all things to me. Absolutely all things.' I took a step outside. 'All this . . . all this beauty. It's nothing without him. Everything looks different without him in the world. My house, my china, my carpets . . . they're mine, not ours. So now they're different. Almost two-dimensional instead of three. I thought you understood, but I see you don't.'

'I do. I do, Jess. That's exactly how I feel, though I couldn't have put it into words. Don't be angry. Please. You will come back?'

'Of course.' I looked round. 'Close the door, Sam. Watt will be feeling the cold.'

He hesitated but then he did close the door. I thought, when Jennifer comes again I will make a joke of this. The first non-proposal I have received. I went past his car and then tried the rear door. It was open. His briefcase was on the seat. I picked it up and put it on the passenger seat of my car and drove off.

Much later, I realized neither of us had mentioned the New York tragedy. It occurred to me that Sam might well not even know of it.

Eight

Four weeks later it was half-term.

Lucy was tired; so was I. I'd made three calls in those four weeks and had two firm orders. Granted, they were both very small: one woman wanted two of her secondary glazed windows replaced and a young family wanted a window out and patio doors in. I felt as though I'd got orders for another Crystal Palace. The woman told me she was delighted not to have to cope with an over-eager salesman, and one of the children in the other house knew Lucy. Job satisfaction extraordinaire. Billy and I went together to take measurements. He said afterwards, 'You can manage that on your own next time, wouldn't you say?' He had a nice grin.

The third enquiry was for a custom-built conservatory. They were 'thinking it over'.

Sam had telephoned and – still stammering – asked me whether I could take care of Watt again.

'I agree that we owe it to Matt to see this job through. After that . . . I don't know.'

I said, 'Can you leave it till half-term? Lucy will be home then and I won't have to do the school run. It'll be easier for me to get back into the swing of it.'

'Of course. Anything . . . anything.' I heard him swallow. 'Are you all right?'

'Yes.' I told him brightly about the two small contracts.

He said, 'I realize now . . . what I said was pretty insulting. I'm sorry, Jess.'

'For goodness' sake, Sam. You suggested a business arrangement, nothing more.'

'But . . . I implied that my grief was greater than yours.'

'Everybody's grief is so different, Sam.'

'Yes, but—'

'Look, we can't discuss it. It's not debatable in any way. Leave it. Please, leave it. I'll see you on the Friday. That's the nineteenth, I think . . . Yes, it is.'

'That's fine. Thank you, Jess.' He sounded subdued and I felt guilty.

Then he said, 'Did you take the portfolio, by the way?'

'Yes.' I tried not to sound defiant. I had photocopied every sketch. 'You can have it back when you bring Watt over. Is that all right?'

'Yes.'

I waited for him to replace his receiver. Instead he said, 'You saw what you wanted?'

'I've got the details I needed. Yes.'

'Right.' And then he put his phone down.

I sat there gnawing my lip. I told myself it was because I was working out details of the child care I would need for Watt.

I phoned Jerome.

'This is Jessica Tavener.'

'I know.' He sounded amused. I waited for the usual enquiries about health but they didn't come.

I said, 'Just to let you know that Sam Clarkson will be back on Friday the nineteenth.'

'I know.'

'Right.' I was going to end the conversation right there if that was the way he wanted it, but he made a sound and I hung on.

'I think I should come and see you, Jess. I've got one or two suggestions you might like to take up. Or you might not, of course.'

'Probably.' I should have told him to stay put as I wasn't

interested in any of his suggestions but caution stopped me. I had come to the reluctant conclusion that we needed him.

He laughed. 'Just hear me out, that's all I ask.'

'All right.'

'Tomorrow?'

I tried not to gasp. 'All right,' I said again.

'I'll be with you at eleven thirty. We'll go out for an early lunch so that you'll be in plenty of time to pick up your little girl. Lucy.' And he put the phone down. I didn't mind. I might have felt bound to argue, but there was no point because tomorrow suited me very well and I would enjoy going out to lunch. I still didn't like him but his energy stimulated mine. And that was good.

He arrived on the dot of eleven thirty and insisted on walking round the garden.

'Matt told me how much you enjoy it.' He obviously didn't know a thing about plants and stared at the massed dahlias without pleasure. He looked up at me suddenly. 'He talked about you all the time. You know that, don't you?'

He'd got under the armour. I said nothing.

'I didn't believe him. He made you out to be a bit of a prig. But Jennifer bore him out.'

I tried to turn him away. 'Lucy sounds a prig sometimes. Then she laughs and you realize it's OK.'

'I haven't seen you laugh much. But already I know you're not a prig.'

I was unguarded enough to say, 'We used to laugh a lot.'

'You will again.'

I shrugged. 'Maybe. Not much to laugh about at present.'

'What about when your exhaust dropped off and you thought you were having a stroke?'

I managed a smile. He was delighted and patted my shoulder. I knew quite suddenly that if I turned into his arms he would hold me properly and let me take what comfort I needed. I shied away from the thought.

'That was a particularly bad day,' I said. 'It wasn't only the exhaust. Everything kept moving. Revolving around me.'

'Dizzy turns. Probably you'd had no breakfast.'

'Things moved slowly, not dizzily. And anti-clockwise too.'

'That's a good sign.'

'Is it? Why?'

'Shows you're unwinding.' He grinned at me. 'And it was when I was with you. You spoke very plainly to me – that's a sign of unwinding too.'

I shook my head helplessly. 'You're incorrigible.'

That made him ebullient. 'Come on. Get your hat and gloves and we'll go. I've booked at the Hilltop.' It was the poshest hotel for miles.

I said, 'Hat and gloves?'

'Jennifer said when you were younger you were the sort of girl who wore a hat and gloves.'

'I never in my life—'

'It's a type. She meant you were a conformist.'

'I suppose . . . perhaps.'

He took my arm. Where his hand held just above my elbow, I felt his warmth.

He said, 'It's a joke. I wanted you to laugh again.'

And, would you believe it, I did. He wanted a laugh and he got a laugh. That was the sort of man he was, I suppose.

I have to say I enjoyed the lunch. I didn't really notice the food, though I knew it was good – parsnip and carrot soup, risotto, apple snow – but Jerome's company was exhilarating, to put it mildly. He suggested a series of advertisements in the local paper and a press release about the windows at Marcroft Abbey. 'Can you link them with any other building? Did Matt talk about his drawings at all?' He was delighted that any future enquiries would be dealt with by me, tape measure in hand. 'Take Sam's baby with you. Nothing like a baby to break down barriers.' I thought he would muscle in when it came to the press release but all he said was, 'Let me see it before you send it anywhere. Just to make sure we don't tread on each other's toes.'

'You're giving me carte blanche?' I couldn't believe this.

'I've already got something for the nationals.'

'May I see it?'

'Of course. We'll co-ordinate them. Listen, bring the children over at half-term. How's that? You can have a look at what Sam has done – it's impressive. It will be good for him to see his baby—'

'Watt,' I reminded him.

'Yes. Watt.' He grinned. 'And Lucy. And we'll go over everything in the office.' He leaned across the table and put his hand over mine. I stopped myself from flinching. 'Listen, Jess. I want you in on this. It's a terrific angle.'

I held my breath, praying he wouldn't start quoting something like 'bereaved widow takes up her husband's work'. Thank God he said no more. And then that seemed almost worse. We sat there, realizing we were practically holding hands. Gently I put mine in my lap.

'I must go, Jerome. Thank you for a marvellous lunch.'

'And you'll come over at half-term?'

'Yes.'

'Good girl.' He looked at me. 'That didn't sound patronizing, did it?'

'A bit.' I looked at him. 'Jennifer is coming at half-term. May I ask her to come with me?'

'Of course.' He held my gaze. 'If you really want that.'

I nodded and stood up. We climbed into his mountain of a car and drove back along the old Wells road. I bided my time until he drew up in Dip Lane; I wanted to do the equivalent of slamming down the phone after I'd said my piece.

The silence settled around us. I said, 'Jerome, there's something I must ask you. It's quite important.'

He became cautious; I could feel it.

'Is it about Jennifer?'

'No.'

Slight relaxation. 'All right then. Fire away.'

'You said . . . before . . . that you had met Matt in the summer of last year. And my father was with him. Are you sure of that?'

'Of course. I'm not likely to forget Matt's first visit.'

'Can you think of any reason why he didn't tell me about that meeting?'

He shrugged. 'Overlooked it?'

'Denied it, actually. Absolutely denied it.'

He shrugged again. 'Shielding your father, I expect. He brought his girlfriend.'

I clamped my mouth shut; my teeth grated. Consciously I unlocked my jaw.

'Was she blond? Rather large?'

'Yes. Yes, she was. Her name was Marilyn George. She was a great girl.'

Well, there was no doubting it any longer. And now was the time to open the door and slide out of the car. I sat as if turned to stone.

He said, 'No big deal, Jess. They'd wanted a day together. Your father was so at ease with her . . . and she with him. She adored him. I think he . . . respected her.'

I moistened my lips. 'How could Matt . . . I thought he loved my mother.'

'Well, it's obvious why he kept it to himself. Look at you.' He leaned forward to stare into my face. 'Jess, we're in the twenty-first century. According to Jennifer, your parents hadn't slept together for years.'

I made a sound of protest and then at last I opened the door and let myself slide to the grass verge. I began to stumble towards the gate. He was behind me. He grabbed my arm and swung me round to face him.

'Stop it!' He held both my arms. 'Stop it this minute, Jess! As far as I can see, no-one has betrayed anyone. And if they have, then who are you to judge?'

I tried to get away but he held me firm. And then he did

what Sam should have done a few weeks ago. He held me against his leather-clad shoulder. He put a hand on the back of my neck and massaged it gently, while his other hand rested on my waist.

I realized I was shaking so I held on to him like grim death. He said in my ear, 'You're cold. Shall we go indoors?'

'No. It's always windy up here. I'm fine.'

He said a rude word and held me closer, trying to wrap me inside his jacket. His shirt smelled like Matt's shirts had smelled. How could Matt have lied to me? Because I was too much of a prig to take the truth? Oh God. I huddled closer to the starch-smelling shirt as if I could shut out everything unpleasant. My father. And Marilyn George.

After a long time he said quietly, 'Look up. Just for a moment, look up at me, Jess.'

So I looked up. I'd like to say the hand that was now in my hair forced me to look up. But I cannot say that. I looked up voluntarily and I let him kiss me. I didn't pull away; I let myself be kissed. My head fell back and I wanted to be kissed. I didn't want him to stop.

He stopped. He looked down at me. Very deeply. 'Now can you forgive? Now can you understand how it might have been for them?'

I was still, returning his gaze. I whispered, 'Lesson over?'

'Is it?' He held me loosely now. 'Have I made it better or worse?'

'I don't know.'

'I shouldn't have told you.'

'Yes, you should. You've been honest. That's what I want.'

'And you'll still come and see me at half-term?'

'With the children and Jennifer.'

'She won't come, Jess.'

'We'll see.' I pushed away slightly. 'I must go. School.'

His mouth brushed mine again but this time I didn't respond.

'Jess—'

But I was gone, fiddling with the gate and then the front-door key. I got inside the hall and closed the door. Then I whispered hoarsely and fiercely, 'Matt, I want you. Here and now. I want you here!'

Nothing happened. The house was silent and I could hear the kitchen clock ticking. I had no time for hysterics: Lucy would be waiting.

So . . . it was half-term.

I couldn't not go to Marcroft because then he'd think I was making much more of that kiss than just a 'lesson'. In a way I needed to see him again to prove to myself that it had been just that . . . a lesson. But it would be good to have Jennifer with me. I didn't think she would come, but strangely enough, she needed no persuasion at all to stay with Lucy and me for a few nights.

I had cancelled my hair appointment before I knew about Marilyn, and the crew cut was growing out very oddly indeed. But Jennifer liked the hair. 'It's decidedly retro. You can get away with it,' she pronounced authoritatively that first evening. 'And yes, I'll come with you to Marcroft and protect you against the dreaded Jerry. I need to face him and realize that it's well and truly over.' She smiled wryly. 'How did you cope with him when he came to see you?'

'Most of the time it was all right. We talked about the business and he had some bright ideas which I can easily go along with. But then it got a bit difficult.'

'I can imagine. Did he make a pass?'

'*No!*'

I was surprised by my own vehemence. Jennifer raised her brows.

'I wouldn't put it past him, ever. But I suppose, in the circs, it would have been beyond the pale. Even for him.'

I decided then and there that I would say nothing about Dad and Marilyn. Jennifer would take it out on Jerome and there would be endless discussions . . . It would be awful. I remembered how curt she had been about Mum and Ray. I didn't think I could bear to hear her talk about Dad in the same way.

She asked lots of questions about Sam and Watt and was disgusted that I had not laid down what she called 'ground rules' for the future.

'Don't get too fond of him, Jess,' she warned. 'Sam will recover and remarry, you'll see. He's an attractive man.'

I'd never thought of Sam as attractive; he was so ordinary. I went on folding the washing. I didn't want to talk about it.

On the Tuesday we woke to a white world. The first frost of the winter, though the sun shone and it didn't seem like winter at all. We all walked around the garden looking at the silvered cobwebs and mourning the blackened dahlias. Lucy loved it; already she had a small bank of memories and this was one of them. Neither of us mentioned it but just after last Christmas there had been a very damp morning when the cobwebs had been pearled and exquisite and Matt had carried her round to look at them. The way she pointed everything out intently to Watt – in Jennifer's arms – we both knew that she was repeating her father's words. Watt surveyed it all with complete wonderment.

That was the day we had lunch at the old schoolhouse; Ray was there and I wondered how Mum had talked him into entertaining both Lucy and Watt. They must have worked hard that morning because everything was in good order: the soup bowls with their small lids, the well-used willow-patterned vegetable dishes, the deep brown casserole, even the elephant napkin rings which took Watt's fancy, all appeared in their turn without delay or fuss. I was glad to see Ray doing his share; we hadn't been to a meal before with Ray much in evidence but I had gathered he wasn't really a child person. Alicia had been so marvellous with Lucy . . . I found myself longing for Alicia.

Ray said, 'We've put some carrots and peas into the food processor, Jess. Or do you think he'd prefer one of his little jars? Monica has some of those too.'

'Oh, I think the fresh food would be nicer.' Just in case he'd done it himself I said, 'That's really kind of you, Ray.'

'Well,' he said, looking suddenly coy, 'if I'm to be one of the family I'd better put in some practice with the children.'

I kept my smile in place but risked a glance at Jennifer, who refused to look at me. Mum came in with the trolley. She passed over a bowl of orange-coloured puree.

She said, 'Don't jump the gun, Ray.' She turned to me. 'D'you want to feed him now, darling? I'll serve you if you like and stick it back in the trolley.'

'Fine. Thanks, Mum.' I was thanking her for slapping Ray down as well. But of course it was me who had the shock in the end because the lunch was an excuse for an 'announcement' and she wanted it to come from her, not Ray.

We finished the pudding, which was substantial, and sat back practically comatose. Probably Mum had planned that too. She looked at us, Lucy as well, and said, 'My three girls. All beautiful. All special.'

Jennifer interrupted brusquely, 'Do we need the violins?'

'Sorry, Jen. It's just . . . I want to tell you something and it's so important to me that you not only accept it but feel pleased for me. It might be difficult at first. You both loved Dad so much and he's been dead only a year.'

Mum started talking about marriage and all the different kinds of happiness around. Jennifer drummed her fingers on the tablecloth and Lucy looked at her and then at me.

Mum said, 'I know Lucy will be pleased by the news because she already loves her uncle Ray. And I think you two will be – for the same reason – but also for my sake.'

Jennifer said crisply, 'Well, of course. The three of us join together in huge congratulations!' She smiled at me meaningfully as she lifted her glass and passed Lucy her lemonade. 'Come on, girls. A toast. To a new member of the family!'

Lucy reached over to clunk glasses with Jen. I managed

to find a spare hand and lift mine in a token gesture. I didn't even know what it was all about. Was Ray moving into the schoolhouse? Surely, surely, surely, they weren't going to get married? I looked at him. Slowly, the room began to revolve around him. Anti-clockwise.

Much later, when Lucy was in bed and Watt was having an illicit bottle to 'settle' him, Jennifer came downstairs in satin pyjamas and a man's dressing gown, wine-coloured with white penny-sized spots.

She said firmly, 'I'll do that. Go and have a bath and relax.'

'I'm fine.' Earlier she had been concerned and cross with me all at once. I had been doing too much; I had not been doing enough to take my mind off things; I must have realized that something was going on between Mum and Ray for a couple of years at least; how was I going to cope with Watt at the same time as wanting to start running the business? She had made sure I was ensconced in Dad's old chair in the sitting room before she suggested that she and Ray go for a walk with Lucy and Watt. Mum had surveyed me from the other side of the old coke stove and asked me outright if I was ill.

'Of course not. I get a bit . . . I don't know . . . what's the word?'

'Mithered.'

'Yes. But it passes.'

'Nothing to do with Ray and me moving in together?'

'Of course not,' I repeated. I was thankful that marriage wasn't on the agenda.

And then she said, 'I know it's a bit strange for people of our age. But you see, darling, if I marry again I think I lose Dad's pension. Not only that, but Ray is not divorced from Alicia. And if she and Marcus split up—'

'My God. Are you saying she'd come back? And live with Ray again?'

She smiled. 'It does sound odd, doesn't it? I don't think

that would happen because neither of them would want it.'
She surveyed me. 'You don't like it, do you?'

She looked so crestfallen. She so desperately wanted me
to 'like it'.

I said, 'It's just that . . . you know. Dad.'

'Well, of course, I understand that. But Dad and I . . .
We'd grown apart, Jess. He was a man of ideas. And ideals
too. And . . . well, you know me. I'm such a practical person.'

What could I say? I didn't know her. And I certainly
hadn't known Dad. So I said nothing and after a while she
jumped up and suggested a cup of tea.

'It would be nice to have it in peace, perfect peace.' She
smiled, already on her way to the kitchen. Yes, she had
always been a practical person. I looked at her as she
disappeared through the door. Her back was ramrod
straight and she still held her head well. I looked like her.
Jennifer was tall and willowy like Dad.

I recalled all this as I plodded up to the bathroom
feeling like an old woman. I said aloud, under cover of the
gushing water, 'I'm so thankful that Jennifer was only
thirteen when we first met, Matt. I'm not the beautiful one,
that's for sure.'

I had a bath and came down in my old nightie beneath
the wonderful, if shabby, alpaca dressing gown Matt had
bought me ten years before. Jennifer was still holding Watt.
The bottle was on the floor by her chair and Watt was fast
asleep.

'Let me put him in his cot,' I said. 'It's all right, he won't
wake up now.'

'Not until about four ack emma,' she said drily. 'No.
Leave him, Jess. I'll put him down when I go to bed. He's
so delightful.' She glinted up at me. 'Perhaps I should get a
cat.'

'Well . . . as you've finished with men, it might be the
only option.'

'Not at all. Women have babies now without going into a
relationship with the father.'

I looked past her head. I couldn't be bothered with one of these flippant conversations tonight. I said bleakly, 'It's not good being a single mum.'

She didn't reply. There was nothing to say anyway. I made cocoa and we talked around the subject of Mum and Ray and then she suggested that I should sleep in her bed and she would be with Watt.

'You need a really good night's sleep,' she said, sounding like Mum. So I left her by the fire nursing Daisy's seven-month-old baby, and I tucked myself into her bed.

It was Thursday, sunny, windy, with scudding clouds; frost all gone. We set off for Marcroft at nine thirty; it was a bit of a rush because of Watt but we would need to get back early. Jennifer drove and she was unusually quiet. I remembered that Jerome had been convinced she wouldn't come. Now I was glad she was here, driving, helping out so generously with Watt too. She was going back to London on Sunday and I was dreading it. But glad too that I was dreading it. Jennifer and I hadn't been close like this for years. I wondered how much of an ordeal this meeting would be. But she had agreed to it almost immediately.

Lucy and I sat in the back. Watt, in the carrier, was strapped into the front seat. He loved being in the car and we knew there would be no demands for food or drink while we kept moving.

It was so different from our 'adventure' of last May Day. The countryside was putting itself to bed; there were plenty of leaves left on the trees but their colours were either fading or going out blazingly. The cow parsley had gone and the heavy gorse-smell too. The breeze coming off Salisbury Plain was fresh and clear. I pointed out the late foxgloves and the huge busy sky. Lucy's hand crept into mine and I waited for her to voice her memories of our last drive.

But she said, 'Will I have to call Uncle Ray Grandad, Mummy?'

I said, 'Is he your grandad?' She shook her head worriedly. 'He's not, Lucy. Your grandad was Donald Not Ray. So I think you'd better go on calling Uncle Ray Uncle Ray.' I laughed but she didn't join in.

'I think . . .' She paused. 'I really think that Gran would like me to call him Grandad.'

From the front seat Jennifer said loudly and swiftly, 'It's entirely up to you, chicken. Whatever you want to call him will be OK with Gran. In fact you could invent a new name for him if you liked. He'd be tickled pink by that.'

That made Lucy think. She released my hand and tugged at her hair and came up with a series of names that made us all laugh. By the time we reached Avebury she had settled on one. 'Bunny,' she said decidedly. 'It's like Watt's rabbit that I gave him before he was born. D'you remember Mummy? And it's got a bit of uncle in it too. And it's cuddly.'

I was surprised. 'Do you think of Uncle Ray as being cuddly?'

'You mean Bunny. Yes. He's good at cuddling. He cuddles Gran when she cries and yesterday he cuddled me when we thought you were ill.'

I glanced at her. She had known two bereavements before she was five years old. She must live in terror of a third.

Jennifer laughed from the front seat. 'That sums up Bunny all right. He cuddles while Mum and me do the slapping and the cold compresses!'

That was interesting. Jennifer might look like Dad but she was as practical as Mum.

I hugged my daughter. 'Bunny is excellent. I like it so much better than Uncle Ray. Thank you, darling.'

Jennifer drove by the Armstrong Arms and then turned down the long lane to the abbey. She knew it so well. Past the arched entrance we followed the track down toward the little wood where we had paddled in the stream such a short time ago. So foolishly, so unknowingly.

It had all changed since we last saw it. These were the main living quarters and as Jennifer drew up at the side door I could see curtains at most of the windows. I started to say to her that Jerry was obviously living here but she totally ignored me – and Watt – and got slowly out of the car and just stood there, one hand on the door and the other, very uncharacteristically, fiddling with her hair. And then the side door opened and Jerome came out and also stood stock still. I held Lucy back for a moment. The sexual tension between them was practically tangible and I expected Jennifer to run into his arms.

But then he said, 'Surprise, surprise. I didn't expect you, Jennifer Maslin.'

She smiled and dropped her hand. 'That's really why I came,' she said.

He made a face. 'You haven't changed a bit. Shame.'

Her smile died. 'I've changed a lot actually. And I think I should thank you for that.'

'If it's true, then it's a pleasure.'

All these brittle exchanges meant nothing to me, but that highly strung moment had certainly passed. Lucy scrambled out to stand by Jennifer and Jerome said, 'Hello, Lucy. How are you?'

Lucy took his proffered hand and said unexpectedly, 'I didn't want to come. But I'm glad now.'

He kept her hand and hunkered down to her level. 'I thought you might feel like that. Thank you for coming.'

She smiled right into his face. 'We thought you were going to take Aunt Jennifer away from us.'

Jennifer crouched too and said, 'Luce. Darling. That was never actually on the cards.' She glanced briefly at Jerome. 'I expect Lucy could do with a bathroom.'

He stood up. 'I want to show you the house anyway. You haven't seen it since it was finished and I moved in.' He looked across the car as I scooped Watt into my arms. 'Can you manage?' But he didn't wait for an answer. I locked the car and followed them inside.

The annexe to the abbey was marvellous. I remembered that I hadn't liked the abbey itself one bit, but this was quite different. It was spacious yet comfortable, almost cosy. I was amazed that Jerome could create such a home. The furniture was absolutely modern and a complete mixture of styles. Some of the chairs were obviously one-off designer pieces, and the enormous glass trestle table in the dining room I had seen in a department store in Bristol. The sofas were huge and squashy and the long, low storage units held the occasional cushion for extra seating. Clinging to the back of the abbey as it did, it should have been a jarring contrast, but it wasn't. In spite of its blatant comfort it was sparse enough that it could have given shelter to a monk or two. I stood, clutching Watt and watching Jennifer walk the length of the sitting room and through an arch into the dining room. Her elegance set everything off to perfection. Jerome watched her too. Presumably they had shown Lucy where the bathroom was.

He turned to me at last. 'Does it work?' he asked. 'You see, if I'd tried to furnish it with reproduction stuff it would have looked fake straight away. So why not proclaim its newness. Nothing to be ashamed of, surely?'

I said honestly, 'It's beautiful. You've got room to entertain yet it's still a home. I like it very much.'

He was pleased. 'It's not finished. You haven't seen the kitchen yet. I didn't want to start it until you'd had a look.'

I raised my brows at that. 'It's out of my ken, Jerome. I need a kitchen that will yield up the cornflake packets without a fuss and a table that can be reached from the cooker and the sink.'

He smiled. 'I'd still like your opinion.'

Lucy came bouncing in to announce her approval of the bathroom, and Jennifer wandered back from the dining room nodding slowly.

'It's super, Jerry. You've hit the right note in every room.'

He repeated that the kitchen wasn't finished. 'It's only

partially new. The main part of it is Victorian, sort of like a vestry, and it was very dark. I couldn't enlarge the windows – they're only on one side in any case. So as we need a new roof, I've asked Sam whether it would be feasible to have a glass one. He seems to think it is. Therefore . . .' He looked at me. 'Perhaps we could do business this afternoon, Mrs Tavener?'

I looked at Jennifer, who was standing just behind Jerome. Slowly and deliberately she moved her head from side to side in negation. I couldn't understand it. I would have clapped my hands if I hadn't been carrying Watt. This was going to be a really big job. Billy would have to come down and we might have to get outside contractors. Well, in the good old days of the double-glazing boom we'd done it. We could do it again.

I said cautiously, 'We could certainly discuss it. I'd like Sam to be with us, of course.' I ignored Jennifer, who was definitely shaking her head now. 'Perhaps we'd better have a look at the area first of all.'

He led the way. The floors were block-tiled a pale golden colour, the off-white walls punctuated with the occasional picture . . . I couldn't take it all in. The double doors to what Jerome called the utility area opened wide enough to take trolleys four abreast. Inside, to the left were more doors. He flung them open to reveal a washing machine and tumble dryer, a table holding a single electric ring and a microwave. Someone had been arranging flowers at the sink and the discarded stalks still lay there. He waited for our comments.

Jennifer said dryly, 'Very minimal.'

Lucy said, 'Where's the cooker?'

He picked her up. 'Not there yet. I want your mummy to help me choose.'

Lucy clapped her hands. 'I'll draw something,' she offered.

We went further into the empty area outside and were suddenly in darkness. The stone walls were blackened by soot, the flagged floor uneven. Along one wall, a line of cupboards looked as if it might well contain skeletons.

'Untouched by human hand,' Jerome emphasized.

'It needs the glass roof,' I said.

Lucy began poking into the cupboards and Jerome joined her, explaining that if the abbey had been really old they would have held robes and prayer books. 'Missals,' I heard him say. And Lucy piped up, 'Is that where mistletoe comes from?' He hunkered again and began to tell her about missals and mistletoe.

Jennifer said in a low voice, 'Don't touch it with a barge-pole, Jess. You'll be under his thumb just like Matt was. Like I was too.'

'Sis, I can't afford to pass up an order like this. Besides, I don't want to. I can cope with this. I've been in on big housing contracts, I know the ropes.'

'You don't know him. Who do you think arranged that furniture, the pictures . . . Who d'you think was doing the flowers when we arrived and has probably been bundled off to the village?'

'One of his girlfriends. All right, I don't like his promiscuity but so long as it doesn't involve you . . . It doesn't, does it?'

'You know damn well it doesn't!'

'You were both fairly bowled over at the sight of each other.'

'He might have been. I certainly wasn't.'

'All right.' I was doubtful. If Jennifer and Jerome decided to be an item again, it would make things . . . different.

He came back and asked for ideas and I threw in a vague suggestion which involved a double Aga along the back wall and storage units in the modern half.

'OK,' he said, 'make some sketches – let Lucy help – and I'll come and see them next week.'

I wasn't overjoyed about that but felt myself nodding. I hoped our meetings weren't going to have to be too regular.

He took us out to lunch at the Armstrong Arms, then back to the abbey. While Lucy and Jennifer went down to the stream, Sam and I sat at the glass table and Jerome spread out what he called a provisional contract for the glass roof in the kitchen.

It was so good to see Sam again. Like finding a fellow countryman in a strange land. He took Watt from me and leaned over his downy head to peck my cheek. I was amazed.

Jerome pointed out the various clauses and assured us that we could get out of the job within two weeks if we had second thoughts about it.

'I suggest the two of you get together next week some time. Go into the costing very carefully.'

I said, 'We need longer than two weeks. I have to contact people, sound them out, get estimates.' I glanced at Sam. 'Much longer than two weeks.' He nodded emphatically. 'The opt-out clause should be a month to six weeks.' Sam nodded again. I wished he would say something. I needed more reassurance than just the occasional nod.

Jerome blustered a bit. 'Too long! Much too long.'

'Well, that's it.' If we lost the job then we lost it. I couldn't possibly sort it out in less than a month.

He drew the contract towards him, took out a pen and changed the opt-out clause to six weeks. 'Will that do for you both?' he asked brusquely. He threw down the pen.

'Fine.' I picked up the pen and signed my name along the dotted line. I had no idea whether this so-called provisional contract was legally binding. But I knew I wanted the job and, apparently, so did Sam.

Jerome signed and then Sam witnessed our signatures while I held Watt. Sam immediately stood up.

'I think I saw your sister and Lucy down at the stream.' He leaned over me and took Watt on to his shoulder. 'I'll join them.'

It was typical of Sam to opt out of any further discussion. I reminded myself how marvellous he had been that time he had driven to Bath and slept in the car overnight to be near Daisy. Yet his elusiveness was probably the best way of dealing with Jerome. I took a leaf out of Sam's book, smiled up at him and let him go. I could fix up our meeting on the phone; he rang nearly every evening to see how his son had been that day. That was what he called him: my son.

Jerome watched him go with evident exasperation.

'A man of few words,' he commented. I nodded and he turned back to the contract. 'It'll be a big job, Jess. You could come across rotten timbers – we've found plenty of them in the abbey – and I want it done really well.'

'Don't worry. We use a surveyor from Bath, who is excellent. He'll look at the work in stages and liaise with the building inspectors. We'll have to contract out the building work, of course. That's usual with big jobs like this. And Matt had built up quite a good network of firms.'

He smiled. 'Jess, I'm proud of you.'

I wanted to tell him he had no right to be proud of me; I was simply doing a job. But it could have sounded smug and I didn't want that. I kept quiet and pretended to be studying the contract.

He sat down next to me. 'Jess, I want us to be friends. After the other week . . . and today . . . I feel we've got a foundation to build on.' He grinned. 'In more ways than one!'

I looked at him. Our lunch at the Hilltop had seemed to lay a foundation for a friendship of sorts, but I wasn't too certain of the 'lesson' he had administered before parting. And I wasn't too sure about today either. I was wondering whether his affair with Jennifer was not as dead as both of them would have me believe.

'We'd better see how it goes,' I said. 'Business and friendship don't always mix.'

'We'll make it work!' he said, so full of energy that he was like a charging rhino. 'Let's start with you calling me Jerry. Come on, say it.'

'Your initials are A. K. Why do you use Jerry?'

'It has a ring. Jerry Jerome.'

I smiled at this frank conceit. 'What does the A. K. stand for?'

'I won't tell you unless you call me Jerry.'

It was so childish. I said, 'What does the A. K. stand for, Jerry?'

'Ah. Thank you, Jess. And I'm not going to tell you.'

'You promised!' I was ridiculously outraged.

'Not quite. And anyway I crossed my fingers.'

'Did you cross your fingers when we signed that?' I nodded at the paper before us.

'No.' He sighed. 'That paper doesn't mean much, Jess. Sam knew it and you probably know it. But it was the only way I could think of to make you realize that I do want you to have the job.'

I smiled full at him. 'Thanks for that, Jerry. If we're to be friends we must at least be honest. However painful it may be.'

'I'm not sure. Afterwards . . . after I'd told you about your father and Marilyn George, I felt pretty rotten.'

I shook my head. 'Don't. Please. You're the only person who could have told me. It's so obvious now that everyone else knew and said nothing.'

He sat there by my side, one elbow on the glass table, looking at me consideringly. And then he said, 'You and Matt. The perfect couple, wouldn't you say?'

I was immediately wary; on the defensive. 'If you are going to jibe about us, Jerry, please stop right there. I'd like to be friends. But there are boundaries. You could never understand Matt and me in a thousand years.'

'I wasn't going to jibe. As a matter of fact, I'm curious. Envious maybe. But I respect your limits and apologize for coming close to them.' He stood up abruptly. 'Let's collect the others and go out for tea. Sam has an electric kettle in the abbey but I rather think Lucy would like an ice-cream sundae.'

We went back to the Armstrong Arms and then it was time to leave. We drove off waving frantically as if to old friends. Jennifer drew out on to the road and said with pleasure, 'Right. I've done it. The lion in his den. I've bearded him.'

I adjusted Lucy's seat belt and leaned over to check on Watt.

'So have I.' I smiled at my sister in the driving mirror. 'Let's go the quicker way home. Through Devizes.'

I could bear to see it again now: the place where Matt and I had been together for the last time.

Nine

The weeks until Christmas were hectic. I often thought of Marilyn's words about needing time to grieve. There was barely time to get through each day. Mum and Ray were wonderful; they had Watt most days and often met Lucy from school. I asked Mum whether Ray minded having the children so often.

She laughed. 'Darling, Alicia didn't want children so Ray isn't going to have grandchildren either, is he? It's a bonus for him, believe me.'

So I'd got the wrong end of the stick there, too. Maybe I then tried to compensate for my ill-feeling; I started to call him Bunny, like Lucy did, and he blossomed.

It was Lucy's birthday at the end of November; she was five, which seemed like a coming of age to me. Matt would have thought of something super but when I asked her what she would like to do she said she wanted to go to the theatre to see *Wind in the Willows* with Bunny and Gramma. She wanted to take Andrew Bearwood, Nat and Tony and a girl called Blodwen. Gramma would pick them all up from school and Bunny would drive them to Bath.

'Nat and Tony? I thought it was Nat at your school?'

'You've forgotten, Mummy. They take it in turns. This week it's Tony.'

I swallowed. They'd got away with it for almost a whole term.

'I haven't met Blodwen, have I?'

'Yes, you have. She's got a long plait and she can sit on it.'

'Oh yes, I remember.' Her mother was a piano teacher. 'I'll get some invitation cards, shall I?'

'Gramma's doing that. And Bunny is seeing to the supper.'

'Supper?'

I was asking questions the whole time.

'You go to the theatre and have supper after. Bunny says that as it's Saturday the day after, it won't matter if we're late home.' She grinned gleefully. 'We're going to the Pizza Place. It stays open very, very late.'

'Oh.'

'And Mrs Sparrow is reading *Wind in the Willows* so we know about it. Bunny says that's good because we won't have to ask a lot of questions.'

'Right.' I looked at her. She was – to me – so beautiful with her straight dark hair and enormous brown eyes. I was glad she was happy, glad she liked Bunny and didn't resent his taking her grandfather's place, but she was growing up so fast. She had a life, as they say. Last spring Alicia and Mum had taken her on her little trike with its restrainer. Now I had got her a scooter with its own brake.

I said tentatively, 'Am I invited?'

'Oh Mummy!' She flung her arms around my waist and butted her head into my fleece. 'I wish you could come! Could Aunt Jennifer come down and take care of Watt?'

I had temporarily forgotten Watt. So . . . I wasn't invited. It was the strangest feeling.

Mum knew how I felt, of course. She said, 'Listen, Jess. This busy time will finish once you've got the glass roof sorted out. And Sam is almost done with the stained glass.'

'How do you know?' I asked. 'It could go on well into the spring. He hasn't said a thing to me.'

'Well, Jennifer seems to think it's almost finished. She was down there last weekend and gave me a ring. Said it looked absolutely marvellous. And once Sam is home he'll be able to take on some of this roof business.'

I raised my brows but made no comment about Jennifer being at Marcroft.

'Sam's no organizer, Mum. He's marvellous on site but he hates meeting people and doing the business.'

'So did you before you had to!' She smiled and hugged my arm. 'We're so proud of you, darling. Ray admires you so much. You realize that, I hope?'

I didn't. Ray had been kept so much in the background during Alicia's time.

It was true that once the actual abbey was finished and the various contractors had given dates for their work on the roof, life would slow down again. It occurred to me suddenly that Sam would then be very much in the picture. He would doubtless keep an eye on the roof at Marcroft but he would be based back at Two Lanes Cottage, so he could take on Watt again. I gnawed my lip at the thought and then put it from me, because I had arrived at the small engineering firm on the coast who had given a competitive quote for the girders that would support the new glass roof. They were a two-man business: brothers, both young and very keen, Steve and George Gully. They agreed to come with me and look at the job and we fixed on 30 November, Lucy's birthday. I told myself it didn't matter because after delivering her to school I was free, and I would be back in good time to take Watt from Mum. But somehow it didn't seem right. Other years I had been making paper hats and laying the table.

Billy from the factory was to come with us. The Gully brothers were waiting for me outside the house when I got back from school. Billy arrived soon afterwards and we set out at nine thirty. It was an awful day, raining yet not a bit cold, almost muggy. I had left the living room full of discarded paper from Lucy's presents and I should have done something about it. The whole thing weighed on me as we drove towards Avebury. A few discarded boxes – as if they mattered. What mattered was that it was Lucy's fifth birthday and I wasn't sharing it with her.

Billy made conversation and the two boys in the back chatted to each other and the journey was soon done. I pulled up at the abbey entrance so that we could see the stained glass. Everything was ankle-deep in mud and the place looked grim and Gothic and awful. I planned to leave them in Sam's hands and drive on down to the house as soon as possible. Jerry had said he would be free from lunchtime onwards but that I was to make myself comfortable. I needed the grand bathroom; I needed some comfort too. I knew exactly what I was going to do: I was going to sit in one of the modern chairs and cry. I knew it was self-indulgent and I didn't care.

Anyway, Sam was sweet and pecked me on the cheek again.

'Don't go just yet – I know the governor wants to talk to you but come and see the windows.' He actually looked me straight in the eye for a moment. 'I think Matt would be pleased.'

He would have been, too. The windows transformed the place; coloured light was everywhere, even on such a grey morning. Bars of gold and orange and purple lay across the nave and bathed the stonework in warmth. The pillars were all clothed in deep red, and I knew that was down to Matt and his careful measurements and sketches. Watching me, Sam said quietly, 'They change with the sun and the seasons, of course. But Matt wanted them all to be the same colour, whatever that might be. It's rather special, isn't it?'

I turned to him, glowing. 'It's wonderful, Sam. You've done a wonderful job. Thank you.'

He shrugged slightly. 'I did it for him.'

I was momentarily surprised he didn't mention Daisy.

'Oh Sam . . .'

He was, after all, closer to me in experience than anyone else, even Mum. And if I was never ever going to feel anything again for a man, then why not take up his suggestion and be with him on a partnership basis? Two parents again for Lucy and for Watt. I knew Lucy would understand only too well why we were doing it. She would be kind to Sam. If only he would let me touch him, lean against him perhaps, exchange some kind of . . . comfort. That word again.

Tentatively I put out my hand. Just as tentatively, he took it. We stood for a moment while the others went up to the gallery to take a closer look at the windows.

I said again, 'Oh Sam.'

He shook my hand gently and released it. 'It's done now. Perhaps . . . we might be able to start again.'

I nodded. 'We'll always be friends, Sam.'

'Of course. I wouldn't want it any other way.'

I gave him an upside-down smile and nodded again. And then Billy called down to ask if he should take any of the lead equipment back home and Sam had to tell him to leave it until he had done the finishing touches. Somehow I drifted off and went back to the car and drove down to the house. I really did need that cry. Sam was different. Something was not quite right.

I went through to the new half of the kitchen, made coffee on the single ring and sat with it at the glass-topped table, then got up and threw it away and went outside and down to the stream. It was colder by the water and the rain was softer, mistier. It was impossible to imagine building dams and paddling. I found a narrow place where I could jump across and I walked up the opposite bank, where there had been bluebells in the spring, and came out of a belt of trees on to muddy fields. The sky was right down on top of the land, heavy and dark. Ideal weather for going to the theatre.

I don't know how long I was there; when I looked at my watch it was well past midday and I wanted to leave for home at three. I hadn't thought of lunch. George, Steve and Billy were going to need feeding somewhere.

I started to hurry back and immediately slipped over. Already my shoes were caked in mud; now my jeans were too. But I told myself I felt better for coming here and squared my shoulders as I jumped across the stream and tried to jog back to the house.

Sam met me halfway.

'The governor came back about an hour ago. Wasn't overjoyed you were missing, of course. You know what he's like. He's taken the others to the Arms for some food. We're to join him as soon as we can.'

He was horrified at the state of me and took my shoes while I went to the bathroom to do the best I could with my jeans. In spite of being determined not to hurry, I sponged the mud off in two minutes flat and found Sam outside, scraping my shoes clean with a penknife.

We scrambled back to the car and I started her up. I was fuming. 'He told me to use the house. I was under the impression he wouldn't be back until after midday.'

'Well, it was just gone midday.' Sam was unperturbed as usual. 'He didn't think much of Billy and me taking the lads up into the roof. Apparently that's your department.'

'Oh . . .' I wanted to swear but somehow I knew Sam wouldn't like it.

He said flatly, 'He kept calling you Mrs Tavener.'

'Right.'

I got the picture. I was the boss and the others were my employees.

We drew up behind his horrible four-wheel drive at the Armstrong Arms and I led the way into the bar. No sign of them. They were in the restaurant of course, Billy, George and Steve looking ill at ease, Jerome being mine host.

I threaded my way among the empty tables.

'This is fun,' I said. 'I didn't expect such a treat.' I settled myself next to Steve and grinned across at Jerry. 'Thanks for giving me the morning off, Jerry. I went for a walk. Crossed the stream and followed the other bank for about half a mile. Very muddy.'

'So I see.' He sounded displeased.

I turned to Steve. 'Did Sam take you to see the job?'

'Yes, Mrs Tavener—'

'Please call me Jess,' I said quickly.

'Oh . . . right. Thanks, Jess.' He glanced at his brother. 'We can do it all right. It'll need several reinforced steel joists to hold that amount of glass. We'll need to know the actual weight, then we can calculate how many.'

Sam was settling himself on the other side of me.

'I've done the measurements, Jess. Billy and I can work it out as soon as I get back next week.'

Billy said, 'The boss can put it through the computer.'

It took me a moment to realize that I was 'the boss'.

'Certainly, Billy.' I glanced at George. 'Are you happy with that, George?'

Everyone seemed happy with it except Jerome, who remained ominously silent.

I said, 'Shall we have something to eat, Jerry? I have to get back fairly soon.'

'Oh. Yes. Lucy.' He seemed to accept that all right, so I expanded.

'Actually, it's her birthday today. She's being taken to the theatre in Bath to see *Wind in the Willows*.' It was a good move; everyone wanted to know about Lucy and I was only too glad to tell them. Then we ordered some food and I had a much-needed coffee and told the others they could have a drink as I would drive again. The food came and we tucked in with a will.

Jerome said, 'You'll need to have a bath by the look of you.'

I laughed. 'I'm not on show tonight, Jerry. My mother and a friend are doing the honours.' I told him a bit about Andrew Bearwood, then found myself expounding about Nat and Tony and their double act.

He said across Sam, 'You're not going with Lucy? On her birthday?'

I swallowed. 'No.'

Sam said, 'Is it because of Watt?'

'Well, yes. But Jennifer would have come up and looked after Watt. It's just a golden opportunity for me to have a rest.'

'Not much rest with Watt around.'

I risked touching his arm for a moment. 'He's much better now, Sam. Some nights he goes right through.'

He didn't look at me and just nodded. I wondered why I made him feel so uncomfortable.

Jerry said, 'Was she all right about it? Lucy?'

'Yes. She's absolutely fine with Gramma and Bunny.' I smiled. 'My mother and her friend.'

I could practically see Jerry putting it all together. He said nothing then, but when it was time for us to go he stood by the car holding the door not quite open enough for me to get in.

'Listen, Jess. Would it help if I followed you home? I could spend an hour with you . . .'

'Good gracious!' I sounded incredibly false. 'Of course not. How could I have a quiet time with you around?'

He ignored my rudeness. 'It's just that . . . you seem so alone, Jess.'

I shrugged. 'I'm so busy I don't notice it.' At the time I thought that was the truth. 'Anyway, once Sam is back home, things will change again.'

He frowned. 'You don't depend on Sam, do you? I mean . . .'

'I know what you mean. Sam . . . no-one will ever replace Matt.'

'Good.' He actually said that. 'Good.' I stared at him and he added quickly, 'Ultimately, Jess, it is better to rely on oneself. That was why I wanted you to get back to work.'

'Oh. Great.'

I managed to slide sideways into the car next to Billy. Jerry shut the door and I wound down the window and smiled a farewell. He stood aside and Sam took his place.

'Cheerio, Jess.' He leaned in and gave me another of his dry little pecks. But it was enough. I felt heartened. It offered . . . something. I made up my mind then and there: Sam and I would make a good partnership. I could continue to run the office, but Sam . . . Sam would be good to come home to. He would never come between Matt and me. Never.

I picked up Watt as arranged and hugged Lucy as she sat at the table in the old schoolroom, having one of Mum's 'snacks' before they set off for Bath. Nat and Tony had bought her a very basic clockwork train set: a locomotive, tender and one coach running on a circular track about a yard in diameter. It was just right for her and she was overjoyed. Andrew had given her an enormous bottle of bubble bath and Blodwen a tiny xylophone.

'How wonderful! Aren't you a lucky girl?'

She nodded violently. 'An' I've got my new scooter too, Mummy! And the drawing stuff from Aunt Jennifer. An' the dolly from Gramma.'

I rolled my eyes. 'Gramma is giving you this lovely birthday treat!'

'No. That's from Bunny.'

It went on and on. Eventually I got Watt into his chair and into the car. The thought of going back to the empty house and the remains of our breakfast was not good, to put it mildly. I hugged Mum and gave Ray a peck on the cheek. It was very dark, no stars, no moon. I promised I would come down tomorrow morning and we would have lunch together. I drew away and turned left at the old stocks and drove straight for the Goose Bump and home and felt awful.

Everything was as I thought, or even worse. The heating had not come on and the house was like a fridge and Watt cried. I cleared last night's ashes and laid and lit a fire with him on one hip, then made tea and did him a bottle as a treat. By the time I'd got my tea on a small table by the chair, Watt's nappy off and him reclining on a towel across my lap with the bottle teat clamped between his top and bottom two teeth, I was exhausted. I juggled his milk and my tea and watched the new flames licking the back of the grate and grimly promised myself a nice new gas fire with the final cheque from Jerry.

The phone went at nine o'clock on the dot. I'd only just put Watt down and switched on the immersion in the hope of having a bath. I thought it would be Jennifer but it was Sam. My heart leaped.

'Sam! Are you home? I should have asked you to follow me back and have a meal . . .' It would have been completely impractical but never mind.

He said, 'I wanted to tell you. Today. Just didn't have the nerve. I know we're friends but I felt so awkward . . . Very difficult. In the circumstances.'

'Sam, please don't – feel awkward, I mean. Watt is such a link between us. Whatever you want to say, just say it. Straight out.' I knew what it was. I was going to say yes. There was just no point in the two of us struggling on separately like this. It would be so marvellous to have someone who could fix the heating and bring in the logs. I felt my eyes fill even though I laughed. 'Sam, we're partners whether we want to be or not. Can't you see that?'

'Yes, of course. As regards work, we're partners. I wouldn't ever let you down, Jess. But I was thinking about Watt. Just about Watt. And then . . . Jess, I know it's early days, but I think I've found someone else. I'm not sure what Daisy would think about it. I'm not sure what I think about it!' He laughed too. 'Golly, Jess. I feel so shattered. I think I'm in love!'

I stood there like a complete idiot, clinging to the receiver, my mouth open in that ridiculous laugh, tears streaming down my face, turned to stone.

He said, 'Are you still there, Jess? Are you shocked?'

I closed my mouth. 'I suppose I am. That's what it is. I suppose I'm shocked. I didn't think . . . I mean you and Daisy . . . six months.'

'I know. I'm shocked too. But it's just hit me, Jess. I try to stay calm but inside I'm – I can't be calm.'

'No. I can tell. My God.' I shook my head to clear it and that damned dizziness started up. Slowly but inexorably. I blurted, 'Is it the same as Daisy?'

'No. I loved Daisy. But now, I suppose I'm in love. I've never felt like this before, Jess.'

'You're very honest, Sam.'

'I wish I could have told you to your face. I intended to. But when I saw you, I couldn't. It's easier on the phone when I can't see you.'

'You never looked at me today.'

'That was because I was trying to tell you. She said I had to tell you. She'll be arriving any minute and if I haven't told you she'll do it herself.'

'Who . . . ? What do you mean?'

Perhaps part of me already knew because the shock stayed exactly the same when he said joyfully, 'It's Jennifer! It's your sister! So now you can understand why I'm so happy!'

I clung to the receiver as the furniture changed places and the floor tilted upwards. I managed to say, irrelevantly perhaps, 'But what about Jerry?'

He laughed again. He sounded completely idiotic. 'I know there have been others. Loads of others, Jess. Jerry Jerome was just one of them. They don't mean anything. They don't mean anything at all. It took her a long time to convince me of that, but she has succeeded.'

I whispered, 'How long? How long did it take?'

'To convince me?' His laughter was almost a giggle. 'She made a pass at me ages ago. When I first came to Marcroft. But then . . . well, Daisy and Watt . . . you know.'

'I know.' I sounded tired. I remembered him driving Matt's car to Bath and sleeping in it outside Daisy's hospital window. Perhaps, then, he had been running away from my sister as well as running towards his wife.

'Then after the accident she stopped coming to Marcroft. For a long time she didn't come. But then you arrived together, with Lucy and Watt. I knew then.' He paused and when I said nothing he rushed on. 'Jess, she loves Watt. Have you seen her nursing him? She's wonderful. Like an earth mother.'

I said wearily, 'Yes, I've seen her. She's very good with him.' I drew a deep breath. 'Sam, be careful. She might hurt you. Quite badly.'

He sobered suddenly. 'I know. I've faced up to that, Jess. But this is something I can't turn from. Even if there's no future . . . I think there is but even if something goes wrong . . . I must still try it. I'm not very adventurous, Jess, but this . . . I feel I'm flying.'

I whispered, 'Oh Sam. Be happy.'

'Thank you. Thank you, Jess. I've never talked to anyone like this before. Not even Jennifer.' He laughed again. 'I feel tired.' He paused and I could hear him breathing deliberately and deeply. I did the same but it didn't help. He said, 'She's driving down tonight, Jess. We're going to have the weekend in Devizes. Then I'll come home.'

I put the phone down. The cruellest cut of all. Devizes.

I managed a cool bath and put my nightie and dressing gown on. Watt slept like an angel. I leaned over him and wondered whether Mum knew about Sam and Jennifer. Then I went downstairs, put my jeans in the washing machine, looked at the television listings and switched on to a quiz show.

When a car drew up outside I almost ran to the door because I was certain it was Jennifer. It was Jock Parslow. Jock had never visited me without Jean or the boys in tow. I knew something pretty dreadful must have happened.

He came in and stood by the fire. His red hair was on end; he wore a donkey jacket and heavy-duty jeans and boots. He put a hand on the mantelpiece and stared into the dying flames. He said, 'Is Jean here?'

'Jean? Good God! No, of course she's not here.'

He lifted his head. He looked terrible.

'I'm in no mood for girlie loyalties, Jess. Jean has left me. I'm not going to argue or pester her or anything. I just need to know she's safe. I'll ask you again. Is she here?'

I spoke slowly. 'No, Jock, she is not here. I would tell you if she was.'

'Did you know she was going to leave?'

'I certainly did not. I saw Nat and Tony this afternoon at my mother's. They said nothing.'

'They didn't know. They still don't know. I got home before they did. There was a note. And Simon knew.'

'What did he say? What did the note say?'

'Just that she'd had enough.'

'There must have been more than that.'

'Apparently Tony and Nat have been running some scam at school. She says she can't go on coping with everything on her own. She's always saying that. I waited for the kids to come in. I thought she'd come home. It sounded like one of her usual outbursts. She's always saying she's going to leave me. I expect you know that.'

'I didn't. She gets tired. Especially when she sits up with Tony and Nat all night. But she has never said—'

'She's had an abortion.'

'Yes. She mentioned that.'

'Didn't that give you a clue?'

'No.' I made to stand up to put some more logs on the fire. The room moved to the left and I sat down again.

He said, 'Are you all right?'

'Yes. Bit of a day. The heating isn't working.'

'I shouldn't be bursting in like this. Sorry. Wits' end.'

'I wish I could help.'

He studied me, frowning. Then he said, 'Where's your boiler? I'll check that for you. It's as cold as charity in here.'

'Kitchen.'

He left me and I could hear him tinkering about. He was gone about fifteen minutes, during which time I got control of myself and felt better. He came back in carrying a tray loaded with a huge teapot – the one I keep for parties – two mugs and the milk bottle. I made protesting noises but he poured us tea and insisted on me sipping it.

'It was the boiler. Pilot light gone out. It was a devil to light but it's all right now.' As if in response to his reassurance the radiators crackled.

He said, 'Tell me about your day. Why weren't you at the theatre? Nat said you didn't go. That's why I thought . . . Never mind.'

I told him about my day. Until nine o'clock that night.

'Poor old Jess. Not much fun, is it? All work and no play.'

He was such a very male presence. His trite remark was the sort of thing I knew would infuriate Jean, but I found it strangely comforting. My problem was as simple as that: life wasn't much fun.

Quite suddenly, I found myself telling him about Sam.

He shrugged. 'Seems like a good idea to me. The two of you hitched up would make a nice little family unit. Why don't you put it to him?'

'I nearly did.' I smiled over the top of my mug. 'Good job I didn't quite get there because he rang tonight to tell me he'd found someone he really loved. Better than Daisy. And much, much better than me.'

He almost smiled. 'Oh God. Who is it? Anyone we know?'

'My sister, actually.'

'Jennifer? Or Jezebel as my dear wife calls her!'

'Does she? I hadn't heard that one.' I laughed and almost spilled my tea. 'Yes, Jezebel it is. She's knocked him for six.'

'Yes. Well, she would. She could have any man she wanted, I should think. Not a bit like you, Jess.'

'Thanks a lot, Jock.' I was still laughing.

'Oh hell. I didn't mean it like that. You're one of the best. It's just that you and Matt were so perfect no-one ever looked at you hopefully. Know what I mean?'

I began to cry. He took my mug away and set it in the grate. Then he sat on the sofa by my side and gathered me to him. He held me and crooned at me and combed my hair with his fingers and then he put his hand under my alpaca dressing gown and on the thin cotton of my nightie and I lifted my head from his shoulder so that he could kiss me.

I felt no guilt. When we lay in front of the fire I imagined Matt telling me that I got down there like a camel and I laughed again and flung my head back, half expecting to see him behind me laughing too. All that happened was that the dizziness accelerated hideously and I hung on to Jock with desperation and he whispered, 'It's all right, darling. It's all right.'

Eventually he put me to bed and locked up and switched everything off. Some time during the night Watt woke and grizzled and I heard Jock creep over to the cot and lift him out and take him downstairs. I slept again, deeply and dreamlessly, and woke when it was late and the grey light was filtering through the curtains.

I lay for a long time expecting to feel dreadful. But I didn't. When Jock came in with the same teapot and the same mugs and two plates holding three pieces of toast each, I wasn't even embarrassed. He grinned at me, a really male grin that I should have hated him for, and I grinned back. He disappeared again and came back with Watt obviously changed and dressed.

'I've had plenty of practice,' he said, propping him against my pillows. 'Eat your toast and we'll decide what to do.'

That part was marvellous. *We*'ll decide what to do.

It turned out that after he'd put me to bed he'd cooked himself bacon and eggs and fried bread. 'I hadn't eaten since I got off the train,' he explained. He'd phoned to ask a neighbour to look in on the boys. 'Then I heard the baby. So I fixed him up on the armchair and I slept on the sofa. Actually' – he leaned over and took one of my pieces of toast – 'for a man whose wife has just left him, I feel pretty damn good.'

I didn't tell him I felt the same. But I did.

Ten

The morning became strangely routine after that. Jock left to see to the boys and then decide what to do about Jean. He was no longer frantic. I went through my usual sequence of fitting Watt into his chair and the chair into the car, wrapping myself up against the incessant drizzle, checking that I'd got a shopping list for Hartford's, locking the house, going back to check I'd switched everything off . . . None of it bothered me. I still muttered to Matt that I must get something done about the garage door but I knew that garage doors were not high on my list of priorities. I was wearing some kind of insulation.

Mum and Bunny – yes, I was thinking of him as Bunny – were delighted to see me. The other children had gone home last night but Andrew had stayed on and they were finding him a bit much. To demonstrate the efficacy of his present to Lucy, he had tipped most of the contents of the bubble-bath bottle down one of Mum's child-size lavatories, with the result that bubbles were oozing everywhere. Bunny had proved himself at least half a plumber and was using Mum's floor mop not only to clear the bubbles but as a giant plunger. Mum told me later that he'd looked at the bubbles, then down at the gibbering and red-faced Andrew and commented, 'Well, you proved your point, old man.'

I delivered Andrew to Stella, who had obviously made the most of her time off and just got out of bed. She was effusively grateful.

'It's been lovely,' she said simply.

I said suddenly, 'How about hiring the church hall and

doing a Christmas party for Andrew and Lucy? They could run about and scream some of the time. And then eat, then we could organize a few games. Perhaps.'

'Well . . . it sounds great. But they need a man, don't they? My husband's not here and you're a widow. It might be really hard work.'

It was the first time anyone had referred to me as a widow without me cringing inside.

'Let's see what we can manage.'

I couldn't ask Sam. But I felt – now – that Bunny would give a hand. And maybe Simon would have a go at disc-jockeying. And I hadn't really registered that Stella Bearwood was on her own.

It was good to go back to Mum's for lunch. Bunny had called in a plumber, who had met this kind of thing before. 'Kids will be kids,' he commented gloomily, surveying the mess. 'Birthday parties, Christmas parties . . . they're the very devil.' It should have made me rethink my plan for Christmas but it did not.

Watt sat on Bunny's knee and was fed. Mum said comfortably, 'Ray is so good with children of all ages.' And Lucy looked at him and said as if in congratulation, 'Grandad was like that, too.' Ray went pink with pleasure.

While Lucy 'helped' Mum to make some cakes and Watt had a sleep, I went to Hartford's and stocked up. It was the first time I'd thought about the week ahead since Jock arrived last night. I had planned to go into Bristol to talk to the surveyor, Brian Edwards, about the supporting steel-work for the glass roof in the abbey. I wanted to show him the specifications given me by the Gully brothers for their reinforced joists and ask his expert opinion. I also wanted to ask him if he would liaise with the building inspector on the whole thing, which would save me a lot of hassle. He'd done this before when Matt had taken on large conservatory jobs but I wasn't entirely sure how things worked. It would be the first time I had met Brian Edwards; I needed to make personal contact.

I chewed it all over as I picked up some blackcurrant juice and Lucy's favourite yoghurts, hesitating over oven chips then putting in two packets with Andrew Bearwood in mind. At that moment, as I collected food in Hartford's, I knew I could do what had to be done with the surveyor. I could drive into Bristol and find somewhere to park and go to Queen Square . . . Yes, I could do all that. What was going to throw me was seeing Sam or Jennifer. Or . . . I stopped next to the rows of baked beans, suddenly shocked by my own blindness. Jean. I had completely forgotten Jean. My best friend. How was I ever going to face Jean again? And where was Jean?

Someone said excuse me because I was blocking the aisle with my trolley. I moved aside and continued to stand and stare at the beans in their neat rows. How on earth could I have forgotten Jean? How on earth could I have forgotten that she had found her life unbearable and run away, and I had taken advantage of her absence and slept with her husband?

After what seemed like ages I wheeled my trolley quickly into the ladies and locked myself into one of the cubicles. I thought I would be sick but I couldn't even do that. I went through the motions, the cold sweat and the near faint, but nothing else happened and after a while I came out and stood by a washbasin and rinsed my face. And then I wheeled my trolley outside, collected the rest of the stuff for next week, paid for it and went out into the damp wintry air to load the car. Someone doing the same thing next to me said to someone else, 'Well, we must expect it to be cold. It's the first of December.' Which of course it was. The day after Lucy's birthday was 1 December. This time last year Matt and I were getting ready for our first Christmas without Dad.

Dear Mum and Lucy provided tea and cakes when I got back. Amazingly, I was able to eat and drink; surely a guilty conscience should reject all sustenance?

Mum said, 'Darling, I've been thinking about Christmas.

Should we invite Sam this year? He's going to be horribly on his own, isn't he?'

I glanced at her quickly. Obviously she knew nothing of the latest development.

I said, 'I don't think he would come.'

'Why don't you sound him out? And you and Lucy might as well come and stay here for a few days. It would be so lovely for us.'

Trust Mum to make it sound like a favour to her. I should have said no but the thought of Dip Lane without Matt at Christmas was too much. I nodded and managed a smile.

She said, 'Jess, are you all right? You haven't got a bit of colour in your cheeks.'

'Sorry, Mum.' I managed another smile and decided to tell her half of it. 'It's just that apparently Jean has left home. I'm a bit worried about it.'

She assumed I'd heard this news while shopping. She was aghast.

'Darling! How awful. Those boys. And they were so sweet yesterday. They really enjoyed the theatre.' She looked at me. 'Where is she, Jess?'

I lifted my shoulders helplessly.

'She might be at your place, waiting for you. Listen, love. Why don't you leave the children here for the night and go home now? Just in case.'

'She won't come to me. We're not close any longer.'

'Rubbish. Just because you don't see each other. Doesn't mean a thing.' She frowned, thinking things out. 'Go round there first, love. See if you can help – a meal or something. She might be back by now. If not, go home. And if she's not there, start making a few phone calls.'

I nearly stone-walled that too but then I knew that I'd got to go round to Acacia Avenue and see what was happening, and I couldn't do much if I'd got Lucy and Watt with me. So I kissed Mum gratefully, left her some of the shopping I'd just bought and went.

Jason answered the door. He didn't immediately let me in.

'Mum's not in at the moment, Aunty Jess. And Dad's gone over to Amberside to see that cousin of hers . . .'

I looked at him. He was a typical teenager with acne and hair waxed into spikes in front. His eyes were puffy.

I said, 'I thought maybe I could do some washing-up. Make you a meal.' I rummaged in my shopping bag. 'I've got some chickenburger things here. Nat and Tony are quite keen on those, aren't they?'

He visibly swallowed; his Adam's apple bobbed like a cork in his neck.

'It's a mess in here. But all right. They'd probably like to see you.' He stood aside ungraciously and I went down the hall to the kitchen. From the living room I could hear the television blaring away. The kitchen was bad. Jock had obviously used the frying pan recently and everything appeared to be covered in a film of grease. I started work.

Jason had disappeared but after a while Simon came in and took a tea towel from one of the drawers. I smiled thanks but said nothing and after a while he put the towel down and switched on the kettle. 'Might as well have some tea, yes? I've got enough mugs here now.' I nodded. He assembled milk and some sugar. 'Bit of a business, isn't it? Jason seems to think she's gone for ever. I said to the twins, get on and watch the match, for goodness' sake. She's in one of her paddies. Doesn't mean a thing.'

'It means a great deal, actually.'

He blinked but came back almost immediately with 'Well, you would think that.'

I held my tongue.

He couldn't leave it. 'D'you know what Mum calls you? Mrs Perfect.' He smiled to take the sting away.

He didn't realize how that hurt, of course. This morning I had felt no guilt from spending the night with Jock; now I did. Retrospective guilt.

I picked up his discarded tea towel and started to dry a

stack of plates. He made tea and put milk in the five mugs. 'Sorry, Aunt Jess. It's just that . . . you don't understand how it is for Mum and Dad. Mum is worried all the time and Dad doesn't really . . . You know.'

Until last night I would not have known. Matt and I had a solidarity which I had imagined all married couples shared. Until Alicia and Ray; Mum and Ray; Dad and Marilyn . . . and Jock and me. So I supposed now I did know.

I said, 'I'm going to put these chicken things in the oven. All right? And I'll peel some potatoes and mash them.'

He nodded vigorously. 'The twins will enjoy that. We've got some beans somewhere.' He rushed around finding me a roasting tin and potato peeler. Then he poured the tea and yelled at the twins.

They didn't want to face me but eventually drifted into the kitchen and sat with tea and biscuits. Simon took two of the mugs and disappeared upstairs. I finished the potatoes and put them on the hob. Then I sat down with the boys and sipped my tea.

'You enjoyed the show last night, I hear?'

Nat looked up, surprised. 'I'd sort of forgotten . . .'

Tony said quickly, 'It was great. Thanks ever so, Aunty Jess.'

'Nothing to do with me. But I'm glad you liked it. You know, with the three little ones, it could have been difficult for you.'

'It was fine.'

We were silent again. The potatoes boiled over and I turned down the gas.

Tony said in a thread of a voice, 'It's our fault, Aunt Jess. She told us it was the last straw and she couldn't take any more. And when we got back from Lucy's granny's, she'd gone.'

Nat began to cry.

I passed him a tissue and said, 'It's not your fault at all. Mum was tired out and worried and not very well. That's what it was. She'll be back home before long and feeling much better.'

Tony said, 'Yes, but we were the last straw. When Mrs Sparrow found out about us she told Mrs Ingram and Mrs Ingram sent for Mum and there was a fuss. Mum didn't know we were swapping schools, you see. So she didn't understand for ages. And when Mrs Ingram said she should have more control over her children, she just ran home . . . didn't wait for us . . . and when we got home she said we could get ourselves ready for the theatre because she'd had enough. And this was the last straw.'

Nat put his head on the table and sobbed. I moved my chair and put an arm across his shoulders. I spoke to Tony. 'What about last night? The asthma.'

He made a face. 'Same as usual. Aunty Betty came round from next door but she didn't hear me. It was better when Dad got home.'

'Oh . . .' I lowered my head. Not that Tony was up to reading my expression.

Nat recovered slowly and we had some more tea and I tried to be reassuring about Jean. We mashed the potatoes; Tony added black pepper and Nat chopped some tired-looking chives he found in a margarine tub in the fridge. 'We always have chopped chives in mashed potatoes,' he said. They stirred the beans and found some plates and cutlery and then called Jason and Simon and we sat around the kitchen table and had supper. The boys ate ravenously. Jason mentioned they'd had nothing since Dad's fried breakfast. I told them that by the look of the washing-up that should have lasted them for two days. Simon glanced at me and grinned unwillingly. And it was at that point that we heard a key in the door and Jock appeared.

He looked absolutely exhausted and I remembered he'd had very little sleep last night, between looking after Watt and making do with the sofa. He smiled at me.

'You couldn't keep away.'

'I came as soon as I heard,' I said repressively.

Jason said, 'Aunt Jess has cleared everything up and cooked some supper. There's some for you too.'

He sat down heavily in between the twins and wrapped them in his massive arms. 'Little Mrs Perfect,' he said with another smile.

I hated it all. I was acting a lie with every move I made. And Jock's teasing was too dangerous, too near the bone, too . . . awful.

I said, 'Now you're here I'll go home and see if Jean has been there.'

'She couldn't get in if she went there, Aunt Jess,' Simon objected.

'She knows where I keep the spare key.'

'I'll come with you.' Jason stood up determinedly. 'I want to do something. I can come with you, can't I, Aunt Jess?'

It meant I would have to return to Acacia Avenue before going back to Mum's, but what could I say? We hugged our jackets around us and ran down the steps to the car, promising to phone if there was anything to report.

It was a very dark night and he was as anxious as I was, both of us leaning forward to peer into the pool of light cast by the headlamps. We drove slowly past the stocks and up towards the Goose Bump and very nearly clipped a car parked too far into the road and without lights. Someone got out of it and stood looking after us. I checked in the mirror that nobody was signalling at me, but the person simply stood there. It was Marilyn George.

The house was obviously empty, not a light anywhere. We unloaded the shopping and I went through the house just for the sake of it. When I came back downstairs, Jason was holding his father's awful old woollen cap in one hand. Before I could say a word, he put it in his pocket.

'Dad said he'd been here to look for Mum.'

He spoke so casually he almost convinced me.

I went out into the garden and down to the shed. It was such a waste of time. I knew very well that Jean would no longer turn to me.

'She's not here,' I said at last.

Jason was standing at the kitchen table folding Watt's clothes into a pile. He grinned wryly at me. 'I used to do this when the twins were born,' he said. 'Mum wanted us to be involved. Simon and me . . . we did all sorts of things. Now we don't do anything. We didn't even know that the twins were taking it in turns to go to both schools.' His grin became wider and more natural. 'Sounds like one of their better schemes.'

'When she found out, your mum told them that it was the last straw. So they're blaming themselves for what happened afterwards.'

He was momentarily surprised, then smoothed the last pair of minuscule dungarees on top of the pile and said, 'Load of rubbish, of course. She's lonely. That's what it is.'

I tried to smile. 'How could she be lonely with you lot?'

'Another woman – she needs another woman to talk to, I suppose.' He shrugged. 'Anyway, we're no company, are we? Si and me at school. Twins the same – in any case they've got each other.' He sighed. 'Si reckons that's why Mum makes such a fuss about their asthma.' He flicked me a look. 'They were OK last night.'

'You kept an eye on them?'

'Yeah. Betty came in from next door but she's cool about it. They were fine.'

So he knew very well that Jock had been out all night. Was that why he had come with me now – to confront me . . . accuse me?

He sighed. 'I dunno. Anyway, d'you want me to iron this lot?'

'Don't be silly. Of course not. We'll have to get you home now. Have another think.'

We got back in the car and drove slowly back to town. We didn't say a word. When we rang the bell at Acacia Avenue, Jock answered and let us in without comment. Obviously we hadn't found Jean; even so, the silence was oppressive.

We went to the kitchen where the other boys were sitting around the table.

I said desperately, 'There has to be a note or something. She could be anywhere . . . Bristol, London even.'

'Has she got Jennifer's address?' Jock asked suddenly.

'I expect so. But she would have phoned, surely? And I know that Jennifer isn't there at the moment.'

'Oh.' He remembered. 'Of course.'

Simon spoke abruptly. 'I'm going to bed. Rugby practice tomorrow.'

Jason said, 'Don't let us stop you.'

'Shut up, you wimp.' Simon slammed out of the kitchen. Nat began to cry.

Jason said, 'Is there something you're not telling us, Dad?'

'You know as much as I do, son.' Jock sounded very tired indeed.

I went and sat down by Nat and put a hand on his shoulder. He shrugged it off.

Jason looked at me. 'They know something is up. We all do. Dad said he went to look for Mum at your place last night. But he didn't come home till this morning. That's why I wanted to come with you just now, Aunt Jess. To make sure Mum wasn't there all the time.' He looked down at the twins. 'She's not there.'

There was a long pause. Jock wasn't sure what was happening. I said to the twins, 'She's going to come home, you know. She would never leave you for ever. She just needs to get herself together.' Nat lifted his head and stared at me hopefully. Tony nodded. I said, 'Let's get you two to bed, shall we?'

Tony said, 'We put ourselves to bed, Aunt Jess. Don't worry about us. Really.'

They pushed themselves upright like elderly men and gave Jock and Jason watery smiles as they went out. Jock yelled, 'Teeth!' at them and they nodded again. He said comfortably, 'They're good lads.'

Jason spoke quietly and shockingly. 'Are you and Aunt Jess having an affair, Dad? Is that why Mum has gone?'

Jock seemed to swell with fury. His face went bright red and he stammered unintelligibly.

I said, 'We are not having an affair, Jason. Stop trying to make a soap opera of this. Your mother is having a hard time at the moment. She has gone away for a few days. That is all there is to it.'

He turned from his father and stared at me. 'He stayed the night with you,' he said.

'Watt was crying. He looked after him while I slept. Both of us hoped your mother would turn up at any time.'

'Was that it?'

'It was.'

Jock said apoplectically, 'None of your bloody business anyway! Young know-it-all! I've heard all about you and that Sally wotsit. Don't judge everyone by your own behaviour.'

Jason nodded at me, turned and gave his father a look then said, 'I'm going to bed. She might be home tomorrow.'

He left the kitchen.

I said, 'I'm going too, Jock. We've done all we can. You need time alone with the boys.'

He made a move to stand up but didn't quite manage it.

'Stay, Jess. Please. Stay with me.'

'No, my dear. The boys don't need me. In fact, the way they are feeling now, they don't want me. They don't trust me.'

'I need you, Jess. I really do need you.'

'I'm sorry, Jock.' I began to wrap up.

Jock said, 'We had something. You let me think . . . you let me think . . .'

'No. You're not thinking straight. Because you're so tired and worried. We – we – *leaned* on each other, Jock. That's what we did.'

'It made us feel good. We felt good. Don't deny it.'

'I'm not denying it, my dear.' I began to feel weary

again, utterly weary. And guilty. And somehow terribly betrayed. 'It was like . . .' I thought back to this morning. 'It was as if you'd given me a nice warm coat to wear in a biting gale.' I tried to laugh. 'But too many coats spoil the broth, Jock.'

He was irritated. 'Stop trying to be clever! I just want to sleep with you again, that's all.'

'Jock, I can't keep this up. I'm going. My mother will wonder . . . I'm going, Jock. I'll phone you tomorrow for news.'

I paused at the kitchen door and glanced back. He looked as I had felt after Sam's phone call about Jennifer: beaten. Even his red hair was duller and flatter against his head. I knew that for two pins I could go back to him and wrap my arms around him. I closed the door quickly and almost ran down the hall. Jason was sitting on the stairs.

I drove to the schoolhouse but didn't immediately get out of the car. It seemed colder than ever but the clouds were moving and now and then a star appeared. The illuminated clock on the dashboard told me it was still only nine o'clock, which seemed unbelievable because so much had happened. I tried not to feel anything but I had to register that my heart was beating hard and my stomach churning. I said quietly, 'What is happening to me, Matt? There were just the two of us. And now . . . d'you remember how I wanted Sam to hold me not long ago? And *now* what do I want from Sam? Marriage? And what about when horrible Jerome actually kissed me? And now Jock . . . am I in love with Jock, Matt? My best friend's husband? I don't know anything any more, darling. I don't know . . . *me*!'

I waited for some time but there was no answer. So, at last, I switched off the engine and went inside.

It was like a real homecoming. Mum and Bunny were watching the news. There had been a service in New York for the souls of the thousands of people killed in the twin towers. I sat down and watched it with them. Mum reached over and took my hand. Bunny said, 'Thank God Alicia was nowhere near New York.' And Mum nodded. I thought how strange it was that their love for her was still there. Undiminished.

Later I went into Mum's old-fashioned kitchen and made coffee and sandwiches. Mum protested but we all ate and drank with relish. I asked about Lucy and Watt and they both replied enthusiastically. I told them that there was no news of Jean as yet.

Mum said, 'If she hasn't contacted you, I can't think who . . . She was particularly alone, was Jean. That was why she latched on to your father. If he were still here, she would be sitting where you are now.'

I nodded ruefully. 'I had no idea until . . . well, not long ago. As a matter of fact it put a wedge in our friendship. She was angry with me in a strange way.'

Mum sighed. 'She was envious, darling. You and Dad were always so close. And – like I said – she had no-one.'

'Yes but . . . even if she was envious . . . wouldn't you think she would want to be with someone who was close to Dad?' I frowned. Something niggled at the back of my mind. The drive back to Dip Lane just now, with Jason. I had seen Marilyn. Marilyn George on the road up to the Goose Bump. And it had been Jean who had first alerted me to Dad's affair with Marilyn. I looked at Mum, wide-eyed, quite unable to ask her whether I was on to something or simply barking up another wrong tree.

Mum said, 'What? Have you thought of something?'

'I might have. I just might have. It's probably a wild-goose chase. But . . . Mum, I'll be about an hour at the most. Go on up to bed and let me have a key.'

They both wanted me to leave it till the morning but I knew there was no chance of any sleep anyway. I wasn't keen on going back out into the cold and dark but it was better than tossing sleeplessly all night long.

I drove carefully back on to the high street and pulled up outside Marilyn's shop. There wasn't a light to be seen but I knocked anyway, first on the door and then on the glass window. I cupped my hands against the glass and peered in. She had a small kitchen and toilet at the back of the shop but there would be no room there for a camp bed. The shop was full of dark shapes but none of them moved. I didn't hang about. If Jean was there she would have to have at least one of Marilyn's wall heaters on and there was nothing, no glow, nothing coming from the shop.

I got back into the car and drove on past the stocks and past Hartford's. I wasn't certain exactly where Marilyn lived but there weren't many cottages on this road and she had been using her car, so the likelihood was that I could trace her house by finding her car parked outside.

Apparently everybody parked on the road. I pulled up and looked into three cars; none of them yielded any clues. At the third car I hesitated for ages then walked up the garden path next to it and knocked on the door and asked for Miss George. They directed me to the third house up. I think I would have known anyway as the car outside smelled strongly of hair spray and the front door had an old-fashioned bell on a spring and dwarves lined the path to it.

I ignored the bell and used the door knocker. Marilyn opened it after a short interval. She was wearing a frilly dressing gown and her hair was in giant rollers. Her face, devoid of make-up, looked raw and vulnerable.

'I said to Jean I thought it might be you,' she said. 'I saw you and her boy driving up to the Goose Bump and I wondered whether you'd seen her.'

She stood aside and after a moment's shocked pause I went past her into the tiny hall.

'No, I didn't see Jean. I saw you. And later . . . I wondered.'

'Well, you wondered right. Come on in. She's not in a very good state but she knows she's got to see you and get

176

it off her chest.' She sighed gustily. 'I think I'd better stay with you. Act as referee.'

I had a momentary flash of understanding; understanding why Dad had liked her so much. She was frank and wonderfully uncomplicated. Jean was in a bad way, angry with me, and Marilyn would try to help. That was all it was.

I followed her into a tiny sitting room absolutely full of bric-a-brac. Highly polished brass predominated but there were books and china ornaments, corner cupboards, deeply upholstered chairs full of cushions, a footstool occupied by a large furry cat – and, of course, Jean.

She looked terrible; her eyes were deep in their sockets and her full mouth was drawn in as if she'd lost her teeth. Her hair, always so luxuriant, was flat against her head. She reminded me of someone: Jock. She looked up at me, squeezed her eyes tightly shut and dropped her head.

She said, 'My God. I nearly said I was glad to see you.'

I put out a hand and held on to the door jamb; I had not expected . . . contempt.

I said, 'Well, I am glad to see you.'

'You shouldn't be. You'll have to tell the boys, won't you? And then they'll know.'

'Jean, what are you talking about? The boys – *your* boys – are desperately worried. They think you've run away from *them*. Is that what you want?'

She sighed, half wearily, half with a kind of exasperation.

'Jess. I know. The laugh's on me, isn't it? I've always called you Mrs Perfect . . . I thought you and Matt . . . first him and now you.'

I held the door jamb very hard indeed. Behind me Marilyn said quietly, 'Go and sit down.' But I couldn't move. I just looked at Jean. Looked until my eyes burned.

At last she glanced up. She frowned impatiently. 'Oh, for goodness' sake! Are you going to hang on to the high moral ground until the bitter end? Do you want to actually hear the words?' She leaned back slightly, her frown deepening. 'My God, Jess. You really believe in that dream you made, don't you? Maybe you're ill. Maybe that's what it is. It's what they do in court, isn't it? Plead insanity.'

Marilyn said warningly, 'Steady on, Jean. Let her sit down.'

But I didn't move.

Jean shook her head as if to try to understand something very difficult.

She said, 'I think I know what it is. You found out. You were shocked by your mother and Ray. Then you found out about Matt and Jennifer. So you flung yourself into the work at Marcroft to try to get at the big boss man. But he was still carrying a torch for Jennifer. Poor old Sam was too ordinary for you, perhaps. The obvious choice. Everyone expects you to marry Sam for the sake of Watt. And you wanted to wreck someone's life just as Matt had wrecked yours.'

Marilyn's voice was sharp. 'Jean, shut up!'

But she was unstoppable now. 'You'd heard – dammit, I'd told you – that my marriage was on the rocks.' She smiled at me. 'That day – was it only yesterday? – your daughter's fifth birthday. It was not a good day for me, Jess. First of all, I hear that Tony and Nat have been making fools of all of us for nearly three months. Then I get a call from Jock to say he'll be home at seven and if I don't behave more like a wife, we're through.' She laughed. 'And then – and then—' She almost choked. 'I find that my best friend has been consoling my husband!'

I shook my head, trying to clear it. Marilyn was behind me, her hand under my arm, holding me up.

Jean sighed. 'Well, it doesn't matter now, does it? I wrote my note and packed a bag and started to walk to the Goose Bump. And you. My friend.'

There was a long silence. I remembered my stupid pique because Sam had fallen in love with my sister. I wanted to be sick. I mustn't be sick on Marilyn's carpet or her furniture.

178

Jean said, 'Well, you know the rest. I'd been walking for an hour when the car passed me. I heard it coming – you do, don't you? Must be the way the road twists and turns those four miles. It's a Roman road, I think. They probably built it like that so that they could hear their enemies coming. Like I did. Except that I didn't know it was my enemy and I nearly stepped out into the middle of the road to thumb a lift.' She gave another of those dreadful laughs. 'That would have been the end. To stop my own car and get a lift with my husband who was visiting his . . . his . . . how do you think of yourself, Jess? As his mistress?'

Marilyn said, 'I can't hold you. Please sit down.'

Jean said, 'She's stronger than you think, Marilyn. Much, much stronger. All of us – we've always thought of her as the one who needs looking after. Sensitive, vulnerable. "Don't tell Jess that, she can't cope with that . . ." ' She shifted among her cushions, pushed her fingers through her hair. 'How long has it been going on with Jock? That's the only thing I don't know. And I'm curious. How long, Jess?'

'Nothing. There's nothing. He came looking for you.'

'And it took him all night?' She snorted another laugh. 'Luckily I had the spare car keys on my ring, Jess. So I sat in the car. All night. I wanted to think he'd gone looking for me – I really wanted that. Well, of course, I'm not such an idiot as to want to lose a friend and a husband in one fell swoop. But it was seven o'clock in the morning and he was still – apparently – looking under the beds for me.'

'He . . . helped me. He looked after Watt so that I could sleep.'

'How touching.'

There was nothing to say.

Marilyn managed to angle me round towards the chair next to Jean. I fell into it.

She said, 'Jean walked back to me. She got here soon after seven thirty. It was Saturday, of course, so I had to go to work. I got her into bed and found her there when I got home at four. We drove down to Acacia Avenue and saw your car outside and came back. That was when you passed us with Jason in the car.' She crouched over us as if we were deaf. 'I'm going into the kitchen to make coffee. Will you two be all right?'

I think we both nodded.

Marilyn disappeared and we sat together for ages in that overstuffed, overheated little parlour saying not a word. When Marilyn came back we were in exactly the same positions.

She said, 'Milk and sugar, Mrs Tavener?'

Jean snorted. 'For Pete's sake, Marilyn! Her name is Jess!'

'I've put some sugar in anyway.' Marilyn stirred at a mug vigorously and passed it to me. 'It'll do you good. Warm you up.'

I took the mug and sipped obediently. Jean took hers and said, 'Thanks, Marilyn. You wanted the two of us to meet. Well, we have. What happens next?'

'I don't know.' Marilyn's voice shook slightly. 'I thought . . . hoped . . . you could be friends again.'

'After she seduced my husband?'

'That's a silly word, Jean.' Marilyn put her coffee on one of the little tables and took mine from me. I realized it was slopping over the rim of the mug. 'Jess has gone through a great deal in the last eighteen months. If your husband could help—'

'Just like her husband helped her sister. Is that what you mean?'

'Stop it, Jean! I told you before. There are some things that shouldn't be—'

And then at last I whispered, 'Matt. Matt and Jennifer?' It was the only bit in Jean's whole diatribe that had registered.

It wasn't true, of course. Jean or Marilyn would immediately deny it. But they didn't and I had to repeat it. 'Matt? My husband? And – and – my sister?'

Marilyn had her hand on my shoulder. Jean looked at

me and then away. She said quickly, 'You know your Jennifer. If she wants something – or someone – she gets it. And she's your sister – d'you blame me for using a word like seduced?'

I made a kind of rattling noise. Marilyn said sharply, 'I told you she didn't know! How could she? For God's sake, Jean. She's going!'

I wondered where I could possibly go. Did Marilyn know of a place where none of this was happening? I tried to turn towards her and ask her but I couldn't make it. It occurred to me that I might be going to faint, which I had never done before. I wanted that. I wanted to faint, to reach a place where I knew nothing . . . certainly nothing at all about Matt and Jennifer. But the shock of thinking I might faint pulled me round and I said, 'Sick. I'm going to be sick.'

Marilyn moved faster than light and a bowl appeared beneath my nose. 'Jean, fetch a towel. Just had these covers dry-cleaned.'

I started to laugh. And then I was sick. Jean held me and wiped my face with the towel. And when it was over and she had put the bowl on the floor, we both laughed.

'It's all right, Marilyn,' Jean called. 'Not a mark on the covers!' And we laughed again. And then I left. I drove back to the schoolhouse, went to bed in the same room as Watt and Lucy and lay awake until Mum brought tea at seven o'clock before she went to the early service at church.

I actually drank the tea. Then I got up and started to get breakfast. I looked out of the kitchen window at the flower pots in the old playground. There was a skimmia in full bloom.

I said quietly, 'Life has got to go on.' When I spoke aloud like that, I had always addressed Matt. This time I did not.

Eleven

Life did go on. It was a waiting time. I kept thinking something would happen to make it all right but nothing did. I went home and got everything ready for school the next day. I listened when Lucy told me over and over again how absolutely wonderful the show had been and how she might not be an artist after all, she might be an actress. I ironed the pile of clothes that Jason had so carefully folded and I stacked them in the airing cupboard on the shelf reserved for Watt. He had his bath in the big bath with Lucy and we laughed together when he smacked the water and screwed up his face at the spray.

After we'd put him into his cot, sung to him and whirled his mobile, we went downstairs for cocoa and a story. Out of the blue, Lucy said, 'Mummy, can I sleep in your bed tonight?'

I was surprised. Since her fourth birthday when Matt had redecorated her room and we had bought her a new bed, she had never wanted to share ours.

I said, 'You're all right, aren't you, love? Of course you can sleep with me. But Watt sometimes wakes up and needs a bottle.'

'I don't mind. I'd just like to be nearer you.'

I wondered whether she felt put out by Watt. I said, 'I'm going to see the surveyor Daddy knew. Mr Edwards. I don't think I'll take Watt. I'll ask Gramma to have him.'

Lucy shook her head quickly. 'No. Take him, Mummy. Please.'

'Why?' I looked at her sharply.

'I don't know.' She frowned, thinking about it. 'You need us with you, Mummy. When you're on your own you look lonely.'

I tried to laugh. 'Most people do when they're on their own,' I said.

'I know. But it seems different now. When we came back from Bath, you looked as if you'd lost something.' She scratched her head. 'Watt and me . . . you've got us, you know.'

'Oh Luce . . . I know. And you've got me. OK?'

'OK.'

She was still scratching. I said, 'Have you got a sore place?'

'No. I expect it's nits,' she said matter-of-factly. 'Everyone's got them at school.'

So, for the next few days it was toothcomb and conditioner time. Life went on. I heard that Jean was back at home and everything was 'fine'. So, presumably, life was going on for her too.

Stella Bearwood and I managed to hire the church hall for 15 December, a Saturday. We got together at Dip Lane the weekend before and filled the freezer with little trifles and cakes and sausage rolls. Andrew and Lucy played at discovering the North Pole. They put up Lucy's tent and dragged tin trays piled with provisions across the wet and windy garden. Andrew's dogs were an unruly lot and he had to yell at them almost all the time in his piercing voice. Stella and I sat in the kitchen and watched them through the window while we drank tea. Watt was with Bunny and Mum.

Stella said, 'I don't know how you manage. I have a job to get out of bed each morning and I've only got Andrew.' She made a face. 'I'm starting at Hartford's after Christmas. Check-out. I've done it before and I quite like it. But what with Andrew and the house and the garden . . .' She grinned. 'Tell me your secret!'

'My mother is marvellous. And she's got a new partner and he's proving to be marvellous too.'

'I heard. Nothing's private in this place, is it? I came from Birmingham ten years ago. It hurt like hell when everyone knew about my husband before I did.'

'Yes.'

She said impulsively, 'I know it must be rotten losing someone. The girl in the hairdresser's – Amanda, is it? She told me how close you were, you and your husband. But at least you can grieve for him. I can't do that.' She paused and said apprehensively, 'Have I put my foot in it? I didn't mean to hurt . . . or anything. It's just that . . . it's so nice to have another woman to talk to. Sorry.'

'Don't be.'

I nearly told her then. About Matt and my sister. But I hadn't even thought around it, let alone voiced it as a fact. So I didn't. Instead, I told her about Lucy's nits and she offered to lend me some stuff she'd got for Andrew that was a hundred per cent successful. 'Apparently, it breaks their legs or something and they fall out when you shampoo the hair.' She looked at me in sudden horror and I put my hand over my mouth and then we both laughed.

Life went on quite well sometimes.

I took Watt with me into Bristol the next day simply because Lucy had asked me to. He was growing into a gorgeous baby and I knew he was better with Lucy and me than he was with anyone else. Mum had referred to him 'grizzling', and the babysitter she had found to fill in for her when she was out said the same. Yet he never grizzled when he was with us. He had a grin that went from ear to ear and showed up his two new bottom teeth to perfection. I looked at him sitting next to me in his little carrier and I felt a terrible pang because Jennifer would take our place in his affections and probably be known as Mummy. I had heard nothing more from Sam and even Mum was beginning to wonder why Jennifer found it so difficult to pick up a phone now and then. In a strange way I was almost curious to know how she would deal with this latest relationship. It didn't hurt me that much any more. The other thing did . . . Jennifer and Matt . . . except that I wouldn't allow myself to think about that.

We drove along the old airport road and dropped down into the city through Bedminster and past Temple Meads station. There were roadworks, of course, and I hadn't driven through Bristol for some time, but I hardly gave it a thought. It was good to find a parking space right outside the surveyor's office. Even better when Brian Edwards emerged from the Georgian front door and came down the steps armed with money for the meter.

He shook my hand warmly.

'It's good to see you, Mrs Tavener. Needless to say we were all devastated to hear about Matt. I'm glad you feel you can come to us again.'

I was glad he could be so direct. He was the same height as me so we could look straight at each other, and he managed to do that too. He had grey eyes and sandy brows, and was wearing a good suit. I hadn't seen a man in a suit since Jerome took me to the Hilltop.

I went round the car and began to unstrap Watt.

'Do call me Jess.' I smiled at his expression when he saw me swing out the baby chair. 'I should have warned you about Watt. I take him with me when I can. It seems . . . important.'

'Yes, of course. I knew about your daughter but not . . .' He led the way up the steps. 'May I help? No? Put him here. Will he be all right?'

I put Watt on the damask-covered chaise longue and the surveyor wedged cushions in front of his chair.

'Thank you – thank you so much. He's no problem, I assure you, Mr Edwards.'

'Call me Brian.' He smiled for the first time. 'I can see that. It will be a real pleasure to have him.' He turned to me. 'May I take your coat? And will you have a coffee? It's perking away next door.'

I smiled back and thanked him again and he hung my coat on a hanger and put it behind the door.

'I'd better make things clear.' I glanced at Watt. 'Watt's mother was killed with Matt. In the same car. Also her mother. He's not mine. Our daughter is at school now.'

His face was a picture of changing expressions but he continued to be very attentive and drew out a chair for me. 'Ah. Yes. I think I remember. And the father is unable to care for his son?'

'His father is Sam Clarkson. You probably met him with Matt. They worked together for some years. Sam is continuing the job that Matt took on. I don't know what will happen in the future.'

'You live day by day. That's a good maxim. Difficult to carry out, I imagine.'

I shrugged. 'Not difficult at present. This job, which has extended itself quite a bit, dictates a day-by-day approach. And then, of course, there's school. And Watt's routine.' I looked at Brian. His eyes were kind. Rather like Sam's. He held my gaze again, then suddenly blinked and looked away. Sam had done that. As if they suddenly spotted the ugliness inside me.

I said quickly, 'I've brought the specifications with me. It's a question of load-bearing. I hoped you would come and look at the job and perhaps do a few sums.'

'You want me to check on the contractor's specs?'

'Well, yes. I trust them completely. They're a two-man firm from Clevedon. Brothers. This is a big contract for them.'

'You're safeguarding them as well as yourself, Jess. Don't feel guilty about that.'

'No. Of course not.'

I took the papers from my bag and spread them out on his desk. The coffee was brought in by his secretary, who was pleasantly informal and chatted to Watt delightedly. I talked to her while Brian went through the figures. He made small, satisfied sounds now and then, so I gathered it was going well.

'Actually, I should very much like to see Marcroft,' he confided, picking up his cup and sipping. 'I've heard about it. Some rather overreaching, overambitious entrepreneur is making another folly out of a folly, I understand.'

'You could look at it like that.' I was surprisingly defensive. After all, he was absolutely right, that was what was happening. 'But oddly enough, it's coming together rather well. Matt's windows are absolutely beautiful. They make the original folly feel like a real abbey! The kitchen is partly Victorian and very dark. If we can support this enormous glass roof it will make all the difference. You'll go from the nineteenth century straight into the twenty-first. Marcroft looked just like a barracks before. The stained glass has transformed it.'

'It's wonderful that you can be so enthusiastic. I would have expected . . . something quite different.'

'Like . . . what?' I was curious. How was I supposed to be reacting?

'I really don't know. I'm so sorry. I think you are just wonderful.' He gave a small apologetic laugh. 'Sorry, Jess. I'm embarrassing both of us.'

I supposed that was what it was: embarrassment. Certainly my face became hot but that was probably because I wanted so much to believe him and, of course, I knew he was wrong. The picture of the grieving widow with her friend's orphaned baby probably was rather wonderful. And so terribly wrong.

I muttered, 'Always nice to get a compliment. Not absolutely accurate but . . . thanks.' I swallowed and looked back at the drawings. 'It's a cantilever construction, as you see. It could be clumsy if it's any bigger – thicker here and here – but the boys have worked out that this thickness will in fact hold the glass. Sam's calculations for the weight of that are on this separate sheet.'

He took his cue from me and pored over the drawings again. 'Reminiscent of some of the grand old railway stations,' he murmured. That showed me instantly that he had got the right idea. We were both enthusiastic after that and I sketched in some rough plans for the kitchen furniture, while he wondered about small portholes on either side of the door leading to the abbey. 'If your entrepreneur intends to use the hall itself for dining, it might be useful for the chef to be able to see when he should serve the next course.'

'I'll put it to him.'

That was one of the better times. For a whole morning I hardly thought of the weight on my mind. When he asked if he could take me out to lunch, it came back with a rush.

'I have to get home early to collect my daughter from school. It's most kind of you.'

'Not a bit kind. It would have been delightful. Perhaps I can pick you up on the way to Marcroft and we can lunch there?'

I smiled some kind of acceptance and asked him when that might be. We got out diaries and made a date for the week before Christmas.

'I'll telephone Mr Jerome just to confirm it.'

Yes, that was one of the better times.

I rang Jerome. He was still edgy.

'I might not be here.' Just that: no excuse or apology. I had forgotten in just ten days how difficult he could be.

'You don't have to be there, Jerry. Brian Edwards has seen the specifications. He's checking them and obviously needs to see the site before he can go further.'

'Of course I need to be there. It's my property.'

'You need to see the completed plans and say yea or nay. But if you can't actually meet the surveyor, it need not delay things. I understood from you that time was of the essence?'

'You don't sound right. Time is of the essence. That's not you speaking.'

I ignored that. 'I shall be with him, Jerry. I won't let him do anything drastic.'

There was a pause. Then he said, 'Tell me about it. In your words, not surveyors' jargon.'

I said, 'Arched glass roof. Cantilever supports. Steel. Painted or not.'

'Not,' he said immediately. That was another thing I had forgotten: he was so quick, he was there before I'd finished.

'Yes, I agree. Portholes either side of the door so that the diners can be seen. Flagstones to be retained. Aluminium fittings—'

'Why not steel to match the girders?'

'Softer. That burnished pewter look.'

'Yes. I see.' Another pause then he said, 'All right, I'll be there.' He sighed sharply. 'Brian Edwards. I'll make a few enquiries about him.'

'No need. This is the surveyor who has worked with Matt before on big constructions. He's good. And he'll organize the building inspector . . . He can save us a lot of time.'

'Keep calm. Not those sort of enquiries.'

'What sort then?'

'I'll tell you when I've made them. Is Lucy all right?'

Surprised, I said, 'Yes.'

'About her birthday. I've bought her a car.'

'You've what?'

'An electric car. She'll love it and there's so much space around here for her to use it.'

'But she never goes to Marcroft.'

'Well, it's here waiting for her when she does.'

I said, 'You can't do this, Jerry.'

'I've bought her a present, Jess. What's wrong with that?'

'You can't buy her . . . her . . . affection or admiration or whatever it is you want from her. Anyway, after a few weeks, once this job is finished, you'll never see her again.'

He was silent, offended. I waited.

Eventually he said, 'I have to go. Sam and Jennifer have arrived.' He replaced the receiver and I stood there holding mine and realizing that of course he knew about Sam and Jennifer. Jennifer was not one to hide things and Sam had sounded – and therefore doubtless looked – incandescent with happiness when I had spoken to him that awful night. I replaced the receiver carefully and lifted Watt into Lucy's old high chair. 'What would you like, sir?' I asked him jovially. 'There's beef and tomato, tuna and peas, apricots, or rice.' He banged his spoon on the tray and I nodded. 'Beef. Right.' I unscrewed the lid and stood the jar in a pan of hot water. 'And after lunch we'll pick up Lucy and go and ask Simon if he will do a disco for the party. Shall we? Shall we, Watt?' I spooned the creamed food into his mouth and he smacked his lips and then let it run out again. 'Let's have another try, Watt. Come on now. Be a good boy.' He eventually swallowed about four teaspoonfuls, but when I was changing his nappy he was sick.

We were late meeting Lucy and she was standing with Andrew and Stella looking anxious.

'Sorry, love. Watt was sick.'

She hugged me rather too hard. 'I thought you might have gone to see Aunty Jean.'

'No. We'll go together, shall we?' I was fairly certain that Jean would make an effort to be her old self in front of Lucy.

She frowned and shook her head. 'Andrew and me, we don't want Simon to do the record thing. For the party.'

'Oh love. Why not? If he agrees to do it, he'll be good.'

Stella said, 'The thing is, Jess, my dear husband has turned up out of the blue. He says he'll do it.'

'Oh well, that's fine. In fact it's great. Isn't it?'

'Oh yes. Andrew is really delighted.'

We began to walk down to where I had parked the car. The children piled into the back. I said to Stella, 'What about you – are you delighted?'

'It's happened before. Andrew's birthday. Our anniversary. He might stay a week. He might even stay over Christmas. Then he'll go.'

'Oh Stella.'

'I know. But I've got a job and I know I can cope now.'

'Good for you.'

I drove her home and went back to Hartford's for shopping, and then I looked at Lucy.

'Home, James?'

'Can we go to Gramma's?'

'She might be out. With Bunny.'

She was silent, staring into the darkness, saying nothing.

'Lucy.' I reached back and put my hand on her shoulder. 'Darling. What is it?'

She turned and looked at me and her eyes were full of tears. She said, 'Nat said I can't ever play with his train set again. And his mother won't let us into the house.' The tears spilled over. 'He says he hates you. Because you stole his father.' She sobbed. 'I told him you can't steal people. But he says yes you can and he just wishes someone would steal all of us and take us right away!' She grabbed my hand. 'Mummy, let's go and see Gramma and Bunny. They love us. They really do!'

We sat there in the dark, holding on to each other, saying nothing. Andrew must have heard all this playground talk, which would mean Stella would also know it by now. Like she said, you couldn't keep anything secret in our little town.

Watt broke the silence by setting up a wail. I released Lucy and leaned over him.

'All right, Watt. If you want to go to Gramma's as well, we'll go.' I started the engine and looked back at Lucy. 'Darling, people say awful things when they're upset. Try not to be hurt and angry with Nat. He's really worried about his mum.'

She sobbed. 'He says that I snitched on him and Tony. What does that mean, Mummy?'

191

'That you told someone their secret. That they were switching schools all the time.'

'I didn't! I really didn't!'

'Nat knows that. It's like when you start a fight. Your fists go everywhere and you often hit people you don't mean to hit at all.'

'Mummy, I hate school now! I wish we could stay with Gramma and Bunny all the time!'

I was utterly dismayed. 'What about your swing in the garden? What about going out on the hills and shouting into the wind?'

'I know . . .' She was still sobbing. 'It's no good without Daddy.'

Bile surged up into my throat, burning, horrible.

I said as calmly as I could, 'It's not Daddy, love. We've been fine at home. Just you and me and Watt. It's all this business at school.'

She thought about it while we manoeuvred out of the car park.

'Yes. 'Cos Grandad is dead too and it's still nice at the schoolhouse.' She sighed deeply, her breath catching on the dying sobs. 'Why do people have to die, Mummy?'

I could feel my hands trembling on the steering wheel. I swallowed the bile and bit the inside of my mouth as hard as I could. Watt had stopped wailing and he suddenly threw up his hands and gave one of his gurgles. Lucy actually managed a laugh.

'Good old Watt,' I said. 'Brings us back to earth, doesn't he?' I drove carefully down the high street, still shaking but in control.

'Listen, why don't you tell Gramma all about it? See what she says. How's that?'

'Yes . . . Yes, that would be good.' We turned off down the school lane and she said, 'I know what she'll say. She'll say that Grandad and Daddy are still looking after us.' She sighed. 'P'raps they forgot to do it for a tiny little while. And that's when things went wrong.'

'I wouldn't be surprised.' The irony of it was ghastly but probably didn't occur to me until much later. I turned the wheel and followed my headlights into the old playground and parked behind another car. It was Jennifer's car. Lucy didn't even see it. She undid her belt and galloped across to the door while I lifted Watt's chair free of the car seat. Mum was there, hugging her and welcoming her inside. And then she left her to someone else and came out to me.

'Darling. Jennifer is here. She says you know. But I can't believe . . . Do you know?'

I said, 'About her and Sam? Her latest conquest? Yes, I know, Mum.' I could hear my voice, unutterably weary. 'Sam phoned me on Lucy's birthday. He was over the moon.'

'Yes. But do you *know*?' She held me back. 'They're expecting a baby! I cannot believe this, Jess! Less than a year since he lost his wife! And Jennifer – can you imagine Jennifer with a baby?'

'Well, if she's throwing in her lot with Sam, she's already got one.' It didn't seem real and I spoke the flippant words – well – flippantly.

'I know what you're thinking. You're thinking that I'm a fine one to talk. It was less than a year for me and Ray. But we'd both lost someone, love. It was different, you have to admit it was different.'

'Mum, I wasn't thinking that at all. I wouldn't dream . . . Look, let's get Watt indoors. It's freezing out here.'

So we went in and there was Jennifer waiting in the old school cloakroom.

She looked different; I registered that much. Her hair was tumbling around her face instead of in its usual chignon. Her face was . . . open. Raw and vulnerable. Still beautiful, but no longer chiselled. And then she did something that the old Jennifer would never have done. She held out her arms to me.

'Oh Jess. Don't you be cross with me – you understand, don't you? Please say you understand, Jess. Please.'

How could I resist that? I put Watt down and went into her arms immediately. We hugged and made funny noises at each other for ages. When we pulled apart she was weeping.

I said, 'Hey. Stop it. I admit I don't understand. But that doesn't matter. You'll tell me and then I will understand. Quite simple.'

Mum had shovelled Watt out of his straps and had him over her shoulder. She said unexpectedly, 'You're beginning to sound like Marilyn George! For goodness' sake let's get in by the fire. This child smells most peculiar.'

I said, 'He was sick and I probably didn't clear it all up.' I looked at Jennifer and drew a huge breath. 'Mum. Give Watt to Jennifer.'

My sister knew what that meant. I couldn't have found anything better to say or do. She almost sobbed, then said, 'Oh Jess . . . Oh Jess, do you mind? I would so love to . . . Oh baby.' Her voice dipped a tone as she cradled Watt. 'Come on in and see Daddy. Come on.'

I watched her go through the door into the corridor and then into the sitting room. There was a glimpse of Lucy already on Ray's knee, then the door swung to. I felt small and mean. Watt might have been a gift but he was also a challenge. He would have to be bathed and changed and fed quite soon.

I said, 'I hadn't expected Sam.'

Mum was still dithery. 'I know. It's so awkward. Everyone expected you and Sam to . . . eventually. This is such a shock.'

I hung back. 'Mum, forgive me but after I've said hello could you possibly bear it if I disappeared for about an hour? Maybe less.'

She looked up at me apprehensively. 'Has something happened?'

'No. Yes. There was a row at school. Lucy is very upset. Nat told her that I had stolen his father away from Jean.' Mum's exclamation interrupted me. I spread my hands. 'I assumed that Jean was settling back in and everything was working out nicely. I shall have to go round and talk to her.'

Mum actually wrung her hands. 'Oh *Jess*!'

'I know. It's all so sordid and nasty and I'm angry that the children are involved.'

'But you can't go round, darling. Not on your own. There will be a row probably and Jean is obviously in no state to be tactful.'

'Yes. But the alternative is to let Lucy go back to school and face Nat again. That's not on.'

Mum continued to stand there, worried and anxious. Then she said, 'Yes. All right. Why don't you go now? I'll explain to Jen and Sam. They want to get back up to Two Lanes anyway. Perhaps tomorrow you can go up there and talk to them.'

'I'd much prefer that. Can you cope?'

'Of course I can cope. I've got Ray, remember.'

Yes, she had got Ray. It was important to have someone. Everything that had happened would not have happened if I had . . . had someone.

I went back out into the raw cold and started up the car again.

By the time I parked outside the house in Acacia Avenue I was actually sweating and completely unprepared. If Nat or Tony had answered my ring and refused to let me in I'm not sure what I would have done. As it was, Jason's face reflected palely under the porch light and he actually gave me a wan smile.

'I told Mum you'd come. For Lucy's sake.' He closed the door behind me and said quietly, 'There are rows all the time. She's using you as a stick to beat him with. But Nat doesn't realize that.'

His words almost exactly mirrored mine to Lucy. I said, 'Is he home now? Your father, I mean.'

He shrugged. 'Pub, I think.' He peered into the kitchen.

'Mum must be watching telly with the twins. She's smothering them as usual.'

At least Jock was out of it. Jason opened the living-room door and said, 'Ma. Aunt Jess is here. Try to talk like a couple of adults, will you?'

She came into the hall. Jason took her place on the sofa with Nat and Tony. Simon came down the stairs two at a time; I was surprised he didn't go through each tread as he landed.

'Got to go out,' he said. The front door opened; icy air came in, then it slammed shut again.

Jean looked terrible. It was ten days since she had come home and in that time her face had puffed up unnaturally and was covered in spots and her hair was lank and greasy.

She stared at me narrowly. 'Well?' she asked.

I swallowed more bile and said, 'Oh Jean. Jennifer is expecting a baby.'

Her stare lost some of its aggression and became shocked. 'Jennifer? Good God. Whose?'

'Sam's. He rang. That night. Lucy's birthday night. Told me he was in love with her and happier than he'd ever been. It must have happened before then. I don't know any more. I don't know anything any more.'

'Jennifer,' she repeated incredulously.

'Yes. I know.'

'And Sam. I always thought . . . eventually . . .'

'Everyone seems to have thought that.'

'Did you think it?'

'I might have done. It was awful when he phoned. Like another rejection.'

She stood there working things out.

She said, 'And then Jock turned up looking for me.'

'Yes.'

She pressed her lips tightly together, took a deep breath and said, 'I see.'

'Do you? Or do you think you see?' I looked at the stairs

196

and wished I could sit down. The newel post was hidden under a pile of coats but I hung on to it as best I could.

She nodded. 'What you mean is, am I seeing it from your point of view? The answer is that no, I am not. I am seeing it from my point of view.' From inside the living room came the sound of machine-gun fire. She said, 'You will probably have gathered by now, Jess, that the past ten years have not been exactly laden with primroses in this house. I have felt constantly ill. I am anxious about the twins – you might have to sit up all night with Watt now and then, but not every night. Not every night waiting for the next breath to be breathed. I know about Jock. When he's away he spends a lot of money on . . . other women. So there's never any left over for us to take a holiday. In other words, life has been pretty grim.'

I said, 'You don't need to tell me all this, Jean. I do understand.'

'Perhaps you do – but I doubt it. Matt was like your father. He might have had a fling with Jennifer but he always came home to you. He loved you, Jess.'

'I don't want to talk about—'

'Well, I do.' Her voice changed and became thin and bitterly ironic. 'I know you're sorry. And I'm sorry for you too. This business with Jennifer and Sam – I can see it's awful. But these things happen, don't they, Jess? We've got to learn to take 'em on the chin—' She started using a dramatic voice, punching the air. It was horrible. 'We've got to learn to live with them. After all, your mum and Alicia were best friends and they seemed to be able to share Alicia's husband quite happily. Maybe we should do the same thing. Maybe I should send Jock round to you now and then. What do you think, Jess?'

My head was on the pile of coats now. I said, 'Hate me if you must. But let it stay between us, Jean. Please. Tell the boys . . . it's nothing to do with them or Lucy. It's a quarrel between us. Please try to limit the damage in some way.'

'Oh, there's a good phrase. It's damage limitation now.'

'Jean. Please. Stella Bearwood knows about it and it'll be all round the town.'

That did check her slightly. She looked at me with a new sharpness.

'What have you told her?'

'Nothing. But Nat told Lucy – presumably in front of Andrew Bearwood – that she couldn't come to his house any more and that he hated me . . .'

'He must have heard Jock and me . . . I haven't told the boys.'

'They're very bright, Jean. You must know that.'

'They're used to us rowing. I didn't think . . .'

'Something they wouldn't get used to. Probably.'

'It's Jock's fault. Suddenly he wants another baby. After that abortion too.'

'Perhaps he thinks another baby would bring you closer.'

She made a noise of total disgust. I was beginning to slip down the newel post.

'All right,' she said almost brusquely, 'I'll talk to the boys. When Jock goes back – after Christmas – come round for tea or something. Meanwhile I'll make sure they go to your Christmas beanfeast.'

'Oh Jean.'

'Don't thank me, for God's sake. We've got to paper over the cracks, I can see that. But don't let's forget they're still there.' She put out a hand and jerked open the front door and I stumbled through it. She closed it. The whole thing was like a slap in the face. I stood on her top step looking into the cold mist that circled the nearest street lamp, and had to clutch at the freezing iron railing to stop myself from falling. By the time I got to the car I was bent double. I got inside it and left the door swinging open so that I could lean out and heave that wretched bile into the gutter.

That was not such a good day. When I got back to Mum's, Jennifer and Sam had gone and so had Watt. Lucy didn't even know about Watt. She was sitting on Bunny's knee, exactly where I had left her only half an hour ago, and they were reading a book about the coronation of the Queen. She told me sleepily that next year would be the Golden Jubilee. 'I like that word, Mummy. Jubilee . . . Jubilee . . .' She struggled to sit up and take a cup of cocoa from Mum. 'Did you talk to Aunty Jean?'

'Yes. And everything is going to be all right.'

That would do for tonight. Tomorrow she could face the fact that Watt was not part of our family any more. Tomorrow perhaps I could too.

The party was not too bad. We were still at Mum's and I had to admit it was so much nicer living with her and Bunny than on our own in Dip Lane. I think Mum and Jennifer got a new relationship going over the phone and Mum must have told her about the party. She came to see me at the factory and asked if she could come and bring Watt.

She said hesitantly, 'Of course, everyone thinks that Sam and me . . . it won't work. Do you think that too, Jess?'

I shook my head but not negatively. 'I don't know what to think, Jen. You're not exactly known for constancy, are you?' I didn't look at her as I spoke. If she'd come here to confess anything to me, I didn't want to know. The only way I could possibly cope with any of it was not to think about it. Certainly not to talk about it.

She said, 'Jess, there's no need for constancy most of the time. There really isn't. It – it's been a bit like—' She laughed and then said, 'Wine tasting!'

I stared at her incredulously. I suddenly wanted to scream at her, 'And what kind of wine was my husband?'

She saw my face and said, 'I'm sorry, sis. I suppose what I really mean is that I don't play by the usual rules. But I've got rules. And now that Sam and I . . . oh Jess, I do love him. He – he's so steady.' She smiled. 'And what is so absolutely marvellous is that he loves me.' She sobered. 'No-one has, you know, Jess. Not before. They've wanted me. But then they suddenly don't any more.' She shrugged. 'My fault. I must have made it plain that I didn't want them either.'

I couldn't talk like this. 'How is Watt?' I said.

'Not very well actually. He's with Sam at the moment. I'm hoping he'll be well enough to come on Saturday.'

'He wasn't very well the day you took him home. He refused his food and he was sick. That never happens. It might be a good idea to let the doctor see him.'

'You don't trust him with me?'

'It's not that. I know him. He's usually so placid and happy. And the other night he wasn't.'

'Oh.' She looked anxious. 'I didn't want to sound as if I were complaining but he has done a lot of crying. I sat up with him the first night and Sam last night. Sam said he was like that before. He thought it was normal for a young baby.'

'Some babies cry a lot. Watt doesn't. I think you should go back home and ring the doctor.'

'Yes. Yes, all right. Maybe I won't be there on Saturday, Jess. Sorry.'

I nodded and went with her to the door. The best I could manage was 'Lucy would like to see you. If you can make it.' I knew I didn't want to see her.

Anyway, she didn't come. But Nat and Tony did.

Stella's husband was called Mick and he was full of surprises. He did some conjuring tricks and produced a fifty-pence piece from behind Andrew's ear. He organized games simply by playing them enthusiastically himself. In fact he was a cross between a leprechaun and a school-boy. He was fine for the duration of a party but nobody could have kept up his routine for longer than that, and it was obvious that Andrew knew it only too well. 'Take it steady, Dad,' he said as Mick raced the length of the hall with a matchbox on his nose and a balloon between his knees. That kind of warning from Andrew Bearwood was amazing.

Lucy loved every minute of it, especially being clamped between Nat and Tony's arms during Oranges and Lemons. She sat between them at the long trestle table and smiled beatifically when they both shared their crackers with her. Stella said, 'They've forgiven her for splitting on them then?' I kept my smile in place. If that was what the gossips were saying, that was fine.

We all got home just after eight o'clock. Mum and Bunny looked exhausted so I expect I looked the same.

Mum said, 'Well, I know we've missed Watt but isn't it marvellous not to have to put him to bed?'

Lucy, overtired, near tears, said, 'He was like a little brother though.'

Mum came to the rescue immediately. 'But he wasn't actually a relative, darling. Now, as soon as Aunt Jen marries Sam, Watt will be your cousin!'

Mum must have talked to her about it before because it was no surprise. 'Have you asked Aunt Jen if I can be a bridesmaid?' Lucy asked.

'Not yet. But I will.'

She kissed Mum goodnight, smiling again. It struck me suddenly that she turned to Mum oftener than she turned to me. Even so, that was one of the less awful times. In fact I might have been tempted to think that things were improving.

Christmas was almost upon us and we weren't ready for it. I wasn't interested but Lucy, Mum and Bunny made up for my ennui. School became one long Christmas party and Mum and Bunny herded me into Bristol to do some shopping. I went to work but there were no new enquiries. Sam didn't put in an appearance. Watt was not well; the doctor said it was a virus and the health visitor said it was his teeth. I thought, without pleasure, that Sam and Jennifer were having a baptism of fire as far as family life went. Billy said they would need Sam once the supporting ironwork was in place but what with Christmas and one thing and another they could manage for a week or two without him. Everything seemed in abeyance. And then I had a call from Brian Edwards asking me whether 21 December was still OK for his inspection at Marcroft.

'I'll check with Mr Jerome,' I said. 'But as far as I'm concerned, it's fine.'

He said, 'I could pick you up in the morning. About nine thirty? We could have lunch afterwards.'

I remembered how nice he had been. 'That would be very . . . pleasant.'

I felt awkward. Like a girl on a first date.

He said, 'I'm looking forward to seeing you again, Jess. Will you be bringing Watt?'

'No. A lot has happened in the family recently. My sister is with Watt's father, Sam. They have taken on Watt.'

'Oh . . .' He paused then went on. 'Oh Jess. You must feel bereft.'

It was the first time anyone had looked at it this way. I said simply, 'Yes.'

'My dear, I am sorry. But presumably you will still see him. As it's your sister . . .'

'Of course.'

Another pause. He cleared his throat. 'I have to say . . . it will be good to be alone with you.'

It was too quick. I knew that but I liked him. I said, 'That's good to know.'

He said goodbye almost lingeringly. I put down the phone and stood looking out of the office window, wondering. I hardly knew what I was wondering about. Perhaps it was just a state of mind. Perhaps something better was going to happen.

What happened that night was fairly drab. I locked up and said goodnight to Bob the security man, and then made for the Goose Bump and Dip Lane. I needed to check that the heating was coming on when it should and I wanted to pick up any post that might be lying in the hall. We were hanging up all our cards in the schoolhouse.

I had forgotten how dark the lane was. No street lights and the neighbours had gone to Spain for the winter. It was very dark indeed. By the time my headlights picked out a car parked by the gate, it was too late to turn back. It was the Parslow car. I didn't want to see Jean. I would have reversed and gone back except that Jean was blocking my turning point.

Someone got out of the car. It was Jock.

My heart plummeted. I wound down my window.

He said, 'Where are the kids? The house looks completely empty.'

'We're staying with my mother until after Christmas. I've come to pick up the mail. I can't stop. They're expecting me for a meal at any moment.'

He leaned on the car door. 'Jess . . . Jess. We've got to talk. Please.'

'Jock, I don't want you in the house. Jean saw you before . . .' I tried to see his face through the darkness.

'Jess. It's over for Jean and me. She knows I want you.'

I was shocked to the core. 'For God's sake! You were frantic when you thought she had gone for good! Now she's home and you've got another chance. What's the matter with the pair of you? I don't get it.'

He opened my door and stood aside for me to get out. 'Please come into the house and let's talk. Properly.' I cut across him angrily and he suddenly said, 'I love you, Jess! And I think you love me, only it's too soon after Matt. But I'll wait . . . I love you. And that's it.'

I was silent. The cold, damp air seemed to hang on to his words. After a moment he went on talking. He said he'd loved me for years. He said we could take the kids and go away and start again somewhere. He said Nat and Tony could come and stay with us. They got on well with Lucy and we'd be one big happy family. We could have our own child too. That would be the most exciting thing in the world. Our own baby.

At that I reached out and grabbed the door and closed

it, then locked it from inside. I started the engine and began to reverse erratically along the track. He was startled but then ran after me and protested again and again that he loved me and I was the only woman he had ever really wanted. I wound up the window, managed somehow to swing round in the darkness and the next minute I was driving for the Goose Bump and sobbing with a kind of horror.

I calmed down before I got to Mum's. But that small incident didn't help one bit. I felt . . . soiled. I felt cheap.

Nevertheless I ate a good tea and when Jock telephoned I told him I didn't want to see him again. Bunny overheard me and raised his brows. I put a finger to my lips. I didn't want Mum to hear about this. She would know, as I knew, that it was my own fault.

That night the bile was back. I took an Alka-Seltzer and managed to settle. I thought of Brian Edwards and how wonderful it would be to have a conventional courtship with flowers and theatre trips and maybe something at the end of it. Maybe not. I slept.

Twelve

I wanted Jerry to say something nice to me. Like how good it would be to see me again. Something.

He said, 'Where are you?'

'The office.'

'I've been ringing your house.'

'I've been staying at my mother's place.'

'Why?'

I should have told him it was none of his business but he was still a client.

'It's easier at the moment. After Christmas we'll go home again. You could have rung me here.'

'I was afraid Sam might be around. Is that why you've moved in with your mother?'

'Because of Sam? Of course not. Why on earth—'

He interrupted. 'I tried to tell you. Last time I saw you. I told him he must say something. But I knew he wouldn't, I knew he'd cop out of it in the end. He's an idiot, Jess. You're well shot of him. I hope Jennifer gives him hell before she dumps him.'

'Jerry! It's not like that!'

'You looked after his kid for seven months, Jess. Of course it was like that. Everyone assumed that you and he—'

I said loudly, 'You obviously did.'

He took an audible breath and let it go. 'Yes. Yes, I did. The business . . . everything. It would have been ideal. And he's so steady and loyal. That would be an essential for you.' He paused then added, 'In my opinion.'

I too took time to breathe deeply.

'Look, Jerry. You are talking about very personal things. You and I have a business arrangement and that is all.'

'When we had lunch that day, I thought we could be friends.'

I said deliberately, 'You offered me consolation and I accepted it and I thank you for it. But that was all. Now . . . what about Brian Edwards?'

'Are they staying at his place? Have they got the child?'

'Jerry.' I made a sound of exasperation. 'Yes and yes.'

'She won't stick it. He'll never take her anywhere. He's the dullest man—'

'But he would have been ideal for me?' I managed to laugh. Then I frowned suddenly. 'Jerry, are you hurt? Do you love Jennifer?'

He too made a sound of exasperation. 'Good God, no! I've never met anyone like her, of course, but I would hate to be in love with her.'

'I'm not hurt either. So that is that.'

'She didn't know you wouldn't be hurt. She is totally selfish, Jess. I know she's your sister and I'm sorry for you.'

I looked bleakly across the office and wondered whether he knew everything.

I said, 'Actually, I think it might work. She's expecting his child. And she's so good with Watt. I think this is the sort of real life she has been looking for.'

'Ha!'

'All right, she didn't know it was what she was looking for,' I began.

He said, 'Yes, yes. I get the message. Now . . . Brian Edwards. The twenty-first is tomorrow, Jess.'

The discussion about Sam and Jennifer was obviously at an end. I said, 'Yes. It will be good to get it settled before Christmas. Let's go for it.'

'No can do. I'm away tomorrow.'

'I told you before, you don't need to be around. He's

curious about Marcroft and he can do it tomorrow. Don't let's put him off.'

I could sense his hesitation. Then he said suddenly, 'All right. Tell him to bring his wife if he wants to. Or anyone. The more people who see the place, the better.' He paused then went on quickly, 'They're printing the articles we did, Jess. In that glossy. Is it called *Entitlements*?'

There was a very long pause. Then I said slowly, 'You made your enquiries about him then?'

'Brian Edwards? Yes. He seems to run a good show. I'm very happy about him.'

My voice was hard and level. 'Did it occur to you that I know his wife quite well? And that in any case I am not about to fall at the feet of anyone?'

He cleared his throat as if in apology. 'You are vulnerable, Jess. People – men – can see that. You are running a successful business, you have a small daughter, you have been generous enough to care for the child of your late friend . . . You are . . . desirable.'

'As in a desirable property?'

'Yes, of course. I didn't mean—'

'Jerry . . .' My voice was now weary. 'You are invulnerable, I suppose. Probably because you are so self-centred. You are also a control freak of the highest order. You're not keen on Sam because he totally ignores you. You think you can control me, don't you?' I sighed. 'It's just as well you won't be around tomorrow. Goodbye.'

He rang several times that day but I picked up the phone and immediately dropped it back in its cradle when I recognized his voice. Then I wondered whether I was angry with him for interfering or with myself for being such a fool.

Sam came in later. He informed me that Watt was much better; Sam himself had had the same virus but was now all right. It was Jennifer who was ill.

'I keep telling her that Daisy was sick all the time. But she says it's too soon. Morning sickness doesn't begin until much later.'

I felt a pang of unexpected sympathy for Jennifer.

'She's got that wrong, it starts almost immediately.' I smiled somehow. 'Perhaps it would be better not to keep comparing her with Daisy. After all, it was only last year that Watt was on the way.'

'Jennifer isn't like that,' he said, smiling back, looking . . . well, besotted. No other word for it. 'She hasn't got a jealous bone in her body. She's just anxious that something is wrong. She did a test the moment she was overdue so she's only about five weeks pregnant and she says that's too soon for all her symptoms.'

It crossed my mind that Jennifer must be good for Sam; he would never have spoken the word 'overdue' or mentioned pregnancy tests before he knew her. I reassured him as best I could, remembering that it was actually less than a year since I'd done exactly the same thing when he worried about Daisy. Somehow I managed to change the subject to work. He promised that come the new year he would definitely get back to things.

'It's been like a honeymoon, Jess.' His smile was back. 'I realize it's difficult for most people to understand, so soon after Daisy . . . You know how cut up I was at first.'

I said, 'Yes.'

'But it happened. It just happened, Jess. She says she fell in love with me ages ago so it wasn't quick for her. But for me . . . it was like a bomb exploding!' He laughed. How did he laugh? Joyously. That was the word for Sam: he was joyous.

He wheeled out a few truisms. 'They say that good things come out of bad, don't they? That one door closes and another opens. And it does!' He was standing as usual and suddenly he drew up a chair and sat on it. His voice became earnest. 'The good thing is, we're properly related now, Jess. I'm your brother. We're part of a family again. That's got to be pretty marvellous, hasn't it?'

I said again, flatly, 'Yes.'

'Business-wise too. Mr Jerome reckons that with the

publicity generated from the abbey, we should get more commissions. And we'll all be able to put in our bit.' He sighed ecstatically. 'Jennifer is going to do a course in history, you know.'

I said heavily, 'Yes. She did say something once before. But I thought . . . What about Watt? And the new baby?'

'She's gone into all that. They have crèche facilities at the university.' He beamed. 'She really is the most marvellous human being, Jess. I am so lucky. I can't believe it.' He laughed. 'I thought my life was over. And it's beginning. It's beginning, Jess!'

I watched him go out into the wind that always blew across the tops, and I felt a pang of pure envy.

After such blatant interference I expected Jerry to be at Marcroft when Brian Edwards drew up outside the porch of the abbey. However, there was no sign of him. The door was unlocked and I led the way inside, crossing my fingers in my pockets.

Brian had arrived promptly at nine thirty and won Mum over immediately by his interest in the old schoolhouse and the fact that she and Dad had left it as it was and not tried to update it in any way. It was a raw day with a nasty wind coming from the east and Brian was all done up in sheepskin and a ski hat. I wore a hooded fleece over several layers and already knew it wasn't sufficient to keep out the cold. I had shivered outside the school while I waited for the bell to ring and the children to go indoors. It was the last day of term; the windows were all frosted and the head of a giant cotton-wool snowman peered at me through the tall classroom window. This was going to be the last day of work for me too for a while. I planned to start again when Lucy returned to school on 7 January.

We got on the main road as soon as possible and maintained a steady seventy for most of the way. The car was air-conditioned, the seats luxurious. I hadn't slept much the night before and could have drifted off if I had felt more relaxed. I have to admit I didn't feel relaxed with Brian any longer; Jerry's discovery of a wife had made me realize what I had been doing. Again. I was angry with myself and very much on my mettle. However, he was the perfectly pleasant man he had been at our first meeting. He asked me if there was anywhere we could have a late lunch and I told him about the Armstrong Arms. He darted me a sideways smile and said, 'I always enjoy these jaunts. They're definitely the best perk of my job. The way people design houses is absolutely fascinating.'

'Mirrors their personality, I suppose,' I agreed.

'Tell me about this man's personality,' he suggested. 'As deduced from Marcroft Abbey.'

I laughed. 'Well . . . he's enormously ambitious if the original building is anything to go by. He has retained the minstrels' gallery, of course. But the stained glass . . . That has made the place feel quite different, as I told you before.'

He nodded. 'What about the living quarters behind?'

'Very modern. Yet surprisingly simple. Straightforward. If he were all ambition I think he would have had a stab at something Gothic.'

'So he's courageous?'

'I'm not sure. He is so . . . certain of himself. He believes that whatever he does will be . . . right.'

'Egocentric?'

'Yes. In some ways. Wait and see.'

Brian laughed. 'All right. We'll compare notes on the way home.'

It sounded fun. And the countryside was delightfully Christmassy. In four days' time it would be Christmas Day.

He said, 'Penny for 'em.'

'I was just thinking I must make it a good Christmas for Lucy.'

'You will.' He took his left hand off the steering wheel and patted my knee. Then he put it back on the wheel again and said, 'Can you tell me more about Watt?'

I found myself telling him. Practically everything. I couldn't have spoken so frankly if I hadn't known he was married. It made him safe. So there were definite advantages to going out with a married man!

He was very impressed with the abbey.

'Your husband was a clever designer. To use the light as he has done – it's marvellous, Jess. How I wish he could see it.'

I said quietly, 'He could see it. When he sketched he could always see how it would be. Foresight. He had it in abundance.'

He said, 'It must have been awful before. Like a barn.'

'I thought it was like a barracks.'

'Yes. Exactly that.' He smiled at me. 'You have it too. You can look. And see.'

There was a knock on the kitchen door. Naturally I thought it was Jerry and instead I was overjoyed to find George Gully standing there.

'Sorry to interrupt . . . Jess.'

'Not at all. I was wondering how we would get through.' I introduced him to Brian and then Steve appeared. They pumped Brian's hand in turn.

'Governor said you'd be coming. We're finishing up today for Christmas. Glad to have the chance to meet you.'

We went through while they explained that the steel skeleton had to go up before the old roof was taken off.

'We're doing it piecemeal, d'you see, Mr Edwards. Prefabbing at the workshop and bolting it together here. We haven't got far yet. We're going to jack down through the flags and pour in concrete for the first joist . . . probably mid-January.'

'Your plans and specifications were fine.' Brian walked around, staring upwards, obviously 'looking and seeing'. 'You know you'll need a building inspection before you bed the first girder? Let me know and I'll make the necessary arrangements and bring the inspector here myself.'

'Brilliant,' Steve said.

Brian said to me, 'You'll need a crane when it comes to fitting the glazing.'

George offered a name and said he would make enquiries. Unexpectedly I began to feel good. I hadn't felt dizzy all morning. I wasn't cut to ribbons by the knowledge that Brian was married although I had almost fantasized about him. Maybe at long last I was building some kind of shell around myself. Maybe after Christmas I would be able to face the fact that my husband and sister had betrayed me, and I had betrayed my best friend.

I must have taken a sharp breath because Brian turned immediately and said, 'All right, Jess?'

'Yes. Yes, of course.' I smiled widely at the three men. 'I'm delighted everything is coming together.'

Brian smiled back. 'Matt would be pleased,' he said.

'Yes. Yes, he would.'

It was not the first time Brian had mentioned Matt and I had accepted it, liked it. So maybe that was part of the answer. To compartmentalize my memories. It would mean I could go on looking at the good ones and ignoring the bad ones.

When we went to lunch I climbed into Brian's car and tried out my theory.

'Matt's idea of a compliment was to tell me I sat down and stood up like a camel!' I laughed as I stretched my legs beneath the glove compartment.

Brian said nothing. Nothing at all. It was, to put it mildly, disconcerting. It improved a bit when we got into the restaurant and he ordered drinks and we looked at the menu. He said it wasn't very warm just as I said how nice it was to see a real log fire, then we both laughed. After that he asked me what I was doing for Christmas and I told him.

'It will be difficult, I imagine. Your first Christmas without Matt.'

'It would be much worse on my own. My mother is great.' I thought about it. 'She's also unobtrusive about it.' I gave a tight smile. 'I had the nerve to think badly of her – not long ago. We live and learn, don't we?'

'We do.' He waited until we were served, then added, 'We've talked very openly today, Jess. Thank you for that.'

'Because I told you about Jennifer and Sam? It's an enormous relief. You don't know them so you're not judgemental. I should thank you.'

'The thing is' – he waved his fork towards the fire – 'the thing is, Jess, I am happily married, but . . .' He took a breath. 'We can't have children. And you came into the office, recently bereaved, two children . . . You were obviously coping very well' – I made an ironic sound but he shook his head and went on – 'I was . . . attracted, Jess. I have to admit it. I felt terrible about it. But it happened. And then, today, you were so natural and sweet. And you spoke – you speak so often about Matt – with the same naturalness. It's wonderful. I can't tell you.'

I looked at him. If he'd been a different man there would have been tears in his eyes. How good life would be with someone like Brian Edwards.

I said quietly, 'Take me off the pedestal please, Brian. We've talked like two old friends, but still you don't know me. And I don't know you.'

'I think you probably do know me. There's nothing much to know. But . . . will you talk about yourself?'

I laughed. 'I can't because I don't know myself. Since Matt was killed, Brian, I have discovered something new about myself practically every day – never very likeable, sometimes quite hateful.' He started to protest but I shook my head. 'We've said enough. You know I sympathize entirely with you about wanting a family. But there are ways round that. You've doubtless talked about all of them. Let's talk about Christmas again. Tell me what you are doing.'

So we did.

When I got to Mum's that afternoon, I had Andrew as

well as Lucy. There had been no sign of Stella outside the school and I hadn't known what else to do.

'Don't worry, Jess.' Mum was already cutting sandwiches and making up drinks for them. 'Stella will know he's here. That husband of hers is still around, poor love.'

The sheer irony of it hit me physically. People who had husbands no longer wanted them and those who didn't have them wished they were back. Or did they? Mum seemed as happy with Bunny as she had been with Dad. And did I really want Matt back after . . . everything? Yes. I did. That much was certain. If only to ask him why he had lied so hard to protect Dad . . . and, of course, why he had . . . loved . . . Jennifer. Why. And what. Exactly what. I had thought I didn't want to know but how could I deal with it until I did?

I said, 'We don't really talk, Mum. Do we?'

She looked up from the bread board, surprised. 'Don't we? We seem to be nattering about something all the time.'

'I mean . . . I don't understand about you and Dad. And you still think I'm Mrs Perfect.'

She laughed comfortably. 'You were always our good daughter, Jess. You know that. As for Dad and me . . . you lived with us. You know about Dad and me.'

I was sure she knew about Marilyn. But not quite sure enough to mention her name. Anyway, Stella arrived then in a flurry of apologies. Mick had taken her Christmas shopping and they'd forgotten the time. And quite a bit later – because Stella waited while Andrew devoured his sandwiches and drank his blackcurrant juice – it seemed as if Mum wanted to make sure we had no chance of a tête-à-tête. Perhaps it was just as well.

Christmas was surprisingly all right. Jennifer and Sam arrived with Watt in time for lunch. Mum had taken Lucy to church on her scooter and Bunny and I worked together in the kitchen getting everything ready for one thirty. Most of us couldn't help remembering last Christmas when it had been our first time without Dad. Now this one was our first without Dad, Matt and Daisy. There was a kind of disbelief among us. Or perhaps it was just me. But I had lived in a state of disbelief for so long it seemed . . . all right.

After lunch we all went for a walk as far as the stocks and back. There were quite a few teenagers hanging around. I thought I recognized Jason and Simon but I couldn't be sure. I wasn't feeling too good and hoped it was nothing to do with the lunch. The others seemed all right.

We got back to the house to find Jerry's horrible four-wheel drive in the playground and he was unloading a bright red child-size sports car. I had never mentioned the car to Lucy so she was over the moon with excitement. I had accused Jerry of trying to buy her approbation; well, he certainly secured it on Christmas afternoon.

'I'd forgotten your grandmother had a playground all of her own,' he said to Lucy as she parked expertly next to a tub of holly. 'It's ideal for driving. I thought you'd have to keep it at Marcroft.'

She shook her head. 'Too muddy there.'

'I'm having it paved right now,' he told her. 'A proper road running all around the place. So that you can make a tour of inspection.'

Her eyes opened wide. Mum and Bunny were exclaiming in crescendo. Sam and Jennifer stood aside. I said, 'Stop it, Jerry. She'll think you had it done specially for her.'

'Well?'

Lucy said, 'Mummy's teasing, Mr Jerome. And you are too.' She went into reverse, an expert driver after just ten minutes. 'This is the very best present I have ever had in my whole life. But I'll let you keep it at Marcroft.' She sighed. 'Andrew would wreck it.'

There was a wealth of experience in her voice; we all laughed, even Jen and Sam. And then we went in for tea while Lucy used the last of the daylight to zoom around between the flower tubs and honk the horn. She was happy. That was all that really mattered to me.

It was 2002. The kitchen roof at Marcroft was well under way. Sam and I divided our time between the factory and the abbey. I was still at Mum's because that was what Lucy wanted. Jennifer drove down most days to give a hand. She was feeling good; her skin glowed and she coped with Watt as if she'd been doing it since his birth. I could have talked to Jennifer; she was sensitive to how I might feel about Watt. I could have told her just how much I wanted – needed – another partner and she of all people would have understood. But obviously I would never be able to talk to Jennifer like that again. I told her honestly that I was glad I no longer had Watt. I hardly knew how to look after Lucy these days, let alone a baby.

She said, 'Didn't you ever go to see a doctor? After that turn you had at Ma's?'

'No. I know what it is, Jen, don't I?'

'What, for goodness' sake?'

'Stress. Strain. Grief. Whatever you like to call it. Nothing physically wrong with me.'

'You can get relaxants and things. Please go, Jess. Think of Luce.'

I thought of her. We were filling her life with love, but she was so intelligent. She knew all about death and how random it could be.

I said, 'If it gets any worse, I'll get something. OK?'

'OK.' She made to hug me and I pretended to lean forward to reach for a pen. But we could still talk like that. It could have been worse. Much, much worse.

Sam now had the energy of ten men and gradually he took over at Marcroft, commuting each day and coming home to get in wood and coal and cuddle Watt while Jennifer cooked a meal. I have to say they were both ridiculously happy. Once I went in and found them chasing each other round the table just as Matt and I had done.

That night I drove back to Mum's and wept nearly all the way there.

I saw nothing of Jean or Jock. Presumably he'd gone back to Scotland and she was fully occupied as usual with the house and the boys. A strict eye was kept on Nat at school, quite literally. He had a mole inside his elbow and it was examined every day to make sure he and Tony didn't switch places again. Mrs Ingram had not taken kindly to that little escapade. Simon had a job stacking shelves in Hartford's. I asked him whether he had left school but he didn't reply.

Jerry was rarely in evidence when I went to Marcroft. Sam told me there was a new woman in his life. She was an interior decorator.

I told myself things were getting better; I listed all sorts of blessings. Underneath it all, I felt I was slipping away, becoming invisible. It was the strangest thing. In February I got a virus of some kind and felt terrible for a week. It took away what little protection I had built up for myself and suddenly I wanted to talk to someone about Matt. The only person I could think of was Bunny. I made up my mind I would tell Bunny about Matt and Jennifer. I felt better already. And then he went down with my virus and I realized how ridiculous I had been. As if Bunny would want to know about . . . that. He might even have thought I was trying to get in some kind of backhander about his relationship with Mum.

One weekend when Lucy was spending the day with Andrew, and Mum and Bunny had gone for their first outing since his bug, I found myself driving over the Goose Bump and stopping outside Marilyn's house. I was on my way to check out Dip Lane. It was a Saturday so I was fairly certain she would be at work. But of course I knew she wasn't when I saw her car outside the gate.

I told her all this as she led me into the overcrowded sitting room and sat me among the cushions.

She said, 'My God. You are a crazy mixed-up kid!' She

laughed. 'I didn't have any appointments so I thought I'd come home and rest the poor old plates of meat.' She pu them on the footstool and looked down at them. 'I'm going to book another cruise, Jess. D'you remember I went this time last year? I met some nice blokes actually.' She looked at me. 'I need a bloke, Jess. You probably understand tha now.'

It wasn't what I'd expected.

All I said was, 'Now?'

'Well, when I was joking about it – that first appoint ment, d'you remember? – I could feel your disapproval And now . . . I guess you're a bit more understanding.'

'It's not that simple, Marilyn.'

She grinned. 'It's as complicated as you want to make it But really, it's very simple. You're all tangled up, Jess. Jus like your dad used to be. You wanted a bloke and there wa Jock so you took him.'

I was shocked. 'It wasn't like that, Marilyn.'

She stopped grinning and put on a mock-serious face 'All right. Let's have it then.'

'I don't know . . . I'm not sure . . .'

'D'you want a cup of tea?'

'Perhaps – yes, that would be nice. Let me get it. Don' put your legs down.'

She let me go into the kitchen and fiddle around in its pristine neatness. I looked out of the window while the kettle boiled.

'You've got snowdrops out. Your garden is so pretty.'

'Yes. You like gardening, don't you? Your dad alway said that. He seemed to think it kept you going.'

I made the tea and then poured and took two cups back into the parlour.

She said, 'Well?'

I said, 'What else did my father say?'

'About you?'

'About anything.'

'He was writing a book about follies. You know, the

castles and hunting lodges rich people built just for fun, like – like a game. There was one he loved. Not far away. Walton Castle. We went there twice. And then Matt told him about Marcroft and we went there twice too. He told me all about follies. They were so many things to so many people. Status symbols. Bolt holes. Love nests.' She stopped speaking. I could guess what they'd been for her and Dad. I still couldn't believe it.

I said, 'I came across a picture of you at Marcroft. Matt had sketched you. He said it was just coincidence. He lied to protect you.'

'Not to protect me. To protect your father. And you, of course.' She mused into her tea. 'I often think that the two of them . . . they would have done a lot to protect you and your mother. But to die . . . that was cruel.'

'Oh Marilyn!'

'Sorry. Sorry. I was letting myself go into a "perhaps" world.' She sighed. 'Your father called it talking hypothetically. I asked him what that meant. He said it was when you started every sentence with the word "perhaps". Well, that's not me, is it? A complete waste of time.' She finished her tea and put the cup down decisively on the coffee table. 'Sorry, Jess. That's all. I'm not going to talk about Donald. He was the best thing that happened to me and it won't happen again. But other things will. I'm definitely going on a cruise.'

I continued to sip my tea. She wanted me to go but I knew suddenly why I had come.

At last I said, 'Marilyn, tell me about Matt and Jennifer. Everything. How it started, how long it went on. I have to know.'

She was silent for so long I thought she was ignoring me as Simon had done in the supermarket. But then she spoke.

'Are you up to it? I don't want to be responsible for you landing yourself in a lunatic asylum.'

'No such things now.' I tried to smile. 'Come on,

Marilyn. I need what the Americans call "closure". And I'm not going to get it until I know what I'm closing.'

'All right. So far as I know, it happened only once. In Plymouth. Before your father died. She came in to have her hair done last year – on her way back to work. She'd been to Marcroft the day before to see Matt. But she'd met someone else. Now I realize it was Sam Clarkson. That's all there is to it.'

I said carefully, 'I think it was Mr Jerome then. I'm not sure. But . . . if she had wanted Matt . . . would she have got him? Just like that?'

She shrugged. 'How would I know? He was weak, Jess. In that way, he was weak. Very like your father. And Jennifer was so terribly jealous of you.'

I think I already knew that. Since my life had been so devastated we had become much closer. She had no reason now to be jealous.

I said, 'Weak? I never thought of Matt as being weak in any way. Nor my father. How do you mean?'

'Well . . . they always *understood* everything, didn't they? They were always there for everyone. People could talk to them. They listened. Donald was certainly like that. He used to listen to Jean for hours while she rabbited on about Jock. Maybe Matt was the same. I think he was.' She shook her head. 'Jean called you Mrs Perfect. Maybe Matt wanted to be Mr Perfect.'

'But . . . he loved me. He *did* love me. I know that.'

'Oh yes. There was no question of that. None at all. But he couldn't turn Jennifer away. She made a dead set for him – he was the only one who understood her . . . blah blah.'

'But he was – he was *deceiving* me!'

'But if he hadn't deceived you he would have hurt you. Ruined the marriage. Maybe left Lucy without a father.'

I shook my head. I would never understand. 'Couldn't he have thought of that before he – before he—'

'Of course, he should have done. But then there was his father-in-law and me – he thought the world of Donald. As far as he could tell, I was making no difference at all to Donald's marriage. Maybe he thought it was all right. In certain circumstances. He could see that Jennifer was terribly unhappy and bitter. Perhaps' – she laughed – 'here I go again being hypothetical – perhaps he thought of it as a kind of therapy?' She laughed again, saw my face and stopped. 'Listen, you've got to accept it, Jess. He loved you. That's all that matters in the end. He's not here to explain. You have to do it for him.' She stood up.

I said, 'I'd better go.'

She flapped her hands. 'I don't know what I'm supposed to say next. Your dear ma knew what was going on between Donald and me. She still loved him . . . was shattered when he became ill and died. Then things happened and she found someone else. That is what will happen for you. That is what you thought was happening when Jock turned up. That's how life is.'

I said I supposed it was. I didn't tell her about Sam and Jerry and Brian . . . Instead I stood up. Which proved to be a big mistake because the whole room upended itself and I went down like a bag of potatoes and hit my head on Marilyn's fender.

I woke up almost immediately to find her bending over me anxiously.

'Are you going to be sick again?' she asked.

If only I'd felt better I might have laughed as Jean and I had laughed that awful night almost three months before.

I whispered, 'No.'

Somehow, with Marilyn's help, I got back on to the sofa.

'I think I should call someone. A doctor.'

'Don't do that, Marilyn. I'm under the weather. Stress and so on.' I adjusted my head and nothing happened; everything stayed in the same place. 'It's all right now. Probably that knock did me good. I'll go home.'

She didn't want me to drive but I did. And when I got to Mum's the phone was ringing and it was Marilyn.

'I wanted to warn your mother,' she said when she heard my voice. 'Are you all right?'

'Of course. And don't worry Mum. She's got quite a bit on her plate at the moment with Ray just recovering from this flu thing.'

'I'll make a bargain with you. You go to see your doctor and I won't breathe a word.'

'All right.'

I had no intention of going to the doctor to report my stressed condition. But when Bunny and Mum appeared I hadn't been able to go and fetch Lucy from Andrew's and Mum looked tired out when she got back from doing so. I realized we should have gone home a long time ago and let her get on with her life.

So I made an appointment and a week later presented myself at Christine Parr's morning surgery.

I hadn't met her before so she gave me a thorough examination and asked a lot of questions. I told her three times that I had suffered dizzy spells ever since my husband was killed and that all I needed was something to help me to relax. She appeared not to hear. She said at last, 'Mrs Tavener, you must know the cause of your current symptoms.' She looked at me. 'You're expecting another child. I would say you are about three months pregnant.'

I would have given a lot to have fainted then.

But I didn't. I walked back through the waiting room without pausing for her to say another word. I was not in the least dizzy and I no longer felt sick. It all fell neatly into place and with the solution came the cure.

I was pregnant with Jock's child. I really had hit rock-bottom. I should have gone back then and there and asked about an abortion. But I had to get away. Run away. Run away from all the sordid facts. Run away from my own rotten self. I did indeed start to run as soon as I was outside the modern health centre. Across the car park to where the car offered some kind of sanctuary.

Thirteen

It was so strange the way I kept feeling sorry for Jock. It would have seemed to him – if ever he knew about this latest abortion – that no-one wanted his children. Yet that was stupid because he had four already. I'd heard of women with a kind of pregnancy obsession, but not men. Jock was obviously the exception. When Christine Parr made my appointment and talked to me about 'other options', I still thought of Jock. When I lied to Mum about having to go to the abbey I was thinking of him still. Even when I went home and garaged the car where no-one could see it, then laid the fire for when I got back, then rang for a taxi, he was still in my head. He must never know. Nobody must ever know. It would be over so quickly and I could come back home and take it really easy and get back to where I had been before. That hadn't been a bad place to be. My talk with Marilyn had done something for me; I wasn't quite sure what because the pregnancy had obscured everything else. But once that was over . . . there might be some kind of peace. That was what I wanted more than anything else. Peace. I had to reach understanding first. But it was within my grasp.

It didn't quite work out that way; in fact it didn't work out that way at all. For one thing I hated the actual . . . procedure. That was what it was called: a procedure. I didn't even like my room, which had enormous windows overlooking treetops that wavered in the sluicing rain. It didn't stop raining that whole day. And at some point what I was doing – the whole thing – washed over me like a wave. I had always wanted another baby. That time in Devizes . . . oh God, that time in Devizes. If only I'd got pregnant then, everything, just everything, would have been so different. Even so, this baby, this tiny germ of life inside me, was mine as well as Jock's. Christine Parr had already pointed that out and I had listened but not heard. I remembered what Brian had said about looking and seeing. How often had I listened and not heard, looked and not seen? How often would I do it in the future?

When I got home, I lit the fire and lay on the sofa and stared at it. The phone rang and I ignored it. Some time during the night I went into the kitchen and made tea and toast. I remembered last summer when the kitchen had lost Matt but had gained Watt. The muddles, the washing and ironing, the way Lucy had rocked him in his little chair. I had deprived Lucy of a brother or sister.

Grey light appeared around the kitchen window and I was cold. I went back and put some wood on the fire and crouched by it. Something was hurting so I lay on the sofa again. The phone rang.

It was Dr Parr.

'I tried you yesterday. Are you all right?'

'Yes. Bit sore.'

'That will go. Have you got someone with you?'

'Yes.'

'That's excellent.' She paused. 'Come and see me. Any time. It sometimes gets worse before it gets better. But it does get better.'

'Thank you. Thank you for everything.'

She said, 'I'll ring again.'

I said, 'No. I'm going to stay with a friend.'

She had to accept that though I could tell she didn't like it.

I stood holding the phone and looking up the stairs to where, about a year ago, Lucy had bumped down, barefoot and content. She was still content. Matt had given her his contentment, the best legacy she could have. She was perfectly happy with Mum, with Bunny, with school . . . I dialled Mum's number.

'How is Lucy?' I asked immediately.

'Fine. Bunny has taken her to school.' She tutted. 'I keep calling him that. It suits him.'

'Mum, would you mind if I went to see an old friend of Matt's while I'm here? Just a couple of days? Can you cope?'

'Of course I can cope. You know how easy Lucy is.'

I didn't argue. I thanked her and rang off before she could ask anything about Matt's friend and where he – or she – lived.

I managed another cup of tea and waited for the fire to die before I left. I didn't close the garage door; it was so difficult to open. I'd been going to do something about it for so long.

The rain stopped, which I chose to see as a good omen. Easter was going to be very early this year and it was as if the flowers and trees knew that because everything was a fresh, fresh green and the hawthorn was budding. Jean and I had called it bread and cheese when we were children; we'd pulled off the tender young tips and eaten them and nothing had tasted quite so good until the cowslips yielded their nectar and then the sorrel with its vinegar taste in full summer. So much happiness. And all the time Jennifer had been eaten by jealousy . . . and Dad and Mum had not quite fulfilled each other so that Mum turned to Ray and Dad turned to Marilyn.

I heard a sob and shook my head and put my foot down. I was on the stretch of road where Matt and Daisy and Daisy's mother had died. I kept going but I wondered whether this was my destination. If any other vehicle had come round the bend towards me then, I think I might have let go the steering wheel in a kind of surrender.

But it didn't. I was through and heading away from our hills towards the open countryside of Wiltshire. And then I came to a junction and knew exactly where I was heading. Devizes.

It took some time to find the right pub. I had to go to the big block of flats where Daisy and Sam had lived for those few weeks, then try to remember where we'd gone after we left them. The trouble was, the girl who had driven to that pub last year was not the woman I was now. I tried to fit myself into her mould and could not. It occurred to me that she was insouciant to the point of being smug. Yes, someone else had called her smug. Jean.

I found it eventually. There had been a monkey-puzzle tree in the garden and that identified it because I hadn't even registered its name before. The Full Quart. And they had a room, though it was not the family room we'd had last time.

'Mrs Tavener.' The receptionist smiled. 'I remember. It's such an unusual name. You came twice, didn't you?'

I said unthinkingly, 'That was my sister. Just before Christmas.'

She showed me upstairs. I had my purse in my pocket and toilet stuff in a polythene bag. I had no plans at all.

I slept most of the afternoon. It was a deep sleep but it didn't heal anything. When I woke up I tried to think logically. I would go down to dinner – if only to separate day and night. Then I would have a long bath and go to bed properly and sleep properly and perhaps dream of Matt. And in the morning I would phone Jerry and tell him I was coming to look at the work in progress. That would make my lie to Mum a bit better. And then I could drive home and start again. Christine Parr had said it would get better and she was a doctor so she should know.

I went down and ordered cottage pie and peas. It was typical pub fare; not bad, not good. I couldn't eat it and felt rotten when my full plate was removed. I went back upstairs and it was while I was in the bath that my mind started worrying around what the receptionist had said.

Two visits by someone called Tavener. And Jennifer was not called Tavener.

I came to it quite slowly but so inevitably; like walking towards a cliff in the certain knowledge that it was there and I would step off it at any moment. Why – why oh why – had Jennifer taken Sam to Devizes? Because she had been there before. When she had been there before, why had she called herself Tavener? Because she was with Matt. It was so simple that it was obviously true. It was why Matt had known where to take Lucy and me that evening last May; because he'd been there before. Just as Jennifer knew where to take Sam; because she'd been there before. Marilyn had told me it had happened only once. In Plymouth. But obviously she wouldn't know about the second time. Only Matt and Jennifer knew about that. And now me.

I got out of the bath and wrapped myself in one of the towels, then lay on the bed. When I started to shiver I got beneath the clothes. I don't think I slept but I can't remember how the hours of the night went by. When another windy day of rain started, I got up and put on some clothes, picked up my bag and left. Someone was cleaning the bar and said she would put the kettle on and make some tea. I didn't reply to her. I fumbled with the door and she ran up and opened it. She said something then looked at my face and was silent.

I got in the car and sat there for a few minutes. I wanted Mum. But Mum meant Bunny. And Lucy. I had to see another human being; anyone would do, Marilyn, Jean . . . not Sam or Jennifer. Jerry.

Jerry would do. Jerry with his big mouth and his quick and intuitive mind. The fact that he was insensitive as well as intuitive didn't matter. He would tell me that this second time made no difference; the deed had already been done. He wouldn't understand about Devizes and I couldn't tell him about Jock and the baby. But he was a very real presence. He knew Matt, he knew Jennifer, he knew Sam . . . and he knew me.

I took the Avebury road.

It was nearly nine when I arrived at the abbey. A grey drizzle seemed to hold it suspended and it looked totally grim. No four-wheel drive outside. I went on very carefully down the side towards the new annexe. I barely registered that Jerry had indeed paved an enormous swathe all round the property. I registered that it was dark enough for the windows to be lit and they were not. No car here either.

I switched off and got out stiffly and went to the door. I knocked and rang half a dozen times before I could believe the place was empty. Another dead end. I was at Marcroft Abbey where it had all started and there were still no answers.

It didn't matter. When it came down to it, I didn't really want to talk about this latest betrayal. I had to find a way to live with it and no-one could tell me how to do that. So I went back to the car and sat there and watched the rain stream off the windscreen so that the view constantly changed shape. I felt a self-loathing that was terrible. From that came a certainty that everything was my fault: Jennifer's jealousy, Matt's infidelity, Sam's hasty liaison with my sister, the baby . . . Jock's baby.

I didn't cry. There was no need, the world was weeping in my stead. I tried to think of Lucy; just Lucy. Her wholeness, her curiosity, her sense of excitement and adventure over small things. Her amazing sense of fair play. After the Christmas party last December she had asked me where she could get farthings. 'Nat and Tony didn't chop off my head when we played Oranges and Lemons,' she explained carefully. 'So I still owe them five farthings and I don't know where there are any.' I'd forgotten all about the farthings. I scrabbled in the glove compartment and found my shopping list and a biro. I wrote, 'Five farthings.' Then I put the notebook away and stared again at the wavering outline of the abbey.

How long I sat there I have no idea. But quite suddenly I

opened the door and got out into the rain. I walked to the little wood where we had had our picnic nearly a year ago, and stood looking around me. The trees had the luminous green of new leaves and there were clots of snowdrops; no bluebells as yet. I actually noticed the thickness of mud underfoot and the heady smell of rain-washed bark. It was a grey weeping day, yet beneath it was the promise of Easter: new beginnings.

I came to the brook and looked at it for a long time. It was brown and peaty; the essence of the Plain. I walked into it. As the water seeped over my shoes and into my socks and then soaked the bottom of my jeans, it felt warm. I leaned down and scooped up a handful and held it to my face. It offered a strange but quite distinctive comfort. I knelt and bathed my face again. The sleeves of my fleece dripped; the backs of my hands were the palest sienna. I was becoming one with the water and earth of countless millennia. It was fascinating. I sat in it and it lapped my hips. There was no sensation of cold at all. I smacked the surface with flattened palms as Watt had done in his bath. Drops flew into the air and were no longer brown but crystal. And then I lay down and let the slow current take my shorn hair, which had been smart once but not for a long time.

I lay on my back and felt the ripples fill my clothes and lap around my ears. The world became all sensation. No thought, no logic. Just feeling. I looked up and could see the grey sky between the willows. I smiled at it. It came lower. Like a blanket. I closed my eyes.

I must have slept. I was conscious of my name . . . someone was calling my name. My full name. 'Jessica! Jessica – where are you?'

And then the tone changed to horror.

'Christ, Jessica! She's here, Helen – she's in the water!'

It was Jerry. Who was Helen? She had a deep and very cultured voice.

'Oh my God. Is she dead? Shall I dial nine-nine-nine?'

'No. She won't want a fuss. And she's not dead at all. She's playing at being bloody Ophelia or something.' He sounded furious.

I kept my eyes closed. When he yanked me up, water poured off my clothes and hair. I must have weighed a ton. He shouted at me to wake up. I smiled to show him I was awake and that made him angrier than ever and he shook me hard.

'You little fool! What d'you think you're playing at?'

I couldn't tell him that I didn't know the name of the game but it had something to do with owing five farthings.

He shouted, 'Grab her feet! I can't get her out on my own.'

And the cultured voice said, 'I don't want anything to do with it, thank you, Jerry.'

I wanted so much to laugh. I could see it behind my closed lids. My saturated body hanging from Jerry's arms and the distaste of the girl, Helen. She might be the interior decorator. I imagined her looking rather like Jennifer used to look, all sleek and groomed. Like a cat at the milk. Only the milk was not Matt any more, it was Jerry. And the cat was Helen.

The thoughts came with the drops of water that must be dripping down Jerry's suit. Random, almost flippant thoughts. Jerry was panting with the effort of carrying my waterlogged body back through the wood. The girl was telling him that he should call an ambulance. He stumbled suddenly and laid me down rather quickly in the mud.

'She wasn't under the water, for God's sake!' he gasped.

'But you can't take her into the house. What are you going to do with her? Let the medics take care of her – that's the main thing, surely?'

He got his breath and said wearily, 'She's Jessica Tavener.'

'The people who are doing the kitchen?'

230

'Yes. Now go and open up and then run a bath, will you?'

There was a pause. I registered the taste of mud and the smell of mud. I was still becoming part of the earth.

The girl said slowly, 'Jerry, I don't know what's going on here, but if she comes in, I go out.'

'What about the job? The bedrooms? The new kitchen?' He sounded surprised.

'I can't afford to get mixed up in any scandal. And this whole thing smells.'

He said, with a smile in his voice, 'It's just the mud, Helen. And it doesn't smell bad. Just muddy.'

Her voice became hard. 'That's it. I'm off. I'll take your car and leave it at the station. If you're still interested . . . in my work . . . give me a ring when all this has blown over. All right?'

He started to gather me up again, straightened painfully, then said, 'All right. But open up for me first, there's a good girl.'

He started to stagger forward again and her voice came from well ahead. 'Open up yourself, you patronizing . . . *oaf*!'

I wished I could have smiled. Her words summed him up so well. He had other qualities, but he was distinctly patronizing. But the mud seemed to have cemented my lips and eyelids together and anyway the urge to smile soon disappeared and I was back to the droplet thoughts and the return of sleep. There was just one thing I needed: the water.

Jerry's footsteps were on the hard surface now; he brought us up sharp against something, either the door or the wall. He set my feet down and propped me against his shoulder. With his right hand he opened the door and I felt my body falling backwards. He grabbed at my clothes and suddenly I was hoisted up, hanging over his shoulder, as we crossed the hall. His breathing was loud; he knocked into something and groaned. I was propped again and then I heard the sound of rushing water and a gout of steam enveloped both of us, and for the first time I realized how cold I was.

When he lowered me into the bath I started to shiver. I felt him gently dunk my face and hair and then begin to pull off my muddy clothes. There was nothing I could do to stop him or help him. I had no command of myself whatsoever. It took him ages to undress me. Then he pulled the plug to let the muddy water go and filled up again. He did that several times. Sometimes he muttered under his breath. I caught some of it. 'What the hell were you doing?' He asked that lots of times. Twice he said, 'Christ, Jess. You're not warming up.'

I heard him moving about a lot. I think he was taking off his own muddy clothes and putting on clean ones. He must have got masses of towels too because when he finally drained the water, he wrapped me in a bundle of them and lugged me out and over his shoulder again, and the next thing I knew was the softness of a bed. A warm bed. And then nothing.

Mum was there when I woke.

Fourteen

The great thing about Mum is, she knows when not to say anything. She didn't say much that day at the abbey. She asked me how I felt and when I just smiled and nodded she let go of my hand – she was holding it when I woke up – and scooped her arm beneath my shoulders and held me very close. I could feel her tears running down my neck and wished I could tell her that I was all right, but my mouth was still not working and all I could manage were the kind of sounds I made to Lucy when she fell down. Eventually Mum sat straight again and let her hand slip round till it cupped my face. With her other hand she stroked my hair and looked at me, smiling through her tears. Then she whispered something that Dad used to say when I couldn't sleep: 'Twelve of the clock. And all's well.' She stood up and began to undress. An open suitcase was on the ottoman and she took one of her cotton nighties from it and slipped it over her head. Then she slid into bed by my side and put my head on her shoulder.

I think she must have slept, though I can't be sure because, curled within her arm, smelling the lavender bags from her underwear drawer, I slept again and didn't wake till it was fully light.

She was not by my side and as I moved to look for her the cold air chilled my body so that I huddled down. I was soaked with my own sweat; I put out a hand to feel my hair and then tucked it down quickly. Outside the safety of my cocoon it felt polar.

The door opened and Mum came in with a loaded tray. I

think she had been crying again. She was dressed and looked as neat as ever.

She put the tray down and came over to feel my forehead.

'You've had a good sweat, Jess. That'll make you feel better. I've run a hot bath and while you're in it I'll change the linen. Jerry has gone to work. He's given me the run of the place.'

She pulled back the bedclothes and for the first time I realized I was naked. I thought of Jerry pulling off my clothes and started, very weakly, to cry with shame. The sheet was stained. Mum ignored it all. She helped me to stand up and together we staggered into the bathroom.

At least it was warm in the bath. I continued to whinge quietly as I washed myself. This had nothing to do with the terrible weight of knowledge inside my head, and everything to do with personal physical shame, but it helped to make that small animal sound of distress.

Mum came back in to help me out and I dried myself laboriously. Mum had been out to the car and got my bag and I put on my own nightshirt and the protective stuff they'd given me at the nursing home. Mum waited while I got into bed and then propped the pillows and tucked in the sheets and gave me a cup of tea. I'd had nothing since that evening meal at the Full Quart in Devizes, probably about thirty-six hours ago. As I obediently ate bread and butter and marmalade, I began to feel better.

'Lucy?' I asked when, at last, she sat down with her own tea.

'She's fine. She's with Bunny – Ray, I mean.' She tried to smile but her face was all over the place. 'If he can't manage, Jennifer will come down.'

'*No!*'

My voice was almost a shout. Mum jumped and blinked and I shook my head in apology and marshalled my voice, words, sentences.

'I don't want Jennifer near Lucy. Not ever.'

Mum was shocked. 'What's happened? She didn't say anything when I telephoned. She sounded eager to help – glad to help. She's changed, Jess. She really has.' She looked at me for a long moment then said slowly, 'My God. No. You were pregnant. Was it Sam? Oh my God, Jess!'

I closed my eyes. 'How did you know? Would Jerry have known?'

Mum understood instantly the enormity of Jerry knowing.

'No. Of course not. I didn't know until . . . then. That was why – no wonder you were so shocked when he fell headlong for Jennifer. I can't believe it of Sam!'

I said, 'It wasn't Sam. It was Jock.'

Her amazement crescendoed. '*Jock?* Oh my darling. Did he . . . force you?' She put her cup down and took mine too, then tried to hold me as she had last night. I drew away. She kept saying, 'What – what, Jess?'

I took deep and measured breaths.

'No. He didn't force me. I was low. He was there. I can't explain.'

'My dear – my dear girl. I understand. Completely. It was almost . . . well . . . an accident.'

I tried to laugh. What an easy explanation of that evening. I tried to tell her about the wonderful aftermath when I had felt so . . . good. Surely no-one felt good after an accident. Then I tried to tell her about the abortion and the awfulness afterwards. The guilt that hung like an albatross around my neck.

'Listen, darling,' Mum said. 'It's done. And you've done what you could to put it right. Think what it would have been like if you'd gone through with it. Jean. And those boys. And Jock himself.'

I nodded.

She went on telling me what the doctor had already told me. This was a reaction and it was quite natural but it would go away.

'You're doing so well, darling. Finishing off the windows

in the abbey and starting to put a new roof on the kitchen. Looking after Watt and then having to give him up. Seeing Lucy into school life . . . that new friend . . .' She was pouring more tea. Gradually, skilfully, her conversation slid into day-to-day things. Jerry's domestic arrangements were pathetic, she said; he had one electric ring and a microwave. That was why there was no toast. But there were tins and he was going to bring in a chicken at midday and Mum was determined to start chicken soup. 'It'll take ages on that ring, but once you've had a bowl of that you'll pick up again. We'll have you back home in no time.'

I thought of home, which would be the schoolhouse of course; I thought of dear Bunny and dear Lucy. I didn't want it. Not yet.

I tried to explain that to Mum too. I used the word closure and she said it was psycho-nonsense.

'We can't impose on Jerry for too long, Jess. He was worried sick about you. He even wondered whether you'd tried to drown yourself!' She managed a laugh. 'As if! In three inches of water, I ask you.'

I closed my eyes and summoned my strength.

'Mum, I can go to the Armstrong Arms. You could take me there on the way home. You must go home, Mum. I'm all right. Lucy needs you. Please, Mum.'

She was silent again, staring at me. I hadn't strung so many words together since she'd arrived. She said eventually, 'Is there anything between you and Jerry, darling?'

'No.'

'Why did you come here yesterday?'

I shook my head; it was too hard to explain about Devizes being the last straw. I whispered, 'Matt was here.'

I finished eating and she gathered up the cups and plates and put them on the tray. At last she said, 'Jerry thinks you should stay here. He seems to think it's to do with Matt too.' She sighed. 'And he used that silly word.

Closure.' She looked at me and said helplessly, 'I don't know what to say, Jess. You certainly can't go to a hotel. And you don't want to come home. Would you stay here?'

I didn't know. I didn't seem to have any will left. I shook my head.

Mum sighed. 'If you would let me stay too . . .' I shook my head again, violently. She said, 'All right, all right. What you said just now – about Jennifer – is that why you want me to go home?'

I nodded.

'Look, Jess. I know that Jennifer has been a naughty girl.' She stopped there and took a breath. 'All right. What she did . . . darling, you have to live with it. You have to know that Matt never stopped loving you. Once you accept that, you will be able to love her again. She has found what she's been looking for all her life, Jess. Contentment. Fulfilment. Call it what you like, but now she's got it. Can you begin to imagine how she feels about . . . it all? All that stuff – stupid irresponsible behaviour – from her past?'

I put my head back and closed my eyes. So Mum knew. Dad must have told her about what happened in Plymouth. But she didn't know about Devizes and even if she did it wouldn't mean to her what it meant to me.

I whispered, 'Please go home to Lucy, Mum. Please – please – don't let Jennifer look after her.'

She just stood there with the tray on one hip, not knowing what to do. I couldn't feel any sympathy for Jennifer and I didn't think I ever would, but I did feel for Mum. She had obviously forgiven Dad and I suppose she had forgiven Jennifer. Anyway, she couldn't stop loving her as I had.

At last she said, 'Let me talk to Jerry when he comes home. He can't be expected to look after you, Jess. Perhaps . . . tomorrow you might feel able to get up for a few hours. We'll see. I want you to sleep again now. And try not to think. Of anything.'

She was gone, closing the door gently behind her. And I pushed myself down in the bed and slept. Again.

When Mum came back she announced it was two o'clock and I'd better have some of her chicken soup. I'd been awake about two minutes and I managed a smile.

She said, 'You'll have to get up and come to the dining room.'

I looked at her; I didn't want to move but I knew this was a test. She helped me to dress. She had washed my clothes and dried them but couldn't find an iron. This worried her ridiculously and I had to force myself to reassure her. But of course it wasn't the lack of an iron that was getting to her; it was everything.

'Listen, love,' she said. 'Jerry has a girl who comes in to clean once a week. He's gone to the village to ask whether she could manage a daily visit. Get some food, do some laundry. But Bunny and I will be coming for you at the weekend. He can drive your car home and I'll drive you.' She saw my face and added, 'Lucy will be with us.'

'Mum, I'm sorry.' I stood up to button my jeans and had to sit down again quickly. 'It's just that . . . I can't face it all. Not just yet.'

Mum was brisk. 'Don't worry. Everyone knows you have to spend time down here anyway. Jerry says work has stopped for a couple of weeks. Waiting for a crane, did he say? When you get back, we'll have a quiet weekend.' She opened the door and I moved towards it. I felt light-headed, as if I had been ill for weeks. As I passed her she said, 'Ray would like us to go away after Easter. It might be good for you to have the place to yourself for a few days.'

I paused, holding the door jamb. Mum was as good as telling me that I was going to have to pull myself together.

I felt much better after the soup. While she was busy remaking the bed, I took my bowl into the kitchen. The Gully boys had hung an enormous sheet of builder's plastic between the old part of the kitchen and the new bit so that the area was relatively free of dust and rubble. The sink was huge and I washed up the few things Mum and I had used. It was all a bit like the so-called kitchen at the office, but it was usable.

Jerry arrived back just before teatime. I heard the car draw up outside and glanced nervously at Mum. She lifted her shoulders helplessly. All of a sudden I realized what an absurd situation this was for Jerry. The whole business of him having to drag me out of the stream and through the wood, put me in the bath and pull off my clothes . . . It was just that: absurd. And if he really thought I'd been trying to drown myself he must despise me completely.

Voices came from the hall and then he opened the door and held it for someone else. I had a horrid feeling it might be the interior decorator, Helen, but it was a woman of Mum's age.

'This is Violet, Mrs Maslin.' He was speaking to Mum. 'It's her daughter who does the cleaning here. She's had some experience of nursing.'

She didn't come into the room. 'Pleased to meet you,' she said formally. 'I know it's difficult here without proper cooking facilities – my daughter has told me all about it. But I've got till the weekend spare. And Mr Jerome says I can microwave frozen meals, so that's no problem.' She smiled at me. 'He said you were having bed rest, my dear.'

I started to apologize to anyone who wanted to listen but Jerry came over and put his hand on my shoulder and Mum said loudly, 'Jess is trying to get her strength back bit by bit, Violet. I'm sure she will be better by tomorrow or the next day.'

I nodded emphatically and moved away from Jerry's hand. He said heartily, 'That sounds ideal.' He went to the door again. 'Shall I show you where everything is, Violet? Here, let me take your case to the other guest room.' He eased her back into the hall.

Mum was even more worried. 'Darling, are you going to be all right? She seemed to want to get you back into bed.'

It was what I wanted more than anything else. I knew suddenly that I shouldn't be here; it was Jerry's home and I had taken advantage of our many connections and landed myself almost literally in his lap. It seemed less obtrusive if I hid away in bed. I let Mum lead me back to the room she and I had slept in, and then I turned and looked at her pleadingly. 'What's the matter with me, Mum?'

'You've just come to the end of your rope. Give yourself time, Jess.' She helped me into my nightie, tucked me into bed and sat next to me, stroking my hair back. 'Be kind to yourself, darling. Please.' She said other things too, lovely motherly things that made me want to cry. But she hadn't really answered my question. There was something in me that was making me do the wrong thing. Every time. Every single time.

Violet came in later with an invalid's supper on a tray. She was glad I was in bed; that was where I should be. She told me that Mr Jerome had bought all this lovely stuff in Avebury and I was to do my best to eat it up. She talked to Mum about me as if I wasn't there and even began to spoon melon balls into my mouth. I took the spoon from her, smiling gratefully, and she actually called me her 'good girl'. Mum thought I would mind and looked at me warily, but strangely I didn't mind. It was so restful to hand myself over to Violet and play the invalid.

Mum left. That was not good. I could have clung to her except that I wanted her to go just in case Bunny was on the point of phoning Jennifer for help. She said she would be back on Saturday and if I wanted to come home sooner than that I was to phone her. She made me promise all kinds of things: I agreed to anything she asked.

Violet came and collected my tray and said Mr Jerome would be visiting me in about half an hour. He had to make some phone calls and eat his own supper and then later someone was coming to discuss the new kitchen. I knew then that I was a nuisance; I had to be slotted into his busy schedule and he wanted me to know it. Violet left me a whistle in case I needed her at any time – 'day or night', as she put it. 'There isn't a bell anywhere. But this whistle was in the drawer and I thought I would probably hear it better than a bell.' She beamed at me. I tried to imagine myself blowing the whistle day or night. I could not.

'Thank you so much, Violet. You are very kind.'

She looked roguish. 'I'm being paid well for my kindness, Mrs T.,' she confided.

There was another thing. I would have to find out just how much Jerry was paying her and reimburse him. My position here was becoming more untenable by the minute. Why I had ever assumed that Jerry would want me to stay on, I couldn't imagine.

He arrived in precisely half an hour. He had changed into jeans and an enormous sweater. He drew up a chair and sat on it and then glanced at his watch. I closed my eyes, opened them and forced myself to look straight at him.

I started with my prepared speech. 'Jerry, I really am sorry to impose like this. I simply felt I couldn't go back just yet. And I couldn't think of anywhere else to go. I shouldn't have done it—'

'What exactly shouldn't you have done, Jess?' he asked.

'Taken advantage of your hospitality.' My voice shook slightly.

'Or tried to kill yourself on my property – isn't that what you meant?'

I repeated Mum's words. 'There are only a few inches of water in that stream, Jerry. It wasn't over my face or anything.'

'If I hadn't come home and seen your car and come to look for you, would you have stayed there?'

'I don't know.' I remembered the sense of peace, of being one with the sky and the water and the earth. I did know.

'I think you would,' he said levelly. 'And hypothermia was in the offing as it was.' He started to get up. 'I know you're in a fragile state, Jess. I mustn't upset you. But you're intelligent enough to know that I'm very angry.' He went to the door. 'You can stay as long as Violet is here.'

He left.

I tried to ring Mum but she wasn't back and Bunny must have been putting Lucy to bed because there was no reply. After trying two or three times, I replaced the receiver and put out the light. And after another hour I switched it back on and fumbled about in my bag until I found a scrap of paper and a pen. And I sketched Lucy. The one totally good thing.

I intended to start ringing again as soon as Jerry left in the morning. But Violet had only just taken away a breakfast tray when there was a knock on the door and he came in. He threw a notepad on to the bed.

'I found it in your glove compartment. I went to look for the keys to your car – I don't want you taking it into your head to drive home today.'

I said, 'Thank you.' I picked up the notepad. It was for my shopping list at Hartford's. On the front page was written 'five farthings'. I said, 'I won't try to drive. But I'll ring my mother and she can fetch me. I'm perfectly all right and I can't think what possessed me . . .' I saw his expression and stopped. 'Jerry, I am so sorry. I had no intention of—'

He interrupted brusquely. 'I think you did. And the fact that you chose Marcroft was a kind of revenge.' He frowned. 'What for, Jess? That's what I need to know. What have I done that is so unforgivable?'

I was aghast. I tried to tell him that my actions had no such motive but he was evidently not convinced.

I said miserably, 'There's so much, Jerry . . . in my head. I went to Devizes and found out . . . something. And then I had to find Matt. And I thought he might be here.' Even to my ears I sounded insane. Perhaps I was.

His frown deepened. He pulled the chair forward and

sat on it just as he had done last night, on the edge, ready to leave. But he was still wearing jeans and jumper, so perhaps he was working at home today. My heart sank.

He nodded at the notebook. 'What does it mean, five farthings?'

'Nothing really. Five farthings is one too many in a way. There were only four in a penny, weren't there?' I drew a breath and tried a bit harder. 'It's from Oranges and Lemons. Don't you remember? "You owe me five farthings say the bells of St Martin's" . . . and then, if they're not paid' – I tried to laugh – 'you're executed.'

I didn't think he'd get it; I didn't get it myself. But he said, 'You're paying a debt, is that it? And you haven't paid it all. So you should be executed.'

I made another attempt at a laugh. 'I haven't quite worked it out yet.'

He sat back. 'Listen, Jess. Other people lose their fathers and their husbands. It's not some kind of punishment and it's not a debt. It's dreadful – ghastly – but it happens.'

I nodded. I wanted him to go. He was going to bring everything into the open and I couldn't bear that.

He waited but I said nothing and suddenly he changed tack.

'You think of this place as belonging to Matt. Is that it?'

'No. But he made it. The actual abbey. It was ugly and he made it beautiful.'

He leaned forward, elbows on knees. 'That's true. That abbey is his memorial. I like that, Jess. I like the thought that you were looking for him here.' His eyes held mine. 'Was that it? Tell me.'

I said miserably, 'I think so.'

'And then, when you lay down in the water . . . did you want to join Matt? Or were you paying out another of those farthings?'

I wailed, 'I don't know! I don't know, Jerry.'

He would not let go. He said inexorably, 'Who told you about Matt and Jennifer?'

243

I could have moaned aloud then; but our society has no place for keening women. I said, 'Jean first. My friend. Only not my friend because of Jock. But then Marilyn.'

His eyes narrowed. He was sifting the information in that jumble of words. He said, 'Ah. Marilyn. Your father's . . . friend. I see.' He sat back. 'And Jean is no longer your friend because of Jock. Who is . . . ?'

I sobbed. 'Her husband.'

'Her *husband*?' He looked outraged. 'You slept with your friend's husband? I knew you were vulnerable. But for God's sake, Jess—'

I closed my eyes and said loudly, 'I was pregnant. I had an abortion two days ago. And then I found out that Matt and Jennifer had been to the Full Quart in Devizes. *Devizes* – do you hear me? Matt took Lucy and me there. It was special – nobody realizes – it was so special. I thought I might have been pregnant after that but I wasn't! But it was still special. The last time we were together – and she has spoiled it all! All of it! Everything!' My voice had risen to a near scream. I lowered my head almost to the duvet and covered it with my hands. I was making terrible noises, choking noises. Suddenly I was no longer speaking to Jerry. I was speaking to Matt. 'There was nothing else to do then, was there? I'd got rid of the baby and then thought – it was my baby. Not Jock's. Mine. D'you hear me, Matt? It was my baby! And I got rid of it! So I ran for Devizes. I found the place, Matt. Where we were so happy. But you'd been there before . . . oh God, oh God, you'd been there before, Matt. So I had to look for you somewhere else. Where you worked. Where you created something so special . . .'

I looked up through my fingers and hair; Jerry was staring at me.

'Yes, I came here, Jerry Jerome. It wasn't only Matt. I wanted to see you. I wanted you to make me tell you everything – just as I've done now. I wanted you to take over like you always do. And you weren't here. So I went to the stream. And I lay down in the water. It felt warm. It was so . . . welcoming. I didn't want to kill myself – there's Lucy – how could I kill Lucy's mother? But I wanted so much to sleep.' I dipped my head again, held my hair, pulled it hard.

There was a sound of movement. I peered again. He was standing up. 'Violet said I could have ten minutes and I've had ten minutes. I'm glad we've talked.' He went to the door. 'Listen, Jess. Let it go now. You've told me and it's in my head. Not yours.' He opened the door and looked back at me. 'I want you to stay. Please don't ring your mother today. Just see how it goes.' I didn't reply and he said insistently, 'Please.' So at last I nodded. He nodded too. And was gone.

That afternoon I got up, showered and dressed. I went through to the kitchen. There was no sign of Violet so I made tea and took it to the sitting room and sat by the window that looked down to the woods. For the first time I noticed the sun and realized it had been shining all day. After so much rain it was marvellous and I looked and looked across the swathe of paving stones towards the snowdrops. Little grape hyacinths like rows of soldiers lined the edge of the woods and the rooks cawed from somewhere inside. I stood up and opened the window and immediately the room was filled with the song of black-birds. Weak tears burned my eyes; had I really wanted to leave so much beauty because I seemed to have lost the knack of living? Jerry was right; if he hadn't come back when he did I probably would have died lying in the stream, wanting to sleep there. I began to shiver again and closed the window. I had to face the fact that I could quite easily be mad.

Violet came in lugging bags of vegetables. She threw up her hands at the sight of me but didn't order me back to bed. She had been to the farmers' market in Marcroft and bought tons of fresh produce.

'All this frozen stuff isn't going to do you so much good

as some young carrots and peas. I said to Mr Jerome, I said, let's look after the body and then the mind can heal itself.'

I looked at the bulging bags lying on the carpet. There were sweet potatoes and corn cobs, young beets and parsnips; another bag of fruit.

I said, 'Am I mad, Violet?'

She stopped being brisk and nurse-like and said gently, 'I don't think so, love. Mr Jerome told me about your 'usband. You're grief-stricken, that's what you are. If that's mad then all of us who've lost our 'usbands are mad. And there's a lot of us. An awful lot of us.'

My eyes were burning again. I whispered, 'Thank you, Violet.'

She picked up the bags. 'Going to take me some time on that single electric ring. I'd better get started.' She paused. 'D'you want to help me clean some of these vegetables?'

I followed her into the barren area of the kitchen and we found paring knives and chopping boards and Violet produced an enormous skillet and began to heat it. We all ate together that evening, Jerry, Violet and me. We sat around the glass table and relished the compote of vegetables in a sweet and sour sauce. I cannot remember enjoying a meal more. I thought of nothing else except each separate taste, each chew, each swallow. Afterwards, Violet took the dishes away and brought coffee then said she would come to help me into bed in an hour.

I said to Jerry, 'You told me to see how it went. I did what you said. The birds . . . the flowers . . . all marvellous, Jerry. I think I'm better. Tomorrow I'll be able to go home.'

He stirred his coffee slowly. 'Stay over Easter, Jess,' he said. 'It'll be just four days more, that's all. It'll make a big difference to you. And to me too.' He smiled ruefully. 'Remember, it's in my head now.'

'Oh Jerry. I'm sorry.' I shook my head as he started to say something. 'It's not your problem. And I mustn't stay.

Mum and Ray are planning a few days away. There's Lucy
. . . the sooner we get back to Dip Lane, the better.'

'But not just yet. Let me talk to your mother. Please,
Jess.' I shrugged. 'Have you rung her today?' he asked.

'No. I promised, if you remember.'

'Has she rung you?'

'No.'

He said nothing for quite a while and I had nothing to
say. He went to the window and opened it as I had done. It
was dark now but suddenly from the wood came the sound
of a bird.

He spoke without turning. 'I've heard that before. Is it a
nightingale?'

'No.' I listened hard. 'I think it might be a nightjar. It's
early for them.'

He repeated quietly, 'Nightjars.'

'They're often mistaken for nightingales. Because they
sing at night.'

'It's a nightjar wood then.'

'I suppose it is.'

'Lucy will like that. A nightjar wood.'

I said nothing. He closed the window gently, turned and
went to the light switch. The wall lights came on and filled
the room with a quiet glow. He stood by the table, sipping
his coffee, and then sat down and looked up at me.

'Jess . . . maybe I shouldn't say this now. It's very soon.
But I've been thinking – thinking hard. And there is
something we could do. To get on an even keel again.' He
sighed and looked down into his cup. 'I can't make up my
mind about the debt – the five farthings. Who owes who.
Perhaps it doesn't matter. But that fifth farthing – it could
be important. It could set us straight.' He looked up
again and suddenly smiled. 'Don't say anything now. But
later . . . perhaps much later . . . would it be a good idea
if we got married?' He held up a hand as I moved involun-
tarily away. 'Please, Jess. Don't worry about it. But you were
considering Sam as a husband in a very practical light. A

father for Lucy, a partner for the business, maybe a kind and undemanding companion.' His smile turned down at the corners. 'Well . . . I think I'd fill the bill in the same way. And – quite important this' – his voice became jocular, removing any kind of threat or danger – 'I've already had my fling with Jennifer and am well over it.' He watched me; my face must have spoken a thousand words. He said quietly, 'I could love Lucy, Jess. That's why I gave her the car, you know. Not to buy her affection but because I knew I could love her.'

I made a sound of protest and he said quickly, 'This is not a proposal that needs any kind of comment, my dear. I've put it to you just in case it's a lifeline. But you need not reply and I won't repeat it unless you tell me to.' I gestured with one hand and he smiled again. 'Then that's all right. Come and have your coffee. Tomorrow evening, if this weather holds, we could take it outside and watch the sun go down.'

I drank my coffee standing and then said I would like to go to bed. He held the door for me and said goodnight and I managed to thank him. I didn't say what I was thanking him for. I lay in the big double bed and watched the moon through the curtains and knew a kind of peace.

Fifteen

I woke the next morning knowing I had had a whole night's deep and refreshing sleep. I hadn't realized that my head had been aching the whole time: it wasn't any more. I got out of bed without having to clutch the furniture and my legs were no longer shaking. I pushed back the curtains on a wonderful morning. It was Good Friday. I had always thought of it as a day of ritual sadness. But not this Good Friday. This Good Friday was saying something else . . . I think it might have been forgiveness. Anyway I showered and dressed before I looked at my watch and saw it was only six thirty. It was deeply satisfying to have woken early like this, found a special time for myself, and to feel almost in command of my own body again.

I opened my door inch by inch and crept into the hallway. No sign of Violet; the house was obviously still asleep. I went through to the kitchen. It was neat and pristine despite its air of a builder's yard. I switched on the kettle and found a mug and the tea bags and some milk in the fridge. It made me feel good assembling everything and then breathing in the subtlety of brewing tea. Just as yesterday the colours of the grape hyacinths and the song of the blackbird had seemed almost piercingly wonderful, so now did these small homely pleasures.

I took my mug of tea and went through into the sitting room; the sun streamed in and there were dust motes dancing on the edges of light. It was beautifully warm. Very gently I tried the key in the french door; it turned in its well-oiled lock and the door opened outwards and the fresh, cold air of morning came in. I stepped out on to the new paving stones that Jerry had said were for the benefit of Lucy's electric car. To the left of the french window there was a brand new wooden garden seat; I sat on it and put my tea on the ground at my feet. There was a slight swinging sensation but nothing like before. I felt myself smiling with sheer pleasure. Nevertheless I stayed very still for a while, letting the surroundings settle into themselves again. Perhaps because I was so motionless, a robin suddenly alighted a yard in front of me, cocked his head and surveyed me expectantly. I had nothing for him so I reached very gingerly for my mug, drank half the tea and replaced the mug as far as I could reach in his direction. He hopped around it for some time and then flew off. I watched him when he reappeared and pecked at the plantings on the edge of the paving. Then he ventured further into the growth around the house and was gone.

I stood up eventually and began to walk to the woods. There was no sense of horror at revisiting this particular place; when I reached the stream I couldn't see it as a deathbed. It was the place where Lucy and Sam had built a dam last year. That was all. The banks were still muddy but after a few days of this weather they would dry out for the summer. I stood there, leaning against a tree, watching the water slip over the stones. It had been peat brown just two days ago, swollen by the rain higher up. Now it was clear and where the sun streamed between the treetops it sparkled. It reminded me so much of Lucy, full of vivacity and excitement for the next day, the next hour, the next minute. I should have yearned for her; a normal mother would have insisted on going back home immediately to see her daughter. But I didn't yearn for anything or anyone. I felt surrounded, and part of so much; the whole world was condensed into this one spot. I was content, more than content. There was a glory in this morning and I was there; it was in me too.

I might have transcended completely – who knows? –

except that a tiny sound made me turn suddenly. It was Jerry, of course, and he caught me before I keeled over. He was understandably annoyed.

'What do you think you're playing at, Jess? It's not eight o'clock yet!'

I smiled at him and separated us gently, wedging myself back against the tree. It would have been very difficult to describe my peculiar oneness with everything that was happy that morning, so I just told him I was better.

'And that's why you fell over just then, was it?'

'Bit dizzy.' It didn't worry me. It was like a zoom lens, whirling me around so that my impressions became panoramic. I said, 'Please don't worry, Jerry. I'm all right now.'

He looked baffled and I realized I was smiling broadly and idiotically. He said, 'I took you in some tea and you weren't there. Looked out and there was a half-empty mug on the patio. Ran here as fast as I could and there you are staring at that bloody stream. What am I expected to think?'

I knew what he meant but I couldn't pursue that line. I controlled my smile as best I could. 'Jerry, please believe me – I was not trying to kill myself. I was trying to – to – *attain* something. I think it's happening now, this morning. And I have to thank you. I don't know how to. I want something to – to show you – how I feel.'

'Well, it won't be here by the water. Sorry, but I'm tempted to culvert the stream.' I shook my head. He said, 'All right. But please come away.'

He took my arm and I didn't try to shake him off. In fact I was grateful for the support; my strength was not going to last long. We began to walk back through the snowdrops and grape hyacinths like two invalids.

'Have you thought about what I said?' he asked.

I couldn't think what he meant. 'No,' I said.

He glanced sideways at me, obviously put out, but said, 'That's all right. I told you not to, didn't I? And I told you I

251

wouldn't mention it again, but I rather hoped that this sudden euphoria was because you saw my proposal as the answer to everything.'

'Oh.' I remembered now. 'The proposal. Perhaps that was why I slept so well.' My smile widened. 'It's part of why I'm so grateful. Thank you for that too, Jerry.'

He stepped over a clump of flowers – I liked him for that. 'This is like walking through treacle.'

'It's not very muddy here.'

'I don't mean literally, Jess. I mean this conversation. Are you thanking me for a good night's sleep or my proposal?'

'Everything. Somehow you gave me today. The sunshine and the sky and the birds and the flowers and the woods—'

'All right, all right. I get the message.'

'But it's your doing – you took on all the . . . terrible things. You took them away, Jerry. You told me they were in your head. And I think they must be because they're not in mine.'

He led me through the last of the hyacinths and on to the patio.

'I'll keep them, Jess. For good and all. How's that?'

I laughed. 'Oh Jerry. It won't be like that. But . . . there's today.'

He said urgently, 'Make it the four days. If you can let me have them for the next three days, you'll be stronger.'

My voice suddenly dropped to a whisper. 'Look. Now d'you see what I mean? We're part of something quite wonderful and very important.'

He looked. My mug sat where I had left it. And on the rim the robin perched fearlessly and dipped his head into the cold tea. We stood very still, watching. When the bird flew we followed it with our eyes, in unison, like the crowd at Wimbledon watching a ball. And then it disappeared into the trees.

I said, 'Yes. Thank you, Jerry. I would like to stay until after Easter.'

I was glad to go back to bed after breakfast. I woke at eleven when Mum rang. Lucy came on the line and asked if I felt better. She sounded subdued. I said anxiously, 'Darling, what about you? You don't sound your usual self.'

'I don't know how ill you are. And Gramma says I can't come and see you just yet.'

'It's only because I'll be home soon.' I was tempted to say I'd come home the next day but remembered just in time that I had promised Jerry I would stay another three days. 'What I would like to do, Luce, is go back home to Dip Lane. There's a lot to be done to get the house ready for the summer. What do you think?'

She was unexpectedly enthusiastic. 'Oh *yes*. We could get out my tent too, couldn't we?'

'It'll need airing. Yes, we could.'

She said earnestly, 'Mummy, I'll look after you. I'll put my stuff away every night and wash up. And – and – I could sleep with you.'

I smiled. 'Like we did before?'

'Yes.'

'That would be nice.'

She said other things; about Andrew's father leaving again after three whole months of living at home. I think she might have been trying to tell me that Matt was still with us in a way. I'm not sure. She was only five, after all.

I spoke to Mum, who was determinedly upbeat; then to Bunny, who asked me why I didn't want Jennifer to see Lucy.

His simple and direct question was like a gunshot.

I said, 'Is there a problem about it?'

He said, 'Frankly, yes. She called in earlier this morning and your mother said she and Lucy were just going out. She kept Jennifer at the door. She was making signs at me behind her back to keep Lucy out of the way.'

I knew I couldn't bring the whole business of Jennifer out of its dark cupboard; not now. Certainly not on the phone. But his words made me realize that some time I would have to . . . explain.

I said, 'Is Mum in earshot? Or Lucy?'

'No. They're in the kitchen.'

'Bunny, I'm so sorry. You've been good and kind to all of us. But there are things you don't know. I will try . . . later . . . to tell you. Not now. But I beg you not to let Lucy go back home with Jennifer. So long as you are there . . . can watch and listen . . . but . . .' My voice trailed off miserably. Obviously I sounded paranoid.

He said heavily, 'All right, my dear. But the problem is, Lucy would like to go and stay there. See Watt again. You must take this into consideration. Later.'

I told him I would and he was so sweet and said I was just to concentrate on getting better. I put the receiver down and swung my legs off the bed. For an instant the sense of total bleakness was there with me again; but then Violet tapped on the door and came in with an early lunch.

'Mr Jerome says d'you mind eating here today. He's got a meeting in the dining room then he's taking some people from the council out for a late lunch.' She smiled. 'He says you're here till Tuesday. Now that's good. If we could get you up and about a bit tomorrow it gives you another two days to get back to normal.'

I was curious about Jerry's meeting with the council, but not that curious, so I smiled and looked at the tray, which bore a bowl of soup and a roll. It smelled delicious. And Jerry was extending my four days to five. I need not think about Jennifer for five days.

I watched him and four other men leave in the car and then I took my tray to the kitchen and washed up. Violet came out of her bedroom wearing her coat and carrying a handbag.

'I thought I'd have the afternoon with my daughter. So long as I see her in the afternoons, I can stay on for a bit.'

254

She hesitated, looking at me. 'Will you be all right? I won't be more'n a couple of hours.'

I was thrilled. It was more precious gift-time. I actually went to see her off, as if it were my house. And then I went into the sitting room and gathered up some glasses and a sherry bottle; washed the glasses, binned the bottle, put the glasses back in the sideboard . . . as if it were my house. I looked around the sitting room and realized that some of the seating units I had noted on our first visit here were actually low bookcases. I squatted and examined the books. Novels, reference books, maps, most of the Churchill volumes . . . If these were Jerry's choice, it proved a catholic taste. I began idly to put them in order. One area for reference, one for light reading . . . another for the pile of maps. I was pleased with the result. I went to the other side of the room and surveyed my handiwork; came back and changed the maps to another bookcase. Surveyed again. Something was missing. I went back to the kitchen and then the little storeroom that served as a utility room. I could not discover one single vase. But there were plastic buckets.

I went outside. The Whitsuntide Bosses were flowering early this year and prolific. I broke off some sprays. There was verbena and mahonia, white and lemon, and a great deal of berberis and other berried shrubs. I took in my gleanings and arranged them in three buckets and stood them around the sitting room. Then I fetched some ivy and trailed it around the base of the buckets. They looked beautiful. I smiled idiotically: exactly as if it were my house.

Jerry phoned at five o'clock.

'It's going to go on for a bit, Jess. I wanted to take you out to dinner tonight but perhaps tomorrow would be better. Are you all right?'

'I'm absolutely fine. I'm having a lovely time, actually. Thank you, Jerry.'

'Don't keep thanking me! And don't wait up. This lot will expect the works and I'll be pretty late.'

I thought I should show some interest and said in a jolly voice, 'What on earth are you doing with the local council members, anyway? Do I smell bribery and corruption?'

He was silent for so long I thought I had offended him and started to tell him I was joking. He said, 'Well, yes. I rather assumed you were. But I'm confused. Who told you my meeting was with the council?'

'I thought that's what Violet said.'

He laughed suddenly. 'I told her it was the consortium. We're looking at tenders for a big project in the centre of Bristol.'

I laughed too. I put down the phone still laughing. I hadn't laughed for so long; it felt good. I went to get myself a cup of tea and decided that I would spend the evening cataloguing Jerry's books. There weren't many and it was probably a waste of time. But I wanted to do it. Make my mark.

Violet came back with what she called 'Good Friday fish'. It was halibut. Too good to fry so we used the microwave and I made parsley sauce with parsley from outside the kitchen door. Violet said her daughter knew someone with a cooker they wanted to sell. 'It'd pay Mr Jerome to get it just temporary like. Ridiculous to have to manage with one ring and an electric kettle.'

I told her about his plans for the new kitchen.

'Ah . . .' She nodded. 'That's why that woman was here, I suppose. My daughter told me about her.' She glanced at me sideways. 'Been a lot of ladies here, Mrs Tavener. I expect you know.'

'I do.' I smiled at her. 'I'm not one of them, Violet.'

'I know that. Mr Jerome told me about your poor husband. And how you've thrown yourself into his work and just plain overdone it.'

It was one of Marilyn's simplifications and I liked it very much. It made me sound almost normal.

We ate the fish and set some aside for Jerry in case he was hungry when he came in. Violet went to her room. I fetched my notebook and found a pen and began to list Jerry's books. I had to lie full length on the floor because of the low shelves and I was just thinking that I must get up and switch on a light when the beam of a car's headlights swept across the windows. I stayed where I was, invisible, waiting for Jerry to come in; I wanted him to see that in order to choose a book this was the position required. I heard his key in the door, then the hall light went on and a female voice called, 'Jess! It's me. Where are you?'

It was Jennifer.

For a long moment I was transfixed. I had felt safe here at Marcroft and in an instant that illusion was shattered. All the silly, impractical plans I had made to cut Jennifer right out of my life were shattered. She was here. The enemy in my midst. My sister. I put my forehead on the floor and closed my eyes.

She called again and began to walk down the hall. I heard Violet's door open and her voice say, quite aggressively, 'And who might you be?'

'I am Jennifer Maslin. My sister is staying here – she's not well. I've come to see her.'

There was a pause; I could visualize Violet sizing up Jennifer. I kept my forehead pressed to the floor.

Violet said, 'No lights on so she's gone to bed. I'll go and see if she's up to seeing you.'

Jennifer began to protest that of course I would be up to seeing her but Violet was plodding towards my door and didn't reply. The next thing was, of course, the discovery that my bed had not been slept in.

'She isn't here, Mrs . . .' Violet couldn't remember the name. She was trying hard to keep panic out of her voice. 'She must have gone for a walk. To see the sun go down. She enjoys the outdoors – birds and things.'

'Are you sure?' Jennifer said. 'Let's just switch on the light – is the bathroom through here?'

The voices receded as they searched the bedroom. I began to feel very foolish; I would have to scramble to my feet, call them and make some excuse about dropping off in the chair. I had actually pushed myself up on to my knees when the voices emerged into the hall again.

Violet said, 'I'll come with you because I know where she likes to go. It's where she had a picnic with her husband and her little girl—'

Jennifer's voice interrupted. 'Oh my God! There's the stream there!'

The front door opened and then closed. They were gone.

This was ridiculous. I knew it even as I stood up and closed my eyes with sheer relief. I couldn't put Violet through this anxiety. I had to go out and call to them and look as stupid as I felt. I was fast getting a reputation as a would-be suicide and it was not pleasant. I certainly didn't want to take that kind of baggage home with me for poor old Mum to carry.

I went through into the kitchen, switched on the light and closed the door behind me, wondering if it would be possible to pretend I had been there all the time. The roof-space was covered with tarpaulin, which would act like a blackout curtain as far as light went. I dithered around like a schoolgirl, going to the table and back to the micro-wave, then filling the kettle and plugging it in so that I could say I was making tea . . . and then I got as far as the heavy-duty plastic sheeting which separated the new kitchen from the old part. I pushed at the edge and got myself through and had to feel my way to the door into the abbey itself. The key was in this side; I turned it and the door opened on well-oiled hinges. On the other side it was horribly dark; I closed my eyes and counted ten, opened them again and could just see the line of windows emerging from the overhang of the minstrels' gallery. I closed the door quietly and shuffled across to the nave. I was fairly certain there was nothing on the floor, but I hadn't been in for some time now; it could be covered in building materials. It wasn't. I came out from beneath the gallery and turned right and went carefully up the curved wooden steps to the gallery itself. Sam's table and stool were still there. I fumbled the stool out from the table and sat on it, my arms on the ledge of the gallery. From here I could see the windows. The colours were changed: the blues were deep purple, the reds black. They took on a new beauty; frightening, almost menacing. I squinted through the gold and tried to find a star; either there were none or the colours would not let them through.

The thick walls of the abbey admitted no sound. I sat there for what seemed like ages, waiting for something to happen, praying that they wouldn't summon the police. I could have put a stop to it by going back in and calling to them. I didn't. My limbs were shaking again and I knew that if I moved suddenly those dark and threatening colours would take on a life of their own and swing crazily around the nave. I stayed very still.

At last there was a sound; someone was trying the main door beneath the enormous porch. The handle clanked as it was turned, and there was a thrust of wood against the metal of the bolts. A voice called faintly, 'Jess! Are you there? Jess – please answer!'

There was nothing for it, no escape. I called something back and trudged down the staircase and down the length of the nave and shot the bolts – again, so easily. Sam had been busy with his oil can.

The door swung towards me and there they were, Jennifer and Violet.

Violet said, 'Oh, thank the good Lord! We wondered where you was got to!' I said nothing and Jennifer just stood there, and now that my eyes were accustomed to the darkness I could see tears streaming down her face.

'Might have guessed you'd be here,' said Violet. 'Your husband's place of work an' all.'

I swallowed. 'I wanted to see the colours at night. They are rather . . . spectacular.'

We waited for Jennifer to make a comment; when she didn't move or speak Violet said, 'Let's go back through this way, shall we? Then we can bolt up after ourselves. Mr Jerome would want everything done proper. This is 'is pride and joy, this is.' She nudged Jennifer forward and I turned and walked the way I had come while they saw to the bolts. I was through the plastic into the brightness of the new kitchen before they rejoined me. I didn't look at Jennifer.

'I need to go to bed soon. Could you wait till tomorrow?'

There was a gulping sound from Jennifer. 'I have to get back tonight, Jess. Sam wasn't at all keen on me coming.'

Again that awful silence descended on us. Violet said uncertainly, 'I'll go back to bed and let you two have a chat. But you're right, Mrs Tavener. You must get your rest. You've been up and about quite long enough.'

Jennifer faltered, 'I didn't realize . . . I didn't know. Mum hasn't said much. I would have come before.'

Violet said much more definitely, 'Mrs Tavener has been very ill. Very ill indeed. She's making a good recovery, as you can see. But she needs a great deal of sleep.'

'Oh Jess.' Jennifer's voice kept catching. 'I'm so sorry. So very sorry.'

Suddenly everything steadied for me. I had run like a frightened rabbit from Jennifer but I couldn't keep it up, not for the rest of our lives. I felt a return of the old weariness; it settled on me, vice-like. 'Let's go into the sitting room,' I said. 'Violet, you go on to bed. I'm sorry about this upset.'

Violet said something propitiating but I was already in the hall walking its length to the sitting room, switching on the wall lights and going straight to the french windows where I knew that, in spite of the blackness, the grape hyacinths still marched towards the clumps of snowdrops. I sensed Jennifer behind me, standing, not knowing what to do. I suppose I should have felt a certain triumph at holding the whip hand for once. But I did not.

She said, 'Won't you sit down, Jess? Please.'

I turned immediately and sat on one of the low book-shelves. I could get up quickly from there. Jennifer squatted on the edge of one of the leather chairs. For the first time I looked at her and understood why Sam might be worried about her. Her face was chalk-white; she had scooped her hair back again but not into the usual ballerina chignon. She had twisted it and clamped it up with one of those enormous hinged combs. Wisps fell about her face.

I said flatly, 'You're not well either. Pregnancy doesn't suit you after all.'

'It's not pregnancy.' She looked at me. 'You can't even use my name, can you, Jess? Do you hate me that much?'

I closed my eyes momentarily. Did I really hate her? My own sister – my baby sister who was so beautiful and clever and talented? I nodded then shook my head. 'I don't know. I don't know anything much any more. I simply don't want to see you or speak to you again. If that is hate, then yes, I hate you.'

She made a whimpering sound. I hoped she would get up and go but she slipped lower into the chair and put her hands to her face. Perhaps I had looked like this in Marilyn's little parlour when Jean had confronted me about Jock.

I said woodenly, 'Please don't be sick on Jerry's furniture.'

She put her head back, closed her eyes and breathed deeply. 'Marilyn told me. Not Mum. I don't want Mum to be blamed.'

'Marilyn.' I made a sound that could have been a laugh.

Jennifer said, 'I went to see her. When no-one would say where you were or what was happening. Marilyn knows most things. Hairdressers do.' She opened her eyes and looked at me. 'You would have given Matt a chance to explain. Why won't you do the same for me?'

'I might have done. Eventually.'

'But . . . what? Did something else happen?'

I looked at her for a long time. Maybe I thought there had been enough secrets in our family. Maybe I simply didn't think anything at all and the words just came out. Anyway, I said them.

'I had an abortion. They told me there would be a reaction and there was. I went to a place where Matt and Lucy and I had spent a night before. A honeymoon night. I thought there might be a baby from that night. But there wasn't. It was all so . . . ironic.'

She breathed, 'Oh my God, Jess. Why didn't you say something? Did Mum know?'

'Not then. No. She does now. She guessed when Jerry sent for her.'

'Who – what happened?'

'Jock Parslow. My best friend's husband. It's incredible, isn't it?'

She was silent, staring at me. Then at last she said, 'So you came here? You and Matt had stayed here?'

I laughed again. 'Oh no. This wasn't the place. The place was a pub. In Devizes.'

She stared for a moment, then her hand went to her throat. She made a low, moaning sound. Then she whispered, 'Jess . . . oh God. Oh Jess. Jess – please – give me a chance – please.'

'I know what you'll say. You'll tell me about falling in love with Sam who was married and therefore completely unattainable. Because Sam would have simply walked away from you. Just as he did from Jerry. There was no way you could seduce Sam. So you turned to Matt. Again. Matt, who was so good at understanding people, comforting them.' I shrugged. 'Well, you were comforted. Twice, I understand. And now you've got Sam. That's all there is to it, surely?'

She was weeping again. I pushed myself up from the cushioned bookcase and started for the door. It was like walking in thick mud.

She said, 'Wait. Just tell me one thing, Jess. One thing.' I paused. 'If Matt were alive,' she said, 'would you . . . make an effort? Would you try to understand and come to terms with it? Or would you leave him – take Lucy and start a new life somewhere else?'

I thought about it but it was too difficult. I started to move again.

She said on a rising note, 'Jess. Matt loved you – he never stopped loving you. And I love you too. I've been jealous of you all my life and I wanted so much to find what you'd obviously got. I shouldn't . . . I know I shouldn't have tried to steal what you had. And of course, I couldn't. Can you believe me if I tell you that Matt was never . . . carried away by me? He knew exactly what I was up to. He was – he was – like a favourite uncle. Giving a naughty niece some sweets.'

Something snapped. I was standing behind her; her face was turned up towards me. I swung round and hit it. I hated her then with all my soul. For speaking of Matt. For speaking of Matt in that way. Almost patronizing him.

It must have been an enormous blow because her head spun with my hand and she rolled right over the arm of the armchair and onto the floor. But she didn't cry out. She crouched there as if waiting for more, each breath a sob, but no other sound.

I'm not entirely certain that I would not have hit her again, but at that moment there was a click as the front door closed and then Jerry came striding into the sitting room and took in exactly what had happened.

He asked no questions. He said nothing at all. He picked me up bodily and carried me out of the sitting room, down the hallway and into my room. He put me gently on to the bed then went to the door again.

'I'll just say goodnight to Jennifer,' he said as if we'd had a pleasant evening together. 'Get into bed, Jess. You look tired.'

I didn't move. I listened with all my ears but he had

closed the door and I could hear nothing. He used the telephone in the hall; I was tempted to pick up my receiver and listen in but he would have known. After about half an hour, he reappeared.

'Sam is coming to take her home. He's bringing your mother's . . . partner. He'll drive Jennifer's car back. Nothing for you to worry about.'

I looked at him. 'Jerry, I'm sorry.'

'No-one ever had any control over Jennifer. We both know that. You cannot be responsible for what she has done.'

'I was apologizing for my own behaviour.'

Quite suddenly he sat on the edge of the bed and grinned. It was a huge grin. 'You did give her a corker, didn't you, Jess? I didn't know you had it in you.'

I couldn't summon an answering grin.

'It wasn't only that. I hid from her. It was cowardly. My whole attitude—'

'For goodness' sake, Jess. You were angry. Isn't that better than being frightened and feeling that life isn't worth living? Anger is positive. It's good.'

'Is it? I don't think so. Not really, Jerry.' I sighed. 'There's some halibut in the microwave. Salad in the fridge.'

He laughed then. Long and loud. Jennifer must have heard him.

'Oh Jess. That's real life. Salad in the fridge . . . flowers coming out every spring . . . robins sitting on mugs of tea. I thought you might have mislaid it again. You do realize that it's your ultimate strength, don't you?'

I shook my head, not in negation but with slow bewilderment. He was taking it all so lightly.

He said, 'I wish I could tape some of your sayings. Especially that one. Halibut in the microwave and salad in the fridge.' Quickly, almost with embarrassment, he dropped a kiss on top of my head. 'I'll take you up on that. It might avoid another row with Jennifer.' He moved to the door. 'Go to bed now, Jess. Please. Think about tomorrow. If the weather's good, shall we have a picnic?'

I looked up at him. I spoke words that would have been foreign to me not very long ago.

'You're a good man, Jerry Jerome.'

'I know,' he replied. And grinned again before going out.

I didn't bother to listen any more. I undressed slowly, heavy with tiredness. Against all the odds, I slept.

Sixteen

I didn't hear Sam and Bunny arrive or leave. And I slept past that magical time of early morning and woke as Violet tapped on the door with a breakfast tray.

She was anxious. 'Are you all right, Mrs Tavener? I was that worried and I didn't know what to do.'

I reassured her as best I could. I was still sleepy and the melodramatic events of last night now seemed far away and simply absurd. But beneath that sense of unreality I knew I felt better. I smiled at Violet and thanked her for the bread and butter and honey and the pot of tea. 'Looks so *good*,' I told her. 'I can't tell you how good it looks – how good everything looks.'

'Well, my dearie' – she put one hand on her hip and the other on the door – 'I do reckon that what went on here last night was like a boil bursting. Poison's out now. Am I right?'

I had a sudden vision of Jennifer crouched on the floor, waiting almost passively for my next blow.

'I don't know, Violet. I've always loved my little sister. Her – her – escapades seemed funny. I never considered that they might hurt other people.'

'She left you a letter. It's propped up on the glass table. She must've sat there and wrote it while she was waiting for her lift to come. Mr Jerome stayed in the kitchen. I got up but he said to leave Miss Maslin alone.' She smiled happily. 'He said he enjoyed the halibut.'

'Oh. Good.' Unexpectedly, I felt a pang of pity for Jennifer, sitting by herself, writing a letter and nursing a sore face where I'd hit her. How could I have actually hit my sister, who was pregnant? I shuddered. 'I'll read the letter later, Violet.'

But I couldn't leave it. I padded barefoot down the hallway and into the dining room. There was no sign of Jerry; he'd probably not gone to bed until the early hours. Poor Jerry. The letter was there, propped against a jamjar of grape hyacinths. I stared at them. There had been no flowers in the house until I filled the three buckets that were in the sitting room. The only explanation for the jamjar of hyacinths was . . . Jennifer. She'd gone out in the darkness and picked them. Why? She hadn't known that they were special to me, surely? I stared at the flowers wonderingly, then I picked up the letter, padded back to my room, sat up against my pillows and read what Jennifer had written. The handwriting said a lot; it was all over the place.

Sis. I love you. Remember that. I don't know where to start, what to say. Anything at all. But I don't want you to blame Matt. I am glad – really glad – that you turned on me like you did. It was my fault, Jess. It was always my fault. I could do it – I found that out when I was thirteen. I could attract men. It's not good, Jess. It's the sort of power that lots of women have and they nearly always abuse it. I've abused it to get what I want. Over and over again. It didn't work with Jerry – he seemed to want to show me what I was doing, what I was really like. He knew all about sex and power and he turned it against me. So I dropped him. Anyway I'd already met Sam and knew he was completely special. He could have hated me, Jess. He knows all about me and he could have really despised me. But he has not and he does not. But when I thought there was no future with him – he had Daisy and a new baby – that was when I turned to Matt. I loved Matt like a brother, Jess. But we haven't got brothers and I thought any

267

kind of love involved sex. It doesn't, does it? Sam and I sit for ages without even touching each other. We are so at ease . . . Perhaps that's what love is? Ease. You and Matt had it. And I wanted it. You and Dad had it and I wanted it. And when I saw Dad and Marilyn . . . Believe it or not, Jess, they were easy with each other. And I thought, why not? That's the way to get it.

Jess, am I making it worse? You must know in your heart of hearts that Matt loved you and I meant nothing to him in that way? He even thought I was mildly comic – like a character in an old film about vamps or something. What I said just now . . . about him giving me sweets . . . I didn't mean he handed out sexual favours to keep me quiet – nothing like that. But it didn't mean anything to him. There was never anything of what you had – he never took a thing from you, Jess, no ease, no fun. You and he were inviolable. I don't think death has changed that, not really. You and he are still inviolable.

Jess, please believe me when I tell you that Matt loved you the whole time. I can't really explain what happened. But, for what it's worth, I loved you too and I still do. Forgive me, Jess.

There was no signature. I found I was crying. I blinked hard and looked out of the window. It was another beautiful day. I knew I had to do something and I didn't know what.

I ate my breakfast eventually, then showered and dressed and took my tray to the kitchen to wash up. Violet was cutting sandwiches. She told me that Mr Jerome had given her the rest of the day off but asked her to make a picnic. I told her to leave it; I would pack everything up and see to drinks. She went off to her room and I started to clear up. It was nine thirty. Lucy and Mum might be ready to go shopping for Easter Day.

Suddenly I knew what I must do. I went back to my room

and dialled Mum's number. Bunny's voice answered: I could tell he was waiting for more bad news. It was up to me now.

I said, 'Bunny, I've been trying to think what to do. You know, to get back to some kind of normal living. I'll tell you and then I'll put down the phone and let you talk it over with Mum and Lucy. You can decide. All right?'

'All right.' He sounded apprehensive.

'You said Lucy wanted to go to see her aunt Jen. If she still feels like that, could you take her over to Two Lanes Cottage? Maybe leave her there for a couple of hours?'

There was a silence. I could imagine him remembering how Jennifer had looked last night: she probably had a very swollen face.

He said, 'We might not be welcome, Jess.'

'You will be. I promise.' I was absolutely certain.

'Are you going to phone her?'

'No. She'll know. She'll understand.'

'I wish I did.'

I said, 'Oh Bunny, I'm so sorry. I think it will be all right one day. Perhaps soon. I'm getting strong, really strong. I can work at it, Bunny. And I will. I promise.'

'That's the second promise, Jess.' But he was smiling, I could tell. 'Will you be strong enough to have Lucy with you in a few days so that I can take Monica away? Just a little break.'

'Yes. That's another promise, Bunny!'

He said something rather sweet then. 'I know you keep your promises, my dear. So thank you.' Then we said goodbye and he put down the phone.

I didn't stand about thinking of what I'd done. I went back to the kitchen and put the sandwiches into a plastic box and found a couple of clean tea towels for a tablecloth and went outside and down to the stream. By the time Jerry joined me it was almost midday. The towels were anchored with stones and the sandwiches sat prosaically in the middle of them. I had been back to the house twice and

269

fetched a bottle of wine and some glasses and a packet of biscuits. And I was standing barefoot in the middle of the stream making another dam.

Jerry came crashing through the trees and then stood, breathing heavily and watching me. I glanced up a couple of times, smiling, and panting because it was quite hard work lugging stones around.

He said at last, 'You can't keep away from it, can you? Has that particular water got some deep, dark, intense meaning?'

I straightened and eased my back painfully.

'This is a happy place.' I looked at him. 'That's all, Jerry.' I stepped over the wall of stones into the shallows. 'That's all it was before, you know. That's why I lay in it. I wanted happiness, quite desperately.' He said nothing and he didn't move. I picked up a slab of limestone and fitted it judiciously. 'Have you noticed that when you go looking for happiness it somehow escapes you? You have to wait for it to creep up on you.'

'I don't think I understand about happiness.'

'Oh Jerry!'

'Truly. I might have experienced it and not realized. But I certainly recognized it in Matt. And I knew it came from you. And that's why I had to look you up.'

I said nothing. I stuffed a handful of muddy leaves into a leak. The water was piling up behind the dam most satisfactorily. The level was halfway up the bank.

'Will that do, d'you think?' I asked.

'Do for what?'

'Swimming. Splashing.'

'Swimming? In that? You must be joking!'

'Of course I'm not. Oh, I know it's too cold now. But later in the summer . . . it needs to be at least knee-deep.'

'It's muddy!'

'Of course. But in the summer it won't be so free-flowing. Then the mud will settle.'

He came to the top of the bank and surveyed it dubiously.

'Whoever heard of swimming in water that only comes to your knees?'

'You thought I was trying to drown myself in six inches!'

'Panic reaction, Jess. But swimming? In thirty inches of mud?'

'I'm not sure. But can you see how good it would be? Lucy would love it.'

'I'll have a pool installed for Lucy.'

'You don't get it, Jerry! She needs to make it herself. Just as I have.'

'You're mad.'

I waded out, slipping in the mud. He ran down and grabbed my outstretched hand, pretending disgust at its slimy wetness.

I scrambled up and flopped down by the spread cloths. 'I think I have been mad. Yes. I'm not now.' I looked up at him. 'Sit down, Jerry. I want to convince you. I am more sane now than I have ever been.'

'Even before? When Matt was alive and you were together?'

'Yes. I think so.' I stopped staring at him and let my gaze drift up to the treetops. 'I was in a dream world, Jerry. Wrapped in cotton wool. When Dad died it was worse – they all wanted to protect me.' I lowered my eyes. 'You want to do it too, don't you?'

'Only for a time. Until you find your feet again. Is that bad?'

'No. It's wonderful. So long as you know when to stop.'

'When will that be?'

'On Tuesday. When I go back home.'

He drew his mouth down consideringly. 'All right,' he said.

I waited, thinking he would bring up his 'proposal' again. But he did not and I was grateful. I said, 'Tuna and cucumber? Or peanut butter.'

'Definitely peanut butter.'

I laughed and handed him the plastic box.

We sat for an hour after we had eaten, talking idly about the new kitchen and what equipment would fit into it. He asked me whether I would do some sketches for him.

'Can you do them to scale, Jess? I'm quite happy about artistic licence but scale drawings would enable me to start ordering stuff.'

'I did them for the glass roof actually.'

'I thought someone said you'd do them on the computer?'

I smiled ruefully. 'I'm one of those people who have to check the totals on calculators. I did my own drawings first and then put them on computer.'

'Sounds a long way round.' He looked at me and added, 'Story of your life?'

'I suppose so.'

There was a long pause which threatened to become significant, so I said, 'There's a new gas-fired Aga which I think we could start with. Let everything else fit in around it.'

He hesitated and I thought he would bring us back to that moment but then he pursed his lips and nodded. 'We have to start somewhere.'

'Sink next? You could keep that lovely big one. But I think you'll need another.' He nodded. 'How do you feel about an island workstation?'

His eyebrows went up. 'I haven't got a clue. Tell me about them.'

So I did. And at the end of that I began to gather up the boxes and glasses. He put the bottles in a plastic bag and then started to laugh.

'Sorry, Jess, but your labours are lost. Look at the swimming pool.'

The water had leaked through my pile of stones and the stream rolled happily on, dislodging another stone now and then, just as it had before. I tried to explain to him the joy of actually building the dam but he only laughed and told me he would make a pool for Lucy.

We went back to the house and sat outside the sitting room until the sun dipped behind the trees. Violet came back and made us supper and the three of us sat at the glass table and ate scrambled eggs; Violet gave us the latest news from the village and Jerry explained things to me: as he put it, 'who was who and what was what'.

Violet expounded. 'Roly Watts in number five is the firstborn of Farmer Watts from the Lower Farm. He married the girl from the Arms. He's expected to take on the farm when his dad retires. But he's got a decent job servicing tractors and she works in a teashop in Avebury in the summer. I don't see either of them wanting to take on that rambling old place.'

Jerry pulled my notebook towards him. 'Look, I'll do a sort of tree. People in the main street. Thirty-five cottages and the new bungalows up on top . . . but they're strangers in there.' He sketched busily, producing a line of boxes into which he wrote names.

I said, 'How do you know all this, Jerry Jerome? You're a stranger – you can't have been here longer than a couple of years.'

He raised his brows. I was getting used to it now; it had seemed supercilious when I met him first. 'I was born here, Jess. Thought you knew that.'

'I had no idea!' I was genuinely surprised. Jerry had always seemed such an outsider – in many senses.

He glanced at Violet. 'Are you going to tell the tale, Vi? You know more about it than I do.'

Violet actually blushed. 'None of my business, Mr Jerome.'

He grinned. 'Come on, Violet. It's no disgrace now. Those days are over.' He turned to me. 'It was when the wall went up across Berlin, Jess. It was supposed to stop East German refugees from getting into West Berlin. It did a lot of harm to the Russians. It was the time of Reds under beds. All that.' He made a face. 'Probably the reason I decided to be a capitalist.'

I wondered where this was leading. Violet patted my arm.

'He wasn't a communist, you understand, Mrs Tavener. Mr Jerome's father was escaping *from* the communists. How he got here, we never knew, 'cos he could hardly speak a word of English.'

I looked wildly at Jerry, who was grinning again.

'He didn't need English to woo my ma. They tell me he was good looking, with a way to him.'

'He looked like you,' Violet put in.

'Anyway, when he heard she was pregnant, he left in a hurry. And my grandparents didn't think much of it either. So Ma got a job as a general dogsbody at Atherton Hall.' He made another face. 'It's in Sussex. It's got a folly. Stained-glass windows. I told Ma we'd have one too. One day.'

There was a little silence. I was amazed. Violet said quietly, 'The two of them – mother and son – came back when Mr Jerome started his business. She knew he had his eye on Marcroft Abbey.' She sighed gustily. 'Fifteen years now, isn't it?'

'Last Christmas.' He nodded. 'I think she'd have approved, don't you, Violet?'

'Oh ah. In fact, I've often thought she had a hand in one or two things.' She patted my arm again. 'Like meeting your husband. And now you.' She saw my face and said quickly, 'I didn't mean . . . like that. I meant that you can carry on the good work. I think you should look at the kitchen. Takes a woman to plan a decent kitchen.'

Jerry laughed and, after a moment, so did I.

He said, 'We were talking about that very thing, Violet, while we had your picnic – for which many thanks.' He stood up. 'Well, that's that, then. Let's go outside and watch the sun go down and have an early night.'

He was doing it for my sake and I was grateful. I needed time to take this in. We stood among the grape hyacinths and looked back towards the west where the sun was sitting magnificently on the flat abdomen of England. I imagined it going down behind the Goose Bump where – perhaps – Jennifer would take Lucy outside to see it . . . and falling into the sea in Clevedon where the Gully brothers might well be watching.

Violet said goodnight and went indoors. And Jerry said, 'Violet was a good friend to my old ma. That's why she's here now.'

I swallowed. 'Jerry . . . I must apologize to you. I got you wrong. Right at the start. I've said some hard things.'

'I think you might have called me a bully. You certainly told me I was a control freak.' I could hear the smile in his voice. He said, 'I haven't changed, Jess. Because I had rather a romantic beginning doesn't make any difference.'

'Maybe not. But I rather think the beginning was less than romantic.'

'Could be.'

'And to understand . . . things. People. Their backgrounds. It helps.'

'Good.' He held up a hand suddenly. 'Listen!' From the wood behind us came a curious call. We waited. The call sounded again. He said quietly, 'The nightjars.' We stood in silence and listened. Then he said, 'He's calling for a mate. They'll be nesting in the woods.'

We waited for the end of the song. I found myself hoping the mate had appeared. Jerry said, 'They've got gaping bills, you know, and bristles inside them. They feed in flight. They're called frogmouths in some countries.'

It was such a down-to-earth remark I laughed. 'One moment we talk of romance, the next of frogmouths! How on earth do you know that?'

'I looked them up. If they're going to live in our wood I want to know about them.' He laughed too and turned back to the house and bed.

Later, just when sleep was about to engulf me, I realized that he had called it 'our' wood. He might not have mentioned his odd proposal again, but he hadn't discarded it. He was still a manipulator.

I woke to church bells the next morning. Easter Day. I got out of bed and pulled back the curtains: a quiet, grey day, no dancing sun-shadows on the paving outside, dampness on the wooden bench to the side of the sitting room.

I pulled on jeans and a sweater and went to the kitchen to make tea. Then I assembled cups and plates and took a tray through to the dining room. I found myself thinking we could buy a toaster and have toast . . . but bread and butter would be fine with boiled eggs. I had put the eggs on and set the timer when the telephone rang. It was Lucy.

'Happy Easter, Mummy!'

'Darling, how lovely. Happy Easter to you too!'

'Are you better?'

'Yes. I'm up and dressed. How about you?'

'I've been up *hours*. Gramma and me are going to our house today. We're going to clean it up nicely and get it ready for us to go home. Proper home.'

My heart tightened. I said, 'Dear Lucy. We'll have a lovely Easter holiday, darling. We'll get the summer stuff out into the garden and we'll have a walk over the hills . . . Don't let Gramma do too much, will you? We can do it ourselves next week.'

'All right. We've got a surprise for you. We're coming to see you tomorrow. I can have a drive in my car. Gramma says he's done the road right round the abbey so I can have a long, long drive.'

I bit my lip. I knew Jerry liked Lucy but this was all a bit much.

I said, 'Is it worth coming all this way when I'm home on Tuesday?'

Lucy said in a small voice, 'I want to see you, Mummy. Aunt Jen says you're getting better and Gramma says you're getting better and you say you're getting better. So why won't anyone let me see you?'

'Oh darling, of course you can see me! And I tell you what: I'll come back home with you and we'll go straight over the Goose Bump to our own little house.' It was breaking my promise to Jerry; I hoped he would understand.

Lucy was overjoyed and that was all that mattered. I asked her – apprehensively – whether she had been to see Jennifer, Sam and Watt yesterday.

'Bunny took me. He said Aunt Jen had had an accident and bumped her face and not to mention it. So I didn't. Watt was pleased to see me. He held up his hands for me to pick him up. He can walk really well now and climb the stairs. I said we'd look after him when Aunt Jen needed a rest.'

'Thanks, love,' I said dryly and she laughed. It would be good to be back home with her; she was tuned in to so much. I was thankful that her visit had gone well.

The eggs were hard-boiled so I cooled them quickly, grabbed my pen and drew faces on them. Violet loved them. She refused to open hers and put it in a plastic bag to take home to show her daughter. Jerry ate his stoically and when I commented on his glumness he swallowed and said, 'I heard you on the phone.'

'Oh.' I was disconcerted. 'Do you mind? She's keen to have another go in the car.'

'Don't be absurd. Of course I don't mind Lucy. I didn't hear that bit. I heard you say you were going home tomorrow.'

'Well . . . yes. She's worried about me. The only way to convince her that everything is back to normal is to . . . get back to normal.' I tried to laugh. Violet smiled and nodded emphatically.

'You're well enough, I reckon, Mrs Tavener. You leave this lot to me and make the most of today. Not a day for outdoors though, is it?'

I looked at Jerry. 'Are you free for a couple of hours? We could walk. I haven't seen the village properly.'

He nodded. I was reminded of the time before Christmas when I had delayed his lunch. He didn't enjoy having his plans changed in any way at all. I breathed deeply. It had been a halcyon time of recovery here; even Jennifer's arrival hadn't spoiled it. I didn't want anything to sabotage my strange sense of well-being, least of all Jerry being difficult.

We walked down the long drive and out into the lane and turned right towards the Armstrong Arms. The cloud cover sat like a pewter lid from horizon to horizon and I could feel my mood descending with it. Jerry strode silently along at a fierce pace and made no attempt to pause at the various marshy bits, leaving me to get up on the grass verge to avoid them. He was wearing boots, and I wore the old shoes I always keep in the boot of the car. As blisters began to threaten I could have wept; it didn't matter how tough his young life had been, how affectionate he sounded towards his 'dear old ma', he was still pig-headed and very nearly a bully.

We passed the hotel – I had hoped we would stop for coffee but when he kept going I felt bound to keep up with him – and the first of the straggly row of cottages appeared, a pair of semis, then the proper village street with its wide grass verge dividing into two around the war memorial. It was not particularly picturesque; like my own little town in the Mendip Hills, it was run-down and tawdry with a few modern additions. A fish-and-chip shop, a takeaway Chinese restaurant, a clutter of supermarket trolleys on the grass. I slowed right down and let him go on without me. This was what I had come to see. I needed to try to turn back the clock forty years to see how it must have been when Jerry's 'dear old ma' was seduced by an East German refugee. I sat on the bottom step of the memorial and looked around me. It was such an unlikely place for grand romance; yet, in these dull surroundings, how glamorous someone from Berlin must have seemed. I imagined him touching her face and saying words she couldn't understand, words that could so easily have been about love and marriage and a new life for both of them.

Jerry suddenly appeared and sat down by me.

He said, 'I know it looks like the village of the damned. It's just that at Christmas and Easter they all go to church and that's where they are now. Easter bonnets and so forth.'

I smiled, grateful for the normality of his words. It made me realize how easy we had felt together these past few days. Ease. Who had spoken of ease lately?

He said, 'That's my grandfather's cottage. There.' He pointed to one of a pair, both in dire need of double glazing. I was surprised the windows hadn't fallen into their overgrown front gardens. 'He didn't own it, of course. All the village belonged to the Armstrong family at the hall.' He straightened his back. 'I was too late to buy the hall. It was a retirement home when we came back here. But they were glad to get shot of the abbey.'

'Your grandfather took you in at last? Better late than never.'

'I was eighteen. A big strapping lad. He thought I would bring home the bacon. Literally. When I disappeared up to London each day, he took it out on my ma. So I told him a thing or two. Some people said I killed him. But when I bought the cottage and then, later, the abbey, they sang a different tune.' He looked at me, his expression hard. 'Money definitely talks, Jess.'

'Does it?'

'Oh yes. If you agreed to our partnership you would soon discover the truth of that.'

I stared over at the cottage where Jerry had learned such hard lessons and decided to ignore that.

I said, 'What about your mother? Did she agree with you about money?'

He looked straight ahead. 'She strived for it the hard way. She thought that my way had to be dishonest.' He stared down at the ground. 'I sail close to the wind. But I'm not dishonest, Jess.'

'She knew that.'

'I wanted to . . . screw the system, I suppose. People . . . most people . . . are such hypocrites.'

I said simply, 'Yes.'

'I know what you're thinking. You feel that everyone you know is a hypocrite. I felt that way about Matt and Jennifer when I found out about them. But I'm not so sure now . . .' He gave a rueful smile. 'It's not that simple, is it, Jess? Not black and white.'

I said, 'No. It's mostly grey.' I leaned back against the granite step until it cut into my spine. 'If he were still alive – and Daisy and her mother too – would they have gone on with their affair?'

'Is that how you see it? As an affair?'

'What else would you call it?'

'An affair sounds too . . . I don't know . . . precise. An affair is surely more than two completely separate incidents?'

'If he hadn't died it could have been many more.'

'But he did die. So it's still just two separate incidents brought about by Jennifer's . . . what would you call it – despair? Desperation?' He sat up suddenly. 'Wasn't that how you felt?' He paused and then said very deliberately, 'About the father of your child?'

My face must have opened with shock. He said quickly, 'I am simply asking an academic question, Jess.'

I said levelly, 'I told you all that when I was . . . ill. I don't want to talk about it again. Ever.'

'All right.' He sounded casual, as if it didn't matter to him.

I sat there trying to get my breathing back into order, feeling my heart pounding in my chest. I really had handed all that guilt over to Jerry. And now he was batting it back at me. The father of my child . . . Jock Parslow.

Jerry drew a piece of paper from his pocket: it was the

little map he had drawn last night. He pointed to one of the boxes and then across the road to the house next to the church. It was one on its own in a good-sized garden with apple trees and shrubs; well painted, with a new-looking porch.

'That's where Roly Watts lives. And his parents' farm is behind the Armstrong Arms. He couldn't have renovated the place without his present job. The farm will never support them so well.'

I looked at the map and then at Jerry. He saw that I wasn't taking any of it in. All I could hear were those brutal words, 'the father of your child'.

He said quietly, 'Sorry, Jess. But tomorrow you go home. I agreed to take on your . . . guilt . . . your five farthings . . . until you went home.' He forced a little laugh at that but he was very serious. 'I can't do more than that, my dear. What has happened – has happened. You can't make it go away or change it. It's there. I had to remind you. I can't send you back like a shorn lamb.' He frowned. 'You do understand that, don't you?'

I nodded dumbly.

He said, 'Right. It was just that. A reminder. I won't be around and everything that has happened will still be with you.' He sighed sharply and waited for a response from me. I couldn't think of one word to say. He flapped the map. 'Come on, have a look at Roly Watts's renovated cottage. Where he will want to stay.'

I swallowed and tried to concentrate. 'So what will happen to the farm?'

He smiled and patted my hand as if in congratulation, then said simply, 'I'm thinking of buying it. There's quite a bit of land. I could get planning permission for half a dozen upmarket houses.'

I hardly took it in; somehow I knew he wanted me to put forward a case for keeping existing farms but my head was still ringing with his previous words.

He thought my silence was disapproval. 'I know what

you're thinking. I know it seems a shame to remove the farm and develop the land but Marcroft is dying on its feet, Jess. It used to have a school, and now the kids are bussed into Avebury. More housing would mean more children and we'd get our school back. It would be a community again.' His voice softened. 'Ma used to talk about how it was when she was young and my father arrived. He picked fruit at the farm and she packed it to send to the canning factory. She wasn't pretty and because she was already thirty her father told her she was on the shelf. But he – she called him Ivan, I don't know what his name was – he thought she was beautiful. He got that across without the need for a common language.'

There was another silence. Then he said, 'Are you crying for my old ma, Jess? No need. She had a great gift. The ability to be happy. It didn't matter what happened to her, underneath all the pain, she was happy.'

He waited but I still could not speak. He said, 'You have it too. That bloody awful brook in the woods . . . You told me that made you happy. The snowdrops, the robin on your mug. The nightjars . . .' He put out a hand. 'Jess, stop it. You're going to drown.' I managed a snuffly laugh and he laughed too. 'That's better. And perhaps it's good to cry. They say it is, don't they? Have you cried much for Matt?'

I shook my head and fresh tears poured down my face. They were unstoppable.

He said helplessly, 'Well, let these be for him. Jess, I'm sorry. I shouldn't have reminded you of everything that has happened. It was pretty brutal, I admit. But you were pretty brutal about it yourself when you told me, so I thought – hoped – you could take it. But when I saw your face . . .'

I shook my head quite violently and he said, 'All right. All right.'

We went on sitting and I went on crying and then the church bells rang again and he pulled me up quickly and walked back down the street and the congregation emerged and began to drift towards the lychgate.

By the time we reached the Armstrong Arms it was one o'clock and my tear ducts had at last given up. We went inside and found a seat in the corner by a window.

'You look a bit like Jennifer looked the other night,' he commented.

'Great.' I managed a smile.

'D'you want to go and bathe your face?'

'No.'

'Oh.' He seemed nonplussed. 'Well then, shall we order some food?'

'That would be nice. But I want to ask you something first. Please be frank.'

'No problem there.'

'No. All right. Well . . . when I was drowning in tears back in the village, why didn't you hold me? Try to comfort me?'

'I don't do that.'

'But you did it. Ages ago. When you were trying to show me how it was for my father and Marilyn George.'

He sighed. 'That *is* what I do. I show people. I show people themselves. I don't offer comfort.' He shrugged. 'I did it for Jennifer. You saw it yourself. I did that – partly – for Matt too. And I did it for you. That's all there is to it.'

'You despised Jennifer. Do you despise me?'

'No. I respect you a lot actually. And I like you a lot too.'

'But you don't love me?'

He spread his hands almost apologetically then spoke an unequivocal 'no'.

'That's good.' I puffed a sigh of relief. 'You would know.' I smiled at him. 'I'm glad, Jerry. Because I couldn't possibly marry you unless you loved me and then I couldn't anyway because I don't love you.'

He stared at me. 'But don't you see, if neither of us is in love, then the partnership would be so much more likely to work. You of all people should be able to see that. My God, you've been let down by all the people you love – why fall down that hole again?'

'Sometimes you are so cruel, I can't quite believe it.' I shook my head, determined not to cry again. 'Listen. I have to learn to live with the people I love as they are. Not put them on any pedestals. Take on their weaknesses as well as their strengths. It's been so easy with Mum. You helped me a lot there, Jerry, and I thank you for it. But Jennifer will be hard. And Matt . . . Matt will be the most difficult of all.' I said nothing about Jean. I couldn't imagine Jean wanting to be near me again. I said, 'You have shown me what I am. And I know now I have no right at all to condemn anyone.'

'That has nothing to do with my proposition—'

'It has everything to do with it. I must stand alone before . . . anything.'

He didn't speak for a while and I was about to direct his attention to the menu when he said, 'And then?'

'Jerry, I simply do not know. You are so impatient. You will meet someone else who doesn't cart a lot of emotional baggage around with them.'

'But if I don't – and if you don't – you won't forget about this?'

'No. I'll never forget it. And what you have done for me. I will never stop being grateful, Jerry.'

'I don't want that. I'm offering you a partnership.'

I could have laughed then and told him he didn't know what the word meant any more than he knew what love meant. But of course I did not.

We ate. We talked about Marcroft. We walked back to the abbey and looked at the grey afternoon through the stained glass and felt the warmth of colour all around us. And then we stood at the edge of the wood and listened to the nightjars.

It was my last day at Marcroft. I had been nursed, cared for, shocked and hurt. But my feet were set now on the road to recovery.

Seventeen

I thought this whole terrible confession thing would end there with me going back home with my dear Lucy the next day and starting the long haul of reinventing relationships and my life at the same time. But it was not quite the end. There was one thing that Jerry had shown me which gave me a terrific boost. That was my ability to be happy. If I could stop looking inside and look out at what was happening in the world, I achieved some kind of balance that was – that had to be – happiness. Even when I had lost Matt – three times over, as it turned out – it had never quite deserted me. The joy of driving over the Goose Bump and seeing the tops of the Mendip Hills spread before me, just as they had been for thousands of years, was never-ending. Putting up Lucy's swing again in the garden was like erecting a symbol of the summer; the weather was very changeable after that Easter and often it seemed as if winter had come back. But there was the swing to tell us otherwise.

That summer I made sure that Mum and Bunny had time and privacy to develop their relationship: I can say honestly that it was a great pleasure to see it happening. I gave up trying to work out why Dad had turned to Marilyn; I still knew that he was a special and unusual man.

I had my old open grate replaced by a gas fire; Matt would have hated it but this was for my convenience. I also replaced the old garage doors with a modern up-and-over one that worked by remote control.

Stella Bearwood and I continued our friendship; she was

pregnant again after her husband's Christmas visit but was hanging on to her job at Hartford's. 'They run a crèche for the staff,' she told me. 'And there are lots of facilities – things for Andrew – so it's well worth keeping it going.' I admired her very much.

Then there was Jennifer.

I would probably never be able to forgive myself for hitting her that time at Jerry's. Or for hiding myself away in the abbey searching for sanctuary. Violet had said it was like a boil bursting and maybe it was for Jennifer. She seemed to think she was due for it and that it might have helped to give her a fresh start. She had changed, there was no doubt about that. Her brittle hardness was gone completely; she cried often and about the most trivial things, telling me shame-facedly that she must be the only person in the country to cry at *Coronation Street*. Sam thought it was lovely. I have never seen anyone so dotingly happy as Sam Clarkson. All down to Jennifer. So, like Dad, she must be a very special person. But why Matt? I still thought that she must have hated me to steal Matt. She had told me she had taken nothing away from me, that Matt had always loved me . . . but, as the Americans so pithily put it, I didn't buy that.

So I struggled on that summer, taking up my old role, trying to add something to it. I was not looking for resignation; I was looking for a moment of epiphany when I would understand and accept. The epiphany would not last, I knew that. But the acceptance might.

I drove to Marcroft when the steel girders were bedded, taking the Gully brothers to lunch at the Armstrong Arms and leaving them there to 'tiddle everything up', as Steve Gully put it. Then I drove across again when the crane arrived to place the glass roof on to the kitchen. Both times I took Lucy and she drove around the whole area in the wonderful electric car that Jerry had got for her. But he was not there.

After what Lucy called the 'crane day', I rang him and

left a message on the machine to tell him I had missed him. He took a week to ring back.

'I wanted to give you space for the work,' he said in his immediate way. 'I trust you completely and I want you to know that.'

'Oh Jerry. Thanks. It went well. Brian Edwards is taking the building inspector down tomorrow but he says there will be no problems. How does it look?'

'I'm not at home, Jess.'

I waited for him to tell me where he was and when he didn't I said, 'Are you all right?'

'Yes, I'm fine. How are you?'

'Fine.'

'How *are* you, Jess?'

'Really, I'm fine. It's as if that awful time never happened . . . No, I don't mean that because I'm glad it happened. That's what I mean. I'm glad it happened, Jerry.'

'What about Matt?'

'Matt?'

'Have you forgiven him?'

'I don't know. I don't even know whether I have the *right* to forgive him. But I need to understand him . . . why he let it happen. You see, if only I could get over the feeling that Jen was trying to hurt me, I could understand her in a way . . . because she turned to Matt perhaps . . . perhaps . . . in the same way I turned to Jock.' I took a deep breath. It still hurt to confront the awful thing I had done. I hurried on. 'I can't give Matt that kind of understanding.' I let the breath go and tried to inject some light into this sudden gloom. 'I've sort of got him on hold.'

'So you're happier about Jennifer?'

'I don't know. But it's necessary, Jerry. She's here, after all. The baby is due soon.'

'Maybe when you've got it straight with Jennifer you'll feel better about Matt.'

I sighed. 'It's so hard to find him now. I thought I knew him. I didn't.'

He said abruptly, 'Jess, I've got to go. What are you doing for the Jubilee?'

'Playground party. Mrs Sparrow has them making hats.'

'Great. Enjoy it. See you one of these days.'

I put down the phone with a sense of loss.

That evening, after Lucy had gone to bed, I talked to Matt as I had done just after he died, calmly and logically. I tried to tell him how cruel it was that we could no longer be face to face so that he could explain to me about Jennifer.

I said, 'I still cannot believe it, Matt. All that . . . what did Jen call it? All that *ease* . . . it seems to have meant nothing after all.' I paused, frowning. 'No, that's not true, my love. It was real and it happened for us both. I do know that. I mustn't throw that away. But if only you'd told me . . . But you wouldn't even tell me about Dad, would you, so it's not likely you would ever have told me about Jennifer. Ever.'

I stopped speaking and sat there remembering how he had lied about Dad. Then I said, 'Matt, was I so . . . *green* . . . that you thought I couldn't take it?' I paused again. 'Yes. Yes, I was, wasn't I? This gift I'm so pleased about . . . this contentment thing . . . it works two ways, doesn't it? My God, was I like some bloody awful Pollyanna person who couldn't take a dose of reality now and then?' I gnawed at my lip. 'All right, I'll take some responsibility . . .' I started to weep quietly. 'But, Matt, you were still unfaithful. I can only accept everything up to a point. Then I think of you and my sister . . . I might have been able to understand about Plymouth, but Devizes . . . perhaps in the same room where we were. What else did you do with Jen? Did you tell her she stood up and sat down like a camel? Oh God . . . oh God, Matt, how could you? How *could* you?'

And as clear as a bell I heard his voice in my head, genuinely regretful but also polite, almost bewildered.

'Jess . . . I'm so sorry . . . I simply put it to one side.'

I gasped and raised my head from my hands and waited. Nothing happened. I wanted to shout, that's not enough, you must explain, you must tell me you love me better than Jennifer, better than anybody in the whole world – but I knew it was a waste of time. That was that. Just as he had forgotten to hide those sketches, forgotten to do the VAT, forgotten to mend the garage door, so he had forgotten to tell me about Jennifer. He had 'put them all to one side'. She had not mattered any more than the garage door.

I sat there, thinking about it. I'd like to say it was instant understanding and forgiveness. It wasn't. But it was a chink in the wall I had put between us. And it was something else too. I didn't know what it was for some time; the only thing that improved immediately was that I slept for longer periods at a stretch. I no longer woke with a slight headache from turbulent dreams. I thought I had been relaxed before – after I came home from Marcroft. Now I was realizing that relaxation comes in stages. I waited hopefully for another stage. I thought it would be a widening of the chink in that wall between Matt and me.

On 2 June, Stella and I laid up trestle tables in the playground while other parents hung balloons all over the climbing frames and sorted out the start and finishing lines for the relay races, then we all had a picnic lunch in the hall with our children. Stella was very pregnant and looking a little lost; apparently Andrew had told her that very morning that he had changed his mind about the baby and didn't want one.

I said, 'Come on, Stella. You know very well all you have to do is to convince him that he'll still be number one—'

'He knows that already,' she said gloomily.

'He also knows he can't cancel the order now. The baby is due in September and that is that. So he's just stirring up some attention for himself.'

She said, still gloomily, 'How's your sister?'

'Any day now. She was hoping it would be on Jubilee Day but she rang this morning to say she would be here for tea.'

Stella said, 'It's all right for her. Devoted partner.'

'I know.' Sam had been bad enough with Daisy; he was

twice as bad with Jennifer. I said unconvincingly, 'You've got me. For what it's worth.'

'It's worth tons. And actually you'll be far more help than Mick would be. But . . . well, he's got more of a vested interest. I suppose that's all it is.' She laughed her big open laugh. Sometimes she reminded me of Marilyn.

The tea went really well and the games even better. Mum and Bunny came over and Sam brought Watt, 'So that Jen can have a bit of a rest.' There was no sign of Jean and her family. I was thankful. I dreaded coming face to face with Jean. She would cut me dead and it would hurt all over again and I had no right to be hurt. When we first came home from Marcroft, I used to wake with a jerk imagining that Jock had found out about the baby and had told Jean. Now I didn't do that any more: but I still felt totally incredulous at what I had done. And I wondered whether Matt had felt like that . . . afterwards.

The strange anomalies of bereavement no longer upset me; in fact they were a comfort. Since 11 September, both Princess Margaret and the Queen Mother had died. Grief was such a universal emotion.

Mrs Sparrow had rehearsed some of the younger ones in a maypole dance and I saw Bunny with a camera as Lucy wove her way past Andrew and Blodwen. For a split second I felt glad because I could show Matt. And then realized. And then smiled, because of course I would show him. Whether he could see was another thing; but I would show him.

Watt was walking well, a strange seaman's roll, hands held high for balance. He wriggled out of Sam's embrace and followed the youngest children as they tottered along with their eggs in their spoons and their faces set in concentration. The field was on a slope and Watt's nautical stagger accelerated until his legs couldn't keep up with his body and he landed with a bump. Lucy abandoned her egg on the instant and ran to pick him up and comfort him. His yell was like a siren for a few seconds, then he quietened and smiled. They were still so close. For Lucy's sake I had to try to love Jennifer again. As my sister. Nothing to do with my husband.

We gathered round the piano for the National Anthem and then trooped outside to watch the lighting of the bonfire on the Goose Bump.

Anna Maslin Clarkson was born in the early hours of the next morning. Jennifer had wanted a home birth with me in attendance. 'Like you were for Daisy,' she had said with a kind of diffidence. Perhaps she hoped it would bring us together and perhaps she would have been right, but it didn't happen that way. Anna was lying in completely the wrong position and after an agonizing and futile labour Jennifer needed a Caesarean section. Sam was with her the whole time and said there would never be any more children; she could not go through it again. I watched her with Anna and with Watt and was not so sure. She was proving to have that elusive quality of 'natural mother-hood'; she had a way of smiling right at the two babies as if they shared a secret. I thought it was more than possible that in time she would want a bigger family. Meanwhile she was still hoping to start her degree course in October. Mum turned her mouth down at this and I found myself saying, 'I admire her tremendously. We'll have to wait and see, of course, but unless things go radically wrong I think she'll manage it.' Mum glanced at me, surprised, then pleased. 'I'm so glad, Jess. So glad.' When I asked her why, she said, 'Because you can admire your sister. Surely that is a huge step?'

The long summer holiday began. Lucy had been at school a whole year and I wondered whether we should take a break and go to the seaside and perhaps take Andrew with us – Stella was on maternity leave from Hartford's and needed to rest. The three of us were talking about it one rainy Tuesday afternoon: Andrew wanted to go to a rainforest somewhere near at hand, and Lucy wanted to go white-water rafting. I wondered just what Mrs Sparrow had been teaching them.

I said, 'Can we keep our feet on the ground. Rainforests don't happen in this country. And white-water rafting is not allowed until you're both forty-five.'

Andrew hooted and Lucy drew her lips in against a laugh. She tried not to laugh at my jokes unless they were really funny and this one certainly was not.

'How about trying to get a caravan at Weymouth?' I suggested.

'What if it rains?' Andrew asked.

'Well then . . . a holiday camp? Lots to do.'

We were still thinking that one through when a car drew up. It was Jerry. I was unexpectedly delighted – but then I hadn't seen him for four months. He entered to what amounted to a fanfare, with Lucy jumping all over him and telling Andrew who he was and me standing there with a big grin.

He was overwhelmed. 'Thanks – thanks, everyone.' He reached across the table to shake hands with Andrew. 'But it all looks familiar. Are you having a meeting?'

Lucy told him and he spread his hands. 'Why don't you come and stay at Marcroft?' he asked simply. 'You can drive your car, Lucy. Maybe Andrew could be a co-driver. And' – he didn't look at me – 'you can build the dam that your mother keeps on about. Did you know she wanted to make a swimming pool? In all that mud!'

'Is it in a forest?' Andrew asked. He glanced at Lucy. 'We could build a raft!'

I protested but was outvoted. We went to Marcroft for a few days while Jerry was in Bristol and when he came home he persuaded us to stay on another fortnight. We had a wonderful time. Lucy showed Andrew the abbey and explained about the stained glass. I admired the new kitchen and the wonderful glass roof. For a whole day, from dawn to dusk, Lucy and Andrew drove 'the circuit', taking it in turns to be on duty at the pit stop, waving a black and white flag. When the weather allowed we went on safari, finding bridle paths across the landscape and making maps in felt tips. Most of the time we worked on the dam, which had to be remade each day. When Jerry came home we did exactly the same things except that he made sure we had 'rest periods'. I was happy. Deeply happy.

Eventually Andrew wanted to go home, to 'check on' his mother.

'She does too much sometimes,' he confided to Jerry. 'When Dad's home he makes her go to bed early. I can do that.'

Jerry avoided my eye. He said, 'Good idea, Andrew.'

'I'm quite looking forward to having a brother,' Andrew went on. 'You know, to teach football to. And things.'

'Not for a while of course,' Jerry said judiciously. 'To start with, it's hard work just keeping everything going. You'll cope though.'

Andrew looked suspicious. 'D'you mean changing nappies? I'm not doing that.'

Jerry said, surprised, 'What a shame. I thought changing and feeding would be just your thing. It's the way to really get to know a person.' He frowned. 'You do realize we're talking about a person?'

There was a slight hesitation before Andrew said emphatically, 'Course I do.' He thought about it and added, 'But I can't change his nappy.'

Jerry shrugged. 'OK. Settle for feeding him then.'

Andrew nodded.

When the children had gone to bed I looked at Jerry hard. 'You appeared to back down then but I've got a sneaky feeling that the feeding bit was what you were after in the first place.'

He said smugly, 'That is correct, Sherlock.'

It was what Matt had called me sometimes. I didn't mind. I said, 'You're clever, I'll give you that.'

'But I'm still a power-mad manipulator?'

'Yes. You can't help it, can you?'

He grinned. 'If you would consider my proposition you'd be around to tell me about it. I think it's called nagging.'

I laughed and so did he. We were a long way from a partnership of any kind; but I had been happy during the past fortnight. What was more, so had he.

We went home and a new term started. Anna was producing a toothless smile; Watt could climb the stairs. Jennifer was wavering about her course.

'I know the crèche is good but after all it's not family. I'm not sure whether I can do it, Jess.' She smiled. 'I know I've always been so prickly and independent, but . . . well, look at them!'

I did. I said, 'Listen. In three years' time we shall need an expert on medieval history. We've already had an enquiry for reglazing a church in Devon. Hopefully they will want replacements only. But in the future, I foresee a demand for new designs with period references. We'll need your knowledge.'

'Oh Jess. I thought you'd be on my side.'

I bit my lip, then said with complete honesty, 'I am on your side, Jen. I will look after the children. You won't have lectures every day and the terms only last ten weeks – surely we can manage that? And I can work from home quite a bit. And you know very well that Mum will step in if there's an emergency.'

Jennifer's face seemed to open. All she said was, 'Oh Jess.' But it was all that was necessary.

Two other things happened that autumn. The first was something I had feared for almost a year. I met Jean head-on in Hartford's. There was no turning away or pretending we had not seen each other. I stood still and waited for her to cut me dead. She hesitated then tightened her mouth in what might have been a smile.

'Hello,' she said.

I said, 'Oh . . . hello.'

We went on standing so I added, 'How are you?'

I could see how she was: pretty good. Her hair was thick and glossy again and her skin was milky.

She didn't answer immediately. Then she took a long breath and let it out tremblingly. 'I'm expecting. And I feel so well. I thought at first I would . . . you know. But then, I couldn't do it again. I went to the clinic . . . just like before. But I started to think . . . it's such a dreadful thing to do, Jess. I've never stopped regretting it, you know. I mean, it's not just Jock's, is it? Half of it is mine. He – he said it was the only way we could really get ourselves together. And I think he's right.' She managed a proper smile. 'I feel wonderful, Jess. And the boys are pleased. Really pleased.' She looked at me. 'You must think I'm such a fool. After all I've said . . . well, and all I've done.' She couldn't stop talking. We wheeled our trolleys outside together and she told me that Jock had 'gone astray' simply because he had wanted another child so badly. She said, 'I don't think you'd better visit when he's around – I gave him a dreadful time, Jess. But when he's doing his next stint, bring Lucy to play with the boys. They often ask about her.'

I watched her drive away. I couldn't believe it. Maybe I could stop feeling guilty about that whole awful business. I got in my car and turned it towards the school. I said aloud, 'Matt, what's going on? Have you got anything to do with this?' But, as usual, there was no answer.

The second thing happened in October when Jennifer had started her course. It was a Wednesday and her only lecture that week started at ten o'clock so she brought the children round at eight in the morning. Lucy immediately left her cornflakes and sat on the floor with Watt to teach him 'See-saw, Marjorie Daw'. Jennifer handed me a typewritten list and a bag containing bottles and jars, nappies, a potty, clean clothes and various creams.

'I want to get off because I've taped my notes and I'll play them on the way down just to get them into my head properly.'

295

I was amazed at her just as I had always been. I waved from the door, Anna on one hip. She slammed the car door, then suddenly opened it again and got out and rushed back. She almost hugged me, then didn't.

'This is awful. Leaving you with two babies and Lucy not much older. I'm so used to you coping that I suppose I imagine you always can.'

I made a face. 'You know better than that, Jennifer,' I said very seriously. But she was serious too and wanted to know if I'd changed my mind. Suddenly I hoisted Anna higher, leaned forward and kissed her left ear where her hair was swept up into its old chignon style. 'Off you go,' I said.

'Is it . . . getting better?' She didn't leave. 'You know. The way you feel about me?'

'Yes.' I meant to leave it at that like Jerry always did. But a gush of pure emotion rushed over me and I went on, 'I just wish – so much – I hadn't hit you. I'm not going to apologize but I wish with all my heart—'

She interrupted. 'Jess, it did me good. Don't you see? It shocked me into seeing exactly what I'd done.' She shook her head. 'Anyway, darling, can't you remember how often I hit you when I was a kid? It was only fair. A long-overdue debt.'

Anna let out a yell of protest; I aimed another kiss at my sister and made shooing noises. She got into her car again and started up. I pumped Anna's hand in her direction. Then we went indoors to sort ourselves out for school.

It meant that when I got home again after shopping, the place was in its old state of complete shambles. And, of course, Jerry's four-wheel drive was parked outside.

We practically synchronized our emergence on to the rough road.

I said crossly, 'How do you do it? Have you ever called and found me properly organized?'

And he said, 'Does this remind you of another time?'

Then we laughed.

He reached into the back of my car and gathered Watt out of his chair and I unstrapped the restrainers of the carri-seat and swung Anna through the gate and up to the front door. He followed me into the chaotic kitchen.

'It's two months since the holiday, Jess. You haven't phoned. You didn't even write a thank-you note. It's not you.'

I was amazed. I put Anna down, fetched her bottle and put it in the microwave.

'It didn't occur to me . . . I'm so sorry, Jerry. We had such a wonderful time. The children loved every minute. And so did I.'

He lowered Watt carefully to the floor and watched as he did his tightrope walk, hands held high. 'I don't want thanks, for goodness' sake! But anything could have happened. The kids could have had pneumonia with all that paddling around in the brook. You could have had another fight with your sister – anything.'

'Well, obviously if anything had happened I would have let you know. And I don't make a habit of hitting Jennifer.' I hoped he was joking about that. 'Anyway, it was you who talked about having space.' I retrieved the bottle and stripped Anna of her nappy. 'Come on, Watt. Let's go into the other room while your sister has her lunch. Show Jerry your digger.'

Jerry brought up the rear. It was the way he walked that made me realize he was in one of his stubborn moods. His greeting and then helpfulness with Watt had deceived me for a time. When I clicked on the gas fire, he made a sound of disgust.

I said, 'I know. But it's so much easier. Aesthetics have to take second place sometimes, Jerry.' I smiled at him. 'Sit down and enjoy it. As soon as Anna has finished, she'll go to sleep for most of the afternoon. I'll get us a sandwich and a nice cup of coffee—'

He interrupted crossly, 'For God's sake, stop talking to

me as if I'm a kid! You accuse me of being patronizing but just listen to yourself.'

I laughed. 'Oh Jerry. Sorry. What's happened? You sound as if the kitchen roof has cracked or something.'

He said, suddenly gloomy, 'Worse. Much worse. I've been talking to Matt.'

I stared at him above Anna's busy rosebud mouth. 'You . . . what?'

'You do it. You told me so.' He was defensive. 'I didn't know it was a private thing.'

'It is completely and absolutely private, Jerry. If you think it's the slightest bit funny—'

'I had to talk to him, Jess! I had to. Dammit – I think I've fallen in love with his wife. And in view of what we . . . agreed, I didn't want to do that. Especially as she's still in love with him. So who else could I talk to?'

'You don't know what love is.' I was deeply angry.

'Absolutely! As far as I could see, when we were thrown together it was because you were miserable . . . suicidal.' He went to the window and looked out at Lucy's swing. 'Then, when you began to get better, it was absolutely nothing to do with me. It was the house and the woods and the bloody, bloody stream! Then when I told you about the village and myself, you cried again and you couldn't stop.'

'You threw Jock at me! Reminded me of what I'd done!'

'I thought we could be honest!' He turned and took a plastic brick away from Watt just as he was about to eat it. Watt yelled and Jerry swung him up and jiggled him. Jerry's face, red and angry, appeared above Watt's downy head. 'Don't you realize that's what we've always had? Honesty.'

I made a rueful face. 'Funnily enough, Jerry, I'm not sure we have had a lot of honesty recently. I think honesty's the opposite of secrecy. And just lately there's been a lot of secrecy.'

He stopped jiggling and set Watt down very gently.

'All right. Secrecy versus openness. We've been open, Jess. Haven't we?'

I nodded. 'You know about me. Yes. But dragging Matt into this—'

'But don't you see my problem? I can be happy with you . . . unhappy . . . angry with you. Anything. But I need to be *with* you. I've tried not being with you. And it's no good. Whether that's love or not, I can't say. And you and Matt . . . you were properly in love. Deeply in love.'

'I thought we were.' I concentrated on Anna. 'I was wrong, wasn't I?'

'No. You weren't wrong. Remember I used to talk to Matt – when he was alive – and he used to talk to me. He was happy with you. And – you have to admit it, Jess – you were happy with him.'

'Fool's paradise.' I was determined not to cry.

He dismissed that with a curt gesture. 'So I talked to him again. Several times. Trouble was, he didn't talk back any more.'

'No.' But there had been that time . . . A chink . . . just a chink.

'What did happen was . . . peculiar.' Jerry sat down suddenly and put his head in his hands. 'It came to me – just like that – that I'd been in love with you for ages. But that you weren't in love with me.' He made a sound that could have been a derisory laugh. 'Big snag. Solution: do what you're doing, keep away, work.' He scrubbed his eyes with the heels of his hands. 'Then came the holiday. It was so wonderful. Surely you felt something? But no. You went back home and didn't give it a thought.'

'I'm sorry, Jerry. So sorry.' I put aside the empty bottle and cleaned Anna up. Then I took her upstairs. When I came down, Jerry was by the front door.

He said, 'I'm sorry too, Jess. I shouldn't have come or said anything. It was simply that I had this feeling that it was what Matt would have wanted me to do.'

I went through into the kitchen and put Watt into the

high chair, washed my hands, put the kettle on, took bread from the crock. Jerry didn't leave; he was now standing in the kitchen doorway, leaning against the jamb.

I said, 'Right. Cheese or ham?' He laughed. I went on, 'Fetch what you want from the fridge. And one of those little jars for Watt.' I waited until he was busy then said, thinking of the chink, 'Matt said something to me not long ago. It's been the only time. I know it won't happen again. It doesn't matter what he said but it showed that he was . . . young. Very, very young. Naive. Perhaps stupid too. Just like me. Two young, naive people.' I took the cheese from him and began to make a sandwich. The kettle boiled and switched itself off.

I said, 'I'm not young any more, Jerry. But I'm just as stupid. I don't do the right thing until I've already done the wrong thing.' I glinted up at him. 'You know about that, don't you?'

'You've got guts. Sheer courage.'

'No. Not really. But I can hang on . . . just keep hanging on.'

'I could help you there. It need not worry you that I love you – but I could help with all this—' He swept the kitchen with his hand and very nearly knocked the kettle over.

I said steadily, 'I need to do it alone, Jerry. But actually, I've known for some time that I love you. And I was pretty certain that you loved me. Otherwise why would you have put up with me last Easter? Your friend – Helen – was only too quick to escape from an awkward situation and you could have done what she suggested and put me in an ambulance. But you didn't. And why did I go to the abbey in the first place? Not because of Matt. Because of you.'

He interrupted. 'Jess! You're saying—'

'I'm saying that I must – I *must* – be able to live on my own first. And I'm doing it. It won't be for ever, Jerry. But we have to know about each other—'

He said a very rude word.

I went on, 'It's so important. When I look back and see

myself jumping around like a flea, trying to find a companion, a helpmeet – anything. It was totally degrading, Jerry. We're worth more than that. I must be absolutely certain that I'm not adding you to that list.' I put the plate of sandwiches on the table and sat down. 'Can you understand?'

'All I understand – or think I understand – is that in the middle of all that – that rubbish, you are saying you love me. Can you confirm that?'

I looked up at him. For such a long time, his appearance had barely registered. He was so obviously good-looking and I had been put off by that. Now I let myself take in the darkness of him, the narrow face, the clever brown eyes, the restless movements. He was a difficult man, a complicated man. Life would not be easy with him.

I said, 'The person I am now – still stupid but perhaps less so – she loves you, Jerry. And she respects you too. She doesn't want you to take on someone who can only just cope. She wants something better for you. So . . . can you hang on? Until Christmas perhaps?'

'Then you'll ask me how Jennifer will manage without you to look after Watt and – and – the new baby.'

'Her name is Anna. And no, I won't say that. Worse than that. I'll ask you whether we can live here in term time so that Lucy can go to school with Andrew Bearwood.'

He looked surprised for a moment then nodded. 'I don't really care where I live if you're there. And actually it would be handy to be near Bristol. For a while.' He waited then said, 'Anything else?'

'No.'

He said, 'Right. Then I've got a present for you. It's not an engagement thing – I promise you I won't do any manipulating about our relationship. I don't honestly know why I'm giving it to you – it seemed the sort of thing that might sway you. But now . . .' He sighed and felt in his pocket. He produced a tiny net bag, the sort that chocolate coins hang in at Christmas. Inside were five farthings. 'I think I had some crazy notion of clearing your debts.'

He put the bag between us and then laid his hands flat on the table and looked at me. I looked at him. That was the epiphany. It happened then. We weren't touching each other physically but it was as if we flowed together. This was the other thing that Matt had wanted to say and could not. I would only ever be able to see Matt through that chink . . . the weak young man who had loved me. But he had made me what I am and what I am is the person loved by Jerry Jerome. The tears eventually overflowed. I rubbed them away with the palm of my hand, then tore off a piece of kitchen towel and leaned across to dry his eyes.

I said, 'I love you, Jerry. And if I had needed anything to show me that you love me, then this is it.'

He picked up my hands and held them to his face. He was still crying.

I am working through the weeks until Christmas though I don't need the extra time to convince me of Jerry's feelings. He appears at weekends and we take Lucy to the cinema or for a walk on the hills. Andrew comes with us sometimes and probably tells his mother all about us, so everyone in the village will know. When I see Jean she tells me about the family. Last week she said coyly that she understood congratulations were in order. She sounded relieved.

At least twice a week I look after Jennifer's children and when she collects them she tells me about her lectures and the utter fascination of the monasteries and the artists who lived in those far-off days. She is overstretched, of course, but she is happy. I am so glad to be able to love her again.

She and Sam, Mum and Bunny, they are accepting the fact that Jerry and I will marry fairly soon; I told Lucy about it and she was really excited and told Gramma. Mum mentioned it only the other day. She said something about the three of us finding happiness 'second time around'. She then laughed and added, 'It's probably fifth or sixth time for Jen!' Then she was still, looking at me.

I said, 'It's all right, Mum. I'm not sure why or how, but it's all right.'

'Did you do what I suggested? Write it all down?' I nodded and she said triumphantly, 'What did I tell you! I keep a diary. Always have. When I read the old ones I get things into perspective.'

Maybe that's all it is. Looking at things from a distance. I'll never take anything for granted again. Not even myself. Definitely not myself.

Stella had a little girl. Andrew was delighted and wanted to call her Forest. Stella won with Daisy. Daisy Forest Bear-wood.

Jerry would like another girl. Or a boy. So would Lucy. Actually, so would I.